PLAYTHINGS

PART ONE OF THE COMING OF AGES TRILOGY

By
LORELEI RUSSELL

Copyright © 2023 Lorelei Russell
All Rights Reserved

Cover illustration by Lorelei Russell
Cover design and layout by David Benson at
Disaster Management & Design

ISBN 9798867735234

No part of this book may be reproduced in any form or by any means, except for the inclusion of brief quotations in a review, without permission in writing from the author.

All characters in this book are fictitious. Any resemblance to actual persons living or dead is purely coincidental.

About The Author

Lorelei Russell is a writer and artist based in London. Her academic background is in ancient civilisations with a particular focus on Celtic history and mythology. Her passion for the magic of the past influences her prose and poetry.

To David, for all of the creative support and technical wizardry;
Jean, for the tireless encouragement and proofreading;
Samantha, for being the first test reader to finish the book;
Nina, for being the first to finish the trilogy;
and Reuben, for a little bit of inspiration along the way.

A (VAGUE) PRONUNCIATION GUIDE

Many of the names in this story have old Irish spelling, and the pronunciation may be unfamilia. This rough guide is included in the hope that it will assist the reader.

Key to my suggested pronunciation:

ee – tr**ee**
o – **o**range
u – m**u**llet
oo – m**oo**n
au – appl**au**d
u – l**u**ck
oh – b**o**red
e – b**e**d
ay – gr**a**pe

Important names and characters:

(The syllables in italics are stressed.)

Aoife – *Ee*fa
Mr. Ó Mordha – Mr. Oh *Murr*ada
Cú Chulaind – Koo *Kull*en
Síd – Sheed
Sídhe – *Shee*da
Eili - *Eye*lee
Étaín – Ay*deen*
Badb – Bav
Fúamnach – *Foo*amnak
Macha – *Mo*ka
Medb – *Med*ev
Nuadu – *Noo*ada

Bres – Bresh
Samildánach – Savilldaunak
Argetlám – Argetlauv
Fidchell – Fidkel
Fomoire – Forwirra
Mag Tuired – Mag Toored
Dian Cécht – Deean Kaikt
Tuatha Dé – Tooatha Day
Lebor Gabála – Lower Gavaula
Brú na Bóinne – Broo na Bohinna
Eochu – Yukoo

Other names that are mentioned:

Noísiu – Neesha
Derdriu – Deerdra
Emer – Ever
Crunniuc - Krinuk
Echu - Eko

PROLOGUE

The butterflies haven't come back. I wonder if they ever will. I've waited, and waited, but perhaps they are not for one such as I am now.

There is no elation or despair for me… Only the odd, wistful memory, from time to time, of playing with small friends in the woods, studying in enchanted libraries, drinking and dancing with gods, or the feeling of a lover's body against mine. As time passes, I find it harder to believe that any of those things happened to me.

I look down on the world, from the places that I now inhabit, with a new perspective, and find that the recollection of its pleasures and tortures has begun to fade.

I do not know how long it has been since I became something… other. I am now beginning to understand that concept of timelessness, which had always evaded me.

I have only one purpose: To wait; to wait, until the look in his eyes is no longer one of purest hatred; to wait, until his excruciating memories are no longer a torment, and the unspeakably dreadful scars in his mind have begun to fade… Scars that *I* gave him; memories that *I* created. It is right that I should be here, frozen in this half-life, destined to wait until the injuries I inflicted are healed, before I can be myself again.

So, I wait, and I follow him, and I watch for any small sign that time has begun to mend what was broken. He never looks at me. Sometimes, I wish that he would. More often, I don't. A cowardly part of me does not like to see the crawling shadows of the unbearable things he has endured, imprinted in his eyes.

I still feel the prickle, somewhere deep inside me, silently sleeping; dormant; waiting for something too. And so, we wait, and we wait, and we wait… and sometimes, we think back to where it all began.

CHAPTER ONE

I can't remember exactly when I began to experience that feeling: That feeling of never being quite alone... As though nobody was there but someone was almost there; of things not quite experienced, but hovering just outside the tips of my senses; of somebody watching and wanting to greet me, but not quite connecting, like a friend across the street, raising a hand to wave just as you have averted your eyes and begun to turn the corner; of creatures and colours half-glimpsed but not quite seen, as though my vision were filtered through a speeding car window. It was a prickly feeling. Perhaps it was uncomfortable once, but I can't recall. I have had it- or, perhaps I should say, it has had me- for so long that, most of the time, it merely feels like a comfortable prickle of... being.

I already regularly experienced that feeling by the time my mother died. I remember the thorny fingers of the prickle burning especially hot on my skin that night, filling every crevice of my senses with scorching, and at the same time, icy shivers of unease. I remember little shadows skittering in the corners of my mind and vision, seen and not quite seen. Had that teddy bear twitched? Had that book of fairy tales rocked? No, they were both sitting placidly where I had left them, the former smiling and benevolent as ever he was, and the latter upright and sumptuously imposing. I remember sitting bolt upright in bed, in the intense embrace of the prickle, when my sister Aoife came in, red faced and crying, to try to explain to me, through gurgling gulps and rivulets of snot, that there had been a car accident, and that our mother was gone.

I was six then- almost seven- and life changed from a warm cocoon of magical bedtime stories and homemade soup, to a somewhat more sombre affair, as a grieving and slightly frayed, seventeen-year-old Aoife tried to keep herself from splitting entirely into shreds by imposing an ordered, joyless schedule on our household.

My mother had been an unusually kind and loving woman, with warmth enough to shine on every little particle of the universe. She undertook every task with the utmost tenderness and care, including the rearing of her children. Of course, by the time I was born, Aoife had her friends in the village, with whom she played after school. She would only come home in the evening for tea, with twigs in her hair and grazes on her legs from tripping over a skipping rope or, as she got older, a suspicious scent which I later identified as a subtle blend of cigarettes and cider. My mother and I, therefore, spent our days together, singing old songs, reading stories about the fairies, and picking berries in the woods. I'm sure we did a lot more besides but, of course, I was very young then, and my early recollections are an all-encompassing, velvet cloak of vivid impressions and favourite activities. One thing I *do* distinctly remember is that every time I whipped my head around, to try to catch a glimpse of some almost visible manifestation of the prickle, I noticed that my mother's head always turned in the same direction, as though she were experiencing something too.

As soon as I turned about four, my mother was happy for me to run about and play outside, while she cleaned or baked. She always warned me not to go too far into the woods and, naturally, I always went a bit further than I admitted when I came home. Something about the twinkle in her eye, and a slight twitch at the corners of her mouth, told me that she knew exactly where I'd been.

Aoife sometimes complained about the amount of freedom I received at my age, and tried to sound very grown up by asking my mother if she thought it was responsible parenting to allow me to wander so freely. "Kathy will be fine," my mother always replied, entirely unperturbed.

One day, when I was six, I went deeper into the woods than I had ever been, and came to a clearing. It seemed quieter than the other parts of the woods, devoid of the usual flurry of insects and four-legged creatures, scuttling clumsily through the undergrowth. Although it was a sunny day- a fairly unusual phenomenon in County Kerry-

The air in the clearing had a slight chill. Fingers of dappled light cascaded through the regal trees, touching a little ring of toadstools with their fingertips, and only the odd, soulfully melodic bird dared to sing.

Utterly enchanted by the place, I danced about, enjoying the spots of sunlight on my face, feeling simultaneously bright, and slightly naughty, as if my carefree twirling were at odds with the sacred, still nature of my surroundings. It was then that I heard a peal of laughter from behind me: A giggle of pure, exuberant joy. I spun around, expecting to see nothing, as usual, but instead, I saw a young girl staring at me, just a few feet away. I can't remember how old she looked, but she was certainly youthful enough not to overly startle me in my playful frame of mind. She had a gently waving mane of lustrous, strawberry blonde hair, which gleamed like satin in the light; shining green eyes; and an exquisite face, bearing the most inviting smile that I had ever seen.

"What's your name?" I asked, grinning back.

"Étaín," she replied.

"I'm Kathy. Do you live around here?"

Her smile broadened. "Would you like to play?"

I nodded enthusiastically and we spent a few hours chasing each other, playing hide and seek- although I never found her, but she always found me- and making daisy chains. Then, she even let me plait her beautiful hair, which felt like the smoothest water, the softest creature, and the most tender caress, in my little hands. She couldn't do much with my straight, chestnut brown locks, which were cropped above my shoulders to avoid tangling. I was not one of those little girls who enjoyed excessive personal grooming. However, she closed one of our daisy chains into a crown, and placed it gently on my head, and I felt wonderful.

The light began to fade, and I reluctantly told her that I had to go home. I rushed through the woods, realising that I might be late for tea. I had never seen my mother angry, and it was an experience that I had long decided I would prefer to avoid.

When I arrived back at our little house, breathless from running, and eyes shining after my lovely day, my mother merely smiled, instructed me to wash my hands, and gave me a bowl of stew.

"Did you have a nice afternoon?" she asked.

"Oh, yes!" I beamed. Then, I remembered that I shouldn't have been so deep in the woods as to have found the clearing, and tried to look a little less exhilarated.

"Did you meet anyone?" she asked.

"No," I replied, avoiding her eyes, and concentrating on my stew with unnecessary attention to detail. However, I glanced up and saw the familiar twinkle in her eye, and the knowing smile playing at the corners of her mouth, and I wondered…

When our mother was gone, Aoife did her best. She dutifully cleaned the house and attempted to engage me in small tasks, like dusting or setting the table, although I tended to begin such projects and leave them half-finished, my mind too full of fairy tales and games to play in the woods. I could read by then, albeit nothing too complicated, and immersed myself in my fantastical, childish books, trying to remember how my mother's voice had sounded reading them to me. People were kind. Mrs. Lynch, from next door, looked in on us regularly, brought us meals, and even sat with me sometimes, when Aoife wanted to go out for the evening. Alan Lynch, her grown-up son, once came in with a few mackerel he had caught, but noting the wild terror in Aoife's eyes, at the thought of beheading and gutting a fish, he had taken them away and had his mother prepare them for us.

Even Aoife's father, Seán, made an occasional effort. He would take us out for the odd drive, although he spent them staring into space and chain-smoking cigarettes out of the window, and invariably looked relieved to have done his duty when he took us home. He had always been "a bit useless," to quote Mrs. Lynch, when I'd once heard her gossiping about us to another neighbour. My mother had met him at school, and Aoife had lasted a great deal longer than their relationship had.

When I began to understand that my mother must have loved at least two men to have had me and Aoife, it didn't surprise me. She was so very full of love that she would have had enough for all the men of Ireland… or, at least, that was how I thought of it in my childish mind. There were whispers, of course. Raising two children by different fathers, alone, wasn't really 'done' in our village. The local priest tended to wrinkle his nose if we passed him on the street, as though he had detected a somewhat displeasing aroma. However, our neighbours were generally kind people, and my mother had been immensely likeable, and not one to take any interest in religion at all, so it never bothered us much. Nor did I give much thought to my own father. If he was anything like Seán, I wasn't particularly interested.

My seventh birthday was an unremarkable affair, with Seán and Aoife, at a garish restaurant off the side of a motorway. Seán was as useless and uninterested as ever. Aoife attempted to look cheerful, although her smile was as fragile as porcelain that might shatter at any moment. Our mother hadn't been gone long. She argued with Seán about buying me a slice of cake, because he didn't want to spend any more money. I got it in the end. I didn't much care.

I had a lot less freedom with Aoife looking after me. She insisted that I be in the house for every meal, and home long before teatime, which didn't give me much opportunity to go too far into the woods, and find my little clearing again, or Étaín for that matter. When I protested that our mother always used to let me stay out for the day, she snapped: "Well, she isn't here anymore, is she? You're *my* responsibility now. What would the neighbours say, if you got lost or hurt in the woods?"

I knew I would be starting school in September: Getting on that big bus into the centre of the village, sitting in rigid seats all day, and missing the feeling of the air on my face, and branches in my hair. It was not a prospect that filled me with joy, but it still felt quite far into the future. Summers seemed to last for about three years when I was little.

The few hours to myself that I did have every day were, of course, spent in the woods, alone. Alone, that is, until, one afternoon, I heard the barking of a dog. I was walking along the edge of a stream, trying to stay as close to the water as possible without falling in, my arms outstretched for balance. When I heard the barking, I assumed it was one of *those* noises, that was almost there, but not quite there. However, when I turned my head to look, I found myself face to face with what seemed like a monster from a fairy tale, with an enormous, hairy head; a wet, black nose; dark pools for eyes; a mighty jaw; and a powerful, muscular frame about three times my size. He sniffed at me inquisitively. I gasped in fright and toppled backwards, head first, into the stream. It was a fairly inoffensive, placid little stream, but the coldness of the water hit me like a thousand winters, and my movement froze with it. I shrieked as the water crept into my mouth like icy fingers, stifling me and choking back my screams.

I felt the sudden warmth of two, strong hands grasping my flailing arms, and pulling me upwards. In a confusing mess of- what seemed like- twenty arms and legs and splashes, I found myself climbing back up on to dry land, spluttering and coughing, and scrubbing my eyes. A hand was thumping me a little too hard on the back, encouraging me to expel the water that I'd swallowed. After a few deep breaths, the serene reality of the woods began to creep back into my consciousness, and I turned to face my rescuer…

And that was the first time I saw him: A tall boy, a little older than me- but not so much as to make me feel shy- with pale golden hair; a wiry frame; and a face almost as impossibly beautiful as Étaín's, yet somehow more… *real*, and far more stern.

"Y-y-you saved my life," I stammered, tiny droplets of stream water flying from my lips as I spoke.

"I doubt that even *you* could have managed to drown in a couple of feet of water," he replied dryly, wincing a little as my spray hit his eyelids, "What on earth is the matter with you? Have you never seen a dog before?"

I stared at him, open-mouthed, most likely resembling a codfish, before stuttering: "D-d-dog?"

He sighed impatiently. "Yes, a d-d-dog," he mocked, "You *do* know what a dog is…?" The pained expression on his face indicated his concern that he might be dealing with some sort of a halfwit.

A little indignant then, I composed myself and snapped: "Well, of course I do, but that beast is like no dog *I've* ever seen!" I glanced in the beast's direction and noticed, to my slight annoyance, that he was now sitting down, wagging his tail, panting happily, and looking exactly like a dog.

The boy whistled, and the enormous hound began to pad towards us. I shrank back a little, and the boy said: "Don't be afraid. He's a gentle soul." His tone too was suddenly more gentle. I timidly extended my hand to pat the dog's muzzle, and received a sloppy lick for my efforts.

The boy smiled a little with satisfaction. "Good boy, Cú Chulaind," he murmured, ruffling his hairy companion behind the ear.

I smiled a little too. "Cú Chulaind?" I repeated.

"Do you know what it means?"

"Yes! It means 'Hound of Culand', from the old story of the hero Setantae, who accidentally slew the great dog who protected Culand's people, and so vowed to protect them himself until he could rear another fearsome hound to replace him, earning him the nickname Cú Chulaind!"

"Indeed," replied the boy, suddenly looking slightly impressed… or, to be more precise, suddenly looking as though my existence were not entirely a dismal failure of the natural order. "Oh, and I'm Liam."

I nodded. "I'm Kathy. Thanks again for sav… er, I mean, *helping* me, even if it wasn't very dangerous." I sighed deeply then, aware of my sodden dress and hair. "My sister will be so angry with me when I go home like this."

He cocked his head to one side and studied me, as though evaluating my worth, before he offered: "You could come to my cottage to dry off. It's on the other side of the woods, that way." He gestured in the opposite direction from my home. "My father makes sure there's always a fire going."

I sighed again. "No, I have to be home for tea, and I'd never get so far away and back in time."

"We'll have to make a fire here, then," he concluded, and set about gathering twigs and sticks, and some sort of moss, and piling them into an architecturally complex structure, before creating the spark by rubbing two stones together.

I watched him, transfixed, as he worked, astonished that anyone could be so competent, let alone a young boy. Before I knew it, a cheerful little fire was dancing merrily in front of us, my shoes and socks were off and drying out nicely, and even my dress was feeling less damp against my skin. Liam had also produced a small blanket of sorts from a leather pack, which I used to scrub the worst of the drenching out of my hair, and then pulled around my shoulders. It felt prickly but, like my own, internal prickle, strangely comfortable. I relaxed and began to hum a little song that my mother used to sing and, to my surprise, Liam began to sing along too, tentatively at first, then with more confidence, getting lost in the tune.

Our voices soared and lilted together, and I began to feel delightfully strange. The prickle inside me, and around me, was at its most intense, yet it was pleasantly warm and blissfully cool, not the scorching fire and ice that I had felt at uneasy times. My face flushed, and a kindly breeze caressed my forehead, as I snuggled further into the little blanket, and our song seemed to sparkle like the tiny embers that fluttered from the fire. Cú Chulaind dozed contentedly at our feet. I stole a surreptitious glance at Liam, curious as to how he was experiencing the moment, and our eyes met meaningfully for an instant, before I hurriedly looked away and continued to sing, at first slightly off beat, and then in perfect unison again.

I became aware of being watched from behind a large stone, on the other side of the flames, and looked up, expecting a fleeting shadow or a scrap of colour. However, I quite clearly saw the top of a tiny head, peering up from behind the stone, cheeks resting on two little hands, and two, big eyes staring at us intently, with an expression both childlike and ancient.

I stopped singing abruptly, and hissed: "Can you see him?" I gestured frantically in the direction of the stone.

Liam frowned. "Stop it, it's rude to point," he snapped, his face stern and disapproving again, though it was evident that the little fellow was visible to him too.

The song was done, the prickle subsided back to its usual level, and the little man behind the stone was gone. I realised with dread, as I noticed the colour of the sky, that it was far too close to teatime, and I was in for an unpleasant confrontation with Aoife.

"I'd better go," I said, quietly, hanging my head as I returned the blanket, and put on my footwear, "Thanks again, though, for the fire and… everything."

Liam's face was aloof as he began to kick loose soil onto the flames, to quench the small blaze. "No thanks required," he replied, stiffly.

I began to scurry back in the direction of home, turning once or twice to get a last glimpse of him, then as I reached the last point before trees would engulf me, I summoned up all of my courage, spun 'round, took a deep breath, and shouted at the top of my lungs: "Would you like to play tomorrow?"

He looked up and shrugged. "Alright," he called back.

I was too far away to be able to tell whether or not his expression was remotely enthusiastic, but my heart leaped into my throat like a swarm of butterflies, trying to flutter out of my stomach, and I ran away as fast as my legs could carry me, grinning all the while.

By the time I got home, I was somehow completely dry. Aoife was stirring something in a pot in the kitchen. She glared at me. "You're late."

"I'm sorry," I answered.

"Well, that's not good enough, Kathy. What on earth must the neighbours think of a child of your age coming home when it's nearly dusk? Our mother was far too easy on you! Here I am, cooking and cleaning, and doing everything for you, and all I ask is that you show a little gratitude! A little consideration for all I do! Is that too much to ask? Well, is it?"

"No," I muttered robotically.

Aoife threw up her hands and groaned. "What did I do to deserve this? What am I going to do with you? You need some boundaries, Kathy, and some discipline. You won't leave this house tomorrow!"

My heart froze in my chest. "I most certainly will," I cried, defiantly.

"You need to learn to obey the rules. Life isn't all about what you want to do, and my mind's made up. You'll stay in tomorrow, and that's all there is to it. Now, you can accept it and eat your tea, or you can go to bed hungry. *That* choice, I will grant you."

I stormed out of the kitchen, bitter tears streaming down my face, telling myself that I'd sooner never eat again than swallow one mouthful of whatever poisonous concoction she had created with her cruel, evil hands. I threw myself on my bed, and shuddered tearfully until I passed out from the effort of angry, disappointed crying.

Morning came and my swollen, saline-encrusted eyes blinked open uncomfortably, reminding me in an instant of what had transpired between me and Aoife the previous evening. *Or, rather, what Aoife did to me when I had done absolutely nothing to deserve it,* I thought with a scowl. I tried to decide between a great show of apology, which might lead to the reversal of my punishment, or sulking for the rest of my life. After some thorough deliberation- and fantasies of poor Liam waiting for me in the woods and deciding that I didn't like him because I never came to meet him, even though he had saved my life and built me a fire- I decided upon the former course of action. I trotted out to the kitchen, where Aoife was wearily sipping a cup of tea.

Clasping my hands behind my back, I looked up at her with, what I hoped, were the widest, most innocent eyes, and said in my sweetest voice: "I'm sorry, Aoife. I'll try to do better."

She sighed softly and put out a hand to touch my cheek. "I'm sorry too, Little One, for being so angry. I suppose we're both just trying."

I nodded enthusiastically, and my expression probably brightened far too quickly.

Her fingers dropped from my face, and she took another sip of her tea. "The punishment still stands, though," she stated.

"*What?*" I cried, incredulously.

"Kathy, I've been reading books on this sort of thing. I need to set boundaries and stick to them, or you'll grow up some sort of delinquent! It's only because I care how you turn out, you know. What would the neighbours say if I raised a child who went off the rails?"

"Y-y-you don't care about me at all," I blubbered, and marched back to my bedroom to resume sobbing. The prickle burned, and it was the first time that I distinctly remember feeling as though it were somehow connected to my own emotions, rather than a mysterious warning, or whisper, from outside my consciousness.

As soon as Aoife went to the bathroom, I raced out of the house, so fast that I had probably reached the woods before she'd even emerged.

Liam was exactly where I had left him, by the little stream. He was picking up small stones, and throwing them out so that they skipped several times along the surface of the water, while Cú Chulaind barked excitedly, and bounced up and down, clearly tempted to follow them, but unsure about getting wet.

I was so relieved to see them that it took me several moments to notice that they were not alone. Two little creatures, human-like but for the fact that they didn't quite reach Liam's knee in height, were standing beside him on the bank of the stream. As I approached, softly, utterly enthralled, I could see that they were joining in his game, skipping tiny pebbles out across the water in place of stones. In the midst of my anger with Aoife, and my longing to see Liam, I had almost forgotten about the one that I'd glimpsed by the fire the day before.

I didn't know how to react, terrified that they might just disappear if I made my presence known. However, some slight sound must have given me away, because they all started, and spun 'round to look at me. The two little creatures' enormous eyes were nervous. They glanced at each other, and their expressions seemed to say: "It's time we were going…"
"Please don't go," I blurted out, "I mean you no harm!"

"I'm sure they know that, Kathy," snorted Liam exasperatedly, "What harm is it that you think you could do them, exactly?"

The two little men chuckled, and looked at each other again, this time with merriment in their huge eyes. With something of a shrug, one of them stepped forward. "Kathy, is it?" he smirked, "Eili's daughter, are you?"

My eyes widened. "That *was* my mother's name."

He nodded his tiny head. "Aye, we knew your mother. Lovely girl."

"She was," I agreed, feeling a little sad, because she was gone, and because she hadn't shared everything with me. Why had she never told me that she knew these little creatures, who could only possibly be fairies? Why had she never introduced us? Were *they* the ones that I always felt, watching? Instinctively, I knew that they were, to a point, and yet not entirely, for they were clearly simple souls, their intent openly written across their childlike and ancient little faces, whereas the prickle was something deeper: Much kinder and yet harsher; much older and yet younger; much bigger and yet of no size at all.

"Your mother," continued the small fellow, "She used to... do us little favours from time to time, you know? What do you think about that?"

"I have no idea what you mean," I replied, sounding slightly cross, "What *sorts* of favours?"

"Ah, she's a bit young for all that yet," interjected the other one.

His friend nodded. "You may be right. Well, we'll take our leave of you, Kathy, but we'll see you again."

"But, wait..." I began, yet before the words had left my lips, the two of them were no longer there.

"That went well, don't you think?" observed Liam sarcastically.

I barely heard him. I was staring, open-mouthed, at the spot in which the little creatures had been, the realisation of the importance of the whole affair suddenly hitting me.

"Fairies!" I exclaimed, "They were fairies!"

"Good grief," groaned Liam, "Don't let them hear you call them by *that* silly name!"

"Well, what would *you* call them, then?" I demanded.

"They are far more than that." His tone softened. "Look, I know it must have been a bit of a shock, meeting them for the first time, but try not to get too caught up in naming them, or deciding what they are. I don't think we can fully understand it all and, you'll find in time, that it doesn't really matter."

I was confused. "How long have you known them?" I asked.

He pursed his lips noncommittally. "I don't know. I think I've always known them."

In a strange way, I felt as though I'd always known them too.

Liam was staring at me with a slight frown. "Are you alright?"

I remembered, then, that I was a tearstained mess, and felt a little embarrassed. I also suddenly recalled that I had run away from the house, against Aoife's orders, and that she would most likely come out to find me, with vengeance in mind, and that I'd better get as far away from her as possible.

"I'm fine. Let's go to your house," I said, brightly.

Liam's cottage was a long walk away... A very long walk away. I walked further than I ever had, even with my mother. I took in all of the parts of the woods that I had never seen before: Serene glades; areas almost black, they were so densely populated by trees; a strange, sombre mound in the earth, which seemed to agitate the prickle; and a beautiful, sparkling lake, in which Liam said that he liked to swim in fine weather. As I became more and more aware of the dull ache in my short legs, my attention began to wane. I did not ask to stop or rest, wanting to save face in front of my companion, who strode confidently ahead on his long limbs, almost keeping pace with his giant of a dog.

Finally, I stumbled over the root of a tree and landed unceremoniously in the undergrowth. Cú Chulaind noticed before his master did, and turned around to look at me with a puzzled whine. Liam rushed back, then, and extended a hand to help me to my feet. As his fingers touched mine, the prickle positively blazed in that heady, blissful way that I'd experienced when we'd sung together. We jumped apart, almost guiltily, and I nearly toppled over again, but just succeeded in steadying myself.

"Come on," he said encouragingly, "It's not far, now."

His hand hovered hesitantly for a moment, as if he were unsure as to whether or not courtesy required him to offer to take mine again, for support for the rest of the journey. I decided that I did not want him to take my hand again. It felt a little… too much.

"I'm fine," I insisted, as chirpily as I could manage, and walked on with my head held high.

Liam's cottage was just beyond the next clump of densely packed, dark, leafy trees. As they began to subside, we burst out onto a riverbank, beside which a small, grey, stone dwelling stood. It looked friendly and inviting, with a little red door, and fluffy puffs of smoke floating from the chimney.

A man was sitting by the river, fishing. He looked quite old to me and, as we approached, I could tell that his features were a more mature version of Liam's, partially hidden under a bushy beard and a large hat. He looked surprised as we reached him. I suspected that Liam did not often bring friends home.

"Well, hello there," he smiled, "And who might you be?"

"My name is Kathy, Mr…?"

"O Mordha," he replied.

"Pleased to meet you, Mr. O Mordha."

"It's a pleasure to meet you too, Kathy," he answered, in that slightly amused, yet impressed, manner that grown-ups adopt when they meet a well-behaved child, "Would you care for a sandwich and a cup of tea?"

"Oh, yes please!" I gasped, enthusiastically. I was excruciatingly hungry after the long walk, and having eschewed my tea the previous evening.

He walked off towards the cottage, to prepare the refreshments. I gazed out at the river, somewhat transfixed by its movement.

"It's beautiful here," I murmured, "I would never have known it existed."

"Not many people do," agreed Liam proudly, and gave me the first real smile that I'd observed on his face.

Those sickening, wonderful butterflies, that had threatened to engulf my throat the day before, began creeping up through me, trying to reach my oesophagus again. I broke his gaze, and something occurred to me.

"Is your mother dead, too?" I asked quietly.

He nodded.

"I'm sorry."

He tossed his head in, I thought, somewhat feigned nonchalance. "I don't remember her, so it's fine really. I'm sorry about yours, though. Our... 'friends' in the woods speak very well of her."

I narrowed my eyes suspiciously. Not only had I not known that my mother was acquainted with these 'friends' in the woods, but it now sounded as though they'd been talking about me to Liam behind my back. Just how much did he know about my family?

Before I could interrogate him further, his father called to us that our snack was ready, and we went into the cottage. I noticed little plates of milk and water around the doorstep, no doubt for the creatures of the forest, as they seemed far too delicate for mighty Cú Chulaind.

Inside was wonderfully, gloriously cramped, crammed with fascinating objects, and more books than I had ever seen. A little table in the centre of the living room had been laid with a slightly grubby, red and white checked cloth, a most welcome platter of juicy ham and tomato sandwiches, and a pot of tea.

"Thank you, Mr. O Mordha," I said, as I took my seat.

"You're welcome, Kathy. Help yourself!"

He did not have to make the suggestion twice. I greedily began to munch on a sandwich, and it occurred to me that some sustenance might keep those pesky butterflies blocked up in my stomach, where they belonged. I almost spat my first mouthful back out, however, when Liam casually announced:

"Well, Kathy met 'you know who' in the woods, for the first time, today."

"Oh, is that right?" Mr. O Mordha queried, entirely unperturbed, "The small ones?" He smiled.

Liam nodded, and took a bite of his sandwich.

After chewing mine, and attempting to swallow, I sat in stunned silence. My food was stuck somewhere in my throat, which seemed to have been rendered unable to perform its customary duties by my shock. It was simply inconceivable to me that Liam and his father shared such secrets.

The latter continued: "And how did you find them, Dear?"

I forced the bread down and sipped my tea, coughing a little before replying: "I- I'm not sure. They said that they knew my mother…"

"Of course." Mr. O Mordha lowered his eyes, a little wistfully. "Eili Nolan. Such a sad loss. Who looks after you now, child?"

For a moment, my astonishment increased. Had *everybody* known my mother? Then, the thought of Aoife distracted me from my shock, for long enough to wonder if he might let me stay here forever, if I lied, and said that I had nobody to look after me. I subsequently remembered that I had already mentioned her to Liam, so I sighed, and said: "My older sister."

"Does she know where you are today?" he enquired, looking a little concerned by my reaction.

A thousand lies bubbled to the surface of my mind, vying for attention, but for some reason, it seemed that I was incapable of lying to Mr. O Mordha. "No. No, not exactly."

He raised his eyebrows. "I'd better give her a ring then. What's your telephone number?"

Again, I considered lying, and telling him that I didn't know it, but I reluctantly recited the number.

He walked to the corner and lifted a few old books off a shelf, exposing an extremely dusty and archaic-looking telephone, which clearly did not get much use. Dread rose in me as he dialled, waited, and then I heard the following, one-sided conversation:

"Hello? Am I speaking to Miss Nolan? This is Tomás O Mordha. I don't know if you remember me, but I have your little sister here… No, no! Calm yourself! My young lad Liam is a friend of hers, and he brought her home to meet me, that's all. Yes, yes, of course I'll tell you where I live! Please calm down, and let me give you directions… No need to worry… Please… Aoife…"

I wondered, for a moment, how he knew my sister's first name, and from what possible occasion she might remember him, but my interest in the conversation trailed off as my heart sank. I looked down at the half-eaten sandwich that I'd wanted so much, but had now been ruined by impending doom, and tried very hard not to cry in front of Liam.

"I'd like to see her find her way here, through the woods," I muttered.

"There's actually a back road you can take by car, if you know where to go," said Liam regretfully, with genuine pity on his face. That explained the aged little car that I then remembered having seen outside.

Aoife didn't have a car, but I was sure that she would find one, just to spite me. Sure enough, some time later, she arrived at the cottage, in the passenger seat of Alan Lynch's vehicle. She jumped out with a face like thunder, and Mr. O Mordha went out to greet her. She just about remained civil to him, until she had bundled me into the car, and instructed Alan to drive away. She remained tight-lipped on the journey home, thanked Alan for his assistance once we'd arrived, hauled me through our front door and slammed it shut behind us.

I won't go into detail about the row that ensued between me and Aoife that night. Suffice it to say that I was not allowed out of the house again for several days, and my movements were very closely policed to ensure that I did not escape. I sat in my room, prickling despondently, and longing for the real life that I had only just found, with a friend, and a dog, and a kind adult, and small, mysterious beings who were somehow linked with my mother.

I tried to sketch the characters who had brought such warmth to my life for the briefest of moments, as though immortalising them in coloured pencil would keep them alive in my mind. Liam, Cú Chulaind and Mr. O Mordha were easy enough to draw, but I found myself frustrated each time I attempted to depict the tiny, magical men that I had met in the woods.

Their enormous, ancient eyes were imprinted in my recollection, but my simple pencils could not quite get the measure of them. Were their other features entirely human? Had their faces been young or old? Had their hair been thick or wispy? Surely, it could not be both! What had they been wearing? I knew that they had been clothed, but somehow, the specifics of their attire escaped me… Had their appearance been entirely unexceptional, or had it somehow blended into their surroundings, to the extent that it was difficult to remember where it ended, and they began?

It was as though, as soon as I tried to focus on a particular detail, it became infuriatingly blurred and fragmented, and left me with only the vaguest of impressions. I scribbled out my failed attempts sulkily, and threw my pencils on the floor. I did not want the memory of the enigmatic creatures to fade.

Then, one day, the telephone rang, and I heard Aoife speaking to someone:

"Hello? Oh, hello. I hope you're well. Oh, I see… Well, yes, I suppose that would be fine, but how would she get there and back? Oh, I see… Right… Well yes, that sounds acceptable. Not too late, mind. Thank you for inviting her. Goodbye!"

She then walked into my room and said: "Kathy, make yourself presentable. Mr. O Mordha has invited you over for tea. He's sending your friend Liam to collect you, and walk you there, and then they'll drive you home later." Without waiting for a reaction, she left.

My heart leaped, and I sprang upright, almost unable to believe what I'd heard. Aoife and I had barely spoken, since our argument after my last visit to Liam's home. I supposed she had decided that she couldn't keep me imprisoned forever, and that an invitation from a responsible adult was more respectable than my running about alone, left to my own devices. I also suspected that she was looking forward to some time to herself. In recent days, she had seemed increasingly uneasy, as though the prickle had reached such heights of frustration that it was emanating from me, and even prodding her a little with its persistent, twitchy fingers.

I dashed about, putting on my prettiest, pale blue dress, brushing my hair until it was glossy- which was a rare occurrence- and surveying myself in the mirror.

When I saw Liam and Cú Chulaind outside the window, those infuriating butterflies made a break for it, surged up through my chest, exploded out of my mouth, flew a couple of laps around the room, and then fluttered back into my body.

We strolled through the woods and, to my surprise and delight, were joined by 'the small ones', as Mr. O Mordha had called them. It seemed as appropriate a name for them as any other. Of course, I had no idea then that he had used the term 'the small ones' to differentiate them from something else entirely.

They walked with us for part of the journey, making pleasant conversation about nothing in particular, but listening carefully when I responded to their seemingly idle questions, and watching me intently as I spoke. Something in their manner seemed surreptitiously deliberate, and made me wonder if they had instigated a random chat only as a pretext to allow them to observe me more closely. I found that I didn't really mind the possibility. *I* wanted to observe *them* more closely too. As we neared the cottage, they exchanged perplexingly knowing glances, excused themselves, and left us to continue on our way.

In the weeks that followed, Liam often escorted me to his house... or, at least, that's what we told Aoife. Sometimes we did go to visit his father at the cottage, and sometimes we didn't. We spent many long afternoons playing in the woods, and sometimes the small ones would join in our games for a while. Although I still had thousands of questions teeming in my mind, in relation to their specific nature, I chose not to interrogate them and, instead, just let them be a wonderful, mysterious little part of my life. After all, I was happy for the first time since my mother had gone, and subconsciously, I believe I feared that questioning it all too closely would cause it to disappear in a puff of smoke.

As Liam and I parted before teatime, I always found myself asking: "Would you like to play again tomorrow?" as though I needed reassurance that it wasn't all over.

He always shrugged and said: "Alright," but by then, he always said it with a bright, beautiful smile.

CHAPTER TWO

Of course, everything changed in September. I had to start school, and it was just as drab and joyless as I had feared that it would be. The deceptively cheerful bus arrived each day, and cruelly drove me to my oppression, as I gazed longingly back in the direction of the woods, and my former freedom. I don't think I'd ever had to sit still for so long, trying to absorb information. I did not mind the information in itself, but loathed the grey, formulaic manner in which it was presented. I wasn't particularly bad at my lessons. My mother had taught me to read and write, and calculate basic sums, at a young age, so I had something of an advantage. This was lucky, as it compensated for the vast swathes of time that I lost daydreaming, or staring out of the window.

At break times, I was overwhelmed by the number of little bodies out in the yard. They seemed so loud, and so juvenile, and so inexplicably *unkind*, pulling each other's hair, tripping each other up, and laughing at each other's misfortunes like a gaggle of little monsters. A small boy tried to push me over one day. I spun 'round, prickling with indignation, and somehow sent him flying halfway across the playground. A fortuitous accident, I supposed. From then on, people stayed away from me. I wasn't sure whether to be disappointed or relieved. *Lucky, lucky Liam*, I thought. Liam didn't go to school.

"Anything that boy needs to know, I can teach him myself," Mr. O Mordha had said during one of my visits, "Why would I send him out into such an unnatural environment?"

I was in no doubt that Mr. O Mordha was a very learned man, and Liam seemed extremely bright and precocious for his age, so that arrangement was clearly working for them. *If only Aoife could be a bit more like that,* I thought, and instantly realised that I was being unfair. She still had a year of secondary school to finish herself.

"All this nonsense of running about with young Liam every day has to stop, now," she had said, "You can see him at weekends but, on school days, you'll come straight home and do your homework. Is that clear?" She had given me a gift of a little red watch to soften the blow. It hadn't.

Fortunately, she had to travel further than I did, to and from her school in the closest town, and had a longer day of lessons, so there was a blissful gap of a couple of hours between the respective times that we got home. Naturally, I spent all of that time with Liam and Cú Chulaind in the woods, and the little red watch proved itself to be very useful, as I knew exactly when to leave in order to beat Aoife home.

The small ones still frequently joined in our games. One day, one of them asked: "How are you finding school, Kathy?"

I sighed deeply in response. "Very, very dull and lonely," I confessed.

"Ah, that's no good! We can't be having that! Would you like us to look in on you there, from time to time, and keep you company?"

"You can leave the woods?" I asked, incredulously. For some reason, without having given it much though, I realised that I'd always assumed that they were trapped there by an ancient curse, or some such.

They burst out laughing, and it dawned on me that my assumption had been a little ridiculous. I'd have spent all of my time in the woods too, if I'd had the choice.

"Thank you. I'd like that," I smiled.

From then on, one or two of them occasionally came to my school during the day. It was instantly, abundantly clear that none of the other children could see them. This made their presence there all the more entertaining. Sometimes, they popped up outside the window and made funny faces at me during a particularly dull lesson, and my classmates stared at me, as if I were a lunatic, when I burst out laughing at inappropriate moments. Sometimes, they even crept into the classroom, and did silly things like hiding someone's pencil or rubber, and I could barely keep myself from falling off my chair with mirth, as I watched the victim's confusion when they noticed that the item had disappeared. More often, they came to me in a quiet corner of the yard, and we played little games like we did in the woods.

One evening, Aoife received a telephone call, and confronted me in the kitchen: "Your teacher has just rung, asking me to meet her tomorrow to discuss some issues with your behaviour. What have you done?"

"Nothing," I protested, indignantly.

Aoife pursed her lips. "Well, I'll find out tomorrow."

It turned out that my teacher was concerned about my mental health, prone as I was to random bursts of laughter in the classroom, and playing 'alone' whilst talking to 'myself.' Afterwards, I received a lecture from Aoife about how our mother had been far too easy on me, and how I'd have to learn how to behave in normal society, or people would think I was deranged, and what would the neighbours say?

Reluctantly, I told the small ones that they had better not come to visit me at school anymore. They understood, and I think it made little difference to them, but it left me extremely disappointed.

Weeks blurred into months. Another exquisite summer of Liam, Cú Chulaind, Mr. O Mordha, and the small ones, came and went, and seemed to last for three years and, at the same time, three weeks, but not at all the three months of its actual duration.

The following years at school were similarly mundane, but thankfully punctuated by holidays, during which I could immerse myself in the woods and forget the drudgery of term time. I enjoyed the escapism of creative writing and art, and dutifully paid just enough attention to the other subjects to avoid concerning Aoife. The less I concerned her, the more she left me to my own devices. She had since finished school, and made a deliberately exaggerated point of telling me that she *could* have gone to university, but had decided to stay in the village to look after me instead, so I should be extremely grateful and cause her as little trouble as possible. She took a job at the local post office and, to my delight, appeared to acquire more of a social life than she'd had for some time. This kept her out of the house, and in the village more frequently. The less time she spent in the house was less time that she knew whether or not I was in it, so the situation suited me perfectly.

For my twelfth birthday, she decided that she should make an effort, and instructed me to invite some friends over for tea and cake. I didn't have any friends at school, so I only wanted Liam, Cú Chulaind, and Mr. O Mordha. Aoife said that she'd have no dogs in the house, and that inviting a grown man to a child's birthday party was strange, so we agreed on Liam.

He accepted the invitation with a certain reluctance, not least because he'd had few dealings with Aoife, and my descriptions of her demeanour were generally less than flattering. I considered inviting the small ones too. After all, Aoife probably wouldn't be able to see them, and Liam and I might have such fun, watching her confusion as they untied her shoelaces, or tickled her ankles under the table. However, I decided to be kind, and not to interfere with her good intentions. The afternoon was stilted and uncomfortable, while Aoife served cake, and attempted to interest Liam in excruciatingly dull conversation.

After a polite amount of time had elapsed, she said, almost pleadingly: "I expect you two will want to run out and play for a while now?"

We nodded enthusiastically and, having thanked her for the tea and cake, burst out of the house with matching sighs of relief, where Cú Chulaind was waiting patiently for us. He sprang up, with a friendly face and a wagging tail, and we all raced into the woods.

We were attempting to play a game of hide and seek- which Cú Chulaind made quite difficult, by finding us before we ever had a chance to find each other- when the prickle, my ever constant companion, began to rise up, and make itself noticed as a sort of disconcerting hum in my ears. I forgot that I was supposed to be searching for Liam, and looked around curiously.

She was standing a little way away, resplendent in her almost impossible beauty, and framed by two majestic, leafy trees. Her strawberry blonde hair quivered in the slight breeze, and glistened in the light.

It had been about six years since we had met, but I recognised her immediately. "Étaín," I exclaimed.

She smiled her brilliantly inviting, infectious smile, and came towards me. "I'm so pleased you remember me, Kathy," she replied.

I extended my hand instinctively... for what purpose, I was unsure. I was far too young to even think of greeting somebody with a handshake, but something about her gentle beauty and shining, green eyes just made me long to touch her... to make sure she was real. She walked straight up to me, and brushed my outstretched fingers with her own, and the prickle turned to velvet for a moment.

Liam emerged from behind a tree, and I suddenly remembered his existence. "Liam," I called, excitedly, "This is Étaín. I haven't seen her for ages!"

Liam approached, but with a stiffness that I had not seen in him for some time. His expression was guarded and aloof, and the tension in his mind was almost palpable to me. His demeanour reminded me of the wary boy that I'd first met, but gone was the sarcastic, mocking sparkle in his eyes and, in its place, was something much harder to read.

He nodded quickly with dutiful, albeit strained, courtesy.

"Liam," exclaimed Étaín in a warm, silken voice, as though he were a beloved friend of hers, "How lovely you are!" She glided to his side and kissed him lightly on the cheek.

The prickle churned uneasily in me, and the butterflies moved in circles around my stomach, but crawled rather than fluttered. I wasn't sure whether I wanted to kiss Liam, or get a kiss from Étaín, or just not to be left out, because they looked so sickeningly, maddeningly beautiful, standing there together.

Liam, however, did not appear in the least pleased by her affection. His fingers twitched spasmodically, but I thought *not* from a desire to reach out and touch her. It almost seemed as though he wished that he could claw her kiss out of his being.

Somewhat relieved that they had not skipped away together, holding hands, and left me all alone, I remembered how pleased I was to see Étaín.

"Would you like to play with us a while?" I asked hopefully, breaking the silence.

"Dearly," she replied, "But I have things to do. I will see you both again soon, though." She flashed us a bright, butterfly-rippling smile, and scampered away.

"Isn't she wonderful?" I breathed.

"She's… something," answered Liam, through gritted teeth.

I looked up at him, puzzled. "Don't you like her?" There was an incredulity in my tone that conveyed my unwillingness to believe that it was even possible not to find her charming.

"It's not that. I just don't…" He hesitated. "…*trust* her." He frowned, as though those were the closest words at his disposal, to denote his feelings, but not quite the ones that he'd been searching for. He changed the subject abruptly, and offered to walk me home soon afterwards.

When we reached my house, and he took his leave, I turned and asked something that I had not asked for some time: "W-would you like to play again tomorrow?" I was surprised to find that I felt a little nervous, as I awaited his response.

He hesitated, deep in his own thoughts and, for a moment, I genuinely feared that he might say 'no'. Then, his eyes met mine and their guarded cloudiness cleared a little.

"Alright," he said, but he still seemed uneasy.

I can't recall at what time I was jolted from my slumber, and sprang bolt upright in bed. The white-hot claws of the prickle were tearing at my cold, clammy skin; and something was positively screaming in my scorching ears, with devastating urgency, and yet no words for me to comprehend. My heart felt like an enormous boulder, hurling itself at the walls of my chest; desperate to escape my body; rattling my bones with its overly fast, rhythmic fervour. Something was very, very wrong… and something was tugging at my sleeve. I looked about wildly, but everything was still, apart from the crawling, thrashing feelings inside me.

"Kathy!" I barely heard my name, through the noise of dread in my ears, but the tugging became more urgent. "Kathy! Kathy! Please wake up, Kathy!"

The words came into focus and began to pry open the narrow window to my consciousness. "Kathy! Kathy!"

Reality rushed through me as I bent down and came face to face with one of the small ones, standing beside my bed and pulling at my nightdress. His eyes were wide with terror.

"Kathy," he repeated, "We need your help!"

Suddenly, everything was very sharp, very calm, and happened very quickly. The claws of the prickle became decisive hands, pushing me out of bed, and to my feet, and propelling me out of the house behind the tiny creature who had summoned me.

Liam and Cú Chulaind were waiting outside, their faces grim as stone. My eyes widened in surprise to see them, and my lips contorted, as a thousand questions prepared to explode from my mouth.

Liam placed his hands firmly on my shoulders. "Later," he hissed, "I'll explain as much as I know later, but for now, we need to move. There's something wrong among the small ones, and they say that you can help."

I turned to the little fellow who had called me from my bed, my eyes pleading for clarification, but found his own expression begging, even more fervently, for me to heed Liam's words and move as fast as my legs could carry me. I swallowed heavily, gulping down my questions, and prepared to run.

The small one shook his head. "We'll keep a brisk and steady pace," he said, "We have a way to go."

We all began to walk towards the woods.

I had never experienced the place at such a strange, dark hour of night. Its hulking, organic shapes were only occasionally visible, by frail slivers of moonlight. Cool dewdrops clung to my- I suddenly realised- bare feet, glittering occasionally in the deep, velvet grass, like tiny trails of stardust in the meaty blackness.

The prickle stirred as we made our way further and further through the woods, and became an inquisitive tingle. It emanated from me, exploring the night with curious fingers, as though it were reaching out to touch something akin to itself, with which it wanted very much to connect. I felt on the verge of tumbling into a sensation not unlike the heady, entranced state that threatened to engulf me, whenever Liam and I touched, but I also knew that this was something quite different, and that made me wary. I decided that, if I had to let something engulf me, I'd prefer it to be that warm feeling I knew, and I reached for Liam's hand. He started a little with the unexpectedness of it, but gripped mine in return, with reassuring strength. The fingers of the prickle retracted and tingled down my arm to where our bodies met, and filled me with such an indescribable sense of inevitability and power, that I seemed to float along in some enchantment, unaware of the passing of time, or the dew drops and tiny thorns on the ground, towards some predestined place, that I both knew and did not know.

The journey melted away, and we stood before the curious mound that I had observed many times on my way to Mr. O Mordha's cottage. I could see it clearly, although it was no more lit by the moon than any other darkened shapes in the vicinity. It was, in many ways, a humble lump on the landscape, and yet the prickle always seemed to reach for it, and whisper to me in its wordless voice, that there was some importance to this place.

"Now, before you go in," instructed Liam sternly, "Don't eat or drink anything in there."

Go in? There was no doorway in the earthen mound. I had seen it from all angles, at various times of day, and I would have noticed something like that! *Don't eat or drink anything*? That warning prised something out of the corners of my memory, sounding familiar, and just like a line from… a fairy tale.

I gasped. "Are we going to the otherworld?"

Before Liam could answer, our small companion clicked his tongue exasperatedly. "*She* doesn't have to worry about any of that nonsense," he sighed, "Now come along, quickly!"

My mother and I had read a great many tales about the otherworld, accessed from a *síd,* or mound: A timeless place, where immortal beings dwelled. As I followed the small one, and passed seamlessly through the earth, as though it were both there and not there, I tried to take in every sight, sound and smell for posterity. However, what I was later left with was a clear memory of the events that took place, but only jumbled fragments of my surroundings, like the recollection of some dream that had felt powerful, but had passed too soon to hang on to a single tangible detail. I sometimes think about those who claim to have passed away and returned to life, and remember colours that they cannot describe, because they bear no semblance to anything from our reality, and I think I know how they must feel.

What I do remember, is a larger group of the small, woodland creatures than I had ever before encountered, gathered anxiously around the lifeless bodies of several of their kind, and stepping back, almost reverently, to let me through, as I passed.

My mouth fell open. "Are they… dead?" I asked, softly, beginning to feel alarm. These beings seemed timeless, ageless, and untinged by mortality, so if some sufficiently dreadful horror had occurred, as to rob them of their lives, how could I possibly be expected to help?

"No, not dead," replied one of the others sombrely, "But cursed to sleep as though dead. Now, please wake them up!"

My jaw stretched further still towards the ground. "How on earth do you expect me to do that?"

"I don't know," she shrugged, "But you have the power within you. Of that, I have no doubt. You just need to find it, girl, and be quick about it, I implore you!"

I felt as though I were trapped in one of those nightmares, about sitting an exam in a subject that I had never studied. I looked around at all of the pleading, expectant little faces, desperately hoping for some helpful direction from any of them, but receiving none. I looked for Liam, but he wasn't there.

Tentatively, I crept towards the dormant bodies on the ground and crouched down beside them. I extended a hand and shook one of them, weakly.

"W- w- wake up," I stammered. Nothing happened. "W- wake up!" I repeated, attempting to sound more authoritative. Again, nothing happened, and I could almost hear the collective sigh of disappointment from those behind me.

I felt around for the prickle inside me, but it was strangely dormant, too. I closed my eyes, and concentrated, and thought that I felt the slightest hum from somewhere deep inside my ears. At that moment, a fly buzzed noisily past me and bumped into my face, breaking my chain of thought. I opened my eyes and swatted it away. I had never seen a fly like it. It was unusually large, and strangely purple, and continued to hurl itself at me, landing on my hair, and skin, and clothing, as I tried to brush it away in vain. I felt utterly powerless, besieged by this infernal insect, at a time when I was attempting a task that I had no hope whatsoever of completing.

I tried to remember the feeling that I'd had on the walk to the *síd;* of power and belonging; of being there, yet not there; of floating through the uncertainty, as though I knew exactly where I was going. The prickle was tingling a little again, and I began to sing softly under my breath, to steady my nerves, and block out the noise of the infuriating, purple fly. For a moment, the small, lifeless creature I was touching moved a little, and his eyelids fluttered as though he were about to awaken. I heard the congregation behind me inhale sharply, in hope.

However, the fly doubled its efforts then, moving so quickly and noisily about me, that it could have been a swarm of the things attacking.

"Liam!" I found myself crying out. If only I had his hand to steady me, and his calming power to focus my mind.

"I'll fetch him," muttered someone from behind me and, moments later, Liam was thrust, somewhat unceremoniously, in my direction. He looked slightly bewildered, yet not so much as one might expect. I wondered if he had been there before.

I continued to sing, fending off the purple fly with one hand, and reaching for Liam with the other. As soon as our hands were joined, my song sounded less shaky, and echoed through the space with more certainty. After listening to me for a little while, to ascertain the melody, Liam joined in, and our voices soared together as they had on our first meeting. A burst of warmth fluttered up from my stomach, as though those butterflies, now a majestic army, were coursing up through my being and exploding from my mouth, in the notes of our little song, encircling all of those present, and driving the fly away into the shadows.

I heard excited murmurings of: "She's done it," and realised that the sleeping ones had woken, yawning and rubbing their bleary eyes, as they rose to their feet. The fly was nowhere to be seen. I let go of Liam's hand and breathed a sigh of relief, feeling sickeningly depleted and exhilarated at the same time.

"Thank you, Kathy," exclaimed the small one who had escorted me there, rushing forward, "Thank you from all of us! You truly are your mother's daughter… and more besides!"

"I- I…" I stuttered. The situation seemed far too strange for such an ordinary phrase as: 'You're welcome.' I gave up attempting to speak. I was utterly exhausted.

Liam gently helped me to my feet, his face concerned. "Can we get her out of here? I think she needs to rest."

"Thank you," I whispered to him, "For everything."

"No thanks required," he answered briskly, "I think I just… steadied your nerves a little. They say you are quite powerful."

My brow furrowed in confusion. "I think you're right about one thing: I do need to rest."

"You can just walk straight back out, my dear," smiled the small one, "I'll take Liam."

He took hold of Liam's hand and walked back the way we had come. I followed unsteadily and, in a moment, it was all over. Wherever we had been fell away, and the cool breeze of the woods at dawn touched my face, and filled my lungs, and I collapsed on the dewy grass, in a bundle of whirling sensations.

Liam rummaged around in his leather pack and produced a flask of water, from which I gulped greedily, as I tried to steady my breathing.

Eventually, I spluttered: "What on *earth* just happened?"

"As you suspected," replied Liam softly, "We've just been to another world. I suppose it's as close to the one from the old stories as really exists. I used to play there often when I was very small. I can't just walk in and out, like you did, though. They have to take me, and touch me for the crossing. They've told me not to eat or drink there. I suppose having anything in your body, that belongs to another reality, keeps you from returning to your own, as the old tales suggest…"

I raised my hand to silence him. I had far more immediate questions. "What happened to the poor creatures who were unconscious?"

Our small friend, who had remained silent since our return to the woods, then spoke: "As we told you, it was a curse. It was intended to force our hand, if we wanted them to recover."

"Force your hand to what? Who cursed them?"

"One of those who fears becoming more like us, and does not want us to be happy with it either."

I frowned. "What exactly *are* you, then? If you live in the otherworld, doesn't that make you fairies? Or… *gods*?"

He smiled wryly. "Or both. Or neither. The words you use, young Kathy, are mortal words which seek to name, and impose your order upon, what cannot be explained by mortal means. There were powerful forces in this country for a longer time than your mind could fathom: Different passions, different energies, and different concerns… A collective, yet a series of functions, which could individually be called down by man, in times of need.

We grew too close to them, bonded to them by rituals and tradition, and let them call us by names, with which we learned to identify. We lost ourselves more and more in the relationship. The goddess of fertility and destruction coupled with the kings of men and, through their union, both sides were responsible for the good of the land, and the bounty of nature. We became lesser than we were, and divided amongst ourselves, in conflict and petty pride, reflecting the flaws of those who worshipped us.

Then, a new god came, and stole their love, and they made us lesser still: Small things in stories, crouching behind mushrooms, and living in mounds… Not gods, but little memories of what had once been, for what is immortal cannot die, but it can be much changed. Only the truly Great Ones, the most powerful among us, are remembered by name, as heroes of a magical race, preserved in human tales, but tainted by contempt.

They are still with us, and they are not small; and now that fickle, faithless men are falling out of love with their new god, the Great Ones want to take their original place again. They want us all to be mighty, and whole, and reclaim that love; regain what we once had, and avenge what we lost.

Some of us are so small now, that our desires are small too. We have forgotten how to want… *more*. We do not want to rise up. We want to stay here, in peace, and remain a little memory. We want a serenity that we lost before time began, and have almost rediscovered in our lack of desire… Our lack of remembering.

However, those who want power will not leave us alone. They seek to frighten us, with their displays of greater magic, hoping that we will flock to their cause in terror. It is after one of those interventions that you find us today."

I struggled to make sense of everything he had said. They were very, very immense and ancient truths to comprehend for anyone not of their world, and especially one of my tender age.

"So…" I reiterated, in a simplified fashion, "You're saying that… you *were* the gods, but the Christian god took over and, because you were ignored, you became something else? And now that the Christian god is less powerful, some of you want to be gods again, and some of you don't, and you're fighting amongst yourselves about your future?"

"Something like that," he smirked, with very little mirth behind the expression, "One of the Great Ones cursed us today, and we were no match for their power."

"Then, how did Liam and I match it?"

"You have magic, young Kathy. Powerful magic."

I considered his words. Magic! Was that what the prickle was? No, I decided. The prickle was the prickle. 'Magic' was far too grand a word for anything that *I* possessed, no matter what he said. I then remembered what one of them had mentioned once, about my mother doing 'little favours' for them, 'from time to time,' and suddenly wondered if those 'favours' were anything like the one I had just done for them in the *síd*.

"Was my mother... like me?" I asked, softly.

"She was... special," he responded warily, "Very special, but not quite like you."

His guarded tone diverted me from that line of questioning. "And Liam," I continued, glancing at my friend, who was listening to the whole conversation intently, as he stroked Cú Chulaind, "Does he have... what I have? I couldn't have done it without him!"

The small one's expression was difficult to read. "We know nothing of such matters regarding Liam, but, whatever the truth of it, perhaps you'll find out together."

I narrowed my eyes, suspecting that he knew more than he was saying, but was being enigmatic, and contrary, and not quite telling me. I opened my mouth to continue with the interrogation, but a yawn groaned out instead. I realised that my tiredness was now so profound that my legs felt like jelly, and my eyes felt as though they might never open again once they'd closed.

"She really needs to rest," observed Liam.

The small one agreed. "Aye. There'll be plenty of time for all of this. Rest well, young Kathy. I take it you'll see her home?"

He looked up at Liam, who nodded. I tried to stand up but wobbled uncontrollably, and he rushed to take my arm.

"I don't know if I can make it home," I admitted, weakly.

"The cottage is closer," suggested Liam.

I nodded. It was the summer holidays, and I was rarely up before Aoife left for work in the morning, so she wouldn't know a thing about it if I didn't go home. She didn't strike me as the sort of person who was likely to be in the habit of opening my door, and peeking tenderly at my sleeping face, before she left the house.

The small one took his leave, and was gone in an instant, as though he had never been there.

"Isn't it maddening, when they seem to know more about you than you know about yourself?" I grumbled, as Liam led me away.

He shrugged. "I've never given it much thought. I've always been here, and I've always seen them. You don't question things so much when you're very little, and I've never thought to question them much since. My father understands. He's always seen them too."

"Your father…" I mused, "He once said something about 'the small ones' in a way seemed as though you both knew about the other ones. Have you seen them? The 'Great Ones'? What are they like?"

"I don't believe *I've* never seen them," replied Liam, "I think my father might have, though. He warned me about them when I was younger. He said: 'If anybody strange approaches you in the woods, other than the small ones, you should be wary, because they could be magical beings with intentions that are none of your concern. They might be very beautiful and intriguing, and you might want to go with them, but they are no fit company for a child.' He hasn't told me much more."

When we reached the cottage, Mr. O Mordha was sitting thoughtfully on the steps outside, the lilac dawn light playing on his sombre features. As soon as he saw us, he was up in an instant, and at my side, taking my other arm for extra support, as he and Liam escorted me indoors. He seemed relieved that we were safe, but unsurprised that we had been out at such an unusual hour. It occurred to me that he and his father truly did not appear to have any secrets between them. *Then, why doesn't Liam know as much about the 'Great Ones' as his father does, and why…? Oh, I'm too tired for this.*

I slumped on a chair, as Mr. O Mordha bustled about, making up a cosy little bed for me on the sofa. Liam fetched me a cup of sweet tea and a biscuit. The former, I drank gratefully, and the latter, I desperately wanted but could not find the energy to chew.

I was bundled into the makeshift nest of blankets and pillows, and my eyes closed instantly. I felt somebody stroking my forehead and decided that the hand was far too rough to be Liam's. As I drifted off into a hazy slumber, I heard his voice, however, recounting to his father what had transpired. Mr O Mordha began to respond, and the tiny part of me that was still conscious struggled to listen to what he was saying, but was defeated by my exhaustion. Their voices were merely a comfortable hum that trailed away, as I sank further into oblivion, and fell into a deep sleep.

When I awoke, it took me only moments to remember where I was, and fewer still to realise that the sun was setting outside the window in a crimson blaze, which meant that I had slept all day. I leaped up from the sofa with a shriek, crying: "Aoife…"

"It's alright," Mr O Mordha, who had been sitting at the table, reading, approached me and placed a gentle hand on my shoulder. "I rang Aoife, and told her that you had come down here after playing with Liam for the day, and that I'd invited you to stay for tea. I'll take you home later."

I sat back down on the sofa with a thud of relief. "Thank you so much, Mr. O Mordha," I breathed, "Where *is* Liam?"

"He's gone out to walk the dog. He watched over you most of the day, though. Hasn't slept at all himself."

"Oh," I replied, feeling guilty, "I'm sorry to have caused so much trouble."

Liam's father raised his eyebrows, in an expression that was extremely reminiscent of Liam when he thought that I was being very stupid. "Why would you apologise, Little One? None of this is any of your doing!"

"He told you what happened?"

"He did."

"Apparently, I have some sort of… power."

"So it would seem."

"Do you know anything about it?"

He sighed, as though I had asked a very weighty question indeed. "I know something of the general situation amongst the old ones, great and small. I have always seen them. I don't know why. It seems quite random. I grew up with six brothers, and not a one of them saw what I saw. The small ones have spent far more time with Liam than they ever did with me, though. I sense that, young as he is, he instinctively understands it all better than I do."

I smiled a little. "That's what he said about you. There *is* something about him, though. Something… powerful. Do you know what I mean?"

Mr. O Mordha continued, not quite answering my question, yet not quite *not* answering it. "Well, he's different from his brothers. They never saw any of it."

Liam had two older brothers, who had moved to Australia shortly before I met him, although they had lived away from the cottage for years before that, only coming home for occasional visits. I wondered if it made Mr. O Mordha sad to have them so far away. It could not be easy for him, particularly with his wife gone. Every mention that I'd heard of her from him was in connection with ill health, and with undertones of tragedy. I was glad that he and Liam were so close.

"But… what about me?" I asked, somewhat timidly, "Do you know anything about *me?* They speak to me in riddles, and hint at something I should know about myself, and I have no idea how to begin to find out!"

"Well," he replied, evasively, "There was always *something* about your mother…"

"They keep saying things like that, but do you know what it was? Did you know her well?"

"I knew her quite well, at one time, but not so well as to understand the whole truth of it…" His voice trailed off, wistfully.

It didn't feel like an unequivocally straight answer. Frustration began to prickle slightly within me, at the unfairness of my mother's untimely death more than anything. *If only she were here to guide me through all of this.* Liam and his father were so lucky to have each other.

"Is it something about this place, I wonder?" I mused, "After all, there seem to be several of us who see them, and the *síd* mound is nearby… Have *you* always lived here?"

"No, I grew up on a farm in a different part of the country, the youngest of a large family. My parents left us the land when they passed away, but there were so many of us that there just wasn't enough work for us all. Some have gone abroad, some tend the farm, one is in Dublin, working as a barrister… and, I travelled as a younger man, and then came here to live a quiet life. There are *sídhe* all over the place in this country, Kathy. I don't know that ours is in any way special above others. If there's anything particular about this place, perhaps it's just that it's lovely!" He smiled a little, evidently attempting to lighten the mood and, I suspected, distract me from my quest for answers.

I continued with my interrogation, undeterred. "What about the Great Ones… Have you seen them? Liam said he thought you had."

"I believe so," he replied, slowly, "I've met a few strange characters in my time. There were some that I took for men and women at first, though they were unusual in appearance, and suddenly saw them completely transform, or simply melt away, before my eyes, and then I knew them to be something… other."

"So, you've spoken to them? What did they talk about? Did they tell you exactly what they want from the small ones, or anything that might help us to help them?"

He shook his head. "They said little of any consequence, at least to my comprehension. Odd, enigmatic phrases, and riddles that I rarely stayed long enough to hear them explain. It's been a long time. I don't give it much thought anymore."

"Where did you meet them?"

He shifted nervously in his chair. "Here and there. Lonely places, usually. Always strange encounters that left me feeling a little… unsettled. I'm glad of the fact that young Liam hasn't come across them. I was worried, when he first told me he'd been to the *síd*."

I peered at him, inquisitively. "Why? Do you think it's… dangerous, in some way?"

"I didn't use to think so," he began, "But, I've known great unhappiness to come of it, for some." His face grew dark, as though he'd been visited by a torturous recollection.

At that moment, Liam returned. When he saw that I was awake, his eyes widened, and his face broke into one of his most brilliant, beautiful smiles.

"Are you alright?" he asked, rushing to me, then stopping short and hovering awkwardly in my vicinity, as though he hadn't quite thought through what he was going to do upon reaching me.

"I am," I beamed back. In truth, I was still feeling exhausted and depleted, not to mention maddened by the mystery of it all, but my friend looked older than his years that day, as though he had been the prisoner of grave concerns, during his long vigil at my bedside. The last thing I wanted to do was trouble him any further.

Mr. O Mordha made us, what seemed to me, the finest tea I had ever eaten. Then, Liam said: "You know, if we left now, I could walk you back through the woods, instead of us driving you home."

"It's no trouble…" protested his father.

"That's a great idea!" I exclaimed a little too quickly, almost cutting him off. Although I was tired, I couldn't imagine being at home in half an hour, sitting in that bland, soulless house with Aoife, and trying to make inane conversation for the rest of the evening, when I felt so confused, and so forever changed. There was nothing I wanted more than a peaceful wander through the woods with my best friend, to give me a little more time to mentally digest everything that had happened.

Then, my face fell. "I've just realised… I'm wearing a nightdress, and I have no shoes!"

Mr. O Mordha chuckled. "I thought of that. I dug out a few old bits that used to belong to my wife. Might be a bit big for you, but if you try to get past your sister before she examines you too closely, you *may* get away with it."

I nodded gratefully. "It's worth a try!"

He fetched the clothes and shoes, and I changed into them in the bathroom. They were not a good fit, but an improvement on my former attire.

"Don't dawdle too much now, or Aoife will be on the phone to me," warned Mr. O Mordha, as Liam and I prepared to leave.

I agreed, fighting back a slight smirk. It was clear from his tone that he was as eager to enter into conversation with my sister as I was.

Liam, Cú Chulaind and I set off, pausing for a moment to look out over the river, before Mr. O Mordha's voice echoed from the cottage window with exasperation, and a little mirth: "What did I just say about dawdling?"

We scuttled hurriedly out of his line of vision, through the elegant expanse of trees that lay between him and the woods, then defiantly slowed our pace.

Liam stretched his tall body, his arms reaching for the sky, with a weary groan of relief. "Well," he said, "That was all a bit dramatic, wasn't it?"

I giggled. "Just a bit!" I grew more serious, then. "Do you think these Great Ones are going to keep coming after our small friends, or might they just leave them alone, now that we've intervened?"

"I don't know," he replied earnestly, "But if they don't back off, we'll be here to help."

I nodded emphatically.

We rambled through the woods, at a leisurely pace, although we did do Liam's father the courtesy of not stopping to rest. We played a game as we walked, which consisted of taking turns to pick a character from the old stories, and answer questions from the other, until they guessed who the character was.

It was easier to keep our minds distracted with light, amusing things, than to draw ourselves deeper and deeper into the spiral of uncertainty and worry that would have accompanied a protracted discussion of the situation among our supernatural acquaintances.

"Are you handsome?" I asked Liam.

"Extremely!" he replied proudly.

"Yes or no answers only," I chided, "Okay… erm… Did you come to a tragic end?"

"Oh, most definitely!"

I shot him a warning look. "Did you get into trouble over a woman?"

"Yes."

"You're Noísiu," I cried triumphantly.

He nodded. "Correct. Right, your turn! Are you a woman?"

"Yes."

"Are you a queen?"

We were about halfway through the woods when I put out my hand to stop him for a moment. A sudden, prickling wave was shuddering down the back of my neck. "Wait…"

"What is it?" whispered Liam.

I looked about suspiciously, convinced that there was some reason for my uneasiness, then shook my head, baffled. "Nothing, sorry. Go on!"

"Are you a queen?"

My shoulders shivered, attempting to shake off the crawling feeling of the prickle. "Oh… Maybe…"

"Yes or no answers, remember?" He paused, and his tone softened. "Are you sure you're okay?"

"Yes, yes. Just tired. You'd never think I had slept all day, would you?" I joked, attempting joviality, "So… erm…"

Étaín was standing right in front of us. I had been so caught up in the prickle, and the game, that I hadn't even noticed her approach. Liam evidently saw her at about the same moment, because he started a little at the suddenness of her.

I was delighted. "Étaín! How lovely to see you again so soon!"

"Kathy," she responded in her glittering voice, my name dripping like honey from her perfect lips, but with a hint of a chill behind the saccharine. There was something slightly different about her demeanour. Oh, she was still radiant as to rival the sun, shining as she did in that moment, in the growing shadows of dusk… But gone was her brilliant smile: That smile, that seemed to wipe all care out of one's head at the sight of it. In its place was *something* of a smile… an *attempt* at a smile… a thin wisp of feigned pleasantry, curling over a somewhat disapproving mouth. If I hadn't known better, I would have been certain that I'd displeased her in some way that she was too polite to mention. Perhaps she'd noticed how awkward Liam had been when we'd last met her, I concluded. She had tried to be friendly, and he'd been positively discourteous, and she was hurt. I frowned at him sharply, and he looked baffled.

"Étaín, I'm *so* pleased to see you," I said, emphatically and, I hoped, reassuringly, "I have to get home, but would you like to walk with us awhile? We've been playing a game…"

I was about to explain it to her, in case she cared to join in, but she interrupted: "Oh, thank you so much for the invitation, Kathy." Her voice oozed with sparkling politeness, and yet… was that a hint of sarcasm hiding in her tone? "I couldn't possibly accept. I had the most dreadful night, with people meddling in my affairs. I still don't feel quite myself."

"My night was… challenging too," I responded without thinking.

Her head snapped up and her eyes held me in a gaze that seemed to extend through my eyeballs, and bore right into my brain. I felt, rather than heard the words: *'Are you mocking me?'* in a searing, seething tone, but her lips had not moved, and she had not spoken. Her gaze released me, and I stumbled a little, as though invisible hands had let me go.

I stared at her, and she was flawlessly composed, fluttering her hand daintily over her beautiful mouth as though stifling a small yawn. She could not have uttered those scathing words. My weary brain must have conjured them in some stupor.

I looked at Liam, and he was watching me with grave concern in his eyes again. Clearly, I was imagining things, and flopping around on the spot like a lunatic. Perhaps I was even more exhausted than I'd thought myself to be.

"Étaín," I said earnestly, "We must get on and head for home, but I really *would* like us to be friends. Tell me we can spend time together soon!"

Her face brightened. Her eyes sparkled, and her smile shone again, as though she were genuinely both surprised and delighted to find that my words rang true. "I'd like that." She then turned to Liam: "I would like to see more of *you* too," she glittered, "I had not expected to meet one such as you again."

He made no response, and she began to float away, through the grass, on her delicate feet, with an enticing wave.

I waved back, then turned to Liam with more than a little disapproval. "You could have made *some* effort!"

He raised his eyebrows in surprise. "I don't know what you mean!"

"She was clearly already offended by how stand-offish you were yesterday, and today you didn't say a word to her! You were so rude that I think she was worried *I* didn't like her anymore either!"

He sighed, as though reluctantly breathing out his feigned innocence. He knew quite well what I meant. "She makes me uncomfortable," he admitted, "I don't know why. There's something unsettling about her. She makes me feel… dizzy, careless, cautious and frightened all at the same time. It's as though she wants something from me that I don't really understand, and her eyes are like prying fingers, trying to reach into my brain and poke about. Part of me wants to give in, and the other part of me is terrified that no good can come of it. It's just strange…" He broke off and stepped back from me, as though the physical distance might somehow mitigate the amount of himself that he had just revealed.

I froze, the meaning of his words hitting me in the stomach like a sack of bricks, and knocking my butterflies unconscious, as it stole my breath and my voice. In the lonely stillness deep within me, where they had been, came the realisation that he did not dislike Étaín at all. In fact, he liked her so much that it sent his thoughts to a place that frightened him: A heady, spinning, breathless place, perhaps even more powerful and passionate than the one I visited whenever I held his hand. I tried to swallow, but the realisation was a lump in my throat. My eyes stung, as though tiny demons had suddenly begun to prick them with saline pitchforks.

"You really don't look alright," observed Liam, no doubt assuming that my odd expression was another manifestation of the strangeness that I'd exhibited earlier on our walk.

I waved his concern away with a flailing, irritated flick of my hand.

He changed the subject. "Let's get you home. Now, where were we? Oh, yes… Are you a queen?"

"I've had enough of that," I managed to mutter, and we walked in silence.

Cú Chulaind padded beside me for the remainder of the journey, keeping pace with me, and glancing at me regularly, with large, soulful eyes. I stroked his head every so often, sensing that he somehow knew I was upset, and wanted to comfort me.

It was dark when we reached my house. Liam looked grave as he said goodbye. "You will be okay, won't you?" he asked, clearly aware that something was amiss but, presumably, putting it down to the previous night's adventures and the long walk we'd just had.

I nodded stoically, and fled inside, desperately hoping that Aoife wouldn't be there. Of course, she was. In fact, not only was she there, but she was not alone. She and Alan Lynch were sitting at opposite sides of the fire, cupping small glasses of whiskey.

"Kathy," she exclaimed, "*There* you are!" There was an implication in her tone that she thought it was a bit late for me to be getting home, but didn't want to discuss it in front of the neighbour, for whom I was infinitely grateful in that moment. She seemed distracted… Distracted enough, I hoped, not to notice what I was wearing.

"It *is* late," I replied tightly, fighting so hard to keep my emotions in check, that I sounded strange, "I'm going to bed."

Aoife raised her eyebrows slightly, clearly thinking that it might be a bit late for getting home, but it was a bit early for bed. She shrugged, sipped her drink, and turned back to Alan. "Goodnight then," she called absently, before resuming her conversation.

I hurled myself into my bedroom and back against the door as it shut, struggling to manage the shaky, silent sobbing that was strangling me, and threatening to turn into a pitiful whine. I didn't have the faintest idea what was wrong with me, but I felt as though I had been eviscerated. He was *my* friend. *Mine...* and so was she. Well, she wasn't even my friend yet, but I *had* met her first! To think of some strong, emotional connection between Liam and Étaín, that didn't involve me, made me feel ill. I'd had few dealings with jealousy in my young life. Aoife had always been much older than me so, even when our mother was alive, we'd required such different things from her that it had never felt like a competition. My relationship with Liam was so special, so unique, bonded by years of playing together, knowing each other's minds, sharing the secret of our friendship with the small ones, and that feeling when we touched, or used our powers together. How could he feel so much for someone that he barely knew in comparison? And yet, part of me understood it. There was something about her… Something that had moved me too, from the first moment I saw her.

Damn them, I thought, Damn them both! Damn them for making me care so much, and want so much from them in order to feel complete! I wish I'd never met them. If only I'd just been a normal girl, and made ordinary friends at school, it wouldn't be like this. I should have known that they were too special for me.

I was surprised to find Liam waiting for me as usual, the following morning. Of course, he had no idea that he'd upset me, so it wasn't at all surprising from a logical perspective, but I wasn't feeling very logical that day. As we wandered in the woods, I did my best to appear aloof and mysterious, answering questions with phrases that I hoped were enigmatic, and when a smile was required, I attempted to make it bewitching and enticing. When I spoke, I tried to make my voice sound musical, rolling syllables on my tongue like nectar. His only response was to stare at me strangely, and express mild concern as to my mental wellbeing. I gave up. I hoped that we wouldn't encounter Étaín, and we didn't. In fact, we didn't for quite some time.

From then on, we occasionally 'did little favours,' as they had once put it, for the small ones. Many of them were minor, such as joining in songs and chants to promote the fertility of the woods, or calming an injured bird as they tended to its wounded leg, but some were more challenging. When an enormous tree fell over in the woods during a storm, they came to us. We held hands and concentrated, and somehow found and coaxed out something in the prickle, that rose invisibly from me with the strength of fifty men. It righted the fallen giant, smoothed the cracks in his gnarled body, and reunited him with the life force that pulsated in the ancient roots beneath our feet.

When some of their kind went missing in the woods, and were nowhere to be found, the small ones approached us again, and their dark mutterings seemed to indicate that this was no ordinary mishap, but some greater force at work. Liam and I held hands, and I let the prickle take control of me, to dictate my path, as we walked slowly through the woods. It took some hours but, finally, the prickle rose to an urgent throbbing and, soon afterwards, we discovered the pitiful-looking group of tiny folk that had been lost, cowering from nothing visible, in a clump of greenery. Their eyes were strange, and blank, and fearful, as we led them back to the *síd*, as though something important had been stolen from their consciousness, and replaced with something unfathomably horrid. I hoped that familiar surroundings, and a reunion with their kinsfolk, would eventually coax them back from whatever bleak place had disturbed their peace.

I took pleasure and pride in helping, and in my bond with Liam, which felt cemented by every task we undertook. I had no idea that far worse tests of my skills were yet to come.

CHAPTER THREE

When I was fifteen, the woods began to die. It was little things we noticed at first, like the birdsong becoming gradually more muted and, eventually, strangely absent. Nuts and berries became less plentiful and, when we did find them, they were shrivelled, warped and sickly. The grass, despite the frequent rain, grew yellow and coarse, and the majestic trees began to slouch and droop, as though they had grown tired of holding their proud heads high.

I dealt with each symptom of the sickening as I found it, mustering all of my concentration to call a flock of birds into a clearing one day, only to find their corpses strewn across the grass the next, or to coax a clump of berries back to ripe, juicy life, only to find them rancid and decaying two mornings later. Try as I might, I did not have the space within me to hold the entire expanse of the woods in my power and keep it safe. Even working with Liam, which usually helped me to focus my abilities and perform feats I had thought impossible, did not seem to have a sufficient effect.

Being in the woods made me feel strange…. Slightly ill myself, as though I were somewhere unwholesome, that I shouldn't be. The prickle didn't like it. It wriggled and churned inside me, and the touch of a branch, or the grass, or an unusually tame squirrel, sent unpleasant chills through my skin, to my very core, as though I had brushed something dangerously unclean.

The small ones were fearful. They had seen themselves as the caretakers of their surroundings for longer than I could comprehend, the wellbeing of the woods somehow bound up with their own. They now felt powerless, and seemed smaller still.

Liam and Mr. O Mordha were even more distraught than I was, their entire existence revolving, as it did, around this small corner of the world. Mercifully, the garden and river around their little cottage remained untouched by the malady that was spreading through the landscape, just minutes away. It was still safe for Mr. O Mordha to fish there, which was fortunate, because he supplemented some savings he had from his younger days with selling fish to local shops and markets, in order to make ends meet. The cottage continued to be a refuge, and a place for us to talk. Sadly, our conversations were most often sombre and nostalgic, and full of longing for our favourite place to be whole again, and such frustration that we could not make it so. If the small ones knew of anything we could do to lift whatever darkness had taken hold of the place, they remained silent.

Before too long, a small part of myself, that I was not entirely proud of, longed to avoid the woods as much as possible. I began to take a little more interest in my schoolwork, because studying was a good excuse- to myself more than anyone- not to venture there every afternoon.

Liam, however, wasn't fooled. "You don't… enjoy coming here the way you used to, do you?" he asked sadly, one Saturday morning, as we wandered through the silent, misshapen mockery of the woods.

I sighed and absently took his hand, concentrating on a patch of wizened grass, and feeling the surge of the prickle course from my electrified palm to my fingertips, through me, and out into the ground beneath us, until it was green and fit for us to sit on. We slumped down wearily. Unusually, we did not immediately let go of each other's hands and, although I was no longer actively summoning my power for any purpose, strands of it rippled across my skin like a luxuriant, playful caress, until I snatched my hand away with an entirely unwarranted glare at Liam, as though he had been *doing* something *to* me.

He merely shook his head dismissively and returned to his earlier question: "You don't, do you?"

"I…" I began, struggling to compose an answer, in the whirling fragments of my shattered peace of mind, "I… don't know how to explain it. Nothing is the same. I feel… empty here, these days."

He winced a little, and petted Cú Chulaind. I could tell that the words had hurt him. I wanted to pour my heart out… To explain that it wasn't him… That he was the dearest person in the world to me, and I never wanted to be without him, but I felt confused, and unsure of my role in this withering, fading place. However, it all sounded far too emotional in my head, and I feared that he wouldn't know what to say in response, and then I would feel even worse, so I said nothing.

Knowing what I knew about matters that most did not even acknowledge as existing, was a heavy weight to bear. By then, I had moved from the village primary school to the bigger secondary school in town, where few of the other pupils knew about the unusual childhood behaviour that had caused me to be such an outcast. Therefore, not everyone avoided me like the plague. I began to speak a little more to my classmates, because their conversation was light, and easy, and unimportant. Everything else in my life seemed far too heavy. I sometimes stayed in town for a while after school, to have coffee with them. Occasionally, I thought of Liam, dejected and alone in the woods with the grieving small ones, and felt guilty for not being with them. More often, I attempted to push such thoughts out of my head, and enjoy the pointless nonsense of socialising with my peers.

One Friday evening, I returned from town to find Étaín lingering by the entrance to the woods near my home. If it had been anybody else standing there, so still and silent on an empty patch of road, I would have described them as lurking aimlessly. She, however, appeared perfectly poised and radiant, wearing an exuberant smile of greeting, as though she had been waiting for me, and had expected me at precisely that moment.

"Hello, Kathy," she beamed, each flawless porcelain tooth a tiny light in her exquisite face.

"Hello," I gasped, "It's been a long time."

"I rarely stay in the same place long," she purred enigmatically, stroking her silken hair with a graceful, ivory hand, "Are you going into the woods?"

"No. It's a little late, and… well… I don't know if you've been there lately, but it's… not as it was."

She nodded. "Sad, isn't it?" Although she spoke the words, her expression appeared anything but wistful. "I've been there these last two days," she continued, "You weren't there. Your friend Liam was, though."

I bristled slightly, as I experienced a small shiver. I did not have time to process my feelings in the moment, but I did not like the thought of them spending time together in the woods, one little bit.

"Oh, really?" I remarked, guardedly, "Did you speak to each other much? I never got the impression that you particularly got on."

She looked a little sad, and I suddenly felt guilty for having been so cruel. She sighed, her breath fluttering in the breeze, like the whimper of a fragile creature that I instantly longed to protect and comfort.

"You're right," she replied, softly, "He doesn't seem to have any interest in my company at all. He just kept asking if I had seen you." Her head drooped dejectedly, and her bottom lip began to quiver.

"Though you and I don't know each other *very* well, Kathy," she continued, "I've always felt a certain connection between us. I can speak to you openly, can't I?"

"Of course you can," I reassured her, hastily extending a hand to touch her pale, silk-adorned shoulder. Though age had tempered my unrestrained infatuation with her, just a little, I was flattered at the thought that someone so special desired to share a confidence with the likes of me!

"I don't know what I could have done to displease Liam," she murmured, "I like him so much, and have done since we first met. Why doesn't he want to talk to me? Are you the only person that he cares for in this world?"

"I'm sure that's not true," I responded, gently, "He just doesn't know you. He lives a very isolated life, out there in the woods, and… he has much on his mind, now that such a terrible sickness has blighted the place."

Her glittering green eyes looked up at me, suddenly brighter and full of hope. "You could mend things between us, couldn't you, Kathy? Oh, do say you'll help! Come to the woods with me tomorrow, so we can all spend the day together, and he can get to know me! Please?"

Her beautiful face was so radiant that, in that moment, I wanted to please her more than anything. However, I still experienced a slight shudder of foreboding at the thought of spending a day in the woods.

As though she had read my mind, she continued: "You know what will heal the sickening of the land, don't you? You know the old tales. We simply must help Liam to see it!"

I had no idea what she meant. Perhaps she knew something of my powers. Perhaps Liam had mentioned something to her in a conversation, to which I had not been party. Perhaps she thought *I* knew how to heal the woods. Perhaps she knew something that I didn't. She *had* always been very enigmatic.

I paused to construct my question carefully, before asking: "What… do *you* think will heal the land?"

"You know, Kathy: The same thing that ensured its fertility for generations."

"By which you mean… what, exactly?"

"A union, of course! A union between king and goddess!"

I frowned sceptically. I resisted the urge to ask what she knew about goddesses, for that risked travelling down a path of conversation that might force me to reveal certain things I knew, but was not yet ready to share with her. I wondered if she were, perhaps, suggesting some ritual in which we attempted to channel ancestral forces… but, if such a possibility existed, why would the small ones not have mentioned it? I also considered the possibility that she was just an overly imaginative girl, who had read too many fairy tales, and had no idea what she was talking about.

Eventually, I simply said: "Ireland no longer has kings, Étaín."

"None that knows to what he was born," she answered immediately.

Perplexed as I was by our conversation, I did not notice the car approaching until I heard the merry honk of a horn and turned to see Alan Lynch driving Aoife up the road towards the house. They waved at me, and I automatically waved back.

"Just come with me tomorrow, Kathy," whispered Étaín urgently, but when I turned back to face her, she was gone.

I barely had time to begin to think about the strange encounter before Aoife called to me to come inside and help her prepare tea, because Alan would be joining us. The fingers of the prickle felt gnarled, thick, and wary around my throat as I obeyed.

I awoke far too early the following morning, and spent what seemed like an eternity gazing up at the slightly cracked ceiling of my bedroom, as the blue of dawn turned to the white light of day on its blank canvas.

Foremost in my thoughts was my current dilemma: My need to make a decision between going to meet Étaín in the woods, and ignoring the whole thing completely. A part of me loathed the thought of the woods themselves, and of watching her attempt to ingratiate herself with Liam while I sat there feeling plain and clumsy in comparison. Another part of me wanted to be there to provide a voice of reason, in case Étaín persuaded him to perform some random ritual in my absence, and called down something unfathomably terrible. I was convinced that he had some power of his own, after all, and had no idea of what he might be capable, with some convincing that he could heal the woods. I was getting to know my prickle a little better, and I knew that I could perform small, magical tasks alone, but I wasn't sure if Liam had ever tried to access any such gifts he might possess, without my being present.

Eventually, I concluded that my reasons for *not* going were cowardly and childish and, as always, my natural curiosity won. I showered and readied myself slowly, however, a slight sense of dread halting my pace.

I came out into the kitchen. Aoife was sitting by the window, drinking a cup of tea and staring dreamily into nothingness. "Oh, good morning," she said with a slight start, "What are you up to today?"

"I'm going to the woods," I replied joylessly.

"Oh, that's nice. Are you going to see Liam?"

"I expect so."

Her brow furrowed slightly, and she turned from her own mysterious musings, to face me directly. "You and he…" she began a little awkwardly, "You and he aren't…? You *are* just friends, aren't you?"

I felt a deep, hot blush rush to my face, as though I had just been slapped across both cheeks. "*Of course* we are," I exclaimed.

"Good… That's good," she smiled, looking almost convinced, though still a little wary, "Because, you know, you're getting to that age now, and he's a little older, and… erm… if there *were* anything more between you, it wouldn't do for you to spend so much time alone in the woods together. What would the neighbours say if you… got into trouble?"

Her expression was pleading with me to acknowledge that I understood her meaning, so that she was not forced to go into excruciatingly embarrassing detail about how she feared that our raging, adolescent hormones might lead to a scandalous, teenage pregnancy.

"We're just friends," I insisted firmly, probably even less eager than she was to continue that line of conversation, "In fact, we won't even be alone in the woods today. Another friend will be joining us." Before she had time to respond, I added: "A girl."

She appeared relieved. "Very well, then! I'm sure you can understand, I have to ask about these things. You *are* my responsibility, after all, and I can't have you running about, making a mess of your life, can I? It's only because I care!"

I nodded woodenly. "I'd better be off." I wasn't sure whether my skin was crawling more at the thought of hearing anything further from Aoife, or of the day ahead.

"Have a nice time!" she called as I left, and I saw her from the window, returning to the seemingly pleasant, sightless trance in which I had found her.

Étaín was waiting for me at the entrance to the woods, exactly where she had been the day before. "Oh, I'm so glad you came!" she squealed enthusiastically, her musical voice ringing like a high-pitched bell. Although she was always as beautiful as to stop one's breath at first sight, I couldn't help gasping, as I noticed that she was looking particularly exquisite that day. Her endless hair was a mass of artful plaits and cascading rivulets, and her body was clothed in a shimmering garment, that seemed to accentuate the gentle curves of her lithe frame.

I almost replied: "I'm not," but thought better of it. I did not want to admit, or explain, how much I dreaded the thought of sitting beside her all day, in my charcoal jeans and vest top, while she flaunted her positively ridiculous beauty and grace in front of *my*… I shuddered, brushing away the silly thought. He was not '*my*' Liam. I had no hold on him whatsoever, and to think otherwise was utterly nonsensical. I blamed Aoife for corrupting my mind with her clumsy, stupid questions.

"Kathy?" came Étaín's silken voice, and I realised that I had been standing there staring, for far too long, without even a word of greeting, "You *are* coming with me today, aren't you?"

"Yes, yes," I said, hurriedly, and she clasped my hand delightedly, tugging me into the woods. Her cool skin felt like a white flame against mine. The prickle trickled down my throat, into my stomach, cold and queasy. I told myself that it was the sickness of the woods I felt, squirming in my core.

As we walked, I regained some composure, gradually dropped her hand, and finally asked: "What exactly did you mean by those things you said yesterday? Were you proposing some ritual to heal the woods and, if so, where did you come to hear of it?"

"The sacred union is a ritual of sorts, yes," she answered, seeming entirely unsurprised by my question, "There is no 'coming to hear of it'. It merely *is*. It is the truth, as it always has been. You know the old stories, Kathy."

"So, you have taken some meaning from a story, and you're now convinced that you know of a ritual that will cure the land of… *this*?" I raised my palms, and gestured with frustration, at the misshapen, pale trees, and the barren ground that surrounded us. "What story is that idea from? If I'd ever read such a thing, I'm sure it would have come back to me, in all of the time that we've been dealing with… *this*!"

"You, of all people, should know not to be so literal," smiled Étaín, "The ancient truths of gods, and men, and the land, were not written down in a factual, prescriptive format. Stories are just stories, containing fragments of truth, which cannot be omitted, because we need them to show us the way: Truths intricately woven, in unbreakable thread, through all the traditions of mankind, discernible only to those who know them. I thought that *you* knew some of those truths, Kathy. You're not just a girl, after all, are you?"

For the second time that day, I felt as though I'd been slapped. "So Liam *did* say something," I exclaimed. How much had he told her about me?

"Liam has said practically nothing to me, on any subject, of any note, at any point," she retorted, suddenly sounding slightly angry.

"Then, why do you sound as if you know things about me that you're not quite saying?"

"I think you understand things quite a bit differently from the way in which most people do, don't you, Kathy? In some ways, we are a little alike."

Then it hit me. "You see them too, don't you?"

"See who?"

"Why, the small ones in the woods! Did *they* tell you these ancient truths? Have they told you about some ritual to save the land? Does it involve you? Do you have some… power too?" My shoulders slumped, as the barrage of questions finished leaving my body. I felt cold… Terrified that I'd said too much, and… exposed too much about myself.

She gazed at me earnestly, looking slightly shocked, and for a moment, I thought that I heard a horrible voice, echoing in my mind, hissing: '*Are you really this stupid?*' Then, her large, green eyes widened in realisation, her shoulders began to shake, and she threw her head back, her hair swirling like billowing swathes of satin in the breeze, as she laughed. It was not the discreet, musical giggle I had heard from her before, but an uncontrollable, guttural sound, which sent one of the last pairs of sickly-looking birds flying upwards from a nearby branch, in surprise, scattering their few feathers as they fled.

The laughter echoed on and on, for what seemed like several minutes, as I stood still, and completely unsure of how to react, until it lessened to a chuckle and Étaín straightened herself, and faced me with something of an eerily mocking smile.

Did she really know nothing of the small ones, or of my gifts? Had she found my questions so hilariously ridiculous, because they sounded like utter fantasy… Or had she been amused for some other reason?

"Oh, Kathy," she breathed, her voice still mirthful, "You really don't know much after all, do you? Yes, I see them: The 'small ones' as you call them… but I don't need *them* to tell *me* about ancient truths!" She chuckled again, her shoulders rippling, as though it were an effort to contain herself from bursting into a renewed fit of cackling.

The prickle spread its claws, tearing at my skin like a beast that needed to escape. "I- I should go," I whispered, "I don't think this was a very good idea…"

Suddenly, she was so still that it was hard to imagine she had ever been so joyful. "You said you'd come with me," she snapped, her voice cold and serious, "You can't refuse me now."

Momentarily, I imagined fleeing in the direction of home, with her chasing me. The idea, for some reason, seemed terrifying. However, the idea of going forward with her also suddenly felt utterly unbearable. I tried to summon the prickle; to allow it to course through, and empower me, as it had at other times; to convince it to stop tearing at my skin, and give me strength instead. However, I found myself weak and trembling, and I wasn't entirely sure why. I wished that Liam were there.

As if on cue, I heard the barking of a dog. *Cú Chulaind*, I thought, with delighted relief, and couldn't help exclaiming out loud: "They're here!"

Étaín positively shimmered with satisfaction, her expression returning to one of beguiling, girlish hope. "How lovely," she remarked, pleasantly, "Now let's have no more of this nonsense. We're friends, aren't we, Kathy? Let's have a nice day together!"

I nodded mechanically, as there seemed to be no other suitable response, and inwardly thanked fate for the fact that, according to the volume of Cú Chulaind's bark, Liam would be coming through the next patch of trees in moments. I still wasn't sure what had so unsettled me. Whatever perceived threat, that had made me want to flee, was feeling less and less real. I knew that I would feel better still, as soon as I saw my best friend.

When I clapped eyes on him, emerging from the trees as predicted, a glorious wave of butterflies fluttered up and down repeatedly between my head and the tips of my toes. I noticed how comforting he looked: Still lean and fair, but tall and strong too. No longer a boy, but a young man.

When our gazes met, he grinned, and I was sure that I saw his blue eyes sparkle, even at a distance. In a heady, thankful moment, I felt the urge to run to him…

But Étaín beat me to it. "Liam," she called, excitedly, and began to skip lightly down the slight slope in the ground ahead, to meet him. I decided that both of us rushing to him like simpering fools would be ridiculous, so I plodded, slightly resentfully, after her, at a steady pace.

When we reached him, I was distinctly aware of how his eyes lingered on her graceful curves and her exquisite face, but I hoped I was not imagining the fact that he looked far more pleased to see me.

I felt Étaín staring at me expectantly, and suddenly remembered that I was supposed to be there to encourage her friendship with Liam, although it was the last thing that I felt like doing. What I really wanted to do was, somehow, spirit him away to a private place, where I could tell him all about the strange things she had said, and the bizarre way in which she had behaved, to see if we could make any sense of it together. However, that was evidently not an option, so I simply said: "We thought we'd come and spend the day with you."

"What do you feel like doing?" asked Liam, directing the question solely to me.

"The stream," suggested Étaín, "Let's go to the stream!"

"The stream is barely there anymore," replied Liam with a certain impatience, "It's more of a pathetic trickle. Kathy, what would *you* like to do?"

"I…"

"I think you'll find that the stream is full today," interrupted Étaín, "I passed it earlier, and it was looking deep, and robust."

"Really?" Liam sounded disbelieving. "It was never deep in the first place, let alone recently! Are you sure?"

"Oh, yes," she assured him, "It was quite lovely."

I had to concede that she made the prospect sound attractive. "Very well, let's go to the stream," I acquiesced.

Liam shrugged, and we turned to go in the appropriate direction.

Étaín had not been mistaken about the stream. It appeared fuller and deeper than it ever had… Almost a rushing river, coursing through that familiar patch of the woods, like an alien invader.

Liam raised his eyebrows. "Where on earth did this come from?"

"It might be a positive sign," I observed, "If this stream has somehow become so healthy, and grown so much, perhaps the plants and animals will follow suit!"

"It could all be healed," observed Étaín, almost smugly, smiling her enigmatic smile.

I frowned. Surely, *she* couldn't be responsible for this? Although I was coming to suspect that she knew something of magic, summoning this vigorous a body of water would be a mighty feat indeed.

"Étaín has some interesting ideas about saving the woods," I announced loudly, for Liam's benefit. If I couldn't tell him about her notions in private, I could at least force her to repeat them for his consideration. "Don't you, Étaín?"

Her lips tightened, as though she were mildly annoyed, but only for a moment. She turned to Liam, who was waiting expectantly for her to elaborate, and bestowed a radiant smile on him.

"Let's not dwell on that now," she chirped, "Things will happen as they must. Here…" She rummaged in the folds of her long gown, and produced- I couldn't imagine from where- a beautiful, golden cup, shaped like an elegant and ornate goblet. She stooped gracefully to fill it from the stream. With a flourish, and a shy giggle, she offered it to Liam. "Have a drink! You must be thirsty after walking all of this way!"

Liam shrank back from the proffered vessel. "No, thank you," he replied brusquely, "I have a flask of water with me."

"Oh, please," insisted Étaín, "You can't refuse a drink from my special cup!"

Liam stepped further back. "I don't want it."

There was something strange in his expression. I remembered how he had warned me not to eat or drink anything in the *síd*, and I wondered if he was suspicious of the origin of the water from this newly invigorated stream. I wasn't so fussy, and I longed to touch the gleaming, golden cup.

"I'll have a drink," I said, and reached out my hand to take the vessel from her.

In an instant, she had emptied the contents back into the stream, and slammed the cup down on the ground, at the water's edge, with a surprisingly dark scowl. She walked to the other side of me, and snapped: "Go ahead. Go and fill the cup, and you may drink from it."

I sighed. She really was a very strange girl. I supposed that she was sulking because Liam had refused yet another gesture of friendship from her. I shrugged, walked to the edge of the stream, and bent to fill the cup.

When I touched the smooth, cool goblet, the prickle exploded against it, sending searing waves of pain up through my arm. I cried out, and opened my hand to let go of the object, but nothing happened. It remained glued to me, as though my palm had been magnetised. I shook my arm through the pain, and felt the prickle rise within me, pushing against the cup with all of its might. The power of the cup was too strong, forcing my arm over the side of the stream, and into the cold water below.

As my hand became submerged, the goblet slipped out of my grasp with ease, yet I still could not break free. The water rose like pale snakes, and its twisted, blue fingers began to crawl up my arm, devouring it with a vice-like grip. The prickle roared in my ears, and became tiny spears on my skin, stabbing at the liquid tendrils that were threatening to engulf me. Though they receded with each blow, they snapped back like elastic, and continued to rise, now pulling and dragging me as they crept across my chest and my shoulders. I saw the water coming closer and closer to my face, and realised that I was falling into the stream.

My body met its surface with a mighty splash, and I flailed in horror, struggling to stay afloat, as my legs thrashed about in the icy nothingness. How had the tiny stream become so deep? The war between the prickle and the watery tentacles raged on, and the prickle fought well, just about keeping my head out of the water, as my liquid bonds continued to pull at me, forcing me down. I managed to scream, before they came up and coiled themselves across my mouth.

I heard Cú Chulaind barking frantically.

I heard Liam's horrified voice, yelling: "Kathy!"

I heard Étaín's silken tone, saying: "Leave her, Liam. It's too late now. She's gone."

"*Let go of me*," he roared.

"She's gone," screeched Étaín, "Do you hear me? She's gone!"

I heard her cry out. The sound was something between a scream and a hiss. Then, I heard another splash. Droplets of water splattered across my eyelids and forehead, the last remaining parts of me that were not in the icy blue. The prickle was tiring. My watery chains were too strong. My vision blurred, as they bobbed across my eyes.

"Hang on, Kathy," shouted Liam, "Fight!" And then, he was there, thrashing about beside me in the crazed stream, wrestling with the watery serpents, and forcing them apart. He took my hand.

As soon as my skin met his, the prickle awoke again, like a white-hot blast, thrusting against the water with renewed vigour. Our fingers clung to each other desperately, as I concentrated. I visualised the prickle streaming out of me, scorching and slashing the things that were trying to drown me. Suddenly, I could see again… Then, I could breathe again… Then I could scream, although what came out was only a strangled whimper. The snakes struggled to keep their hold on my shoulders, like a deathly harness, but the fingers of the prickle pried them, off with grim determination, and they slipped away into the depths, like a dying octopus. The water bubbled as they sank.

Then, there was ground beneath my feet again. Liam and I were standing, ankle deep, in that pathetic, sickly trickle of a stream, that we had come to know, clinging to each other and gasping, in our sodden clothes. The golden cup lay innocently at our feet.

Étaín was staring at us, and my skin crawled at the expression on her face. Her eyes were huge and glittering, as though filled with tears, and her face was a perfect mask of horror. I truly wanted to believe that she had been stricken by concern for our welfare, but the downturned corners of her beautiful mouth seemed to indicate only bitter disappointment at our success.

Liam dragged me to dry land, and released me roughly, before spinning 'round to face Étaín. His fists clenched, and he bristled with an utter fury that I had never seen in him.

"What did you think you were doing?" he bellowed, his voice positively feral.

Cú Chulaind rushed to me, and snuggled into my lap.

Étaín's eyes widened still further, wincing slightly at the strength of his words. "I- I didn't do anything," she protested weakly, and somewhat unconvincingly.

"Y-y-you…" he stammered, as though trying to contain even more rage than he was displaying, "You tried to stop me from saving her!"

"I was just concerned for you," she whined pitifully, "I didn't want *you* to go in there!"

"But you were happy for *her* to die?" he demanded.

Étaín fidgeted with one of her perfect, strawberry blonde plaits. "The land wanted her gone, don't you see? She's not the one to save it! She's on the wrong side! She's just distracting you from your destiny, and getting in the way of things that she doesn't understand…"

"You…" interrupted Liam, his voice dark as rolling thunder, "You *lunatic! Stay away from us!*"

She parted her lips, as though to respond, then closed them again, and narrowed her eyes. "This is not over," she snapped venomously and, pausing only to snatch up her golden cup, stormed away.

Liam took a deep breath, and exhaled heavily, as though trying to expel some of his anger, before throwing himself down beside me, his arms around my shivering, saturated body.

"Oh, I thought I'd lost you," he breathed, "Are you alright?" He pulled himself back to survey me with concern, his hands still firmly on my trembling shoulders.

I nodded jerkily, trying to be brave, although I felt as though I were about to cry, and then die of cold. "That's t-t-t-twice you've saved me from the stream," I managed with a smile, through chattering teeth.

His expression softened, and he almost smiled back, though he looked close to tears himself. "Come on," he instructed me, hauling me to my feet, "We're going back to the cottage."

I nodded weakly. That was clearly the only logical course of action.

Mr. O Mordha's face was grim as death itself. His cup of tea lay cold, and near-untouched, on the table. Liam had just finished recounting the day's events and I, after more than one hot drink, and the aid of about a thousand blankets, had managed to tell him and his father about Étaín's strange ramblings, and the erratic behaviour that had so unsettled me when she and I had been alone.

"Good grief," he muttered, "I'm so glad you're both okay." He touched his son tenderly on the shoulder and patted my hand.

"*'She's on the wrong side,'*" I repeated, "That's what she said about me, when I came out of the stream. It must be something to do with the small ones... Something to do with the fact that I help them. Do you think she's different, like me, but is using her powers to help the Great Ones instead?"

Liam nodded. "Very possibly... but what on earth does she want with *me?*"

"You've been helping the small ones too."

"Yes, but she didn't want *me* gone. She wanted you to die in the water, and me to remain!"

"Perhaps she was hoping that, without me, you'd use your strength to help her cause instead, the way you give me strength." I gazed at him, thinking how grateful I was for his existence.

"But all of this 'king and goddess' talk," interjected Mr. O Mordha, "And the very strange business with the cup... It concerns me." His expression was dark. "You know the old stories, in which the goddess offers the future king a drink from her cup, to cement his sovereignty?"

I frowned. "Surely, you don't think she's...?"

"Perhaps that was the ritual she was trying to re-enact," suggested Liam, "With her standing in for the goddess and me..." He shuddered. "For the king."

I drew in my breath sharply. "That actually makes some sort of twisted sense."

"I wonder if it would have worked," Liam mused, "Could I have healed the land, if I had just taken that bloody drink?"

"Don't even think about it," snapped his father, sternly, "Who knows what you could have got yourself into if you'd gone along with it? I want you both to promise you'll stay away from this Étaín."

We both nodded vigorously, neither one of us remotely keen to see Étaín again any time soon.

"However, the small ones might have some light to shed on this," continued Mr. O Mordha.

Liam shook his head. "We haven't seen much of them lately. I think they've gone to ground, either weakened, or too saddened, by what's happening to the woods."

"Kathy," Mr. O Mordha turned to face me, staring into my eyes intensely, "You can walk into the *síd*. Would you consider going there to speak to them?"

I began to shiver again, although I was no longer at all cold.

"You can't expect her to want to go into the woods again, so soon," exclaimed Liam protectively, "Not after what just happened!"

His father lowered his head. "You're right, I'm sorry. That wasn't fair of me to ask."

I studied my fingernails, ashamed of the part of me that longed to be brave, and accept the challenge, but was too weak to speak up and do so.

"I'll drive you home, Kathy," offered Mr. O Mordha.

I nodded thankfully. He and I stood up from the table, and walked towards the door. I paused, and turned to look at Liam. I owed him my life. What words could I find to express that?

He rose from his seat, came to me, and took my hand. The prickle began to pulsate at his touch.

I opened my mouth uncertainly.

"It's okay," he reassured me, "I know. No thanks required. All part of a day's work for a king!" He smiled playfully.

I smirked back. "I don't know what you're talking about. I wasn't going to thank you. I was going to say that you *could* have saved my life a bit sooner. It wasn't very pleasant in there, you know."

His smile broadened to a grin. "I'll come and see you tomorrow."

"I'd like that."

He was suddenly serious. "I love you, Kathy."

A terrified blankness swept through my mind, as I searched for some response. I flashed him a blinding, somewhat manic smile and, in a strangely high-pitched voice, I cried: "Of course you do! We're best friends!"

I squeezed his hand weakly, and rushed out of the cottage to join Mr. O Mordha in the car.

Liam did come to see me the following day, and the day after that, and the day after that. We avoided the woods. Sometimes, Mr O Mordha came to collect me, and took me to the cottage for the day. Sometimes, Liam and I just spent time together at my house, sitting on my doorstep, chatting and playing word games. One Saturday, I suggested taking the bus into town for coffee. To my surprise, he agreed. From then on, we went into town every so often, and sat in coffee shops, or went to the cinema.

He sometimes took the bus to meet me after school on weekdays. He even met some of my classmates. He always seemed a little stiff around them, and underwhelmed by their company. They, however, appeared to find him positively fascinating. To them, he was a mysterious older boy from the woods, who had manly skills like fishing and making fires, with a sarcastic and nonchalant air that made them long for his approval, and vie for his attention in conversation. Sometimes, I thought that he was purposely manipulating them, just a little, for his own, relatively harmless entertainment.

After a particularly sarcastic comment, he sometimes caught my eye, and I would find his expression twinkling with slight mischief. I would smile a little too broadly, and raise my cup to my lips to hide my amusement. I knew, deep down, that he didn't really want to be there, and appreciated the effort that he made to remain a part of my life.

CHAPTER FOUR

Aoife and I had never been what you would call 'close.' By the time I was sixteen, as long as I didn't do anything to potentially upset the neighbours, she mostly left me to my own devices. I barely gave any thought to her personal life at all, and as a result, it had entirely escaped my notice that she and Alan Lynch had become practically inseparable.

That year, she decided to have a few people over for drinks on New Year's Eve, and asked for my assistance in preparing the house for the gathering.

I was dutifully polishing glasses, to put out on the dining table, when she walked over to me and just hovered in my vicinity, looking nervous, and a bit timid.

I frowned, and paused in my task. "Did you want something, Aoife?"

"No, no," she replied a little too quickly, but lingered in the same spot, twisting her fingers together awkwardly. "You know... Alan and I are... a couple now."

I raised my eyebrows and dropped the polishing cloth in surprise. "Alan Lynch?"

"Yes."

I gasped. I didn't immediately know how to feel about the news. On closer inspection of my emotions, I concluded that I didn't feel much about it either way. She deserved a little happiness, I supposed. I couldn't really see anything particularly attractive about Alan Lynch, but then, *I* didn't have to go out with him. I shrugged.

"I'm pleased for you, if you are," I told her.

She smiled with obvious relief. "Thank you, Kathy," she exclaimed.

Perhaps she had expected a teenage tantrum. I couldn't think why. What she did in her own time made very little difference to me. She went back to preparing canapés, and I returned to setting the table.

The guest list for the party wasn't exhaustive: A few of Aoife's work colleagues, her useless father Seán, Alan

Lynch and his mother, and another couple of neighbours. I had been allowed to invite one friend and, naturally, had chosen Liam. Aoife had finally agreed to my inviting his father as well, when I made her feel guilty at the prospect of leaving the widower alone on New Year's Eve.

However, when I had extended the invitation to Mr. O Mordha on the telephone, he had sounded as if he didn't know whether to laugh or cry, and had eventually replied: "A night with your sister and her friends? Thank you, Dear, but I think I have other plans. I'll collect Liam afterwards, though."

Liam was one of the first to arrive, along with the Lynches. Cú Chulaind sat dejectedly outside the house, having refused to stay behind, and waited for his master, with his muzzle buried in his big paws, and his huge, sad eyes fixed on the door.

I gazed at Alan Lynch, wondering what Aoife saw in him. He was quite a few years older than her, and slight of build, with a weather-beaten face, a few chicken pox scars, and slightly sly eyes. He always wore a cap and unkempt, woolly jumpers. Aoife favoured plain, modest clothing, but was always perfectly styled and coiffed.

"They make a strange couple," I muttered under my breath.

"What did you say?" asked Liam.

I hadn't really been addressing him, or anyone in particular. I shook my head absently. "Oh, nothing. I was just saying that my sister and Alan Lynch are an odd match."

"Who, *him?*" Liam gestured at Alan surreptitiously.

I nodded.

"Really?" His slightly shocked tone indicated that he agreed with my assessment.

Unsurprisingly, the evening was rather dull. Aoife's friends talked about mortgages, at quite some length. Alan spoke, for an extended period of time, about the best way to sand floorboards. Aoife spent about forty minutes explaining a work dilemma, and her colleagues reassured her that she absolutely *should* point out the error in the spreadsheet to their manager. Seán chain smoked. Mrs. Lynch expounded on how the village priest's sermons weren't as good as they used to be. Even the other guests appeared rather bored by that topic. Liam looked as though he would quite like to cut off his own head.

I spotted two, unattended glasses of wine, subtly picked them up, and whispered: "Come with me!"

We slipped out of the house, drank the wine, and threw a ball up and down the road for Cú Chulaind to chase.

Eventually, I sighed. "We'd better go back in, before we're missed. It's close to midnight."

We crept back into the house, and I stopped to put the empty wine glasses in the kitchen, before re-joining the gathering. Liam looked back at me from the doorway as I approached. His face was expectant and frozen, as though awaiting my reaction to some shocking occurrence.

I looked past him and saw Alan Lynch, in the middle of the living room, down on one knee in front of Aoife.

"Yes!" she squealed, "Of course I'll marry you!"

Alan stood up, gathered her into his arms, and swung her around, before the other guests rushed forward, babbling excitedly, to embrace and congratulate them.

I stood still as a statue, unable to quite believe what I was seeing.

"Are you okay?" asked Liam.

"I- I don't know," I replied, honestly.

"Must be a bit of a shock…"

"You… *could* say that. I only found out that they were seeing each other today!"

Aoife bounced up to me, then, shrieking and flashing her finger in my face, though she was moving so quickly that I couldn't quite make out the aesthetics of the ring she was displaying.

"Oh, Kathy, I'm so happy," she cried, breathlessly, throwing her arms around me and hugging me tightly. I returned the gesture weakly, patting her shoulder with all the excitement of a dying fish.

"Congratulations," I muttered, sounding anything but festive.

She was completely oblivious to my lack of enthusiasm, and bounced off again, exclaiming: "Oh, no! I've just noticed, it's gone midnight! Happy New Year, everyone!"

I went out of the house again, as invisibly as I could, with Liam in tow.

"Married? She's getting *married?*" I hissed, "To *him?* It was one thing for her to have a boyfriend, but a *husband?* Is he going to have to live with us? Are we going to have to live with him?"

Liam touched my shoulder gently. "It's going to be okay."

I threw up my hands in exasperation. "I don't know… I suppose it was bound to happen sometime. I just never really thought about it."

"I'm sure they'll try to make it as easy on you as possible."

"Have you actually met my sister?" I snapped, and instantly felt guilty for my harsh tone. "I'm sorry, I know you're only trying to make me feel better."

"Is there anything I can do?"

"Do you think you could steal the whole bottle of champagne, and bring it out to me?"

He laughed. "I think they might notice that."

"Yes, I suppose they would," I conceded with a rueful smile, relaxing a little.

His hand was still on my shoulder. It slipped lightly down onto my upper arm. "Happy New Year, Kathy," he said softly, looking earnestly into my eyes.

Suddenly, I was certain that he meant to kiss me. I froze in terror. Had the world gone mad? Aoife was engaged, and now my best friend was contemplating something that would change everything in the entire world, forever! I couldn't let myself imagine how it would feel to kiss him… To be pulled so far into that heady, spinning place that accompanied his touch, that I might never find my way out.

I jerked away from him abruptly.

"Happy New Year," I replied tersely, almost tripping over my own feet as I staggered hurriedly backwards.

He looked as though I had punched him. "I- I didn't mean…" he stammered in astonishment.

"It's fine," I snapped.

"But I…"

"I said, it's *fine*. Just leave it."

"I can't leave it like this," he protested, "I don't know what you thought…"

"Just stop! Please!"

A car roared up the road, its headlights flooding our faces and startling us out of the intensity of the moment.

"Liam," called Mr. O Mordha, "Are you ready to go home?"

Liam stared at him, open-mouthed, as though the basic question were not quite permeating his brain.

"Perfect timing," I cried, struggling to make my voice sound bright and carefree, "Happy New Year! Goodnight!"

Without a second glance at Liam, because I knew the expression on his face might break my heart, I ran back into the house, and shut the door firmly.

I slipped, unnoticed, through the merry throng, cooing over Aoife's ring, and into my room. Once there, I threw myself across the bed, buried my face in the pillow, and hoped that if I lay there long enough, the entire evening would disappear from history, or that I might at least suffocate to death.

In the morning, it became disappointingly clear that neither of those things had happened. I opened the door of my room and saw Aoife sitting on Alan Lynch's lap, giggling like a witless fool. I presumed that he had stayed the night. I wondered how many times he had stayed here before, and crept out at the crack of dawn with Aoife's voice ringing in his ears: "What would the neighbours say if they saw a man coming out of the house in the morning?"

I didn't see Liam that day, or the day after that, or the day after that. Initially, I was glad, because there was little I wanted to do less than have an awkward conversation about that clumsy, embarrassing moment between us at the party. Eventually, though, I missed him, more and more each day, until I felt as though one of my limbs had been amputated, and I floated miserably through my existence, going through the motions of attending school, and doing homework, and having bland conversations with classmates, and attempting to be civil to Alan Lynch, who now appeared to be a permanent fixture in my home, attached to the sofa like an ungainly, cancerous lump on the upholstery.

Aoife tried to interest me in planning her wedding, which she appeared to be organising with startling rapidity. I paid little heed to the details, although I did casually remark that I would brutally murder her in her sleep, if she thought of forcing me to wear a salmon pink dress.

One day, I came home and found her in tears. Alan Lynch had, presumably, been surgically removed from the sofa, as he was nowhere to be seen. I groaned inwardly, knowing that protocol dictated I take an interest in her distress.

"What's the matter, Aoife? Has he left you?" I enquired, trying to conceal the hope in my tone.

She shook her head, sniffling unattractively. "His mother has said she won't come to the wedding unless it's in a church," she wailed, "And it just doesn't seem right to have it in a church. We're not religious people, and I wasn't even christened as a baby!" She began to sob.

I wasn't sure how to respond. "Oh dear," I offered, hoping that it would do.

"But we *can't* get married without his mother there," she blubbered, wiping her nose with the crisp, white cuff of her blouse, "That doesn't seem right either!"

I sighed. I rarely offered advice to anyone, but I couldn't help myself. "Aoife, why don't you stop focusing on what *seems* right or *looks* right, for just a moment, and try to think about what you actually want?"

She stared at me as though I were speaking some strange language that she had never heard before. She wrung her hands. "I'm so fed up that, at this point, what I actually want is to get married on a beach in Barbados, wearing a bloody coconut shell bikini!"

I tried to contain a smile at the mental image, then a shudder at the thought of her betrothed in his swimwear. "But you won't do it, though, will you?"

She shook her head miserably. "No. I suppose I'd better go and speak to the village priest, to find out what the rules are."

I rolled my eyes.

"Would you come with me, Kathy?" she asked, pleadingly.

I was so startled that I jumped slightly. "Me? Isn't that something that you and Alan Lynch should do together?"

"I'd prefer not to mention it to him, until I know what I'm dealing with," she replied, "And you're going to have to start calling him 'Alan' instead of 'Alan Lynch'. He's going to be family."

Not my *family,* I thought, darkly. However, my life was so empty at the time, that a visit to the local church was about as interesting an invitation as I could expect to receive, so I said: "Alright, I'll go with you to visit the priest."

The prickle, which had been about as lacklustre as I'd been of late, began to whisper to me in its wordless, rasping way, as Aoife and I walked from the bus stop towards the church… At first, so weak that it was almost indistinguishable from the sound of the breeze, gently rattling the tree branches, and then with more fervour, burning my ears with its urgent tone. I shuddered, as a cold shiver trickled down my neck, over my shoulders, and crawled slowly down my spine. Some external force did not want me on that holy ground, and something within me did not want to be there. The feeling of foreboding grew stronger with every step we took towards the pretty little grey, stone church. It looked utterly innocent, standing proudly in spite of its small stature, its unnecessarily tall spire stretching elegantly towards the clouds.

I glanced at my sister and noticed that she was trembling. I wondered if she was merely overwrought, due to the glitch in her wedding plans, or if she was experiencing anything similar to my instinctive discomfort. Something suddenly occurred to me.

"Aoife, have you ever actually been inside a church?" I asked.

She thought about it for a moment. "No, I don't think so."

I shivered with a renewed sense of icy dread. "Neither have I…"

As the words left my lips, a freakishly strong gust of wind flew at us, swiping at us like an enormous, ungainly paw, knocking the breath from us, as our bodies were forced back several steps. We pushed forward, against the unnaturally vigorous gale. Its power was such that I felt as though a pair of strong, blustery hands were pushing me backwards. Aoife shrieked and flailed, as though she might simply blow away at any moment.

The prickle burned. I narrowed my eyes, barely able to see, as the wind whipped and pummelled them with tiny fists of dust and broken twigs. I squared my shoulders, as though preparing to fight an assailant. Though the icy blast was crazed and ferocious, the heat of the prickle felt like a warm ball in my very core, smouldering with a calm determination to do battle. I willed the heat out from within me, out to the tips of my fingers and toes, out through my skin, visualising a glowing orb of power all around me, and around Aoife, protecting us and our path ahead.

A red-hot explosion erupted from me, blasting through the wind, and decimating the whirling dirt and foliage, with volcanic intensity. Time seemed to slow down for a moment, as I watched the fearsome manifestation of my power with fascination.

Then, the air was almost still again. We were safe. A few pebbles and fallen leaves fluttered around my ankles, with all the ferocity of a toddler waging war with a toy sword. My body tingled all over, alive and triumphant.

Aoife smoothed her hair and adjusted her jacket, staring around wildly in all directions, then regained her composure with a dismissive cough.

"Such strange weather for this time of year," she observed, only a slight tremor in her voice betraying the fact that anything out of the ordinary had happened.

"Quite," I concurred with a touch of sarcasm in my tone, "Strange weather indeed."

"Shall we?" she gestured towards the steps of the church just ahead.

Although I still felt distinctly unsettled, I suddenly knew that whatever lay inside was of no threat to me. I shrugged and nodded. It was strangely quiet as we pushed the large, wooden doors open. For a moment, I was relieved that we had not happened to walk in during a religious ceremony. Then, the stench hit me. There was no other word to describe it: Decay. The cool air was heavy with putrefaction, as though the entire building were a mass of rot.

I took in the elegantly vaulted ceiling, the beautiful paintings that adorned the walls, the exquisite stained glass of the pointed windows, and the ridiculously ostentatious decoration of the altar, which contrasted starkly with the dark, solemn pews and confessionals. It all seemed a little sad: A monument to something barely clinging to life with rancid, weakened fingers… A grandiose mausoleum to house a living corpse.

"Good grief, is there a body in here?" hissed Aoife, covering her airways with her sleeve, as she wrinkled her nose.

I was a little surprised that she was experiencing the same, revolting odour. I had thought that it might be one of my more instinctive, sensual exaggerations: A reaction to something other than what was really there.

"Can I help you?" called a sharp voice.

We looked up to see the priest coming out from a mysterious little door beside the altar. He strode down towards us, looking irritated, and stopped some feet away, as though some invisible barrier had halted him in his tracks. He bristled, as his beady eyes devoured us, and his expression warped into something of a repulsed grimace.

"Eili Nolan's daughters," he snarled, "What are you two heathens doing in the house of the Almighty?"

Aoife cleared her throat, bravely. "Good afternoon, Father. I've recently become engaged to be married…" she paused, as though she were expecting some words of felicitation from him, but none came, "And- I- erm…was wondering about the possibility of…"

"Having the ceremony here?" he interrupted, with a loud guffaw.

"Well, yes. My future mother-in-law, Mrs. Lynch, would dearly love her son to have a religious wedding…"

"There is no other kind!" he snapped, "Do you mean to tell me that *you're* engaged to Mary Lynch's son? By all the saints, his mother is a pious and god-fearing woman. She must be devastated by all of this!"

Aoife's eyes gleamed a little, with rising indignation. "The religious aspect of the marriage is important to her, yes, but I don't believe that she objects to anything else about the match!"

"Too soft on that boy, she always was," muttered the priest, "Dear, oh dear…"

"To return to the point," interjected Aoife, coolly, "Could you please furnish me with the necessary information, in relation getting married in this church?"

He shuddered. "Oh, *you* won't be getting married in this church, young lady, under any circumstances. For me to entertain such a notion would be an affront to our saviour and the blessed virgin."

"But, surely…" she protested.

"Good day to you, Miss Nolan," he barked.

"But, Father…"

"I said, *good day!*" He turned on his heel, and stormed back towards the altar, muttering darkly about "foul, unclean, unnatural things." As he reached his mysterious little door, he shouted back: "It would be just as well if neither of you came to the house of God again… unless you are seeking salvation!" Under his breath, he added: "Though I doubt you'd receive it." He slammed the door behind him, and was gone.

I wandered idly up the aisle, curious to examine the richly decorated altar. I climbed up and stood upon it, running my hand over ornate carvings, of which I'd never seen the like. I was not sure whether I had imagined the slight tremble beneath my feet, as though the ground itself were shaking with fury at my presence in this sacred spot.

"Kathy, get down from there," snapped Aoife, "We're leaving!"

I skipped irreverently down the steps, back to the aisle, and strolled down to meet her, with a slight smile. Something about the church, simultaneously revolting and beautiful as it was, made me feel… *superior*. Proud to be free of all the superstition and artifice, and the rules and regulations that this god demanded from his followers. Yes, I had taken part in rites in the woods with the small ones, but I had not been *worshipping* them. I had simply been honouring the land, from which all things were born, and willing it to be fruitful and healthy for everyone's benefit. I had merely been honouring a timeless truth.

It was no wonder that the reign of this god was coming to an end, I decided, as we left his house. The whole building seemed to breathe a putrid sigh of relief, as though exhaling hard, with its mouldering breath, to hasten us out of its system. Whatever fragments of truth there had been to this religion seemed to have been lost in layer upon layer of stifling embellishment… *Though that could be said of many truths,* I mused.

It struck me that this may have been how the old gods had felt, when the Christian god replaced them in their followers' hearts: Dying; weakened; so reliant upon a rich tapestry of traditional worship, that they did not know how to let go of it, and merely be the eternal truth of what they were. The small ones had let go, though they had let go of a lot of their powerful essence in the process… But the Great Ones… Had they been wandering, so unsatisfied, lost and decaying, all of these years, looking for a chance to claw their way back to life? For the first time, I felt a little sympathy for their plight. Perhaps their quest was not some petty matter of doing harm for the sake of malice or retribution, but a question of the only way in which they could envision their own… "Survival," I whispered out loud.

"What?" barked Aoife absently. She was scratching at her wrists and her neck, as though scrubbing off the clinging remnants of decay from inside the church.

"Oh, nothing," I muttered, though I remained deep in thought as we trudged back to the bus stop.

As it happened, the priest was not mistaken about Mrs. Lynch's kind heart. Once she heard that Aoife had taken steps towards having a religious wedding, but had been refused, her attitude softened, and she conceded that the girl had tried. She attempted to intercede with the priest on Aoife's behalf but had no luck, and ended up a little affronted by his attitude towards her future daughter-in-law. Therefore, she agreed to attend a legal ceremony at the registry office in town. She had always been fond of Aoife, after all.

However, when the day of the wedding finally dawned, that fondness did not prevent Mrs. Lynch from muttering incessantly: "A sad day! A sad day! A marriage without God's blessing!"

Her rants were punctuated by the disapproving click of her teeth, and the shaking of her head. The older woman had come to the house in the morning, as tradition dictated, supposedly to rejoice with the bride and other womenfolk, while they prepared themselves for the wedding ceremony.

I watched Aoife grow angrier and angrier, as she attempted to get ready, and sip champagne with cheer, only to hear: "A sad day!" echoing from Mrs. Lynch's chair in the corner.

My sister held her tongue, but I could tell that the comments had all but ruined her morning. Her lips became positively pursed when she put on her smart, cream wedding suit, only to hear Mrs. Lynch say: "It's like something you'd wear to work in an office! Not like a wedding dress at all!" Aoife's mouth contorted further, into a thin line of fury, when she overheard the elderly woman add: "And she's not in white, I notice! Young women nowadays! A sad day!"

In truth, I too was finding it a sad day, though not for any of the same reasons. I did not relish the thought of being forever bonded to Alan Lynch one little bit, and I was dreading the moment that he and Aoife returned from their honeymoon, because it would mean that he would never leave my house again. I had once heard an old adage, along the lines that women always married their fathers. This seemed to ring true: Alan appeared to be every bit as useless as Sean.

Fortunately for Aoife, two of her work colleagues were also bridesmaids- though, as tradition dictated, I was the reluctant 'maid of honour'- and they remained cheerful and disproportionately excited throughout the proceedings, gibbering at the pitch of cartoon chipmunks about her hair, make-up and outfit.

We took a large, six-seater taxi from the house into town. Although I tried to sit Mrs. Lynch as far away from Aoife as possible, it was even harder to ignore her dismal mutterings in the confined space of the car.

By the time we arrived at the registry office, even the two, simpering bridesmaids seemed a little less jovial, as though Aoife's future mother-in-law had literally sucked some of the life out of them.

We entered the unexceptional building, and encountered the groom and his party in the foyer. He staggered slightly as he slurred a somewhat crude compliment at Aoife on her appearance.

"He seems drunk," I whispered to her in alarm.

"It's tradition," she snapped, protectively.

The ceremony passed quickly and blandly. The registrar did his best to inject a little humanity into the proceedings with smiles and kind words, but Alan was too drunk to participate any further than was absolutely necessary, and Aoife seemed tense, and eager for it to be over before he did anything to embarrass her…

And, before we knew it, they were husband and wife. My *sister* was a Mrs. Lynch. While the others clapped and cooed over the pair, I shuddered, and swallowed a mouthful of bitter bile that had crept up into my throat.

We moved from the registry office to a nearby pub, in which an area had been reserved for the occasion, and decorated with slightly grubby, 'lace effect' plastic table cloths, and platters of sandwiches, sausage rolls and little cakes. The dank aroma of many years' worth of spilled beer in the carpet washed over us, as we crowded a little awkwardly around the somewhat sad, festive spread. Mrs. Lynch- the elder- picked up a limp, salad sandwich, and wrinkled her nose in distaste.

"They should really have done something classier, in a hotel," she whispered to me, conspiratorially.

I shrugged. "Our mother didn't leave us much in the way of savings," I replied, longing to add: "And your son is completely useless," but biting my tongue.

As if on cue, Alan began to sing a rowdy song with his drinking buddies, who were the closest things he had to friends and had, therefore, been roped in to act as groomsmen. They all laughed horribly, and clinked their glasses together, adding more spillage to the already sodden old carpet.

I glanced at Aoife, wondering if she was at all beginning to realise the extent of the mistake that she had made. She was chatting politely and animatedly to her guests, as though she hadn't a care in the world. I knew better. She was holding herself stiffly upright, and her eyes were just a little too bright. I recognised that stance. Nothing was as she wanted it to be, but she had to believe that, if she controlled herself from the roots of her hair to the tips of her fingernails, and made sure that everything *seemed* right to those around her, her world would not come crashing down.

After the reception, Aoife and Alan were taking a bus to West Cork, where a friend of his owned a little holiday cottage. He had granted them the use of it for a week's honeymooning.

Before they left, my sister took me aside, still looking so rigid that I thought I could snap her in two, with only a little force. "You will be alright while we're away, won't you, Kathy?" she asked.

"I'll be fine," I assured her.

"Don't go keeping strange hours or anything, will you? What would the neighbours say?"

"I doubt I'll get up to much at all, Aoife."

"Mrs. Lynch will look in on you, in case you need anything. You will be polite, won't you? She's family now, you know."

"Yes, Aoife."

"And I'm sorry again that we'll be away for your seventeenth birthday. You don't mind, do you?"

"I really don't." That was entirely true. I had no interest whatsoever in some depressing celebration with her and her *husband*.

"Make a nice day of it," she advised me, "You only turn seventeen once! I've left you some money in an envelope, in the top kitchen drawer. Do something nice with Liam or someone, won't you?"

"Thank you, Aoife," I said evasively. She clearly hadn't noticed that I hadn't seen Liam for months.

I couldn't help breathing a sigh of relief when she and her husband finally left to catch their bus. I wanted nothing more than to take a bus home myself, but lingered a little at the reception, simply to avoid having to spend any longer in Aoife and Alan's company on the way to the station. After a suitable period of time had elapsed, I muttered my excuses to the others, who barely noticed, and I slipped away. I hardly remember the journey home. I felt as though I were on autopilot, going through the motions, until I found myself inside my front door. I opened the kitchen drawer, and found Aoife's envelope, on which my name had been printed in her neat handwriting. It had also been ripped open, and only a small amount of money remained inside.

"Alan Lynch…" I sighed aloud, rolling my eyes, "Well, happy birthday to me!"

I felt a saline lump in my throat, and a slight mist across my eyes. For a moment, I wasn't entirely sure which was worse: Being stuck with Aoife and her thieving spouse, or being so completely and utterly alone.

The following day, I decided that I had better go into the village to buy some provisions with my meagre funds, so that I wouldn't starve to death in my sister's absence. I took the bus to the local market, entered, and picked up a shopping basket. I glanced around at the bewildering array of produce on offer, unsure of quite where to begin.

"Kathy?" came a familiar voice from behind me.

Startled, I spun 'round and came face to face with Mr. O Mordha. I was so flooded with relief to see his friendly smile that I almost hugged him. Tears sprang to my eyes, and I dropped my head to hide my embarrassment.

"Are you alright, Dear?" he asked with concern.

I nodded my head jerkily, breathing deeply as I tried to compose myself. "I- I'm fine," I stammered, "It's just… so nice to see you!"

He beamed kindly. "It's lovely to see you too, Kathy! It's been too long." The slightly pointed note in is tone was hard to miss, and left me in no doubt that he had received a full account from Liam, of the mortifyingly awkward events of New Year's Eve.

I hung my head even lower, my cheeks burning with shame, and whispered: "I miss you too."

"So, how have you been?" he continued brightly, "You must be on your summer holidays now, are you? And don't you have a birthday coming up?"

"Yes," I replied, a little sadly, "My seventeenth."

"My, how the years fly by! I still can't believe Liam is all grown up!"

"Is he well?" I asked, carefully.

"He is, thank you. He's been helping me with the fishing. In fact, he's really taken to it. We've bought a little boat and we go out on the river together."

"That's nice."

"I'll tell him you were asking for him, shall I?" Mr. O Mordha's eyes twinkled mischievously.

I can only imagine, from the scorching sensation I experienced in my face, that I had turned some sort of beetroot colour. "And how's Cú Chulaind?" I queried, desperate to change the subject.

"Oh, he's as healthy and full of energy as ever!"

"And… the woods?"

"A bit better, as a matter of fact. Things seem to have improved since…" he lowered his tone conspiratorially, "All of that business last year."

I knew that he was referring to my near-drowning. "I'm glad to hear it."

"Mmmm…" He looked grave, as though he had some further thoughts on the subject, then shook his head, as though he had decided that it was not the moment to share them. "Is Aoife not with you?"

"No, she's on her honeymoon."

"Honeymoon?! Goodness! Time flies…"

I fidgeted a little with the handle of my shopping basket, as I racked my brain for something more to say.

However, Mr. O Mordha broke the silence. "Come down to us in the cottage for your birthday, won't you?"

"I- I'm not sure," I gasped, "I…"

"I'll come and collect you, and make you a nice birthday lunch."

"I- I don't know…"

"Nonsense! It'll be no trouble! We'd love to have you."

"B-but, I…"

He sighed deeply, taking a moment to pause before speaking, as though he were trying to decide whether or not he should be frank. Evidently, he decided in favour of it. "Look, Kathy, whatever misunderstanding transpired between you and my son at the party is no good reason to throw away such a special friendship. I told him that he should have contacted you at once, to explain himself, but the two of you are as pig-headed as each other. Now, I'll be at your house around midday on your birthday, and we'll all have lunch. Is that clear?"

"Yes, Mr. O Mordha," I agreed, meekly.

"Right! That's settled, then! I'll leave you to your shopping. So nice to see you!"

"You too," I murmured, as I waved goodbye in a half-trance. After he had gone, I spent about twenty minutes staring sightlessly at some seedless grapes, until a member of staff enquired as to my state of wellbeing, and I scuttled off hurriedly.

Two mornings later found me staring out of the kitchen window, waiting for Mr. O Mordha's car. Part of me felt that it could not arrive soon enough, and the other part of me hoped that it would never appear. I wrung my hands nervously, filled with an uneasy half-longing, half-dread. I was simply *dying* to see Liam, and simultaneously wanted to throw up at the very thought of it.

When I saw the car approaching, my stomach churned with an unnerving mixture of butterflies and bile. As it drew closer, however, my whole body grew rigid with white-hot shock. Mr. O Mordha wasn't driving. I had prepared an entire scenario in my mind, of a leisurely drive to the cottage, where Liam would be waiting to greet me politely, before we made small talk and had a civil lunch with his father, and everything might magically just go back to normal. All of that now disintegrated in my head, and I felt only panic, and a desire to run to my bedroom and lock myself in the wardrobe.

The car stopped and the driver got out. Our eyes met through the window. *Liam,* I shrieked internally, *Oh no, it's Liam!*

Now that he had seen me, there was nothing to do but go and greet him. He was on the doorstep. I wasn't sure whether he had grown more beautiful in the last few months, or whether I was so pleased to see him that my brain had turned him into some sort of godlike, blonde statue.

"You're driving," I observed. I silently took a moment to congratulate myself on having said something normal and innocuous.

"Yes, my father taught me," he replied, "He also told me to come and collect you for your birthday lunch. He's running a bit behind, and wants to finish making your cake."

"Oh! He shouldn't have gone to so much trouble…"

"He's happy to do it. Actually, I probably shouldn't have mentioned the cake. He might have meant to surprise you."

"I'll do my best to seem utterly astonished."

"Thanks."

There was a moment of silence, as great and deep as a dusty canyon in a desert, utterly desolate but for the lonely whistling of the wind.

"Liam…" I began, at precisely the same moment as he said:

"Look, I…"

We both stopped, and smiled awkwardly.

I tried again, and this time, he let me. "Liam, I'm sorry I behaved so strangely on New Year's Eve. I was in shock about my sister's engagement, and I should have handled it better when you tried to kiss me…"

"Kathy, I was only going to give you a peck on the cheek," he replied.

I stared at him, open-mouthed, struggling to make sense of my feelings. Had I really just made myself miserable by avoiding my best friend for so long because, in my conceit, I had misinterpreted a friendly gesture as some sort of romantic advance?

"I'm such an idiot," I blurted out.

"It's okay," he said, kindly. *More kindly than I deserve*. "I should have known that you were all over the place emotionally, after Aoife's news. I should have tried to explain…"

"You *did* try," I cried, "I didn't let you! All of this could have been avoided if I'd just let you speak!"

"I should have called the following day, to talk it through, but I was a bit offended by the way you acted, and with each day that followed, it felt more and more difficult to pluck up the courage to speak to you…"

"I felt exactly the same way," I confessed, "But it was *my* stupid mistake! I'm *such* an idiot! I'm sorry."

"Well, I'm sorry too. I'm glad my father bumped into you the other day. He said we were both being stubborn over something very silly, and he was right."

"He was."

"Speaking of which," said Liam, "He'll be expecting us. Shall we?" He gestured towards the little car. It was only then that I noticed Cú Chulaind, crammed into the back seat, panting and squirming excitedly, as though he were dying to jump out and say hello.

"I've missed him," I smiled, as we approached the vehicle.

"He's missed you too," replied Liam, "Happy birthday, Kathy."

As we drove towards the cottage, we made small talk, both of us smiling and obviously relieved to have overcome the hurdle of first contact, but still a little wary of over-familiarity. I told him about Aoife's wedding, and about my pillaged envelope of birthday money, to which he reacted with suitable disapproval, and he told me about his father's boat and their fishing trips.

When we arrived at our destination, Mr. O Mordha came to greet us with a smug smile, and it occurred to me that he hadn't been too busy to collect me at all, but had orchestrated the whole thing to force me to make peace with his son before lunch.

I narrowed my eyes at him momentarily, my expression playfully rebuking him for his crafty betrayal, and his smug smile just broadened.

He had outdone himself in making my birthday lunch, and presented us with a three-course feast of mussels in white wine sauce with homemade bread, roast lamb with vegetables from his garden, and a sumptuous coffee cake, complete with seventeen candles. He and Liam sang as I blew them out, and Cú Chulaind howled along tunelessly. I could not believe that my birthday, which I had expected to be one of the most miserable of my life, had turned out so perfectly.

After our meal, Liam declared that he needed to walk Cú Chulaind and asked, a little shyly, if I would care to join them. I realised that I hadn't been in the woods since I'd been half-drowned in the enchanted stream, early the previous year. It seemed high time that I overcame the fear of my memories, and returned to the place that had practically raised me.

"I'd love to," I replied.

As we approached the woods, I became exquisitely aware of the fact that the place was no longer silent. I heard bird song, and rustling in the undergrowth. The trees, though still a little sparse, no longer drooped like dying giants.

The grass was patchy, but healthy in parts. I smiled, took a deep breath to gather my courage, and extended my hand to Liam. "I'd like to try something," I announced, "If you don't mind?"

Intrigued, Liam took my hand. The sensation that rippled through my body shocked me for a moment. I had forgotten the intensity of our connection. I took another deep breath to calm my mind, and closed my eyes. I imagined the prickle creeping down through me, into the ground below, down through the earth to the cool, dark place where the beginnings of life occur, and, with careful fingers, coaxing each blade of grass up, up through the earth, out into the sunshine. As I focused, I felt my whole being tingle with power. I heard Liam gasp. I opened my eyes, and beamed with satisfaction as I realised that the entire ground, as far as the eye could see, was fully clothed in a rich, velvet carpet of vibrant green.

Liam stared at me, wide-eyed. "Kathy, your powers have grown," he exclaimed.

"I know," I smiled, excitedly. Then, I told him about the strange experience, when Aoife and I had visited the village church, and something had tried to turn us back.

He appeared suitably impressed by my tale of triumph. Then, he asked: "How does it feel to be… back here?"

"Wonderful," I replied, "In fact, I think I rather fancy walking the whole way home!"

"I'd like that too," he grinned.

We strolled on, and I took in every familiar sight with relish.

"I wonder why the woods are healing themselves," I mused out loud, "After all, whatever ritual… *that girl* had in mind, never happened." I shuddered as I recalled Étaín.

Liam frowned. "My father and I have wondered the same thing. We couldn't help thinking that there may have been some plot to destroy the woods so completely, that I would be driven to participate in the ritual when the time came. When it became clear that my loyalties lay elsewhere, whatever power created the sickness of the land may have just… stopped bothering."

"That's an interesting theory. I wonder if we'll ever fully understand it, or exactly what Étaín was up to…"

Liam shivered a little. "Or why she was so fixated on me," he added.

"I wonder if it's actually over. Have you seen… 'them' at all, recently?"

"I have. They still come out and walk with me. I tried to ask them about the situation, but they were strangely guarded and didn't seem to want to discuss it. I also asked them directly what they knew about Étaín, but they just looked terrified, and clammed up completely. I thought they might relax a bit, now that the woods are growing healthier, but they still seem uneasy… as if they're waiting for something."

"They've been through so much lately, after countless centuries of relative peace," I said, "Perhaps they're just still a bit wary, and reluctant to become complacent."

"True," Liam concurred, "But something as great as the most mighty of the old gods' struggle for power is unlikely to be over so quickly. Perhaps the small ones know that there's more to come."

I prickled at his foreboding words. Then, I tried to push my misgivings aside, and focus on the moment. "It's been such a nice day," I said, gently, "Thank you."

"No thanks required," he replied, with his characteristic nonchalance.

We reached the stream. It was no longer the pathetic trickle that it had become in the harshest of times, but, thankfully, it was not the deep, enormous, watery chasm of the day of my near-death, either.

"It's strange," I sighed, "I have such conflicting memories of this place now… All of those nice ones, of our meeting here when we were little, and then…"

"Well, yes," he nodded understandingly. Then, he fumbled in his leather pack and pulled something out. "When my father told me you were coming today, I made this, because I thought you should have a birthday gift. Sorry it's not much."

He handed me a beautifully intricate little wooden carving of a tree. My jaw dropped as I cradled it in my palm. "You do woodwork now as well?!" I exclaimed.

He shrugged. "It's been a hobby for a long time. As I say, it's not much."

I decided not to embarrass him by telling him that to me, in that moment, it was *everything*. Instead, I said: "I think it's beautiful. Thank you."

"No…"

"…thanks required?" I guessed, finishing his sentence cheekily.

He laughed.

Suddenly, I was overcome by a bitter sense of disappointment, which I couldn't quite explain. "I'll be fine walking home alone from here," I said, convinced that I needed a little thinking time on my own, to make sense of the strange feeling that had just come upon me, "After all, this is always where we used to meet, and leave each other, when we were little."

Liam nodded, apparently entirely taken in by my excuse of nostalgic tradition as a reason to part company. "Well, seeing as we're finishing each other's sentences," he smirked, "Can I just steal your line entirely and say: Would you like to play again tomorrow?"

I giggled delightedly, surprised and flattered that he remembered. I shrugged exaggeratedly and answered:

"Alright." I then stuck my tongue out at him, and raced away, in the direction of home.

I turned back once to look at him. He was looking back at me too. We waved, a little awkwardly, and then I continued on my way.

I turned my thoughts to my strangely bittersweet feelings about the day in general. It should have been almost unequivocally wonderful. Apart from realising that I had been a complete idiot on New Year's Eve, everything had been perfect. I had been reconciled with my dearest friend, had a delicious birthday meal, enjoyed the woods again for the first time in years, used my powers with great success, and received a beautiful birthday gift. I looked down at the delicate little wooden tree in my hand.

Suddenly, I realised what was bothering me. Liam hadn't tried to kiss me a few months ago. With a loud internal groan, I realised that I was beginning to wish he had.

Oh, no… I thought. At the very moment when the pieces of my life appeared to be falling into place again, I had to go and spoil it by having silly feelings that seemed completely out of my control.

I was so engrossed in my own thoughts that I barely noticed the prickle trickling down the back of my neck, in its customarily warning fashion. Registering my lack of reaction, it began to stab me more urgently, with angry talons, until I took notice and bristled, knowing that I needed to turn around.

Oh, please don't let it be Étaín… I thought. That was all I needed!

I turned. It wasn't Étaín. It was a tall, somewhat spindly man, walking with a staff, though he did not appear to need it. He had dark hair, and an intriguing face. He was almost unnaturally beautiful, but for his eyes: Wide-set eyes, like dark pools, so full of knowing… so full of *everything,* that it was difficult to decide whether or not to like them. They left me in very little doubt that he was not an earthly being.

"Good day," he said, politely. His voice was smooth and silken.

"Hello," I replied, my body still prickling with suspicion.

"That's a nice trinket you have there." He gestured towards my little wooden tree.

"I- It was a gift," I stammered.

"Is it your birthday?"

"How did you know that?" I snapped.

"Just a guess. Would you like to walk with me?"

"N- no, thank you, I have to get on. Someone is expecting me, just up ahead." I hoped that the lie would deter him from any thoughts he might have of brutally murdering me, or the like.

"Very well." I was relieved that he had accepted my rejection calmly. "I hope to see you again." He bowed to me in an old-fashioned manner, and began to walk away.

I was alarmed to find that a part of me longed to go with him. Those eyes were imprinted on my very core, their ancient, swirling depths scorched across the inside of my eyelids, and filled with all the ills and all the wonders of the world. I wanted to know more about him. It made absolutely no sense, but something about him felt impossibly familiar. I tried to shake off the feeling and, quite unnecessarily, began to run for home.

As I rushed through the last patch of the woods before the road to my house appeared, some words of Liam's from many years ago began to repeat themselves in my mind: 'If anybody strange approaches you in the woods… you should be wary, because they could be a magical being with intentions that are none of your concern. They might be very beautiful and intriguing, and you might want to go with them, but they are no fit company for a child.'

I shivered. "But I am no longer a child," I whispered into the empty air.

CHAPTER FIVE

I was delighted to find that Liam was waiting for me by the stream the following day. I was so eager to tell him about my strange encounter with the spindly man in the woods, that I'd almost forgotten about the silly emotions that had preceded it. He listened intently, as always, and remained thoughtfully silent after I had finished my account.

"I wish I had gone with him," I gushed, "It might have been my only chance to ask him directly what he was doing here, and what his purpose was. He seemed so gentle, and polite… Perhaps he would have answered me honestly, if only I'd just gone with him…"

Liam spoke up then: "Well, I'm glad you didn't! Who knows what malice he may have had in mind? If he was one of 'them', he may have been as ill-disposed towards you as Étaín was! *She* seemed gentle and polite too, once, didn't she?... And now, it's clear that she's working for the other side!"

"There was a kindness to him," I mused, "And, yes, a certain malice, but I didn't feel that it was at all directed towards me."

"And what if he wasn't a magical creature at all, but a strange-looking, murderous man who was out hunting for victims?"

"Well, yes, that occurred to me too… but I'm quite capable of looking after myself."

Liam sighed. "In any case, I'm glad you didn't follow."

"I think I might if I met him again."

"Don't!"

"We'll see. There's only so much we can do for the small ones, if we keep fighting against random curses and acts of aggression against them, without knowing anything about the other side."

"We know enough! The small ones are out here, minding their own business, and not doing any harm to anyone, and these other forces just come crashing in at random, to do despicable things, and torment them. I have no interest in their motivations!"

"I don't think it's as simple as that. I think they're afraid of some sort of… half-death, or near-oblivion, if they don't make a stand and take their power back."

"And where did you get that idea?"

"I don't know… it was just something that came to me after I had been to the church, and sensed the fading glory of the Christian god. I suddenly thought that I understood how that loss of power might feel."

Liam looked unconvinced. "Well, even so, why do they need to terrorise the small ones into complying with their plans? Why can't they just get on with whatever they want to do, and leave unwilling participants out of it?"

"Well, it was all a collective power once, wasn't it? The small ones told us that. It was a power that became more and more fragmented, as time went on, and then was ultimately cast aside. If the Great Ones really want to regain everything that they lost, they'll need all of it, won't they? All of the facets of that diminished power are needed to make it whole."

"You're beginning to sound like Étaín," snapped Liam, disapprovingly, "With this enigmatic nonsense about truths that you can't possibly understand. How could you know what they might or might not require?"

"Well, I could be more certain, if I had the opportunity to ask them," I scowled in response, "Which, to go back to my original point, is *why I wish I'd gone with the spindly man*!"

My friend sighed exasperatedly.

I didn't want us to end up estranged again, within just a day of our reconciliation, so I racked my brain for some compromise, to temper the conversation.

"After Étaín nearly drowned me," I began, "Your father suggested that I go into the *síd* to ask my questions. I couldn't face it then, but I think I'm ready now."

Liam stared at me, open-mouthed and clearly wary, yet I read his silence as a reluctant acquiescence. After all, he'd been in the *síd* more often than I had, and we'd both emerged unscathed.

Eventually, he said: "But, I won't be able to go with you, unless one of them happens to turn up and take me."

"Maybe *I* could take you."
"Maybe…"

When we had walked, in tense silence, to the mound which we had experienced as the gateway to the otherworld, I grabbed his hand firmly and, with every step closer we took, his body felt more and more like a lump of lead, trailing behind me. I struggled and pulled but, eventually, had to conclude that I couldn't take Liam across.

"Are you sure that you want to go in alone?" he asked with concern, "We could wait for one of the small ones, or we could try to summon them, somehow…"

I shook my head. "I need to do this now, before I lose my nerve."

"I'll wait."

"You don't have to. Your cottage isn't far. I promise I'll come and see you afterwards."

"I'll wait."

"Very well." With a slightly nervous nod, I turned and moved forward, melting effortlessly into the *síd* .

A whirl of sensations hit me. I was hot. I was cold. It was dark. It was light. I was somewhere familiar, but I can't recall quite where. My eyes began to adjust, as though to a deathly gloom, or a blazing light. I was unsure which. Gradually, I began to feel more comfortable, and the prickle pulsated gently across my shoulders like a reassuring caress. I steadied my breathing.

Somebody was there. I squinted, struggling to focus my vision properly. I expected to see one of the small ones. Instead, I saw the spindly man I had met the day before. He was seated beside an enormous, bubbling cauldron.

I stepped back slightly, in surprise. "You!" I exclaimed, "But I thought… The last time I was here, I…"

"Here?" he repeated quietly, fixing me with an unrelenting gaze, "Where's 'here'? There are many realities to find, when you step outside of your own. Would you care for some refreshment?" He gestured towards the contents of the cauldron.

"N- no, thank you. I was looking for…"

"Someone else?" He almost looked a little disappointed, but those knowing eyes positively glittered, as though he knew exactly who I had been seeking.

"Are they here?" I asked, my voice a little shaky.

"Where's 'here'?" he repeated.

I bristled. "Have you done something to them?"

He raised his eyebrows. "Why would I do anything to them?"

"Y-you're one of *them* aren't you?" I demanded, "One of the 'Great Ones'? The old gods?"

"Some might call us that."

"You've been coming here for years, causing trouble for the small ones! You've cursed them, and sickened the land, and sent Étaín to kill me, so that I couldn't help!"

He chuckled softly. "Étaín?"

"So, you admit that you know her, then!"

"I know many things by many names."

"Stop it!" I cried, raising my voice in frustration, "Just stop it! I'm sick of these riddles, and this enigmatic nonsense! *What* are you doing here?"

He appeared genuinely astonished. "I'm just… being. Not… doing. *You* came in and found me. What is *your* purpose?"

I sighed, struggling to compose myself sufficiently to formulate a sensible response. "I want some answers. Why did you come to the woods?"

"I came to reconnect with parts of myself that I have longed for. Kin, you might say."

I could only assume that he meant the small ones. "You want them to re-join you, so that you can feel more powerful again. Am I right?"

"If you like."

I groaned, then accepted that this might be as close as I could hope to get to a 'yes'. "Why can't you just leave them alone?"

"'They' are not separate from me. 'They' are a part of me. Do you ever argue with yourself? Have you ever struggled to make a decision, as though there were more than one part to your consciousness? Eventually, all of those parts have to agree, or you wouldn't be capable of putting one foot in front of the other."

I shivered, imagining my different internal voices all becoming tangible beings... Several different personalities, in fully functioning bodies, that I had to defeat every day, in order to move forward with even the simplest of actions requiring decisive agency.

He continued: "I sense that you're beginning to understand a little. The ones that you know from the woods aren't even the worst of it. Some parts of us are so separate that they squabble amongst themselves like petty children. Reining them in will not be easy... but we must be made whole, or we serve no purpose. What good are we to the land, or to man, or to anything, for that matter, if we are off serving tiny little fragments of ourselves?"

His words made a strange sort of sense, yet I felt uncertain. "But the small ones *are* being useful! They care for the woods, and try to keep the land safe. *You* almost killed it, and then tried to kill *me*!"

"Oh, that was no doing of *mine*. I sent her to your small friends to convince them to hear us. She came with a noble purpose, hoping for the same things as I do: Unity, peace and strength among us."

"Who exactly are you talking about now?"

He merely looked at me with his knowing eyes. As they shimmered into every crevice of my soul, a creeping, icy tingle of realisation crawled down my spine. *Étaín.*

"*She's* one of *you?*" I then hurriedly adjusted my question to suit his manner of speaking: "She's... a part of you too?" *Good grief, I played with her as a child!*

He shrugged. "She is a part of me. I am a part of her."

I wondered if a part of *me* had always known it deep down. There had always been something about her...

"But her actions have been anything but peaceful," I exclaimed, "She has cursed and abused the small ones, and tried to kill me, and... Is she responsible for what became of the woods, as well?"

"Her methods may have been a little heavy-handed, and born of frustration, to begin with," he conceded, "But, then again, she had a terrible time of it, many moons ago, and she was much damaged. Perhaps she was not the right one to send. I hope to remedy my error now, and speak to them myself. As for her dealings with you... Alas, she has strayed far from her rightful path. Her head was turned by your young man, you see. She had not thought to encounter one of such lineage again, and when she did, it created a wistful longing in her, for an earthly union, and a new attachment to the artifice that is her face, and to the mortal traditions of her guise. She fought you for him, and left like a bitter, common woman, having failed to defeat a rival for human affections! Shameful!"

"What young man's lineage?" I repeated in astonishment, "What are you talking about?"

"It is of little consequence. If he does not choose to be king, he cannot be compelled to become one."

"Kingship again," I sighed, "Don't any of you know that we no longer have kings in this country?"

"All could be restored."

I groaned inwardly at the familiar, enigmatic refrain. "What are you going to do now?" I asked simply.

"What needs to be done," he replied.

"Are my small friends at risk?"

"At risk of what, exactly? Healing? Becoming one with themselves? I cannot comprehend why you would not want that for them."

I was utterly confused. I needed to discuss it with *them*. "Where are they? Please tell me!" I begged, "Why aren't they here? They were here before!"

"Do you think the *síd* is like a set doorway, to a certain room in a mortal building?" he asked, "When you enter our realm, all things exist at all times. All times exist in one moment. All places exist in one space. One merely encounters one reality of that space, or another. Today, this is what you have encountered. If you come back tomorrow, it might seem to be something quite different."

"What can I do… to help them?" I asked, pleadingly.

"Do?" He looked surprised. "Do what you will. Things will happen as they must."

A chill slithered down the back of my neck. His words reminded me of Étaín's. "I don't accept that. I have interfered before. I have some power. I may not comprehend it, but I know that it can have an effect. Why else did… 'she' see me as such a threat?"

"You're right," he admitted, a little sadly, "You could interfere. I hope you won't... But I would never harm you, Kathy. At least, the shameful, self-serving fragment that is *me* would not. And that is as much as I am prepared to tell, for now."

"How do you know my name?" I demanded.

He looked down dismissively, and began to stir the contents of his cauldron. His message was clear: My audience was at an end.

My lips bubbled with a hundred questions, but there were even more thoughts teeming in my mind, that I needed to retreat and process. His stubborn expression told me that he was not about to be of any further use to me, anyhow. I turned to walk back out of his reality, into my own, and the world began to melt away.

Then, the air was a cold slap across my gasping face, as things and colours that I could recognise swarmed into my consciousness, with a dizzying hum. My head pounded.

"Kathy!" somebody yelled.

As I fought to focus on my surroundings, I dimly thought that it should be Liam's voice, but it didn't sound quite right...

I became aware that I was in a heap on the ground. I scrabbled about to get a grip on the earth beneath me, and pushed myself clumsily to my feet.

Mr. O Mordha rushed towards me. "Are you okay, child?" he asked, anxiously.

"I- I..." I stammered, shaking out my limbs, as I fully embraced the reality of the woods, "I'm fine. Where's Liam?"

"He's down in the cottage. We've been taking shifts. Ye gods, Kathy, you've been gone three days!"

My eyes widened. "*Three days?* But, I just had one, short conversation with..."

"There's no time for that now," snapped Mr. O Mordha, "Come quickly. They're all over the woods."

"Who?"

"*Them.*" The expression in his eyes chilled me to the bone. I did not question him further, as he ushered me ahead of him urgently, and I moved as quickly as I could towards the cottage.

The prickle raged as we walked through the woods and approached the familiar stone dwelling. Its thorny fingers twitched with panic… Or was it excitement? I couldn't be sure. For all of its twisting, churning unease, a certain simultaneous thrill rippled through me. I felt invisible tendrils reaching out from me, as though searching frantically for… some part of itself.

Cú Chulaind was sitting rigidly on the doorstep, like a dutiful sentry, guarding his home. I expected him to run forward to greet us, but he merely registered our arrival with a slight twitch of his ears, and remained solemnly at his post. Liam was sitting outside by the river, his face darkened both by shadows, and sombre thought. He leaped to his feet as we neared him.

"Thank goodness you're alright," he exclaimed, "What on earth happened to you?"

"Not much, really," I responded a little sheepishly. If I had indeed been gone for three days, part of me wished that I had a more fantastical tale to tell than that of my brief conversation with the spindly fellow with the cauldron. I should have had a story of epic adventure to relate, from an enchanted forest, or a fairy tale castle, complete with legendary heroes, and a quest, and some form of final battle that would decide the fate of a magical kingdom. However, this was clearly no time for fantasy.

I merely said: "It felt as though I had only been gone for a few minutes."

"Well, that's the paradoxical nature of the otherworld for you," shrugged Mr. O Mordha, "I suppose we should be thankful that you weren't gone for twenty years!"

"What's happening?" I asked. I looked back towards the cottage and noticed, to my surprise, that many, tiny little faces were pressed up against the windows, peering out at us.

"They're *here,*" I cried, "No wonder I couldn't find them!"

Liam nodded gravely. "They came to me a couple of days ago, when I was waiting for you to come out of the *síd* . They wanted your help, but they couldn't find you here… *or* there. They're afraid. The Great Ones are all over the woods, determined to bend them to their will. All I could think to do was to bring them down here, and hope that you would come back soon."

"I should go and speak to them," I concluded.

Within moments of my entering the cottage, I was utterly swarmed by small ones, crowding around my legs, tugging at my clothing, and practically hurling themselves at me for attention. They were babbling excitedly, with so many little voices speaking at once, that it was impossible for me to comprehend a single one of them.

"Calm down," I beseeched them, "Please, calm down! Can *one* of you explain the situation?"

They relaxed a little, and looked towards one of their number, who stepped forward with as authoritative an air as I had ever seen one of them adopt.

"We need your help, Kathy," he said simply, his tone grim and pleading.

"Yes, that's evident," I replied in an exaggeratedly patient voice, "But can you tell me why?"

"The Great Ones are here to destroy us!"

"Oh, but you're so wrong! They don't want to destroy you! They just want to unite…"

The little fellow leaped back from me with a hiss, as though my words were boiling water that had just scalded him. "You've been listening to them! You've turned to their cause!"

"No, no. That's nonsense. I *do* want to help you, but I think I know more about what they want now, and it's not what you think…"

"Oh, they've turned your head, with their pretty words, and their beautiful faces!"

"They want to be useful," I insisted, "They want what you want: To protect the land, and to…"

"Oh, is that right?" he spat, exasperatedly, "Then, would you please be so kind as to explain *that*?"

With a tiny, quivering finger, he pointed at the window, his face aghast. My eyes widened as I turned to look towards the woods. Fire was blazing from within the leafy expanse, billowing smoke cascading from the bright haze of the flames.

"I have to go," I gasped, rushing for the door.

"Don't go in there," exclaimed Mr. O Mordha, grasping my arm.

I shook him off determinedly. "I have to! I can do... something... Put out the fire, or... *something!*"

"I'm going with you," said Liam.

"So am I," added the small one, to whom I had been speaking. Several of his fellow creatures clustered around him in agreement.

"You stay here with the rest of them," Liam told his father, "We have to try to save the woods."

Mr. O Mordha swallowed heavily, knowing that we would not be dissuaded, while tears of concern welled up in his eyes.

"We'll be back," I said, gently, wishing inwardly that I were entirely sure of that myself.

There was no time to speak further. Every wasted moment was an opportunity for the fire to spread, and engulf its surroundings entirely. I strode purposefully out towards the terrible light, with Liam and the small ones in tow.

I expected the air to be thick with the stench of smoke, and the bitter, ashen taste of burning, but it was sweet and clear as it had ever been.

"The fire must be further away than it looks," I remarked as we rushed forward, "That's a good thing. There may still be time to stop it."

Once the majestic trees had swallowed us up, I could no longer see the light of the flames.

"Where is it?" hissed Liam, "I don't know which way to go!"

I shrugged. "We'll have to split up. If we go in different directions, one of us will be more likely to spot it."

"But how will we alert each other?"

"We can sense it if either one of you calls out for our help," the authoritative small one assured us, "And we can be anywhere in a moment, to notify the other."

I nodded grimly. "I'll go this way."

Liam's eyes met mine for a moment, full of unspoken hopes that this would not be our last shared glance. There was still no time for words. I merely hoped that my expression said as much as his did, and set off on my chosen path.

I ran, and I ran, and when I couldn't run anymore, I walked as fast as my shaking legs would allow. I pleaded with fate, in my mind, to brighten the sky ahead of me with flames, but I saw only the complex shadows of the darkening forest before me. I balled my hands into fists and pummelled my own thighs in frustration.

I must have gone the wrong way. If we could see the fire clearly from the cottage, one of us must have encountered it by now. Who is it? Is Liam standing before a wall of flames, crying out for help? Why haven't the small ones come to get me? Has something happened to them? Why didn't I go a different way?

I saw a figure ahead. *Who's this, now?* I remembered Mr. O Mordha's warning: 'They're all over the woods…" The figure was not moving, but standing very still in my path. It was not the spindly man. It was female, and her exquisite clothing shimmered in the half-light before I could make out her face. I begged fate, in my most pleading inner voice, not to let it be Étaín… and it wasn't. At least, not quite. They could have been related though. *And, in a sense, they are*, I thought as I reached her, for there was no doubt in my mind that she was one of *them,* with her breathtakingly ethereal features, and her huge, knowing eyes, framed by a cascade of fair hair.

I told myself sternly that I didn't have time to be fascinated, or enthralled, or to make enigmatic pleasantries… That was, assuming she wasn't waiting there to kill me.

"Where is it?" I demanded directly.

She raised her perfectly formed eyebrows, as though surprised by my lack of courtesy. "Good evening," she replied, a pointed note in her tone suggesting that I ought to have led with something similar.

"Where's the fire?" I growled, "You think of yourselves as powerful guardians of the land, yet this is what you do to it? Show me where that fire is, before it destroys everything! You must know that would be wrong!"

"Destruction… Creation… Neither one is right or wrong," she answered in a pleasant, sing-song voice, "Both must be, and we must be both."

"*Where* is the fire?!"

"There is no fire here."

"There most certainly is! I saw it from my friend's cottage, just minutes ago."

"You once saw a deep river where there was a tiny stream too, didn't you?"

"How do *you* know *that?*" I narrowed my eyes suspiciously, suddenly doubting myself. Perhaps she *was* Étaín after all… though I thought I remembered her slightly differently, in my mind's eye. "What's your name?"

"Brigit," she replied.

I reassured myself, just slightly, that while the Great Ones tended to be maddeningly enigmatic, they hadn't, in my limited experience, been given to outright lying.

"Are you sure there isn't a fire here, Brigit? Are you sure you haven't been sent to detain me? To stop me from helping?"

"Quite sure. I only wanted to see you. Won't you take tea with me?"

"Tea? *Tea?* I've rushed in here, to face a raging inferno, and you want me to pause for *tea*? I need to find my friends!"

"They'll come and find you, if they need you, won't they?"

"Unless they've been burned to death, or detained by another one of your kind," I replied sharply, "And they couldn't find me for days when I was in the *síd,* talking to that spindly one with the staff and the cauldron!"

"Ah, Father," she responded with a smile.

I gasped in surprise. It hadn't occurred to me that, among these fragmentary beings, there could be something so human as familial relationships. Had they become so debased from their origins that they had actually gone so far as to couple and procreate, and physically give birth to parts of themselves?

"I promise you that your friends are safe, and that I mean you no harm," she continued, "They will join us presently, and you will see what you could all be part of."

"My friends are joining us? How can you be sure?"

I should have known better than to expect anything other than a knowing smile in response. "Come along, my sisters are waiting!"

Sisters? What's going on around here? Some supernatural family reunion? Then, I remembered that, in many ways, it was very much like that indeed.

With a sigh, I concluded that I had as much of a chance of finding Liam and the small ones by following her, as I had by rushing aimlessly around the darkening woods alone, searching for some now-invisible fire, that may or may not have ever existed.

She led me through a densely packed maze of trees, their silhouetted shapes deceptively flat against the gloomy sky, while their three dimensional reality brushed against my tingling skin. Though I was wary and concerned, the prickle was positively purring in anticipation, and straining the boundaries of my caution like an eager tiger, desperate to escape its leash.

My head whirled a little for an instant, as the foliage seemed to melt away, in favour of another reality. I wondered if she could possibly have taken me back into the Otherworld without my noticing. Fear gripped me: Fear for my friends, rather than for myself. How long might I be gone this time? Three days? Three years? Thirty?

Then, I realised that my new surroundings, though strange, were very clear to me. My eyes did not need to readjust, and the air was cool and fragrant with the familiar scent of the woods. I was in a clearing, still in my own reality, and the grass was green beneath my feet… But an enormous wooden table had been placed in the centre, carved with intricate detail, and laden with an astonishing feast of succulent roasted meats and vegetables, aromatic stews and broths, exquisite cakes, and dozens of ornate goblets and jugs of drink.

Decorative tapers, holding lit candles, were scattered amongst the refreshments, and standing candelabra surrounded the clearing, casting a bright, golden light across the space. Dozens of chairs were laid out around the table, while a large throne sat at its head, also made of dark wood, and even more intricately carved, with shapes that suggested animals and trees, and the occasional sparkle, as though it were also adorned with gemstones.

Another light glistened through the surrounding trees, although I could not understand quite from whence it came, as though tiny bright balls had been hung in the very air, on threads of nothingness.

Was *this* the light that we had seen from the cottage? Could we have mistaken *this* for a fire? I had been quite certain that I'd seen flames, but perhaps my panicked imagination had given extra detail to something quite benign...

Two females, identical to Brigit, were floating about gracefully, arranging the plates and drinking vessels on the table. I concluded that they must be her sisters. They greeted me in unison with courteous nods and inviting smiles. I was so enthralled by the scene before me, that I barely responded.

As I continued to look on in astonishment, more strange figures entered the clearing, their regally erect bodies seeming to glide on weightless feet: An elegant, wispy procession of beautiful features, and enormous, ancient eyes. My mysterious, male acquaintance was among them, carrying his staff. His expression bored through me with a certain familiarity that brought a flush to my cheeks. A dark-haired female was hovering, almost nervously, at his side. Though she too was striking, her beauty seemed somewhat fragile... Her skin just a little too pale, her face just a little too skeletal, and her eyes just a little too large and anxious in her head, as though they might burst out of it at the slightest provocation. She fixed me with a gaze that brought dark images to my imagination, of writhing snakes and old bones. I shuddered.

Then, I cried out with relief, as I saw Liam and the small ones arrive. He looked wary. They looked petrified.

He rushed to me immediately, and clasped my hands for a moment, as though making sure I was real, before exclaiming: "You *are* here! Thank goodness. I wasn't sure whether or not to believe them."

"Neither was I," I whispered, "I'm so glad you're all safe!"

Brigit was suddenly at my side... Or perhaps she had never left it. "I told you they would be," she beamed.

The small ones had reached us by now, their eyes skittering about frantically in all directions, as though expecting something dreadful to happen at any moment.

"Th-the fire..." stammered one, "It wasn't real... An illusion to draw us here..."

"Calm yourselves," said Brigit reassuringly, "Don't let your small fears spoil our reunion. You have been separate from us for too long. Why, look how tiny you have become: Misshapen by the whimsical fantasies of mortals, into something amusing and inconsequential!"

"We are all misshapen," retorted one of the small ones sharply, summoning his courage, "You wear one guise, and we wear another, but not a one of them is the truth. You let mortals dictate your alluring forms many centuries ago and, yes, we let them dictate ours further still, but there was a time when none of us had faces. Do not forget that."

"Ah, yes. You speak the truth... and it is that time, when we were at our greatest, to which we must return," agreed Brigit.

"Such lofty realms are no longer for the likes of us."

"Don't you remember when kingdoms rose and fell at our command? Don't you miss it?"

"We don't wish to remember," he snapped stubbornly, "Look at what such memories have brought you: Nothing but dissatisfaction and longing. We want no part of it."

Brigit smiled stiffly and glided a little way away, as composed as though she had been exchanging pleasantries with a guest at a cocktail party, and now needed to move on, to lavish attention on the other attendees. She touched Liam's arm gently, and he bristled with unease.

"Come along," she said, lightly, "Let's be seated. Liam, won't you honour us by taking the place at the head of the table?"

He surveyed the richly decorated throne with surprise, and a certain suspicion, perhaps remembering- as was I- all of the nonsense with Étaín, and the cup, and the kingship ritual.

"I don't think that is my place," he answered, guardedly.

"Oh, but it could be," she smiled, her tone still mild and courteous, but with just an edge of insistence.

Still looking unconvinced, he allowed himself to be led off and seated on the throne. Somebody ushered me towards a chair further down the table. Suddenly, as I gazed up towards him, Liam seemed very far away. I couldn't quite make out his expression… And who was that sitting beside him? My stomach churned. Was it *Étaín*… or Brigit… or some other lookalike?

The spindly one with the staff was still staring at me disconcertingly, as was his ghostly female companion, though while his expression was benevolent, hers brought to mind destruction and decay, and I could not fathom why.

They were clearly important for, when everyone had taken their seats, all of the assembled immortals looked in their direction, as though waiting for them to dictate the next stage in the proceedings.

The spindly fellow rose to his feet, and surveyed the gathering with a natural air of authority. He looked to the small ones, and smiled.

"Welcome, my friends," he began, "It is wonderful to have some of you with us, though tragic that it has taken so long to orchestrate a meeting. We have wanted to discuss important matters with you for such long time."

I looked to my right. One of the Brigits- she and her 'sisters' seemed somehow interchangeable- was sitting beside me.

"What is his name?" I whispered, I hoped quietly enough not to cause offense.

"He has many names. He is often called The Dagda," she whispered back.

The Dagda. I repeated the name in my mind, as I watched him waiting for a response from the small ones.

Their apparent leader, who had spoken to Brigit, piped up boldly: "We did not wish this meeting. Your concerns are none of ours."

The Dadga looked genuinely hurt, and I could not help feeling sorry for him, as I remembered our conversation in the *síd*, during which he had seemed so benign and magnanimous in his desires for his kind.

"I do not understand why you wish to be estranged from us," he sighed, "We can serve a purpose, if we are united. What gives your lives meaning now, scattered about this once great land like little shadows?"

"We don't seek meaning," replied the small one, "Our time is over. We accept that, and merely want to *be*."

"But, being *something* is surely better than just being. This is the time to make ourselves felt… To ensure that all of our voices are waiting to answer together, when they call us back to them."

I could only assume that he meant *us:* Mortal men and women. He wanted the old ones to be powerful enough to give *us* what we wanted, as soon as we finally turned away from the Christian god, and embraced our ancient deities anew. I wondered if he was being a little overly optimistic, in his conviction that things would unfold precisely as he intended.

"But, how is that to be achieved?" demanded the small one, "How do you propose to remind them of the bond that was lost? Are you planning to go from door to door, visiting potential worshippers, and asking them if they might be interested in your godlike services? They are not seeking them. They are seeking a reality beyond immortal forces that meddle with their lives: One of logic, and self-determination! The only way to change that is with…"

"Fear," concluded the skeletal female beside The Dagda, leaping to her feet, with an unsettling enthusiasm, her raven hair billowing almost blue against her pale gown, as her eyes shone with a horrible light, "They must be reminded of what comes of ignoring their gods. Who will pray for food without famine? Who will pray for peace without conflict? We must bring them to their knees, and then they will call out for us to save them!"

I gasped in horror, and looked about, to gauge the others' reactions. To my slight relief, a number of the Great Ones also looked uncomfortable at her outburst.

"You see, Kathy?" cried the small one, "Is that the future you want to bring down on humanity? This is why we resist them! This is why…"

The Dagda raised a hand. "Now, that proposal was far too extreme, and not what we truly want," He looked directly at me. "You must excuse Badb. When our kind fragmented from the collective, some of us came to govern different matters... different domains. Hers is... darker than most. It will be tempered, when we are whole."

Badb scowled, almost sulkily, and slumped back down into her seat, with a defiant flick of her midnight hair. I could see that there was something different about her... Something horrid in her mind...

And yet, I recalled The Dagda's words when he had spoken of Étaín in the *síd:* "She is a part of me, and I am a part of her." For every individual urge that they might denounce or disagree with among themselves, was it possible to for them to do so entirely, when that collective thread of commonality still ran through them at their core?

"What exactly *are* you planning, then?" I found myself querying, my tone wary.

"I'm glad that you asked," replied The Dagda with a smile, and raised his hands. "My brethren, I propose that we simply let go: Let go of these mortal trappings that have imprisoned us. Let go of our faces, and our petty concerns. Let go of our thoughts, and return to the air, and the sun, and the moon, and the bounty and deprivation of the earth; become only our united will, limitless in its power; become... everything. Mortals put another in our place once, but there is room in the sky for us again."

Some of the immortals still appeared uncomfortable, as though the magnitude of the transformation he was proposing was somewhat beyond even their understanding, or not quite to their taste.

"I know that it is difficult to recall quite what it was that we once were," he continued, his enormous eyes shining, "I know that many lifetimes have come and gone, and taken us further and further from that peace, and grace, and power... but it will not be difficult, if we choose it. Casting off our human guises will not be painful. It will be a release from the burdens of loss and longing that we have come to carry: Those things that were never meant for us. We shall merely sink back into the velvet tapestry of all things, and we shall know true belonging."

"I'll join you," declared one of the Brigits, "You speak the truth. Here we are, dining at a wooden table like mortals, when the whole world should be our banquet." Several others murmured in concurrence. Others still looked uneasy and uncertain.

The Dagda turned to the small ones. "And what of you, friends? Will you accept the release, and the reunion we offer you?"

"We will not," replied the authoritative little fellow stubbornly, "We will accept you going away and leaving us, and this piece of land, in peace."

"I'm sorry that you don't yet understand," replied The Dagda, "But we cannot leave even you behind. You are a part of us. I truly hope that, someday, you will come to us willingly..."

"And if they don't?" I asked, sharply, "Is it to be more intimidation, and curses, until they bend to your will?"

"I desire none of this enmity," said The Dagda earnestly, "Won't you help them to see, Kathy? Won't you help them to come to us? They trust you."

"I've heard plenty about *your* desires," I replied, suspiciously, "And how you long to be great again… but I've heard nothing about what positive changes your divinity would bring for mankind. Is there any benefit for us in swapping one deity for another? I've studied the history of Ireland, and I'm quite sure that there was plenty of suffering and conflict at the time when you *were* worshipped here. Why should I believe that things would be any better if you controlled our fates again?"

"Well said!" cried one of the small ones.

The Dagda looked disappointed. "Your mortal upbringing clearly limits the scope of your vision."

"My concerns are just common sense," I snapped, "I have seen you do terrible deeds in these woods, to further your own agenda. I have almost been murdered by one of you, when I got in her way. I understand that these are the selfish acts of fragmented beings, and I have some sympathy for your cause, but how can you prove that all of those unnatural impulses, cultivated over countless centuries, would just disappear if you took power?

You speak as though you want to re-absorb the old ones back into some benign, faceless collective, but others of you speak as though you want men to be at your mercy...

At your command, to be played with like toys! And, furthermore, you haven't answered the question of how you expect to convince mankind to become reconciled with you! The only strategy I have heard involves war and terror! How do you expect me to advise my small friends to rally to your cause, when you haven't presented me with a future that I would wish to see?"

"Ah," said The Dagda, "Yes. The matter of our reconciliation with mankind. Even without words, they will hear us, as did the first men who called down thunder, and rain and rejoiced in the harvest… but you could help us to talk to them, too. You and your young man could help us. Let me show you something…"

A large group of people began to walk slowly into the clearing, dressed in fine and extravagant costumes from a bygone era. They were not immortals. They were also not quite real. They had a certain shimmering, transparent quality to them. Ghosts? Memories? An illusion? I could not be certain. To my astonishment, each one, in turn, walked reverently towards Liam, and bowed deeply to him, before moving on to take their places at the table, which seemed to have completely emptied of the Great Ones without my noticing. The new arrivals spoke amongst themselves, their faces bright and animated, as they helped themselves to refreshments from the sumptuous spread.

A man stood up, and raised his goblet in a toast. "All hail the king of the land," he proclaimed loudly, looking at Liam, "A wise and just ruler, who has brought about peace and harmony in our times."

"All hail the king!" repeated the others, and took a drink.

"All hail the gods," continued the speaker, "Our ancient benefactors, guardians of the land, who ensure its health and fertility, and have bestowed their sacred gift of kingship upon our rightful ruler!"

"All hail!" the others chorused again.

Even at such a physical distance from Liam, I could tell by the saucer-like shape of his eyes that he was utterly bewildered. One of the company approached him with an ornate sceptre, an intricately woven cloak and a gleaming golden crown which, like everything else, seemed to have appeared from nowhere. The crown was placed respectfully on his head, the cloak was draped around his broad shoulders, and the sceptre was thrust into his hand.

"Your majesty," the speaker said with a bow, "Our beloved regent; protector of the realm; consort of the goddess; seventh son of a seventh son of a seventh son: We give you thanks, and beg your favour. Won't you honour us with a few words?"

I watched in astonishment as he rose to his feet, looking every inch the magnificent ruler they thought him to be, standing tall and strong, and wearing his finery with confidence.

He tapped the sceptre lightly on the ground to command attention, though every eye was already upon him. The sound echoed chillingly across the clearing, as though the grass beneath us had turned to stone.

He began to speak, his tone clear and imposing: "Good subjects, I honour you in return, and welcome you to this feast, to celebrate peace and prosperity in the land. I am but a humble representative, appointed by the gods to serve you. By their grace, we enjoy this golden age of serenity and bounty. No hunger, no conflict, and no disease mar our lives. Let them continue to favour me with the wisdom to guide you, and to favour the land with the ability to nourish and protect us. All hail them!"

"All hail!" cried his subjects excitedly.

Where on earth had Liam's words come from? Was this not *my* Liam, but some phantom constructed to look like him, and placed in a fantasy that had been forced into my mind? There was something most unreal about it all and, though everything was beautiful, I felt distinctly on edge.

I stood up and strode down towards him. As I approached, he peered at me curiously, some slight recognition in his eyes piercing through a haze of enchantment.

"Liam," I exclaimed sharply, "Is that you?"

The men and women around the table gasped, as though appalled by my over-familiarity with their 'king'.

Liam appeared confused. He shook his head, as if trying to dislodge it from a fog. "K-Kathy?" he stammered, uncertainly, looking about as though he had just woken from a vivid dream, "Kathy, what's happening?"

In an instant, the entire scene melted away. The night air of the woods felt cold. The courtiers were gone, as were the table and the feast. An eerie glow still lit the clearing, though the friendly candlelight was absent. The immortals were back, and all staring at me with ancient, expectant eyes.

I hugged myself against the chill. "What *was* that?" I demanded.

The Dagda stepped forward. "It was a possibility, Kathy: A potential reality; something that could be. Would you not want that for your friend? Would you not want that for your country? A time of happiness and plenty, after centuries of suffering and conflict?"

"But…" My mouth opened and closed incredulously, before continuing: "That scene bears no resemblance to the mortal realm that we inhabit now! This is the year 1997! Where are the cars, and the jeans, and the radios? Your prospective new subjects don't feast in banqueting halls! They drink cappuccinos in cafés. I think that vision was a fantasy of *yours*! *Your* idea of a golden age! That time doesn't exist anymore, and I'm not sure that it ever really did. Besides, you put my friend into a trance, and elicited behaviour from him that was not his own! That sort of life is not what he wants… Is it, Liam?"

He shook his head fervently, still looking deeply unsettled by the experience.

A shadowy shape appeared behind him: A female. One of the Great Ones. She placed a gentle hand on his shoulder. "You wouldn't have to do it alone, Liam," she said sweetly, and the saccharine of her voice was unmistakeably Étaín's. "I could be at your side. I could be your consort, and your friend. I know what to do. I know how the seasons change."

Liam shuddered, and drew back from her with something akin to revulsion.

"Leave him alone," I snapped, "Can't you see that he wants nothing to do with you?"

"Yes, leave him alone," agreed The Dagda, a menacing note of warning in his tone, "I will not have all the seeds that I've begun to sow, ripped out and trampled by your petty, carnal desire for this mortal boy. Go!"

Étaín drew back with a frustrated hiss.

"Kathy," said The Dagda, his tone softer again, as he faced me, "Just promise me that you will consider what I have said. Somewhere deep inside, you know the truth. Étaín, and Badb, and even I myself, are not as we should be. It is precisely the things you dislike about us that I would seek to eschew, but we cannot do it without our kin."

"What is it that you want me to consider? Everything that you've said has been shrouded in mystery. Everything you've shown me has been intangible and unrealistic. If I am forced to choose between you and the small ones, I will side with those who have spoken more plainly."

"Someday, I hope you will understand."

I was about to burst out with frustration, that there was nothing for me to understand, when I had been presented with only half-truths and enigmatic displays, but then realised that I was looking at an empty space where his face had been. The other Great Ones were gone too. Liam, the small ones and I were standing alone in the clearing.

"Is that it?" whispered one of the small ones, his tone treading a fine line between relief and caution, "Is it over?"

CHAPTER SIX

As though on cue, a horrible, rumbling sound burst out around us, and an alien voice began to screech in my head. I could not see her anywhere, but I knew that it was Étaín's.

"How dare you?" she rasped, the words throbbing in every crevice of my mind, with a searing pain, "Who do you think you are, to meddle in our affairs, time and time again? Well, you came looking for a fire, and a fire you shall have! They may think you're special, but I'll prove that you are nothing!"

I closed my eyes and fell to my knees in the grass, my hands pressed desperately to my ears, to drown out the sound, though it was utterly fruitless, as she seemed to be shouting from inside me. *"Nothing! Nothing! Nothing!"* echoed in my body, each syllable a glass shard stabbing at the inner walls of my flesh.

I was suddenly hot. My eyes snapped open. A wall of flame had sprung up around me, and this time, I knew that the fire was real. The pungent stench of burning grass engulfed my airways, and I spluttered, gasping for breath. I curled further into myself, my arms wrapped around my head, as the smell grew more sour, and I heard the crackling of my own hair beginning to catch alight, and then the scorching feeling of the skin on my forearms beginning to burn.

I heard Liam crying out for me. *Focus on his voice,* I told myself, reaching deep inside myself for the prickle… Visualising a cool blast rising within me, and spilling out to protect me from the flames. I felt its icy fingers slithering up my throat, seeping out onto my sore skin, with a comforting coldness, and emanating from me, to block me from the fire. The cool tendrils of my power extended to battle the angry flames, creating a horribly beautiful tangle of writhing shapes, lapping at and dancing with each other, until the fire was engulfed and, with a final, venomous hiss, sizzled into nothingness.

Liam was upon me in moments, the small blanket from his pack wrapped around his nose and mouth, and his face and arms black with soot. He had clearly been trying to fight through the fire from outside, to reach me.

I wanted to say something, but I could only cry pitifully, as the pain of my burns grew more and more real. He scooped me up from the ground as though I weighed nothing, and carried me out of the blackened, smouldering circle. I could feel vicious blisters actively erupting on my arms. My throat was as raw as if I had feasted on an army of wildcats, who had it clawed it to shreds as I swallowed them.

Once we were out of the clearing, and somewhere that felt safer and more secluded, Liam stopped. He did not let go of me, but slumped down against a tree, cradling me in his lap as I clung to him, his charred shirt wet with his sweat and my tears.

He pressed his face into my neck, and whispered: "Fight, Kathy. Fight!" His voice sounded as though it might break into pieces, and I only cried harder, as the realisation dawned of how badly injured I must be. Every part of me seemed to hurt, but for the place just below my ear where his soft, cool lips were murmuring against my skin.

He pulled me even closer to him, and though the pressure on my burns was excruciating, I did not pull away. My body felt as though it wanted to crawl into his for comfort. As he held me tighter and tighter, I became aware of a strange glow through my half-closed, tear-filled eyes. I was sure that it was not coming from me. I opened my eyes wider, and realised it was emanating from him. He looked just as surprised as I was. The gentle light was radiating from his hands, and reaching out slowly, to cocoon me. It felt wonderful as it crept across my skin, caressing every inch of me, and soothing my scorching agony. I saw Liam looking at me in astonishment, as my pain began to subside. The caress of his light on my body tingled and rippled pleasurably through me, to my very core, and deepened in intensity until it became almost unbearable. With a gasp, I sprang back from him, feeling more alive than I ever had. Everything around me seemed crisp and clear, a whirling array of delicious sensations. I examined my perfect arms joyfully, seeing not one sign of blisters or burns. I looked up at Liam, and the expression on his face confirmed what I suspected.

"You… you healed me," I breathed.

He grinned. "I don't know how… I just felt… something, and…" He laughed delightedly. "You're perfect!"

I stepped towards him, and tentatively picked up his beautiful hands in my own, studying them inquisitively for some sign of how they had performed such a feat. I felt only the familiar prickle humming in my ears as we touched, spreading through me like electricity, until that exciting, heady feeling threatened to engulf my senses. This time, I did not step away.

I threaded my fingers through his, and let them writhe there intimately for a moment, before pulling his arms down on either side of me so that our bodies were pressed together. My chest thumped with boulders, and butterflies, and everything that I had ever felt in my life.

"Those hands," I whispered, "I want to feel them all over me."

I had barely spoken the words when he kissed me: Gently at first, but it was only moments before our desire for each other spilled out, and our lips and tongues explored each other hungrily. The prickle burned with an exquisite ferocity, as the whole world disappeared, but for that heady, spinning place where only Liam and I, and our bodies, existed.

With a deep breath, I began to pull at his T-shirt, peeling it away from him, and gasping when I felt the taught, warm skin of his chest against my fingertips. He slipped off my top effortlessly, his movements sure and deliberate, as though it were the most natural thing in the world. I felt no shyness. I wanted him to see me, and I wanted to drink in every inch of him. My bare chest and back tingled almost unbearably where he touched me, and I could not contain a cry of excitement when he began to kiss my neck, then my shoulders and then, more gently, my breasts. I near-fainted backwards with pleasure, but his strong hands caught me in a swift movement, and we tumbled joyfully into the cool grass.

We lay there, our forms intertwined, like some beautiful painting of lovers, as we caressed and teased each other with our curious hands and tender lips. Before I knew it, my jeans and underwear had been skilfully parted from my body, and I was eagerly helping him to remove his. We became suddenly still, as we stared into each other's eyes, realising the magnitude of what was about to happen. We had touched nearly every part of each other now, and there was almost no closer we could get.

I nodded breathlessly, as I felt his hardness against me. He was clearly ready, and I hoped that my expression could convey the fact that there was a longing inside me that would not be satisfied until we had shared *everything*.

He touched me gently first, as though giving me a little time to be entirely sure of what I wanted. I knew exactly what I wanted. I wanted *him*. I felt too impatient to use any words. I nodded more urgently, throwing my arms around his neck, and wrapping my leg around his, almost pleading for him to take me…

And he did. The yearning, deep inside me changed, to the most natural rhythm, urging me to move against him, and the pleasure and the prickle engulfed my writhing body, devouring it with sensations that I could not have imagined existed. We clung to each other, pulsating together, and kissed so intensely that I thought I might lose myself in that kiss, and never find my way out.

Something new began to rise inside me, coursing through my body with greater and greater strength, and a ravening inevitability. Something was about to happen. Part of me wanted it to be over, so that I had felt it, and yet another part of me never wanted it to come, because its approach was like standing on the edge of a precipice, in the most beautiful place I had ever been… And then, it came: The crashing, soaring release of all of my desire. I cried out, and pressed my mouth to Liam's chest to muffle my screams. Within moments, his body began to shudder with the same, uncontrollable power, and he buried his head in my neck, moaning fiercely with pleasure. Then, he kissed me, and kissed me, and kissed me. He tasted of wonder and awe, and ecstatic relief.

I felt the warmth of him inside me. I stroked his golden hair, as the spasms of our climax began to subside, and held him to me, not yet ready to experience the moment when our bodies were no longer one.

Eventually we moved, just a little, so that we were staring into each other's breathless, shining faces.

Liam gave me one of his characteristic smirks, and said brightly: "Well, you should get burned more often, if this is your response!"

I opened my eyes wide, in mock indignation, and swatted his arm playfully. Then, I thought about it more seriously, and replied: "I want you to know… this didn't happen because of the fire, or the fact that you healed me. I have… feelings."

"Really? I wanted to kiss you ages ago…."

"But… you said that you were only going to give me a peck on the cheek!"

"I lied. I thought it would be better to have you back as a friend, than to lose you completely."

I swatted him again, a little harder. "You made me feel like such an idiot!"

He laughed gently, and stroked my face. "You're so beautiful."

"Me?" I exclaimed, incredulously, "Not in comparison with you!"

"Well, you must not be able to see yourself as I see you," he concluded, and the way his eyes rested on every aspect of my face made me feel utterly exquisite, for just a moment.

The muted blue light of dawn was creeping over our surroundings by now. I shivered a little, as the crisp air rippled over my bare skin.

He stretched a protective arm further around me, stroking me briskly to warm me up. "I'm sorry my little blanket is a bit the worse for wear."

"Oh, because it got damaged when you tried to fight your way through a magical inferno, to rescue me?" I replied, sarcastically, "How thoughtless of you."

"Would you like me to make a fire?"

"Tempting, but I think I've seen quite enough fire for one day."

"That's fair. Do you want me to take you home?"

I smiled, and stretched luxuriantly, hoping that my body would excite him. "Not yet."

He grinned and threw himself on me in a passionate tangle of kisses.

It was quite some time later that he did walk me home, and the morning birds were singing brightly against a sunlit sky.

We strolled slowly, our fingers intertwined, pausing every so often to kiss. His touch still tingled, and enflamed something inside me, but I no longer feared it, for I now knew what the culmination of that heady feeling was, and it was the loveliest thing in the world.

"I've been trying to enjoy the moment, and avoid this, but…" he began.

I sighed. "I know. Me too. There's so much to talk about, after everything that happened with the Great Ones."

"I still don't even know what happened to you when you went into the *síd* ."

"Not to mention all of that nonsense with the shared vision of you as the king of Ireland. Didn't they say something about a seventh son of a seventh son of a seventh son?"

"Actually, my father *is* a seventh son, and his father came from a large family too, but I only have two brothers, so they must be mistaken."

"Where does that healing power come from, then? What you did for me was… incredible!"

"I don't know. Nothing like that has ever happened before… Then again, I've never felt so desperate as I did in that moment, watching the girl I love suffering in my arms, covered in burns."

I stiffened. Was he even aware that he had just said 'the girl I love'? I decided not to draw attention to it, but my smile broadened. There was no point in pretending. You couldn't know somebody so well, and do what we just had, without calling it love.

"Shall we talk about it all properly after we've actually rested?" I suggested, "We can't do much about it now, in any case."

Liam nodded. "That sounds like an excellent idea."

We had come to the edge of the woods closest to my house, and I longed to invite him home with me, even if it was only to sleep… at first. However, I knew that his father would be frantic to see him, and be assured of his safety.

"I'll be fine from here."

"Okay," he replied, gathering me to him, in a swift movement, for one last, passionate kiss.

I looked up at him with a smile. "Would you like to play again tomorrow?"

We both burst out laughing. He could barely keep a straight face as he attempted to look nonchalant, and shrugged: "Alright!"

Another flurry of kisses later, I finally rushed for home, my butterflies putting on party hats inside me, and releasing streamers as they danced a merry jig. I beamed and closed my eyes, feeling the warm sunshine on my happy face, as I came out of the woods, onto the road, then opened them again.

I froze.

It couldn't be. How could it be? How was it even possible? *Oh, ye gods.* With a sickening retch of realisation, it dawned on me that my having been in the *sid* for three days meant that it had been about a week since Aoife's wedding… and that was why Alan Lynch's car was parked outside my house, and my sister's angry face was glaring at me from the kitchen window, with a ferocity that I had never before seen.

Her stare held me in a vice-like grip, pulling me towards her, though all of my instincts told me to turn and run back into the woods. Like a puppet on a string, I pushed the front door open and faced her, head lowered in dread.

Her eyes were bulbous with rage. Her hands trembled. With a deep, furious breath, she exploded: "*Where* have you been?"

"I… I…" I had absolutely no idea of what to say.

"Where have you been?!" she repeated, "We spoke to Mrs. Lynch when we got back, and she hasn't even seen you! What on earth must the neighbours be thinking? Where have you been, and..." She paused, taking in my charred and rumpled clothing and my dishevelled hair. "*What* have you been doing?"

A thousand lies presented themselves in my mind, each one more ridiculous than the last, like an array of utter nonsense passing me on a conveyer belt. Dancing 'round a bonfire? Learning fire breathing? Saving children from a burning building?

"What have you been doing?" she echoed herself, fingering my clothes in horror, "Good grief! Your top is on backwards, and *why* is it singed?"

"I- I left my clothes too close to a campfire, that's all..." As soon as the words had left my lips, I realised my mistake.

"Why on earth were your clothes *off*?! Have you been...?" A look of shock spread across her face.

If only I had thought to say: "Because I went for a swim." However, in my panic, my mouth merely fell open, and a fierce flush rose to my cheeks. She knew. Oh, ye gods, she knew!

"You have, haven't you?" she demanded, "With *him*, I suppose?"

My expression clearly confirmed her suspicions.

"How long has this been going on? If it started before you were sixteen, I could have him arrested for sex with a minor, you know!"

I gasped. "N-no! It only just h-happened, and... I'm seventeen, now!"

She groaned in exasperation. "At least, tell me that you were... safe."

With an inner shriek of panic, I realised what she meant. I stood there, frozen and gaping.

Her eyes narrowed. "You *did* use protection, didn't you, Kathy?"

"I- I... didn't think..." The alarm in my voice was entirely genuine, and not at all for her benefit. I had spoken to plenty of classmates about such things. How had it not even occurred to me to bring up the subject of contraception? Well, in truth, I knew exactly how it had happened, in that magical, carefree moment, blinded by near-death and miraculous healing, and overpowering lust…

"That irresponsible boy," snapped Aoife, "He should have been prepared!"

"It wasn't his fault! He wouldn't have been expecting to… I started it, really…" I protested.

She grimaced and raised a hand. "*Please,* Kathy! I do *not* need to hear the gory details. No matter what you did, he should have had more sense!"

"Don't blame *him,*" I pleaded, terrified that she might try to stop me from seeing him, if she disapproved.

"Well, go and get changed," barked Aoife with weary resignation, "We'll have to go straight to a pharmacy to get you the morning after pill, and then on to the doctor's to put you on a contraceptive." She walked away from me, scowling dismissively, and muttering: "Some homecoming!"

I could hear her shouting at her tumescent new husband, as I showered and changed. It seemed that he had wasted no time in terminally reattaching himself to the sofa.

"Come on, Alan, get up! You'll have to drive us to the pharmacy, and the doctor's surgery. No, we can't take the bus! We need to go to the pharmacy in the next town over, so we won't be recognised! What would the neighbours say, if it got back to them? Come along, now! Move!"

I felt ill at the thought that Alan Lynch knew something so intimately personal about me, but I was in no position to complain. As soon as I appeared, Aoife marched me out to the car, where he was waiting for us, looking grumpy.

In the morning, I rose early and prepared to leave the house. The previous evening had been silent and tense. I had gone to bed early, feeling unwell from the medication, and completely overtired and, thankfully, had succeeded in sleeping.

As I crept out of my bedroom, I prayed inwardly that Aoife and Alan might not yet be up. Of course, they were. He was back on his sofa. I wondered if, had I looked closely enough, I would have seen some protrusion emanating from his body, burrowing into the upholstery, like a giant tick.

Aoife was in the kitchen. She eyed me coldly as I approached. "Going out, are you?"

I nodded, nervously.

"Out to see *him*, I suppose?"

"Y- yes."

"Well, you tell him from me, that I'm appalled at his recklessness."

"He's not to blame…"

"Enough!" she snapped, sharply. "You just tell him."

I hung my head in acquiescence.

"And try not to burn your clothes this time," she added, "These things cost money that I worked hard to earn."

I fled from the house, and into the woods, my heart pounding with relief to be away from her, and anticipation at the prospect of seeing *my*… Yes, I could call him that now. *My* Liam.

He was by the stream with Cú Chulaind. When he saw me, his face lit up like the sun.

Entirely forgetting myself, I ran to him and leaped into his arms. He swung me around and kissed me. I wrapped my legs around his body and clung to his neck, not wanting to feel the ground beneath my feet again just yet. Surprising even myself, I suddenly burst in to tears.

"Kathy, what's wrong?" he gasped.

I sobbed noisily, unable to speak.

"What's the matter? Please tell me!"

I still could not respond.

"Let me guess: Aoife's back?"

I nodded jerkily, and then the entire story of the interrogation, and the pharmacy, and the doctor, came spilling out of me, punctuated by sniffs and shudders.

He hugged me tightly, then put me down and wiped my tearstained face with a gentle hand. "Oh, my beautiful girl, I'm so sorry."

"Y-y-you don't have to apologise," I blubbered.

"Yes I do. Your sister was right! I should have thought… All sense disappeared in that moment… I should have…"

"I know! I was there! You shouldn't have done anything differently. I wouldn't take it back for all the world…"

"Neither would I. But if only you had, at least, rung me after you spoke to her, *I* could have driven you to the doctor's, instead of having you humiliated in front of that oaf she calls a husband. I'm sorry."

"I wish I *had* thought of doing that, but I was just so panicked in the moment…"

"I know… Well, I don't. I can't even imagine."

My breathing was becoming more regular again, as I began to calm down. "Well, on the bright side, it's just as well she thought of it, and now everything has been sorted out medically," I observed, attempting to sound brighter.

"I'm so sorry."

"*Please* stop saying that. I'm not."

We both sank down into the grass and held each other, kissing each other's faces and necks and stroking each other's hair. Cú Chulaind investigated curiously for a while, but somehow sensed that his participation was unwelcome, and padded off to nap a short distance away.

We lay in the grass silently, for some time.

Then, I remembered to ask: "How is your father? Were he and the small ones okay?"

"Fine," replied Liam, "The ones who came to the woods with us had made their way back to the cottage, and told him about your burns, so he was extremely relieved to hear that you'd been healed."

"Did you tell him how it happened?"

"I told him everything…" He paused, with a playful smile. "Well, *almost* everything!"

I giggled. "And how did he respond?"

"He told me something very strange: Apparently, my mother was not a well woman, who struggled to have a successful pregnancy. My brothers and I were the only three healthy babies she had… out of seven. The others died."

My spine tingled. "All boys?"

"Yes."

"So you *are* the seventh son…"

He nodded uneasily.

"And your grandfather was also a seventh son?"

Again, he nodded.

I sighed deeply. "There's a lot of mythology around that, isn't there? I wouldn't have imagined that such things had any truth to them, but then, given the reality of our lives, I don't know why anything surprises me!"

"It must be why my father and I can see supernatural beings… and, perhaps, why I was able to heal you…"

"I was always sure you had some sort of power within you."

"I know. I didn't really believe it, though. I always thought it came from you."

"Did it never occur to your father that this was why you and he were different?"

Liam shrugged. "He said it's crossed his mind, once or twice, but he pushed it aside as nonsense."

"So, that's why the Great Ones want you to be king," I mused.

"Most likely because they want a ruler of men, with whom they can communicate directly, to bend him to their will," he muttered with a certain bitterness.

"I think it's because you're special, and they see the qualities in you that I do," I said gently, "I really do believe that The Dagda wants peace and harmony, even if some of the others are a bit more… difficult."

"The Dagda?" he repeated, puzzled.

"Yes, the one who did most of the speaking at the feast. I was told he is known by that name. He's the same fellow I met in the woods a few days ago, and again when I went into the *síd*."

"We haven't even spoken about that yet."

"I know. It seemed so quick to me… just a brief, enigmatic conversation… and, yet, somehow, I trusted him. I don't think he means me any harm."

"Well, why did you nearly burn to death, then?" snapped Liam.

"I don't think that was his doing. We spoke about Étaín a little. I got the impression that she's particularly fixated on you, and that there's something a bit… damaged about her, that causes her to behave the way she does."

"Deranged, you mean?"

"Well… he said that she'd been through a difficult time…"

"She's not a girl who was born on the wrong side of the tracks! She's a bloody goddess! She should be able to exercise some wisdom, or at least some self-restraint. If many of them are anything like her, I fear that they're very dangerous indeed, and certainly not to be trusted. You heard that chilling rant at the feast, by that female- Badb, was it?- about her dreams of fear and conflict!"

"She *was* a bit scary," I concurred, suppressing a slight shiver as I remembered the wild eyes in her sunken face, and the dark and twisted images they had brought to mind.

"Well, at least they're gone for now," sighed Liam.

"But for how long, I wonder?"

I didn't have to wait long for an answer to my question. Having decided that I had better make some show of good faith to Aoife by not staying out all night, I reluctantly said goodbye to Liam at sunset, and walked towards home, the warm, ghostly memory of his lips still tingling on mine.

I wondered what would happen in the future. I had one more year of school left, and after that, I was determined to get out of my house under any circumstances. I had always found living with Aoife a bit oppressive, but now that Alan Lynch was on the premises, it was utterly unbearable. My teachers had mentioned my applying for university, but how could I, when it would take me so far from Liam? Perhaps I could find a job in the village, and rent a room. Perhaps Liam would even come with me, and we could have a little flat of our own. He could still drive out here every day to work with his father…

The prickle trickled down the back of my neck, and I immediately knew that someone was there. I spun 'round to see The Dagda standing behind me.

"Oh, it's you," I observed, not feeling in the least threatened, but attempting to sound cold and wary, so that he wouldn't think me someone to be toyed with.

"Kathy," he said quietly, "I wanted to see for myself that you were well."

"I am," I replied, "No thanks to Étaín!"

He looked a little sad. "I know. I am glad that… your friend was able to rescue you."

I wondered if he was speaking the truth. He looked genuine enough. "If I hadn't had powers to fight the flames, and he hadn't been able to heal me, I would most likely be very much dead," I snapped.

"Well, I'm pleased to see that you are very much alive."

"Why would *you* be pleased? If I weren't around to interfere, your goals would be more easily achieved."

"I hope that our goals will be the same, one day," he replied earnestly, "But, either way, I would never wish you harm."

"Very well. If you say so." I nodded curtly. "Is that all? I must get on."

"Yes," he said, still sounding unhappy, "Farewell, Kathy. I hope to see you again."

"Well, I don't have much of a choice in that, do I?" I instantly regretted having been so unkind, when his concern for my welfare, though baffling, seemed entirely in earnest, but I turned and walked away, determined to retain my appearance of strength and aloofness.

I didn't tell anyone that I had met him again. The exchange had felt, somehow, entirely unrelated to broader events, and strangely personal.

Liam surprised me, the following day, by arriving at my house to apologise to Aoife in person, and to reimburse her for the medical expenses she had incurred on my behalf. I cringed in the hallway, wilting with mortification, as they spoke. Initially, she was as dismissive and judgemental as I would have expected, but eventually she grew more civil, and by the time the excruciating interaction was over, I was forced to conclude that she sounded just a little impressed by his maturity, in taking responsibility for his part in the matter. She and I never spoke of it again.

In the weeks that followed, he surprised me still further with regular, romantic gestures, like a meal in town, and the odd, thoughtful little gift. Of course, we also spent many, blissful hours in the woods, exploring each other's bodies and giving each other so much pleasure that I wondered if it were even possible for anyone else in the world to feel the sensations that we had.

He took me out on the lake in his father's little boat. We swam together, before falling into each other's arms in a secluded spot. The boat rocked us gently as we held each other, and little dappled spots of light reflected from the water and sparkled on Liam's beautiful form. Wherever we were, the way he looked at me made me feel as though a light of pure, exquisite joy were shining between us, and radiating out onto the whole world.

CHAPTER SEVEN

One day, as I entered the woods, I saw a strange, old woman standing in my path. Although she was positively hag-like, with wizened features and a hunched back, and not at all graceful and ageless, like the other immortals I had encountered, I sensed that there was something magical about her.

As I approached, her wrinkled face creased still further, into something of a withered smile, and I got the impression that she had been standing there deliberately, waiting for me, in that maddening way to which her kind was prone.

I halted with apprehension.

"Do I scare you, Dear?" she croaked.

"No," I replied, defensively.

"Of course not," she crooned, "It would take more than a little old thing like me to frighten a brave girl like you!"

I narrowed my eyes, her flattery making me warier still. What did she want with me?

As though she had read my mind, she said: "I came to offer my sympathies for all of the horrid things you've been through, at the hands of that wicked Étaín!"

"Oh?" I raised my eyebrows, "You know about all of that, do you?"

"I keep an eye on what she's up to," she clucked, lowering her tone conspiratorially, "Nothing but trouble, that one!"

"Have you…had dealings with her yourself, then?"

She sighed hoarsely, as though the saddest remnants of a thousand, cursed lifetimes were passing through her memory. "I'll say! She stole my husband, you know. Wouldn't give up until he was hers!"

"That doesn't surprise me."

"Indeed. And now, she's after *your* young man, I hear. What a pity."

"You speak as though she had succeeded in coming between us! Liam is his own person, and he has no interest in *her,* whatsoever."

Her jaded eyes filled with something akin to sympathy. "I don't wish to upset you, Dear, but she will stop at nothing until she gets him."

"I refuse to believe he'd ever go to her willingly."

"Believe me, she'll have him, willing or otherwise."

My eyebrows shot upwards in alarm. "Is there anything I can do to keep her away? Wh- what did *you* do?"

"Oh, I used all of my considerable powers to force them apart, after she'd bewitched him… But she wouldn't give up! Not that one! I tried everything: Turned her into a pool of water. Turned her into an ugly, purple fly. Years, she spent that way, and she *still* kept coming back to ruin things!"

My heart sank. If this account were true, I could wave goodbye to any hopes I might have had that my small success, in staying alive, had thwarted Étaín's determination to destroy my happiness.

"Do you think, then," I began, "That it's only a matter of time until she comes back?"

The crone sniffed. "You mark my words, she's lurking in the shadows, waiting for you to regain some tiny semblance of peace of mind, before she returns to shatter it into smithereens!"

"What should I do with your warning?" I asked.

"Well, if you like…" she crooned slowly, "You and I could put our heads together, and see if we can't come up with some way in which we could combine our powers, to stop her in her tracks…" Her eyes flicked slyly in my direction, as she trailed off, as though carefully gauging my reaction.

I couldn't help thinking that her speech was very deliberate, despite her disarmingly feeble and benign voice. I wondered if she had come to me with the expressed intention of joining forces against her ancient enemy, and was presenting it as a casual afterthought, in order to lull me into a false sense of security. Still, it was the first offer of help with Étaín I'd had from an immortal, so I replied:

"I… *might* be open to such things. What did you have in mind?"

Her wrinkles splintered into a thousand lines of pleasure. "I'll think on it," she grinned enigmatically.

I pursed my lips, entirely unsurprised that she was reluctant to suggest anything straightforward until some unspecified period of time had elapsed.

"I take it you'll find me when you have," I sighed.

"I will," she assured me with satisfaction.

There was a long pause.

She spoke again: "I'll see you soon then, Dear."

"Very well. Who are you, by the way?"

"You can call me Fúamnach." She shuffled off, on foot, but disappeared from view far sooner than could be considered natural, in accordance with my eyesight.

Of course, I told Liam all about the strange encounter and, as usual, he was extremely wary.

"Have we not had enough trouble with Étaín, without actively seeking to poke her with the magical equivalent of a stick, in alliance with someone who she most probably hates just as much, if not more, than she hates you?"

"Well, I didn't promise Fúamnach anything," I shrugged with a slight defiance, "But I might as well hear out what she proposes, when she comes back to me…"

Liam groaned. "Kathy, I know you! You always jump straight into everything, as soon as soon as the opportunity presents itself. At least, speak to me *before* embarking on some hare-brained scheme with this crone, won't you?"

"I will," I promised.

We were in Liam's car, as he drove me home after a pleasant evening meal at his father's cottage.

"Aoife and The Tumour are out for the evening, drinking with friends in the village," I remarked, changing the subject, "Would you like to come in for a while?"

He looked at me suggestively. "You mean, I might actually make the acquaintance of your bed?"

"You might," I smirked.

"Well, I can't turn *that* down, can I?" He removed his hand from the gear stick, momentarily, to caress my knee. I loved the feeling of his touch on my skin. I had made an effort with my appearance, and had actually worn a skirt that day, which was a rare occurrence.

The car turned the corner and I sighed deeply. "Oh, no," I exclaimed, "The lights are on in the house. They must have come home early."

"Well, that's disappointing," concurred Liam.

"You could still come in, but…"

"For an awkward night with those two? Fond of you as I am, Dearest, I think I'll pass."

I giggled slightly at the sarcasm. "Fair enough."

He stopped the car and pulled me to him tightly, his strong arms around my waist, and I melted into his kiss. When I could finally bear to leave him, despite a pulsating longing to introduce him to my bed, I bade him goodnight, and went inside.

To my horror, Alan Lynch was sprouting bulbously from the sofa, but my sister was nowhere to be seen.

"What are you doing home?" I scowled with distaste, "Where's Aoife?"

"Came home early," he slurred, "Bitch said I'd had too much to drink. She's still out." He punctuated his eloquent speech with a distinct burp.

I sighed deeply. Of course, he had probably started drinking in the morning, so it was no great surprise. On behalf of my gender, I rather took exception to the term 'Bitch' in reference to Aoife, but I decided that it was pointless to argue with an inebriated sloth, and turned to retreat to my room.

"Come here, Kathy," he hissed drunkenly.

The prickle slithered icily about my shoulders, as I turned back to face him. "What do you want?" I asked coldly and cautiously

He gestured for me to draw closer. "Come over here, I want to talk to you."

I edged slightly in the direction of the sofa.

He slapped the empty seat beside him, exaggeratedly. "Sit down, girl! I won't bite… much!" He laughed loudly, clearly far too pleased with his own joke.

Suppressing a shiver of repulsion, I decided that politeness dictated I sat down, though I did so gingerly, and as far away from him as possible.

"What do you want, Alan?" I repeated, impatiently.

Suddenly, he moved his body to cover the space beside me, and placed his hand unceremoniously on my thigh.

"Ah, Kathy. You're a good girl, aren't you, Kathy?" he mumbled.

I bristled. "Could you remove your hand, please?" I snapped.

Instead, he twisted his body to lean over me, and placed his other hand on my shoulder, holding me firmly in place. "Ah, Kathy, we should be friends, shouldn't we?"

His hand moved, slowly and deliberately, from my shoulder to my chest, his grubby fingers squeezing my breast roughly.

For a moment, I froze in utter horror, then gathered my thoughts and screamed: *"Get off me!"*

Before I could even begin to struggle properly, he had lunged astride me, both of his legs, and the hand that wasn't groping me, pinning me firmly and painfully in place. I shouted for him to leave me alone, but he pinched me so hard that I shrieked, and he licked my neck like a slobbering dog, before his voice rasped harshly in my ear:

"Ah, stop teasing, Kathy. I know you're up for it. Been doing it with your fellow in the woods long enough now, haven't you? Come on, show me what you've learned."

Before I knew it, his hand had moved again, and was crawling up my thigh, his fingertips burrowing into my flesh as his body squirmed against me. He reached my underwear and yanked it aside, before plunging, what felt like, fifty, sharp fingers inside me.

I screamed in agony and outrage, my voice sounding somehow outside myself, like the faraway cries of a dying animal. I pushed against him to no avail. Suddenly, his claw withdrew, and he began to fumble busily with the buttons on his trousers.

He means to force himself on me.

I retched. A fiery anger rose inside me. *"No!"* I screamed.

"Ah, come on now, Kathy, don't be like that, we're only having a bit of fun…" His repetition of my name made me want to vomit. He pulled his underwear down and wriggled heavily on top of me, his unbearable weight stifling my breath.

Never before, and never since, have I had a feeling that matched the horror of that moment. Drowning in the lake did not come close. Burning to death paled in comparison. There were a great many dreadful moments to come, that I could not then have foreseen, but not a one of them has inspired quite the same feeling of helplessness, degradation, or violation, as Alan Lynch did that night.

He was flying through the air, his head bouncing off one wall and slamming into another, before I even began to realise that the prickle had risen up with the wrath of a thousand, angry gods, and that *I* was controlling Alan's limp, pathetic body, as it ricocheted off every available surface.

There was blood. There was screaming... Not mine. Not his. *Good grief, it's Aoife.* Alan fell to the floor with an unceremonious thud, and I gasped. Aoife and Liam were standing in the doorway, her face an ashen mask of disbelief and terror. I felt cold. Alan groaned. *Oh, he's alive.* I didn't much care.

Liam ran to me, extending his arms with the intention of comfort, but I shuddered, and pushed him away with a trembling, yet authoritative, hand. He looked hurt. I could not think clearly, but the only thing I knew in that moment was that I did not want anybody to touch me.

Aoife screeched, throwing herself down on the floor beside her bleeding husband. She was hyperventilating. She raised a hand, as if to caress his mangled face, but slapped him instead, and recoiled from him, crumbling further into the floor. *She must have seen enough...*

She stared about her, wildly, then fixed her gaze on me... or, rather, *through* me, as though I weren't quite real.

"You... you..." she panted, "What manner of creature are you? What manner of *monster*...?"

"I'm sorry," I whispered, "I had no choice. He was about to..."

"She knows," stated Liam, his voice dark. "I saw her walking from the bus stop when I drove off, and offered to give her a lift back. We heard you screaming from outside the house. We saw what was happening, when we walked in, but you… reacted before we could help."

I began to shiver. He instinctively moved to embrace me, but then thought better of it, and lowered his arms, looking worried.

"We had better call an ambulance," he muttered.

Aoife nodded slightly, hugging herself, as though she were the only thing that she could be certain of, in all the world.

"You'll be up for murder, if he dies," she hissed, vehemently, casting me another strange look.

"Nobody will believe that Kathy did this. Look at her!" Liam's jaw tightened. "They'll assume it was me."

"Just as well we found him like this when we got home, then," I said, the clarity of my voice surprising even my own ears. "He left the pub drunk. Who knows what happened to him on his way back? Perhaps he had a fall. Perhaps he got into a fight. He was like this when we got home. How fortunate that he made it here, for us to find him, and didn't bleed to death out on the road somewhere… Don't you think?"

Liam nodded gravely.

Aoife muttered something about monsters, but hung her shoulders deflatedly, in weak acquiescence.

"Help me move him into the kitchen," sighed Liam, "The emergency services mustn't see all of the damage to the living room when they arrive, or it'll raise suspicion. Then, I'll call an ambulance."

I took a last look at Alan Lynch, in his current position, moaning helplessly at our feet, his features purple and bulbous, and his bare bottom hanging out of his trousers. His pathetic and undignified state seemed entirely fitting.

With very little emotion, I assisted Liam in dragging him to the kitchen. We helped Aoife up, and positioned her at the kitchen table, although she shrank from my touch as though I were indeed a monster, and not her little sister at all. We closed the door to the living room, and waited for the ambulance to arrive.

"His injuries are inconsistent with a human attack," they said. "A person couldn't possibly have inflicted them," they said. "He must have had some sort of a fall. His trousers were open. Perhaps he stopped on his way home, to urinate, and stumbled over a cliff in the dark. His blood alcohol level was extremely elevated. It's a miracle that he made it home. He will live."

Aoife, Liam and I were at the hospital, talking to the police. Well, Liam and I were doing most of the talking. Aoife was looking blank and traumatised, and clinging to her own cardigan, as though she wanted to curl up inside it and disappear.

"Thank you for the information," said Liam before they walked away. When they were further down the corridor, he turned to me. "Are you sure you don't want to tell them… something? Don't you want to get justice for what he did to you?"

"I rather think I have," I replied, mirthlessly.

It was a strange thing I noticed in the days that followed the incident. Everything had become a little greyer. It was as though a dark filter had been forced across my eyes in my sleep, and fixed with invisible, unbreakable threads, and I could not remove it for all the world. The sun's rays seemed to shine less brightly. The taste of food was just a little less intense. The motivations of those around me became just a little more questionable, and I felt warier of strangers. Alan Lynch's bulbous face, sweating on top of me, popped into my mind at the oddest, most inopportune moments, when I ought to have felt as much at peace as any person could: Relaxing in the bath, strolling in the woods, or reading a favourite book. Everything felt spoiled, and marred, and I did too. It occurred to me that I might not owe my new outlook to invisible lenses of darkness, but that a youthful visor of naïvety, that made everything a little brighter, had been ripped away. I wondered if I would ever recover it. Looking back now, I'm glad I did not know the truth at that raw, fragile time: That I would never get it back; only learn to live with the duller hue of reality, and forget to be sad about it… At least, most of the time, but for those moments in which I would hear the jingle of an ice cream van, or see children building sandcastles on the beach, and would remember carefree days, when the sun shone brighter, and shed a bitter tear of grief for the unadulterated version of myself that was lost forever, and for the better world in which I'd once believed I lived.

I could not imagine anything worse than my body being touched in an intimate way ever again. That feeling did pass, in time, but back then, it was all that I could do not to mistake Liam's hand for a bunch of crawling worms, if he did so much as hold my hand. I would not let him near me. He said that he understood, and we filled our meetings with games, and food, and excruciating small talk, but I spent more time alone, because I could sense his sadness, and it made me angrier still… with myself, with the world, and with him, though he had done nothing to deserve it.

Oh, the anger. I often replayed the memory of Alan Lynch, bouncing around the living room, getting bloodier with every blow, and wished fervently that I could do it again. He was still in hospital. He would be for some time. Aoife and I did not speak of it. She skittered around the edges of our home, looking half-there, and half-mad, and half-terrified. At night, I could hear her crying, as though her heart might burst: A deep, eerie sobbing, that wailed of the end of her world. I sometimes felt some compassion, but then I would remember that her emotion stemmed from her affection for the repulsive creature she had married, and my thoughts would crawl back down to the scarlet, swirling depths of anger.

My leaving certificate exams were approaching at school, after which my options were to go to university, find a job, or face unemployment. I sat angrily through my classes, feeling grey and uninspired, but still succeeded in achieving quite favourable results, due to my unusually good memory. One of my teachers produced forms to fill in, for those students wishing to apply to universities. She urged me to take one, saying I was a bright girl and had potential.

"No thank you," I replied, "I plan to find work in the village." *And live in a little flat with Liam, and be happy,* I added silently. Suddenly, my fantasy seemed laughable, because I couldn't possibly imagine sleeping in close proximity to another person, not to mind being happy! I felt only a bland greyness about the future, and my constant anger was the only spark of life in me.

"Are you sure?" asked the teacher, "You could fill in the form anyway, and decide later. Nothing's set in stone!"

Now that I could see no reason not to, I shrugged and applied to study history at Trinity College in Dublin. *I most likely won't go,* I told myself, *But if Liam gets fed up of being with such a cold and angry girl, I might need something to do.*

I gave it little further thought.

One Saturday, I took the bus into town. My anger was feeling particularly angry that day. I desperately wanted to distract myself by getting out of the house, but did not want to risk bumping into Liam, or the small ones, in the woods, so a lonely beverage in a café seemed my best option.

A poster in a window drew my attention. It was an advertisement for kickboxing classes. My dull heart brightened by a hair's breadth of a shade. *A way to fight without using my powers?* I thought, excitedly. It had long been a fear of mine that, if the wrong person witnessed my supernatural abilities, I might end my days as an experiment at a distant NASA base.

"Yes, please!" replied my anger, "Where do we sign up?"

The answer to that was the community centre, and I went straight there to make a booking for the next class. I threw myself into the training, in the months that followed. Nobody feels quite right about begrudging someone the opportunity to exercise, so Liam didn't protest when I spent several evenings a week in town at classes, though I knew he knew me well enough to suspect that it was a calculated avoidance tactic. While I was merely grateful to escape my normal activities, my anger thoroughly enjoyed the fighting itself. The fact that I was fit, and naturally wiry, was an advantage. My anger liked to assign foreign faces to the punching bag, or my sparring opponents, so that every sharp punch, or skilfully executed roundhouse kick, I dealt, collided with Alan Lynch's face, or sometimes

Aoife's… or sometimes, even Liam's, though I knew that to be incredibly and entirely unfair.

Aoife still floated about the house, wraith-like in her despair, and avoided any unnecessary interaction with me, as though I were carrying the plague.

One day, I returned home, just in time to hear her on the telephone. I froze, and made no further sound, lingering in the doorway in the hopes that she might continue her conversation, unaware of my presence, and reveal some shred to me of the inner workings of her current mindset.

"Yes, I see," she was saying, her voice cold and stiff, "Well, you'll have to contact his mother to make those arrangements. I'm no longer involved… No, she won't be able to care for him at home. She's far too elderly. You'll have to put him in a convalescence home… After that? I really don't care what becomes of him… Yes, I'm fully aware that I'm still listed as his next of kin, and I will be taking steps to rectify that terrible mistake as soon as possible, I assure you. Yes… Right, okay, thank you. 'Bye."

I heard the phone fall into the receiver tray, with a colossal thud, as though the interaction had sapped all of her energy. Then, I heard Aoife burst into tears.

Alarmed, I rushed into the hall, and found her in a little ball on the floor, her hands over her saline-stained face.

"Aoife?" I ventured cautiously, not wanting to frighten her.

One large, weeping eye peered at me from between her tense fingers. "I suppose you heard that, did you?" Her voice was still cold, but her communication was more coherent than it had been of late… towards me, in any case. "He's not coming back here."

I crouched down so that my face was level with hers, but did not creep too close, lest I startle all sense out of her. "Is it… because of me?" I asked.

She took some time to answer, and when she did, she positively spat: "Well, of course it's because of you!"

"I… I'm sorry." As the words left my lips, I realised that I actually was: Not sorry for my part in the proceedings, and the retribution I had wrought on her disgusting husband, but sorry for Aoife. She had her flaws, but life hadn't been easy for her either, and she deserved better than to end up this broken shell of a woman. If she hadn't been doing her duty, by looking after me all these years, she might have had a very different life; other opportunities; the chance to find someone better than the useless and pathetic next-door neighbour.

Her shoulders slumped. "It's because of what *he* did, too," she croaked, weakly, "What *you* did… I don't even know what…" She took a breath, as though to steady herself. "But I know what *he* did, and I won't have that monster back in this house. I feel sick to think that he… I … Oh, god."

Her parted fingers clamped shut again, and her shoulders began to rock with sobbing.

I felt utterly powerless. Tentatively, I placed a hand on her arm, and was relieved when she didn't shrink from my touch. "I- I know it's awful now," I murmured, gingerly, "I know *everything* is awful. B-but… it will get better. I *have* to believe it will get better…"

"Ha!" shrieked Aoife, startling me a foot backwards, "Ha! You don't know…" She began to wail again.

"What is it, Aoife?" I asked gently, "What don't I know?"

Her hands suddenly fell away from her, limply, and she fixed me with the full horror of her stricken face. "I'm pregnant."

She promptly erupted into a fit of harsh, mirthless laughter, for which I was oddly grateful, as I felt faint, and blank, and entirely devoid of language. Pregnant! The spawn of that *creature* was nesting in my sister's belly… Some parasite, burrowing into her very insides, the way its father had attached himself to our sofa.

After a long time of listening to her oscillate between laughing and crying, I realised that these things could be dealt with. Growths can be removed.

"It's okay," I assured her, "We'll go to England and sort it out. We'll pretend it never happened. We'll…"

"It's too far gone for that," she answered, her voice now a despondent whisper.

"Okay," I nodded fervently, giving myself time to think, and determined to remain pragmatic, "We'll go… somewhere. We'll go away. We'll give it up for adoption, and *then* we'll pretend it never happened…"

"I don't think I can do that," she sighed, hoarsely. "I can't have it out in the world without me, when I know it's there… It feels wrong, and I don't think I could live with it. It's mine now, and perhaps I can do better this time…"

The unspoken words sank in: "…than I did with you." They didn't even offend me. It had not remotely occurred to me that she might *want* it… That she might *want* Alan Lynch's offspring to grow fat and juicy inside her, and claw its way out, and gulp milk from her nipple, and defecate all over her. I shuddered, and thought I might be sick.

"But, Aoife, surely you can't…"

"I'm not asking your permission," she snapped, "I'm having a baby. I know it's not ideal, but you'll have to get used to it." Then, she stood up from the floor, tapped her cheek a couple of times, as though she were shaking off the memory of a mildly unpleasant dream, smoothed her hair and her skirt, and walked off into the kitchen. She looked stronger, and more in command of herself, than she had done for months. Getting the awful truth out of her system had been cathartic, I imagined.

Well, I thought, *I'm glad it's been positive for* someone. Then, another thought struck me: There was absolutely no way, in any form, or dimension, of reality, that I was prepared to live with that child when it came.

I told Liam the news in the woods. He was suitably aghast and in fear for my emotional health.

"I can't share a home with it," I insisted, "I just *can't!*"

"I understand," he assured me, "You won't have to. We'll figure something out. You could come to stay with us. My father loves you like his own… Or, perhaps we're a bit old for that now. Maybe it's time to start thinking about that plan we had, to get a flat in the village, or in town, or…"

I winced, and he ceased to speak, as if I had unceremoniously stuck a big cork in his mouth.

"I'm sorry, I…" I attempted, hoping that an explanation for my reaction would magically emanate from me, on the coat tails of my meaningless words, but none presented itself.

"You don't want to do any of that, do you?" Liam sighed.

"I… don't know."

"Do you even want to be with me anymore?"

"I…" Again, words failed to materialise. I felt the sharp sting of tears pierce my eyes, and worryingly large globules of saline quivering on my lower lashes.

He smacked his hand against his forehead. "It's okay. I'm an idiot. I shouldn't be pressuring you, at a time like this, after everything that's happened. I know you need my patience. How can I expect you to know exactly what you want to do right now?"

"Thank you," I gulped, and patted his hand weakly. "I know it's hard for you too. I wish everything could just go back to the way it was, before…"

"I know," he said, and put a protective arm around my shoulders. I didn't recoil, more for the sake of politeness than out of any desire for affection.

The truth was, there was only one thing that I knew I wanted to do, and that was to get to a kickboxing class, and imagine every blow colliding with Aoife's stomach, pounding the thing inside her to a pulp.

And so it was that, one day, the hag Fúamnach appeared to me again on the path home from the woods, and my anger positively squealed with delight.

"Oh, I'd quite forgotten about her," cried my anger excitedly, "She was interested in collaborating in some mischief, wasn't she? Mischief might be just what the doctor ordered!"

Of course, Fúamnach couldn't hear my anger, because it was audible only to me, so I greeted her with a little less enthusiasm.

"Kathy," she positively crooned, her voice like too many spoons of honey on a meal of dry brambles, "I trust I find you well?"

"Well enough," I replied tersely. My anger may have been pleased to see her, but my sense was cautious. Everything else in my life was so broken that some new, potentially dramatic entanglement with the otherworld, seemed the least desirable turn of events imaginable.

"You haven't had any more trouble from that wicked girl Étaín, I hope?"

I shook my head. "No, she's been mercifully absent of late."

"Good, good," Fúamnach's ancient eyes crinkled into a million wrinkles, in some semblance of a grin. "Of course," she added, "You can't be too careful with that one, can you?"

"No, I suppose not," I conceded, "Just when you think she's gone for good, she turns up and wreaks havoc."

"Oh, believe me, I know that very well! Be thankful you've only had to deal with her machinations for a few years, and not for centuries, as I have."

"Yes, you mentioned that she pursued your husband?"

Fúamnach rolled her eyes and clicked her dry tongue in exasperation. "Mercilessly," she whispered conspiratorially, though there was no one else visibly present to overhear, "The lengths she went to! The things I had to do! Why, just look at me: A withered husk of my former self. I was beautiful once too, you know… but my battle with at Étaín took its toll." She sighed deeply.

"Why did you fight so hard?" I asked, surprising myself a little with my lack of romantic empathy, "Why didn't you just let him go? He was only a man."

She looked astonished, and I noticed a flash of anger dart across her eyes, before she hurriedly sought to control, it with another sycophantic smile. "He was a *king*," she said, "And *my* husband! I couldn't abandon him to the likes of her! Would you be happy to see your young Liam in her clutches, even if his foolish head were turned, for even a moment, by her charms?"

"No, I wouldn't," I admitted.

"So, you see that we shall have to do something about her then, don't you?"

"Should we not wait until she does something to do something about?"

"It could be too late by then," Fúamnach's brow furrowed into countless, deep chasms of concern. "She gets closer to killing you every time, doesn't she? What if she succeeds? Who will protect your young Liam from her then?"

I groaned.

She continued animatedly: "Who knows what she's planning? Who knows how close she is? She could strike at any moment! We must make sure she doesn't get the chance!"

"Hurrah! A vengeful plot on the horizon," cheered my anger.

I coughed slightly to silence its voice in my head. "And, do you actually have a course of action to propose, this time?"

"Well, as a matter of fact, I do," replied Fúamnach in a disarmingly 'Oh-now-that-you-mention-it' tone, "You and I together could call her down, I'm sure, and bind her powers, and end this tormented incarnation of hers once and for all."

"And what would become of Étaín?"

"I have been given to understand that you know something of these matters. Étaín, as we know her, is just a fragment in an endless sky of power… A bottomless sea of might. Her individual form may be extinguished, but her power will go where it belongs."

"You mean, re-absorbed into the collective?" I queried, "Like The Dadga wants?" Though I could not claim to understand the right or wrong of such great and unfathomable things, a part of me still felt something akin to liking for The Dagda, and a confusing desire to help him or, perhaps, seek his approval in some way.

"So, you *do* understand," she nodded reassuringly.

"By what means would we achieve this?"

"I have a spell. Your powers will help to ensure that it does not fail, this time."

"So… you've tried this before?"

"Oh, yes, but just look at me! I'm a frail, wizened shell, and you are a young, powerful woman. With you by my side, I know we can succeed!"

"And if we don't?"

Her parched, twig-like fingers suddenly reached out and grabbed my wrist imploringly. Her skin felt cold, and hard as bone. "Well, we *have to* try, don't we? Think of poor Liam! I've heard mutterings, amongst my own kind, that she is not done with him!"

I frowned, thoughtfully. "Fúamnach, surely whatever was between Étaín and your royal husband, is long dead. What have you to fear from her now? Why are you so determined to assist me in this matter?"

She did not reply, but my anger read something familiar in her guarded expression and whispered it to me: *"Revenge."*

"Think on it, Dear, and meet me here, three nights hence, when the moon is full, if you wish to partake in this deed," exclaimed Fúamnach briskly, as if she were eager to be rid of my company, now that I had begun to ask too many questions. "Think well, and think wisely, but do not forget that it may be your last chance!"

"Or, perhaps, yours…" I commented, but she was no longer there.

I thought, and I thought. I do not know if I thought well, or wisely, for my more cautious instincts were constantly disturbed by my anger's fire, and zeal to unleash its full potential in a magical battle with our enemy.

It occurred to me that I hadn't felt the prickle in quite some time, as though there was not room enough for both it and my anger in my consciousness. Had anger pushed it aside, as it had my more authentic musings, or had I used it all up with the force of my attack on Alan Lynch? He was only a mortal man, though, I reasoned. I had fought otherworld forces far more fearsome than he was. *Then, why is he the one who creeps into my nightmares?* I had healed the woods, and defeated water and fire. *With Liam's help.*

I considered turning to Liam for advice, but immediately dismissed it. His caution would almost certainly counter my more impulsive instincts, and once I knew his thoughts, not following his- likely, wise- counsel would feel like even more of a betrayal than staying silent.

I wondered if my powers would even function, without Liam there to help my focus. I soon remembered fending off the supernatural assault, outside the village church, and decided that I was, at least, somewhat capable without his assistance.

I tried to be as honest with myself as possible about what I hoped to gain from this endeavour with Fúamnach. Were my motivations genuine concern for Liam, and for my own life, or was this matter just another happy, distraction from my personal misery? Was I moved by revenge, as the hag was, or simply a desire to lash out at anything I could?

Étaín would certainly be much safer neutralised, and swallowed back into a timeless, faceless cloud of all things, than running about in her too-human incarnation. The small ones in the woods would no longer be at risk from her either, which would be one less trouble for them. Her powers would be back in the collective, with The Dagda to guide them, and for some reason, I believed that he would guide them well.

I thought, and I thought again. I thought for three days and, unsurprisingly- for, caution was never my strong suit, was it?- found myself waiting for Fúamnach in the woods, when the moon was full.

I'm not sure if I imagined the anticipatory atmosphere in the woods that night. It seemed that the gnarled branches of the trees had paused in their swaying, the animals had taken a deep breath and halted in the undergrowth, and the moon herself had drawn closer to the mortal realm, to give her full attention to what was about to happen.

When she appeared, our rapt, lunar spectator bathed Fúamnach's ancient face in her light, and lit up every excited twinkle, dancing in her timeless eyes.

"I knew you'd come," she beamed, gleefully.

I nodded. It was not the time to rebuke her for being presumptuous. "Where is this spell to take place?" I asked.

"Follow me!" Though her appearance was hunched and crinkled as ever, she appeared to glide lightly across the ground, her gait agile and vigorous with hunger for the deed ahead.

The woods continued to hold their breath expectantly, as we wove our way through the graceful frame of their limbs, their tips barely twitching in the muted breeze.

Fúamnach led me to a familiar glade. I had spent a delightful day playing there with Étaín, as a child. I felt the air whisper against my neck, and remembered the place bathed in sunshine. How different everything was now, in the moonlight and shadows of the night. The crone's choice of location seemed a little too deliberate.

"What now?" I enquired.

"Leave that to me," called Fúamnach reassuringly, and from the seemingly endless folds of her shawl, produced one small, curious object after another. She arranged them on the grassy floor with care and attention, each movement exquisitely calculated, like a dance.

The moon's eyes felt too prying. The ritual felt somehow private… Shameful… Unwholesome: Something to be done in the darkest recesses of another reality; something best not witnessed by a good-natured squirrel, or an innocent hare.

Fúamnach continued with her work, and an intricate web of items soon carpeted the glade. I could not quite identify a single one of them, for they seemed misshapen and crooked, like dark, crawling mockeries of things that were familiar.

She motioned for me to step forward, and I did so, fighting an instinctive sense of revulsion, as I entered her magical space. Wordlessly, she made it clear where I should stand, and then took her own place opposite me. Between us was a clear circle, ringed with her strange, black accessories.

I suddenly felt a familiar caress on the back of my neck. It was light and tentative at first, then ice and fire as it trickled down my arms and spine. My ears buzzed, and I felt slightly faint.

Fúamnach had begun to speak.

I did not understand her words. I had learned Irish at school, and there was some familiarity to her strange mutterings, but these were words, or versions of words, that I had never heard before. I knew instinctively that they were older. All words change over time, but Fúamnach's words were the words before the words… The truth of the words… The instruments of the source of a power beyond my comprehension.

Her harsh voice rose and fell, not in song, but with a rhythm of inevitability and foreboding. The prickle raged about me now, simultaneously a live shroud of protection, and a wild beast, waiting to be unchained.

Fúamnach's words seemed to materialise then, as though their power were too great to remain sounds alone. They were something more, and they needed to be heard, felt, seen, and touched. They spilled from her cracked lips like a smoke of abstract shapes, pouring into the glade and surrounding us with their dancing rhythm, their soft yet biting edges whipping lightly against our faces as they swirled.

The voracious, angry part of the prickle longed to join them. I could feel it reaching for them as they passed, ravenous to become one… To couple with the magic. The longing penetrated my very core, to excruciating arousal until I, and it, could resist no longer. My unseen, hungry power reached out to intertwine its fingers with Fúamnach's magic, and laughed and soared in the heady dance.

A deep, sensual part of me roared inside with the crashing completeness of a thousand climaxes. A blinding light, or darkness, engulfed my vision, and when the explosion was over, the space between me and Fúamnach was empty no more.

Étaín was in the circle. Her beauty was maddening as ever, but marred by a jerky, frantic quality to her movements. Gone was her poise, and wide were her eyes, as she thrashed and squirmed in the sacred space, in which we had trapped her. Her golden hair swirled, as she struggled. Her face warped from fear to anger, and then to the most bitter, empty, aching despair.

Fúamnach's words changed shape then: Became gaping jaws, in place of dancing forms. The fingers of the prickle, so enmeshed in their grasp, grew teeth to match them, and hungrier still, ready to devour any spare morsel of the hag's meal.

Étaín's light spilled from the circle in two beams, one facing the crone, and one facing me. Fúamnach moaned gutturally with pleasure, as she ate Étaín's power, draining it, taking it into herself. My prickle lapped greedily at the rest of it, and I felt Étaín enter me too, coursing through my veins, filling my skin and flesh, inside and out. It was wonderful. It was ecstasy. I had never felt so whole… So powerful…

Yet, deep inside, an urgent voice told me something was wrong. I watched Étaín as her shape grew fainter. Her form grew transparent. Her eyes were empty. She was disappearing… but this was not the benevolent release, of her troubled incarnation, that I had expected. We were *consuming* her. Fúamnach and I were draining her into ourselves, not returning her to the lofty, faceless collective of timeless truths, where she belonged. We were hungrily, greedily feeding on her.

"No!" I cried, jumping away from Étaín, and upsetting some of Fúamnach's dark ornaments with my foot, as I leaped, "This is wrong! I don't want her inside me! That power is not meant for me, but for something far greater." My prickle jerked its fingers away from the magic, and retuned to me, slithering around my shoulders like a warm and comforting snake.

Fúamnach's eyes opened, wide with a thousand horrors. She did not look quite as old, or as decrepit, as she had upon our first meeting. Sucking the life out of Étaín appeared to agree with her. She screeched: A sound so desperate as to curdle, not just the blood, but to pulverise the flesh and bone, and then curdle them as well.

Étaín gasped, and I turned to look at her. Some expression had returned to her eyes, and some realisation crept into her expression. Looking considerably less transparent, she stepped out of her circle and surveyed us with utter fury. She was free.

"You foolish girl," shrieked Fúamnach, "You idiot child! What have you *done?*" Her voice sounded as if it were about to crack, and she were about to begin weeping.

"You tricked me!" I retorted angrily, kicking one of her ritual instruments out of my way, deliberately this time,

"You let me believe that we would release her, not have her for tea!"

"You chose to believe what you wanted," snapped Fúamnach, sulkily, now almost a laughable, pitiable figure in her childish temper.

"I should have known not to trust you," I grumbled, "If you had wanted the same thing as he does, you would have been at The Dagda's feast, not lurking around on your own, to waylay me in the woods, like a coward, motivated by nothing but bitterness and conceit!"

Fúamnach pulled at her wispy, grey hair in frustration. "Do you realise the power you've given up? Power I was willing to share with *you,* you ungrateful wretch! I could have been beautiful again…"

"You will never be beautiful, because you're made of vengeance, and trickery, and…"

"Ahem." A small cough interrupted our heated exchange. I had quite forgotten about Étaín, for a moment, but she was still there, looking from one of us to the other, her face a mask of seething, venomous hatred, painted with slight, false amusement. "If I might interject," she began, her tone mockingly sweet, "I believe I may have a thought or two to contribute to the conversation."

"What could *you* have to contribute to anything, you painted whore of a…?" fumed Fúamnach.

"Étaín," I cut in, "I did not intend this. You may choose to believe me or not, but I was misled. I…"

"Oh, I believe you, Kathy," she replied sweetly, her voice like a nectar-tipped dagger, "I've heard enough to make a pretty good guess as to what's going on: You wanted to obliterate my consciousness, didn't you? Now, why would you think it makes any difference to me where it went, when I was gone?"

I shrugged defeatedly. "Okay, Étaín, do your worst. Conjure up another deadly lake, set us on fire, whatever. There's no point in standing about talking, when I'm quite sure you want us both dead, whatever I say."

She narrowed her beautiful eyes, and spun 'round to face Fúamnach. "*You,*" she seethed, "Are such a pathetic, loathsome hag, that you are not worth my time. The best revenge on you I can think of is to let you go on existing, with your unhappiness, and the memory that your husband wanted me instead. You are not worth my further attention."

Fúamnach hopped from side to side with fury, her small, crooked frame a bizarre shadow, bouncing in the moonlight. She tore at her hair again, and this time I could see pale, brittle strands come away in her hands. With a final shriek, she was gone, and all of her twisted little magical objects with her.

"Now, *you,* on the other hand," continued Étaín, returning her gaze to me, "Are quite a different matter."

I sighed. "What are you going to do to me?" I was so tired, and so fed up of the magical drama, at that point in the evening, that I did not care nearly as much as I should have.

Étaín looked even more annoyed by my nonchalance, but her response was unfalteringly saccharine: "Give me time. I'll think of *just* the thing!"

The brightness in her tone left me uneasy, and in no doubt that, whatever she next brought against me, would be unfathomably dreadful. She was gone before I could respond. *Just as well,* I thought. I'd had quite enough dealings with the otherworld for one night.

CHAPTER EIGHT

I awoke the following day, shaking off the remnants of a nightmare involving angry wasps. For a moment, I was relieved, but as my own reality sank in, I almost longed for a few sharp stings instead.

Liam and I were in a difficult place, my sister was terrified of me, and pregnant by my would-be rapist, and now a goddess- who hadn't been particularly fond of me to begin with- had essentially threatened me with the full weight of her wrath, at any moment that she saw fit. *What a delightful state of affairs,* I mused.

Then, I rose mechanically, washed and dressed, and wandered into the kitchen, to prepare myself some breakfast, and further contemplate my impending doom. Strangely, considering recent occurrences, I felt unusually well. Concerned, certainly, but extremely healthy, as though my blood were pumping through my veins with just a little more vigour; my eyesight was just a little clearer; my skin was just a little smoother; and my hair a little more lustrous. Perhaps that small sip of Étaín's power had agreed with me too. The prickle was back to stay, it seemed. It whispered tenderly across my skin, nuzzling me like a cat who had just returned, after straying just a little too far from home. My anger was still there too, but was just slightly less demanding of my attention, as though it had finally learned its place, and no longer fancied itself sole master of my inner domain.

I was nibbling distractedly on a slice of toast, when I heard the wheels of a car speed up the road, and screech to a halt outside. Surprised by the seeming haste of the driver, I looked out of the window, and saw Liam jump from his car, and stride purposefully towards my front door.

I hadn't been expecting him, but found myself quite pleased to see him, though slightly curious as to his seeming urgency. I walked to the door to greet him, and found myself more curious still, when I took in his expression.

"Liam," I exclaimed, "Is everything okay? Why so serious?"

He raised his eyebrows. "*Why so serious?* Are *you* serious? What on earth have you done?"

"What do you mean?"

"Please don't lie to me, Kathy. What did you do in the woods last night?"

"Ah, that." I sighed. I had rather been hoping to find my own way of telling him about Fúamnach and the ritual, in my own time, but I should have known that nothing would stay secret for long in the blasted woods, with curious little eyes peering every which way. "The small ones saw something?"

"Yes, they certainly saw *something*," he confirmed, "If their account is to be believed, they saw you participating in some dark, magic ritual to destroy Étaín, then change your mind and let her go on her way! What on earth is going on? Is it true?"

I groaned. "Not here," I hissed, aware of small sounds behind me that suggested Aoife was up and about. I stepped outside, and went in the direction of the woods, motioning for him to follow me.

As we walked, the whole, sorry tale spilled out. By the time I had finished my account, it occurred to me that I had seen Liam frustrated by me, disappointed with me, perhaps even completely perplexed by me, but never truly angry… until now.

"What were you thinking?" he demanded, his hands balled into fists and his voice stern, "You consider yourself a protector of these woods, yet you brought Étaín back here, and made her even angrier? How irresponsible can you be? You promised me you wouldn't act against her without speaking to me first!"

"I know, I know," I protested, "But I didn't realise what Fúamnach was really planning. I thought I…"

"But *why* would you trust her? If one were asked to describe the epitome of an untrustworthy sort of person, I rather think it would sound like her! You haven't been yourself lately, and with good reason, perhaps, but this is a step too far! You put yourself in danger, with no thought for anyone who cares about you. You put the woods, and the small ones, in danger. You put everyone who is even remotely connected to this in danger, and you just don't seem to care!"

"I'm sorry," I responded, simply. There seemed little else to say.

"Yes, I'm sure you're sorry: Sorry for having upset me, and sorry you made a mistake, perhaps, but are you really sorry you did it? Are you really sorry for keeping secrets, and lying, and for having risked everything without even trusting me enough to talk it over with me, before you acted?"

I wasn't sure, and he could see it.

"Kathy, I need some time," he said, his eyes downcast.

"Okay," I agreed, weakly, "That's fair."

He looked exasperated. He opened his mouth, as though he were about to speak further, perhaps to rebuke me for not having more to say for myself, or for not being able to find the words to reassure him, but he clearly thought better of it, and stormed away. He didn't look back.

I sat down on a nearby stone. I sat there for quite some time, thinking very, very little.

Somehow, I had done well enough in my final exams to be accepted for the history course that I'd applied for in Dublin. When I went to school to collect my results, I couldn't have felt more numb.

"Congratulations, Kathy," cried my teacher, brightly, "You did very well!"

"Thank you," I muttered robotically, accepting the envelope with all the enthusiasm of someone picking up a particularly wilted banana skin.

"Aren't you pleased? Are you going to accept your place at university?"

"I doubt it."

"I hope you'll reconsider," she said, "It would be a shame to waste the opportunity."

Some of the girls from school went drinking, and invited me to join them. I was sure that Aoife would have disapproved, as I hadn't yet turned eighteen, but I didn't much care. I remembered her reeking of cider when she was younger than I was. A little pointless escapism seemed quite the thing, so I decided to accept my classmates' invitation.

They babbled excitedly about how much they were looking forward to leaving Kerry at the end of the summer, and starting their respective university or training courses. Their chatter made me think about it a little too. I imagined living in a city, far away from everything familiar. It seemed impossible to picture myself being anywhere without the woods on my doorstep, or Liam and Mr. O Mordha a walk away. However, it was also far too easy to envision myself somewhere without so many memories, far from Aoife and her impending offspring, and a world away from my life as it currently was. I made up my mind to accept the place at university. If Liam forgave me, and I found a way to be happy in the meantime, I simply wouldn't go. If nothing could be solved, I would have an escape route.

My classmates' conversation turned to matters of the heart, as two drinks turned into five. By the sixth, they were pouring out their very souls about their unrequited loves, recent break-ups, or new romances. I made a quick exit, and took the bus home, not wishing to be interrogated about Liam, whom they had, of course, met. If *I* had no idea what the situation was between us, how could I be expected to explain it to them?

When I got back to the house, Aoife raised an eyebrow, taking in my slightly unsteady gait, but, mercifully, said nothing reproachful.

"Well?" she merely asked, "How were your results?"

"Quite good, actually."

"Congratulations," she said stiffly, "Are you going to go to Dublin?"

"I- I don't know," I stammered, cursing myself silently for slurring a little, as I spoke.

The expression on her face was difficult to read. I wasn't sure if she wanted me here, or wanted me gone.

"It won't be easy, financially, if you go," she said, eventually, "But if you want to, you should. I wish I'd had the chance to go."

So, there it was: A dig at me, and a surprisingly generous comment, and then another dig at me.

"Anyway," she continued briskly, "You'll probably want to be getting to bed."

I nodded, thankfully. I really was quite tipsy, and concerned that if I attempted to speak further, my words would come out as though my tongue were wrapped in cotton wool.

A few days later, Liam rang to ask, rather tentatively, if I would like to do something for my birthday.

"I'm surprised," I admitted, "I didn't know if you wanted to see me."

There was a long silence. "I- I wasn't sure myself, but... we've been through so much together, and it *is* your eighteenth."

"Okay, I said, nervously, "That would be nice."

I assumed that he would invite me to the cottage for dinner, but instead, he suggested a picnic in the woods. I wondered if Mr. O Mordha disapproved so strongly, of what I had done with Fúamnach, that Liam thought it best to keep me away from him.

Aoife dutifully asked about my birthday plans later that day, and I was only too glad to be able to say that I had agreed to spend the day with Liam. She seemed relieved too.

It astonished me that she had never once asked about the powers she had seen me use, on the night that Alan Lynch had attacked me. Wasn't she curious? Was she so afraid of having to accept the reality of what she had witnessed, that she preferred not to know? Was she really capable of not thinking about it? I tried to tell myself that there was no point in wondering, because understanding Aoife was beyond anyone's capabilities, but I could not quite stop it preying on my mind.

My birthday dawned. Aoife politely presented me with a glass of sparkling wine, and a new pair of jeans, which I had to concede was kind of her. Her pregnancy was quite visible now, although she tried to conceal it beneath loose cardigans, and I tried not to look at it, for fear of retching.

"Happy birthday, Kathy," she said, attempting a smile, though it could not hide the coolness in her voice, "Eighteen today! All grown up! Who would have thought this day would come?"

I couldn't help but wonder if her true meaning were something along the lines of: "Thank goodness you're an adult now, and no further responsibility of mine. I thought the blessed day would never come!"

I decided against verbalising the sarcastic retort that sprang to mind. She was, after all, making an effort, and one way or another, we would be rid of each other soon, because I was still determined to leave home before that baby arrived… just as soon as I could figure out where on earth to go.

I was glad to escape the farce of our feigned harmony, when it came to the time to meet Liam, even though I suspected that ,our reunion would be no less comfortable.

I was right.

Liam was sitting where we had agreed to meet, with a beautiful picnic of sandwiches, chicken, little cakes and wine all laid out on a blue, chequered blanket. He had clearly gone to some effort, but his demeanour was stiff and uneasy.

He wished me a happy birthday, and presented me with a glass of wine and a slightly awkward peck on the cheek.

"This looks lovely," I observed, gesturing towards the picnic. He made some appropriate response.

We conversed, excruciatingly civilly, for a spell, then as we drank a little more wine, fell into a marginally more natural conversation. I reminisced about a few carefully selected fragments from our lives, that had nothing whatsoever to do with the otherworld, or our romance. Some of my recollections brought a genuine smile to his face.

Even so, I thought I detected a certain relief in his expression when we had finished the wine, and eaten as much of the food as any two people could reasonably be expected to consume, and he had packed the leftovers away in his rucksack.

"Was there anything you wanted to do with the rest of the day?" he asked, his face guarded, and leaving me with no clue as to whether he was hoping I would ask for his company, or take my leave.

"What more could I want? This has been lovely," I replied, diplomatically.

"Would you like me to walk you home?"

"No need for that! You've gone to quite enough effort! Thank you for a lovely birthday."

"No thanks required." Again came an awkward peck on the cheek.

As I left, I turned back to look at him, and found that he was looking back at me too. My memory was suddenly flooded with all of the times that my heart had stopped at the sight of him, and I longed to ask him if he wanted to play again tomorrow, or run to him and take his hands, and beseech him to tell me that we would be okay, or… *something*.

Instead, I just waved cheerfully, and turned to make my way home. How I wish I had done… *something* instead.

That night wasn't the first time that the prickle had woken me, and it wouldn't be the last, but as soon as I grew conscious, I was in no doubt that it was one of *those* times. I glanced about hurriedly, half expecting to see one of the small ones, pleading for my help, or someone about to give me some dreadful piece of news, but I was quite alone… Alone, that was, but for the urgent, hissing teeth of the prickle, as it gnawed at, and rattled, me with a message I could not quite read.

Without further thought, I rose. Something was wrong and, whenever something was wrong, it was likely only to be dealt with by my going into the woods. As I crept through the house, towards the door, the whisper of the prickle grew louder and hotter in my ears, cementing my suspicion that it wished me to go out into the night, to seek the source of its unease.

There was no moon that night. My sense knew that she must be there, lurking behind a thick, dark cloud, but it felt as though she were entirely absent. Relying on my familiarity with the path, I wound my way through the thick, meaty blackness, enduring the sinister touch of unseen, feathery branches and clumps of earth underfoot.

The volume and violence of the prickle's unease continued to rise, simultaneously a grave warning, and an insistence that I must press on. I knew that my arms were lightly scratched by thorns, that I could not avoid in the gloom, and my hair dishevelled by unexpected collisions with trees and cobwebs, but I barely felt them, consumed as I was by the certainty that there was something I must find.

For a few moments, I thought that my eyes were adjusting to the dimness, as I began to pick out shapes in my path with a little more precision, then noticed the flickers of light dancing up ahead, glittering through the silhouetted leaves. Somebody had built a fire.

I took a deep breath and rushed towards it, bursting out of the trees, and into a small clearing. The cheerful fire was thriving, and illuminated the sight that met me well enough, but at the same moment, the moon whipped off her mask, and her bright face peered in to brighten the scene. She might as well have accompanied her arrival by shouting: "Surprise!"

For, it was indeed a surprise: Nestled in the grass, his naked skin glowing in the warmth of the flames, was Liam. He was not alone. A girl was cradled in his arms.

I did not move or speak, in utter astonishment, and Liam did not notice that I was there. The girl, however, lifted her head, and propped herself up to meet my gaze, with a knowing smile.

I felt cold. I was looking at myself. It was *me*. My face staring up from Liam's embrace, with an audaciously triumphant grin. Was this a vision of another time? A dream? And yet, the increasingly uncomfortable stinging of my scratches, and the fortitude of the prickle, seemed to indicate that I was awake, and truly there.

I stood, frozen, unable to understand. Then she… I… The 'other me' began to laugh, and cried: "Oh, poor Kathy. You just don't know *what* to make of it all, do you?"

The prickle recognised her before I did, bristling with a protective warmth, yet simultaneously craving another exquisite taste of her. Her dark hair melted into a cascade of strawberry blonde, her face changed shape, and her pale body heaved with new, gentle curves. *Étaín.*

Startled by her laughter, Liam turned to her, and his eyes widened, and widened, and widened further than I had known was humanly possible, when he realised that the woman he was wrapped around was our old nemesis. He stared at her, then stared at me, and a guttural cry escaped his lips, as he sprang away from her like a scalded cat.

"Come now, Liam, don't be coy," purred Étaín, utterly unashamed in her nakedness, as she reclined, and stroked her silken hair, "Not after what *we've* just done."

"But…" he muttered, weakly, "It wasn't you, it was…" He turned to me imploringly. "W- w- wasn't it?"

In that moment, I knew everything: This was her revenge. She had taken my form, and taken my man. Her tongue had been in his mouth. His hands had been on her breasts. He had been *inside* her. She sat there, luxuriating in the sensation of his expended warmth, still within her. Her eyes were firmly fixed on me. I was not sure that she was even bothered about Liam anymore, or at least not as much as she was ecstatic in her victory over me.

"Well done, Étaín," I finally croaked, "Well done."

I turned and fled.

I heard Liam's bellowing voice echoing through the woods, beseeching me to come back. I ran faster. His cries did not subside, and I could hear the grass moving behind me as his frantic footsteps approached. I ran, and I ran, but I could not outrun him. I found my wrist in his grasp, and his strong arms turning me to face him. I did not want to look at him. I noticed that he had, at least, had the good grace to pull on his trousers before he chased me.

"Kathy," he said desperately, his hand on my face, forcing me to meet his eyes, "I thought it was you!"

"I know."

"I would never, *ever* have…"

"I know."

"I was walking home after the picnic, and I heard footsteps running after me, and it was *you!*"

My stomach turned. She had been with him for all of those hours, since the picnic? Exploring every nook and cranny of his body, for *all of that time?* My revulsion got the better of me. I crumbled to the ground, and vomited a puddle of chicken, cakes and wine right at his feet.

He barely noticed and, tightening his grip on my arm, yanked me back upright, desperate to be heard. "It was *you!*" he repeated, "And you said all of the things that I'd longed for you to say, and you wanted me so much, and I was so happy, and…"

"Thank you, the rest is self-explanatory," I replied, coldly, "You lay with Étaín."

"But it was *you!*"

"But it wasn't me, was it? I mean, *really?* You didn't have even the slightest inkling that something was different? Am I truly such a one-dimensional, cardboard cut-out of a person, that anything that looks like me will do?"

"That's not fair, Kathy! How could I have known?"

"I know. You couldn't." Then, it hit me why I had suddenly become so angry. "She was better than me."

"What? No! What are you talking about?"

My voice remained steadily icy. "You said that she told you everything you wanted to hear, and made you *'so'* happy, which is a damn sight more than I've done lately, isn't it? Therefore, she was better than me, and you wanted to believe that the new and improved version was real."

"Kathy, this is nonsense. I love you!"

"And if I hadn't turned up, and she hadn't dropped her glamour, you'd still be back there with her, whispering sweet nothings in her ear, and listening to her better words, and taking her over and over again…"

"Stop it! I feel sick…"

"I know the feeling." I gestured unceremoniously towards the pile of vomit between us.

"This isn't my fault!" he shouted.

"I know."

"It's probably because of what *you* did to her the other night, that she did this to me!"

"I know."

"Then, stop looking at me like that… *Please!*"

"I need to leave."

"Okay, okay," he raked his free hand through his golden hair, "Let me just get my things… or, no, never mind my things, let's just go… somewhere, away from here, and talk about this…"

"You misunderstand me," I stated, "I need to be alone."

"No, you can't… please… we need to talk about this!"

"I know." I unwrapped his hand from me, and discarded it with distaste. "Not now."

"I love you, Kathy."

"I love you too."

"Then, please don't go."

"I have to." I walked away in, what I imagined, was a dignified manner, but soon broke into a sprint. I expected to hear his footsteps echoing my own, but this time he did not follow.

I wondered what he was going to do. Was he going to collect his things from the clearing, and end up talking to Étaín? Was he going to go home and tell his father the sorry tale? Was he going to sit dejectedly in the woods until dawn, racked with grief?

I sat dejectedly on my bed until dawn and beyond, racked with horror. I had to hand it to Étaín. She had gone above and beyond this time; inflicted the sorts of wounds that do not heal. Pictures in the mind's eye do not scar and fall away. They stay, like mental tattoos, fading a little with time and exposure to sunlight, but always there.

I considered trying to summon Fúamnach, and to convince her to try the ritual again, this time to completion. However, I found that I had no stomach for vengeance. My anger had retreated. I was spent. I was done. She had won.

What *had* she won? Had Étaín's dreams of a union with Liam now been fulfilled? Was she planning to rule Ireland with him as her consort? I dismissed the idea. He wouldn't go along with that, even with all of the magic in the world to beguile him.

Liam. Poor Liam. He was as much a victim in this as I had been, when Alan Lynch leaped on top of me and undid his trousers. I knew it, and yet I couldn't unsee what I had seen, and I couldn't unhear what I had heard. She had made him *so* happy. *She* had said the right things. I never seemed to say the right things anymore. He claimed that he loved me, but was it just a memory of me with which he was infatuated? I wasn't sure how well he liked me as I was now, let alone how well he really knew me. *Not well enough, apparently,* I grumbled inwardly, *He didn't know me well enough to know that it wasn't me he was rolling about with in the woods.*

Then, there was the guilt. This turn of events was clearly the retribution that Étaín had promised, after the rash mistake I'd made in taking part in the nonsense with Fúamnach. My decisions had put Liam in this position, as certainly as if I had plotted the horrid affair myself. Fúamnach had convinced me that our actions were to protect him when, in fact, they had led to the only time he had ever really been hurt.

I knew he was hurt. I knew that, even though he may have had a splendid time romping with Étaín for those hours in the woods, the truth that he now knew would mar the memory, and haunt him for the rest of his days. He deserved my sympathy, not my resentment… but I was too human, and his words rang in my memory: "I was so happy…"

How could I forget that he had been so happy with her, when I could not recall the last time he'd been happy with me?

He was waiting for me outside in the morning. We didn't go into the woods. Every branch; every blade of grass, would just be a cruel, mocking reminder of all of the wonderful and terrible times we'd had, and we both knew it.

We sat on the wall opposite my house. He had clearly been home, as he'd showered and changed, since his last, bedraggled appearance of the previous night. I wondered if he had told his father what had happened. I wondered if they had enjoyed a good laugh, and he'd received a pat on the back for bedding a goddess. Of course not. Liam and Mr. O Mordha weren't like that.

Cú Chulaind sat quietly between us, his ears down and his expression sombre, as if he knew that it was not a day for games, or balls, or happy things.

"I'm sorry," I said, "It's all my fault."

Liam nodded. "You didn't mean things to turn out this way. I know that."

"And you didn't mean to sleep with Étaín. I know that."

He shuddered slightly at the thought. "So, where does that leave us?"

"I don't know. Something feels…broken."

"Broken, like a limb that will heal, or broken like a crystal vase in splinters?"

"I wish I knew. I can't look at you without seeing you and *her* together. I know it's unfair, but I can't help it."

"I understand," he nodded, "If I had found you in a similar situation, it would have broken my heart."

"It's not all about us either, is it? You were deceived, and taken advantage of, in the most intimate, personal way. You must be hurting."

He looked down. "I'm not sure what I feel about it yet. I haven't been able to stop thinking of you."

"You need time to make sense of your own pain."

"I suppose so."

"Perhaps I *should* go to Dublin…" As soon as it was out of my mouth, I realised my error.

"Dublin?" exclaimed Liam. It was, of course, the first he'd heard of it.

Another thing I've kept from him, I thought with an inner groan.

"Yes, Dublin. I applied for a course at university there. I didn't really plan to go."

"But, you thought about it?"

"Yes…"

"And you didn't tell me!"

"It was after… the thing with Alan Lynch. I felt lost, and I didn't know what I wanted, and nothing made me happy anymore, and I thought I might as well keep all of my options open…"

"I understand all of that," he said, "But why didn't you tell me?"

"I don't know. I didn't want to hurt you. I knew I was already hurting you, by being distant and unhappy."

"The only thing that's really hurt me is the secrets."

"I'm sorry."

"I know... but it feels as though you already have one foot out the door. You made sure that you had 'options'... I never gave up on us."

"You said that you needed space," I pointed out.

He looked me straight in the eyes. "There's a difference between a bit of time to lick your wounds, and running off to the other side of the country."

"I should have told you about Dublin."

He sighed deeply. "You should have. The worst thing is that I'm not even surprised you didn't. I sometimes feel as if I don't know you anymore."

"You don't," I snapped, my petty, defensive, bitterness getting the better of me, "You spent the day with me, and the evening with someone else, and couldn't even tell the difference!"

He spread his hands and let them fall, exasperatedly. "And here we are again."

"I don't know what to do, Liam. I can't stay here with Aoife's baby. You and I are clearly not in a place to be contemplating cohabitation..."

"Clearly," he interjected, his eyes now distant, and his mouth guardedly set, "Perhaps you *should* go away, if that's what you want."

"I don't know what I want!"

"Well, that's the problem, isn't it? When Étaín was pretending to be you, she knew what she wanted, and *that's* what made me happy!"

I wished that he had slapped me, instead of uttering those words. "And there we are. She *was* better than me. You claim to love me, but I think you're actually in love with who you'd like me to be."

"How can you even say that, after everything..." He paused, and swallowed heavily. "*Everything* we've been through together?"

165

"Everything we go through changes us, and I don't think you like who I've become on the other side."

"This is madness."

"Everything in our lives is madness. Normal people don't have to deal with the things that we do. How are we expected to overcome them? It's just too much."

"So, your answer is simply to walk away? What makes you think your life will be less eventful anywhere else? You're not exactly normal, are you?"

"Perhaps not, but surely things would be easier somewhere far away from these woods, and these memories!" If I could go back in time, and wander into that moment between Liam and my younger self, I would exclaim: "Oh, the irony!"

"…And far away from me," muttered Liam through gritted teeth, "That's what you're really saying, isn't it? You want a life without me."

I burst into tears. "No, I don't! B-b-but I do want a different life!"

"So, do you want me to go with you?"

"To Dublin?" I gasped, "Of course not!"

"Right, that clears that up, then. Thank you very much."

"No, I didn't mean… I mean… How on earth would that work? I don't think you could bear to be so far away from your father, and the small ones."

"I don't think I could bear to be away from you either."

"I think you'll bear it. You're far stronger than you think you are."

"Oh, so it's decided then? You're just leaving?" His voice was suddenly cold.

"I don't know what else to do."

He stood up. "Well, we don't have anything further to talk about then, do we? That's it." He walked towards his car.

I leaped up and followed him, still sobbing. "Liam, please wait. We can't leave it like this…"

"You seem to have made your choice, Kathy. Please do me the small courtesy of allowing me to make mine." He yanked open the car door, waited for Cú Chulaind to jump in before he did, slammed the door shut behind them, and sped off.

My internal butterflies found a cold pool, deep inside me, in which to drown themselves. One by one, they fluttered in, squirmed and died.

Some achingly empty weeks later, I went for a walk in the woods. I sat by the stream and waited, hoping that they would somehow sense that I was there, and come to me. They did.

Their tiny faces looked sad, as they approached. They knew.

"I- I've come to say goodbye," I announced, in as steady a tone as I could muster, though the sight of them swelled my throat with a bitter, churning lump.

They nodded in unison.

"We heard you were leaving," said one, "We'll be sorry to see you go."

They had heard? From Liam, I presumed. I longed to ask them how he was, but stopped myself, and instead attempted to sound jovial. "Oh, I'm sure you'll have a much quieter life around here, without all of the drama that seems to follow me!"

They were not amused. "We'll miss you," stated another one, simply.

My mask of nonchalance fell away, and my eyes filled with tears. "I'll miss you too."

They came to me then, one by one, and wished me well, and extended their tiny hands. I clasped each one in turn, not wanting to let go of any of them. I wondered if I would ever see the small ones again.

I desperately wanted to say goodbye to Liam and Mr O Mordha. I rang Liam to ask if we could meet. He said that he couldn't bear it. I asked if I could visit his father the following day.

"Fair enough. I'll be out." he replied.

When I arrived at the cottage the next day, the first thing that literally struck me was Cú Chulaind, bouncing down the path, and leaping on me in an excited greeting. He planted his enormous paws squarely on my shoulders, and waggled his tongue in my face, as he panted happily. I petted and fussed over him, whilst extricating myself from his doggy embrace, wondering if his presence meant that Liam had changed his mind, and decided to meet me after all. However, I saw only Mr. O Mordha, sitting on the front step of his home, his expression sad but, as always, simultaneously benevolent.

As I approached him, I sensed that Liam wasn't there, but had had the kindness to leave Cú Chulaind behind, knowing that I would want to say goodbye to him too.

"Mr. O Mordha…" I began, then faltered and found no words with which to finish my sentence.

"It's alright, little one," he replied, getting to his feet and extending his arms for a hug.

I gratefully melted into the comforting wool of his jumper, then pulled back, so as not to moisten it with impending tears.

"Tea?" he suggested.

I nodded and followed him inside. Of course, being Mr. O Mordha, he produced far more than tea. He had prepared a juicy salad, topped with thick slices of roasted ham, and delicious homemade biscuits for dessert.

Though I hadn't had much appetite of late, I was glad to have one last taste of his cooking, and our munching helped to fill the cavernous silence.

Finally, he said: "So, you're off, then?"

I sighed. "I am."

"We'll miss you."

"I hope you know how much I'll miss you in return."

He nodded. "These things are never easy, and all of the unusual aspects of this situation make it even harder, but you have a chance now, young Kathy, to have new adventures, and learn interesting and important things. I never regret having travelled as a younger man. Let yourself enjoy it."

"It's hard to enjoy the idea when I know I'm making… people I care about so unhappy."

Mr. O Mordha smiled, clearly aware that I was referring to his son. "It's difficult for him. He's never had that desire to leave… but what's right for one person isn't right for another, and only time and experience will tell what life has in store for either of you. Allow yourself to have those experiences. I'll look after him."

I smiled a little. "Thank you… and thank you for your all of your kindness."

"My pleasure. There will always be a cup of tea and a biscuit waiting here for you, Kathy, however far you roam, or wherever life takes you."

"Thank you," I replied warmly, though as I took my leave of him, I had the most irrationally heartbreaking feeling that I would never share a meal with Mr. O Mordha in his cottage again.

He offered to drive me home, but I assured him, as cheerfully as I could manage, that I was in need of a long walk after scoffing so many of his lovely biscuits.

Before I left, I pressed a note into his hand.

"Could you tell him…?" I began, then shook my head, "Please just give him this."

"I will," he promised.

I walked home the long way, down the dull back road, instead of going through the woods. They felt like Liam's place now, not mine. I had said my goodbyes.

I packed my favourite clothes and books, and marvelled at how empty my little room looked without them in it.

"I might need to move some of your other bits into the shed, if I need more space for the baby," commented Aoife.

I was about to snap at her that there were three bedrooms, which should be more than sufficient, but I held my tongue. I didn't envision spending time in the house again, with my sister and her demon offspring, so the location of any possessions I left behind was of little consequence.

"Would you like me to go to the coach station with you tomorrow, to see you off?" she asked.

"No, I'll be fine, thanks," I replied.

"Kathy…" Though she had said my name, her voice trailed off, and her expression grew distant.

"Yes, Aoife?" I prompted.

She finally met my gaze, and narrowed her eyes. "Kathy, I don't want to know anything about any of your… strange goings-on, but you know I've… seen things, and I don't think you're… normal."

My eyes widened in astonishment. This was it! *Some* acknowledgement of what she had witnessed!

"So…" she continued, "Be very careful in Dublin, won't you? Watch your behaviour. Don't give into any of that… weirdness, will you, or what will they think of you in the big city?"

My mouth fell open a little. So, that was it. Magical powers had been reduced to some sort of obstreperous behavioural issue, in her mind.

"Don't worry, Aoife," I said with a jaded smirk, "I'm expecting to have a far more… normal life in Dublin." This is another moment which, if I could travel back in time and witness it again, would cause me to exclaim: "Oh, the irony!"

Aoife nodded, with a certain satisfaction, and scuttled away from my 'weirdness', and the distasteful conversation that she had clearly felt was her duty to instigate.

The following afternoon found me at the coach station, bowed under the weight of a rucksack full of books, and clutching a suitcase.

I had arrived early, hoping he would come.

My departure from home that morning had been oddly jovial. Aoife and I had both been practically manic with barely-disguised relief at the fact that we were about to be rid of each other. We had joked and laughed hysterically and, if she hadn't been pregnant, I'll warrant she might have cracked open a bottle of champagne.

As she was giving me a stiff and dutiful hug goodbye on the doorstep, however, I had thought, for just a moment, that there was some emotion other than sheer glee in her expression. Perhaps it had been a little regret for the friendship that we might have had, if she hadn't had to become my mother.

I sat on a cold, metal bench at the coach station, hugging my rucksack, and squeezing my suitcase between my legs, very much aware that I was alone, and that my luggage was all I had left in the world.

I checked my watch. *Will he come?*

I tried to think of other things. I tried to imagine what Dublin would be like, or what the hotel I was staying in that night, in an area called Temple Bar, might be like. It wasn't expensive, but it was a lot for Aoife.

"You won't be able to stay there for more than a few nights," she had warned me, "You'll have to find something cheaper as soon as possible."

Where is he? My eyes skittered towards the corner, and my stomach churned at every glimpse of fair hair.

My coach pulled up. The driver hopped out, and checked that everyone had the correct ticket. He loaded our suitcases into the luggage hold. There were not very many of us.

The official departure time was ten minutes away.

"I'd say this is everyone," observed the driver, "We can leave early."

I leaped to my feet. "But, I…" I cried, aghast.

He smiled broadly. "Are you waiting for someone, Love? Some nice young man coming to see you off?"

I felt the colour of embarrassment spring to my hot cheeks. "I- I…" I stuttered.

"Tell you what," he chuckled, "I'll smoke a fag, and then we'll be off. Is that okay with you, Missy?"

I gulped, still horribly mortified, and aware of the other passengers staring at me with impatient annoyance. I nodded hastily.

"Right," agreed the driver, and produced a packet of cigarettes from his jacket pocket. "We'll give your fella a few minutes to make his entrance."

I pressed my lips together, trying not to cry. *He isn't coming.*

The note I had passed to Mr. O Mordha for Liam had contained my departure information, my dearest pleas for him to come and see me off, and all of my love.

Had he read it, or discarded it? Had he chosen not to come, or not wanted to know?

The coach driver mimicked a polite cough, in a sarcastic manner. I noticed that he was stubbing his cigarette butt out, with the sole of his shoe.

"Well?" he enquired, cheekily, "Are we ready to be off?"

"I- I suppose so," I replied, meekly.

"Right!" He opened the coach doors, and the passengers filed on.

I turned once more to take a last, desperate look towards the corner, in case Liam were to walk around it at that very moment. He didn't. I stepped onto the coach.

"Not to worry, Love, plenty more fish in the sea," said the driver with a salacious wink.

I shuddered, made my way to the very back of the coach, and flopped into a window seat, placing my rucksack on the empty seat next to me: A sentry to keep all others away.

He didn't come.

I heard the barking of a dog. It seemed familiar. It couldn't be…

I gasped. Had he come after all, but arrived too late? Should I jump off the coach and run to him? Should I look back and wave? Should I…?

The dog continued to bark. It could have been Cú Chulaind. Then again, it might have been any dog.

The engine started, and the coach began to pull out of its parking bay.

Should I look back?

I wondered what I would see if I did: A dejected and lonely Liam, gazing at me with sad, reproachful eyes, or an empty space where he might have been, but wasn't, because he hadn't come?

Suddenly, I was not sure that I wanted to know. I didn't look back.

The coach sped off, away from the station and around a sudden bend. I had missed my chance to look back. I might never know if he had come.

CHAPTER NINE

And, so it was that I arrived in Dublin. I surveyed the enormity of the dirty, industrial coach station in astonishment, looking for an exit. There were several. I wandered in the direction of a bus stop, but realised that there were many, and I had no idea which bus went where, and I began to feel quite light-headed, so I scuttled towards a taxi rank instead. I knew that I couldn't afford to make a habit of it, but I desperately wanted to get somewhere safe with my luggage, so I hopped into a cab and asked to be taken to Temple Bar.

I was dropped off just outside the area, on a vast, grey, busy road, the like of which I had only ever seen in fims, and the driver gave me instructions to walk down an alley to reach my hotel.

I began to drag my suitcase in the appropriate direction, tentatively at first, then with increasing curiosity. The alley wasn't long, and there seemed to be a more open area at the other end. Smaller alleys led off the little street I was on, from both sides, and I peered down them in wonder, hearing human merriment echoing from, what I could only assume were, drinking establishments. I spied one little pub, halfway down the tiniest street of all. There were a couple of people outside. I couldn't make out their features, but I found myself stopping to stare. The pub seemed to pique the prickle's interest too, and it chirruped like an excited cat in my ear. I resolved to find the little pub again later, once I had divested myself of my luggage, and perhaps treat myself to a 'welcome to Dublin' drink.

I suddenly burst out into an enormous square, which was positively teeming with people of all ages, sizes and colours. I wondered whether some festival was taking place, or if Temple Bar was always so busy.

I glanced about frantically, taking in a number of bars, so full of patrons that many of them had spilled outside, to converse and enjoy their drinks. The sounds of live music wafted from several of these, clashing clumsily with the warbling of some competing, nearby street performers, singing with guitars. There were shops too, filled with interesting, eclectic clothing, and other wares. Fortunately, before I began to feel light-headed again, I spotted the sign for my hotel, and rushed towards it with as much speed as I could manage, given the general bustle.

My room was clean and comfortable and, to me, seemed quite luxurious. I showered and changed, and nibbled at some sandwiches that Aoife had packed for me to eat on the coach, but for which I'd had no appetite. I could still hear the raucous sounds of the throngs outside, as evening drew in, and was simultaneously enthralled and wary. I determined to give into the lure of my new surroundings, and go out for a drink.

The lights and life of Temple Bar positively glowed in the dusk, a whirling, heady cavalcade of adventures to be had. However, I immediately retraced my steps to find the little bar that had so intrigued me on my arrival.

An hour later, I paused defeatedly. I simply couldn't find it. I had been up and down the first alley, and the neighbouring alleys, and all of the connected or parallel alleys that I could find, and there was no sign of the pub that I had been drawn to.

I shrugged, concluding that I had made a mistake in my directions, and decided to look for it another day, when I wasn't so tired. I wandered into a bar next door to my hotel instead. I hoped that, if I remained close enough to my accommodation, it would be impossible for me to get lost again later. A small band was playing lively music inside, which I found pleasant enough.

I ordered a beer at the bar. A group of friendly, American tourists were having shots, and invited me to join them. It seemed rude to refuse- and foolish given my financial limitations- so I didn't. They found it utterly charming that I was from a small village in Kerry, and that it was my first night in Dublin, so they bought me several drinks. Eventually, one of the men in the group began to stand a little too close to me for my liking, and compliment my appearance a little more than I appreciated. His interest in me made me think about Liam, and the stale smell of alcohol on his breath reminded me of Alan Lynch, so I made my excuses, and went back to the hotel.

As I walked the few feet between the buildings, I suddenly had a familiar feeling. The prickle perked up, and wound itself curiously around my shoulders, making me shiver a little with its unexpected excitement. In the corner of my eye, I thought I saw a tiny shape, running across the square, but when I turned my head, I saw only human revellers, enjoying the night air. For a moment, I was a child again, unable to shake off the feeling that something was there, yet not quite there. Then, I laughed a little to myself. *What nonsense! Do you really think it likely that the small ones would have followed you up here from Kerry?* I decided that I must be tipsy, so I went to my room, drank lots of water, and went straight to bed.

Several similar sightings/not sightings happened in the next few days. It wasn't just small ones I saw, or didn't see. Liam too haunted me. I constantly glimpsed his tall, fair form, and wondered, momentarily, if he had decided to follow me to Dublin, and walk the streets until he found me, to profess his undying love… And, every time, I found that I was mistaken, and that there was nobody in my vicinity who could be described as looking even remotely like Liam. Eventually, it hit me that they weren't in the city at all, but that I was missing them, and my imagination was conjuring up these little spectres of the past, in an attempt to fill the void in which they had been.

I went to Trinity College- which was quite a short walk away from Temple Bar- a week before my induction, in the hopes that there might be somebody around who could help me to find long-term accommodation. I paused, in awe, in front of the gates, wondering if it could possibly be true that *I* was destined to spend time in this wondrous, magical world. Dame Street outside was wider than any road had a right to be, and unequivocally grey. Yet, the college beckoned, from the other side of the gates, as if the entrance were a portal to another world from fairy tales: An inviting labyrinth of sprawling grounds, and regal, historic buildings, which reminded me of castles.

I entered the campus, slowly and reverently, intoxicated by the sight of every old brick and stone, and each statuesque tree. The place was vast, and I felt a solemn quality in the air… Not sad, but weighed down with history, and truth, and great importance. This was not a place to be taken lightly. The most wonderful, and the worst, of ideas had been incited and discussed here, and I fancied, for a moment, that the buildings were sighing slightly, jaded by, but fastidious, in their task of housing centuries of secrets.

There were few people on campus, as the term had not yet begun. Of those, some were clearly tourists, marvelling at the history and architecture of their surroundings, with cameras at the ready.

A small group of young people was sitting on the steps of a building, chatting animatedly, and looking so comfortable there, that I concluded their awe had worn off, and they must be existing students at the university.

I approached them shyly, and stood beside them for a few moments, before I had the courage to say: "Excuse me…"

They all looked up.

"How can I help you?" asked a dark girl, in a friendly tone.

I smiled, relieved that they did not appear to be about to laugh at, or make fun of, me. I don't quite know why I always assumed that peer groups were going to behave like judgemental, jeering toddlers.

"I'm about to start a course here, and I need to find accommodation," I explained, "So, I was wondering if there was an office, or a notice board around, where people might leave details of such vacancies?"

Another girl with honey blonde hair, and an enviably curvaceous figure, fixed me with a strangely intense stare, as though I were a puzzle that she was trying to work out. I wondered irrationally if I had said something wrong.

"Ah, a newcomer!" stated the first, friendly girl, "Welcome! Yes, there's a notice board in the hallway of that building over there." She pointed. "There should be a few people looking for flatmates at this time of year. Good luck!"

"Thank you so much," I beamed, inwardly relieved that my query had been deemed in the realms of normality.

The honey blonde, however, continued to stare at me, her gaze not unfriendly, but alarmingly penetrating. I fidgeted for a moment, wondering if she were about to address me, but shyness overcame me, and I hurried off in the prescribed direction.

The notice board was covered in hand-written notes, advertising everything from second-hand course books, to mutual interest groups and societies. Fortunately, I found several advertisements for inexpensive rentals. There was a payphone nearby, so I began to ring them, one by one. The first two didn't answer.

The third rang for some time, and I was about to give up when a rough voice snapped: "Hello?"

"Oh… erm… hello," I stammered, "I'm ringing in response to your ad for student accommodation. I'm about to start my first term at Trinity College, and I…"

"Oooh, *'ringing in response,'*" the voice mimicked, mockingly, "Aren't we fancy?"

"I… um…"

"Ah, I'm only joking, Girlie," he chuckled, "Now, what's your name, and can you pay your rent?"

"M-my name is Kathy," I answered timidly, "And yes, I think I should be able to manage…"

"Can you pay it or not? I have better things to be doing than chatting on the phone, if you can't afford it!"

I was tempted to slam the receiver down in offence, but then I remembered that I was really rather desperate, so I sighed and said: "Yes, I can pay it. May I come and see the room?"

"Right, so. Where are you?"

"I'm at the college."

"I'll collect you there, and take you out to see it."

He gave me instructions on where to wait, and I slinked off to find the appointed spot, with very little enthusiasm. He sounded extremely rude, and far too old to be a student, and I wondered what on earth I was getting myself into.

I was so lost in my trepid musings that I did not notice the tugging feeling at first, until my bag was violently ripped from my shoulder, and my heart began to thump to the beat of fleeing footsteps. I spun 'round in shock, and saw a youth hurtling down the footpath, clutching my property.

Without a moment's hesitation, my instincts propelled me after him, shouting: "Stop! Thief!" He was running fast, but I could run fast too, and, as I chased him, I felt a thunderous prickle rise inside me, furious and indignant, spurring me on at a speed beyond human, until I had almost caught up with the miscreant. The invisible arms of the prickle burst out of my body, and their enormous hands grabbed hold of the thief, raised him off the ground, shook him like a rag doll, and then discarded him unceremoniously, leaving him in a ball on the ground. He leaped up, his eyes wide with terror, but made to continue running.

"Give that back," I yelled, springing at him with a kick that knocked him off his feet again.

He kept hold of the bag, attempting to kick me back as he squirmed and tried to right himself, shouting obscenities as he struggled. I blocked him, and continued to fight, until a well-aimed blow to his arm caused him to loosen his grip, and I yanked my possessions from his grasp, with a final kick for good measure.

Another voice shouted from nearby. The thief suddenly sprinted away, realising that the fracas had drawn somebody's attention, and tore around the corner, out of sight.

I tried to steady my breathing, clinging to my bag protectively, as the owner of the new voice reached me.

"Gosh, are you okay?" she asked anxiously, "Shall I call the police?"

"N- n- no," I murmured, my body still shaking, and the prickle still grumbling in my ears, "He'll be long gone by the time they arrive."

Only then did I think to look at my would-be helper. I gasped. It was the honey blonde girl, who had stared at me so curiously on campus, when I had asked for directions. She was looking at me with a mixture of awe, fascination and bizarre delight.

"You were amazing!" she exclaimed.

I was suddenly anxious. How much had she seen? Had she witnessed me using my powers? She didn't look afraid. I presumed that she had only been present long enough to watch the physical fight.

"It was nothing," I muttered, "I- I'm a kickboxer."

"Oh, is *that* what it was?" She smirked audaciously, her eyes knowing and intrigued.

Oh no, perhaps she did see more!

"We never introduced ourselves earlier," she continued brightly, as though sensing my discomfort, and deciding not to dwell on the specifics of the altercation, "I'm Alice."

"K- Kathy," I replied.

"Nice to meet you, Kathy. You must be quite shaken after all that. Would you like to come for a cup of tea?"

Her gaze continued to unnerve me, boring into me, as though my eyes were windows that she was desperate to peer inside.

I stepped back slightly. "No thanks, I'm fine…" I began, then suddenly remembered my appointment, and checked my watch in alarm, "Sorry, Alice, I have to meet someone nearby. Thanks for your help, though." I attempted to smile politely, as I took my leave.

"We must have a drink next time," she called after me, a little too eagerly.

When I returned to the spot from which I was to be collected, a small, battered, green car was waiting, flashing its lights and blowing the horn impatiently. An unkempt, gangly man was leaning out of the driver's window.

When he saw me, he shouted: "Are you Kathy?"

The brusqueness of his tone did little to steady my nerves, and I merely nodded meekly.

"I'm Tom. Alright then, get in and let's go."

With a deep breath, I clambered into the car.

Tom's house was about a half hour drive from town. As we pulled into his parking bay, he pointed out the bus stop across the road that would take me close to the college, if I chose to rent the room.

The house itself was small, unexceptional from the outside, and identical to the other homes in the area, albeit a little shabbier. The inside boasted a mouldy aroma, faded, old-fashioned decor, and a bathroom that looked like it hadn't seen a good clean for a decade. Tom led me upstairs, and opened a cupboard door, to reveal another narrow staircase, then gestured for me to go up.

"Had the attic done up, you see," he muttered, "All nice and new. Thought I could make a bit of spare cash renting it out to students."

The attic was tiny, but to be fair, did seem much newer and cleaner than the rest of the house. It contained a single bed, still wrapped in plastic, a small chest of drawers, and a desk and chair.

"So, do you want it or not?" he barked, impatiently, "I don't have all day!"

I barely had time to think. "I- I suppose so," I replied weakly.

"Right so. I'll take the deposit now, and you can move in tomorrow."

I nodded mutely, and counted out the deposit from the money in my purse.

He yanked it out of my hand greedily, and stuffed it into his grubby pocket. "So, you'll be off now?" It was somewhere between a question and an order.

"I suppose so."

"You remember where the bus stop is?"

"Oh! Erm… yes… okay." He wasn't even planning to drive me back to town!

I left in something of a daze, and waited outside for twenty minutes before a bus arrived. As I stared out of the window at the bleak suburbs, on my journey back, I tried to make sense of how I felt about my new life.

The university was wonderful, but my dismal new accommodation, the theft, and my conversation with Alice, had left me feeling uneasy and deflated. I closed my eyes, and imagined sitting in Mr. O Mordha's warm, cosy cottage, drinking a comforting cup of tea, and chatting about my day. I opened them, and felt very alone.

On my college induction day, I awoke in my small bed in the attic, and felt a sense of excitement. The plain, cramped room did not depress me nearly so much as it usually did. I showered, trying to avoid looking too closely at anything in the bathroom, lest the true magnitude of its filth should overwhelm me. Then, I dressed, and ate a biscuit for breakfast, from the packet that I kept in one of the drawers of my dresser. As soon as I'd investigated the kitchen at Tom's house, I had decided that cooking anything in it was not an option, if I valued my health. There were… *things* in there, which I could not quite identify, and may have been living or dead, or somewhere in between. Due to my finances, therefore, I was left with a very limited and meagre diet. On this day, however, not even the thought of the kitchen, or my impending, slow, crowded journey into town on the bus, could dampen my spirits. Something important was finally about to happen.

There was an entrance to the college campus closer to my bus stop than the one I had used on my first visit, but I walked a little further to access the same, elegant archway, and slip through, as though into another reality of indescribable, detailed beauty. Today, the campus was filled with life, and swarms of excited students scuttled up and down the paths, most of them, like me, studying college-issued maps, and trying to choose the right building for their respective inductions.

I made my way to the history department, and inhaled deeply as I entered. The very air in the spacious, old building was thick with knowledge. I did not need to search too hard for the correct lecture theatre, for the anticipatory hum of the chatter of nervous, new students, positively echoed from the spot. The room was enormous, and plain but grand, with wooden, graduated seating rising up in three directions from the speaker's area. I felt very small in the vast, solemn space, but took a deep breath, picked a seat, and pulled out a pen and notebook, so that I could jot down any important information.

The department professor, an eloquent man with piercing, blue eyes, welcomed us, and produced a stack of hand-outs to be passed around, containing a course overview, term and exam dates, reading lists, and the like.

Then, a number of lecturers took turns to introduce their subjects. I was particularly captivated by the description of a module called 'Early Irish Myths and Legends', which was to be taught by a Dr. Herbert, who was a petite and very animated, middle-aged woman, with large, excited, dark eyes, a warm smile, and a crumpled cardigan that was just a little oversized, and kept falling over her hands as she spoke.

When the introductory session was over, we were instructed to go to a different building to collect our ID cards, and some forms to fill in, indicating our choice of historical subjects to pursue in our first year. We were allowed to take a week to decide, but I ticked the boxes and returned the paperwork within minutes.

"Have you chosen already?" asked the receptionist, raising her eyebrows. "Are you sure?"

I nodded.

She shrugged, and took the form from my hands. "Well, you're the first!"

"Somebody's eager," remarked a friendly voice, from behind me.

I turned and saw Dr. Herbert smiling at me. "Mind if I take a peek?"

I shook my head, and she picked up my form, absently stroking a dark curl that insisted on escaping from her slightly untidy bun, as she read. Her smile broadened.

"Well, it looks as though we'll be seeing quite a lot of each other," she concluded brightly.

I nodded, and grinned back at her. Unsurprisingly, I had chosen early Irish modules, with a particular focus on anything related to religion and mythology.

"Nice to meet you…" she glanced down at the paperwork again, "Kathy."

"Nice to meet you too, Dr. Herbert," I replied.

"Right, I need a coffee," she declared, "Go and enjoy your lunch!" With another beam, she left and bustled down the hallway.

I went to the cafeteria, and looked longingly at sandwiches, lasagne, and stew that I couldn't afford, and bought myself a small bag of nuts and a cup of tea. I sat down at a table, peering shyly around me, hoping that I wasn't the only person sitting alone.

"Kathy!" exclaimed Alice, startling me as she suddenly materialised at my table, pulled out a chair and inserted herself in it, without so much as a by-your-leave. She fixed me with her annoyingly inquisitive stare, and observed: "That's not much of a lunch."

"I- I had a large breakfast," I lied.

Alice shrugged. "Well, I expect that's why you're so thin."

I did not imagine that she meant it as a compliment. I frowned, feeling a little irritated. "What are *you* doing here?" I asked, then realised how rude I sounded, and added: "I had the impression that you were already a student here, so why did you need to come in for induction day?"

She nodded. "Yes, I'm in my second year. I have a bit of work to finish on a project, before term begins, so, while I'm here, I offered to do some of the introductory tours of the library, after lunch, for new recruits to the department."

"And what do you study?"

"History."

Of course she did. There was to be no escaping her.

"So," continued Alice, leaning across the table to draw closer to me, studying my features with shameless fascination, "That day, when your bag was stolen, I could have sworn that I saw something very strange…"

My body stiffened. Oh ye gods, she saw. Why isn't she terrified of me? What on earth is wrong with her?

"I'd prefer not to talk about that day," I snapped, no longer caring how impolite I seemed, "I found it all quite traumatic."

"Did you really?" Her tone was sympathetic, but her expression suggested she didn't believe a word of it. "You poor thing. We must make sure to give you a better introduction to Dublin than that. There'll be free drinks at the history department later. Will you come?"

I was about to say no, but she pre-empted my refusal, and added: "Oh, there'll be food too. You simply *must* join us!"

My eyes widened. Food? However annoying she was, I couldn't possibly turn down free food. Fantasies of food had begun to plague me on a near-constant basis.

"Okay then," I conceded, "See you later."

"Well, in the meantime, I'll see you at the library for your tour after lunch, won't I?" Her smile was slightly smug.

I froze. "How did you know I was studying history?"
"Oh, just a feeling."

She smirked audaciously, as I gathered my belongings, muttered something about the ladies' room, and fled.

I paced the beautifully manicured grounds outside, grumbling under my breath. What *did* that girl want with me? She had evidently seen me use my powers, but instead of running from me, or reporting me to NASA, she seemed to find me utterly riveting, and wanted to get to know me. Was she just downright strange, or did she know something of magic herself? I stomped frustratedly through the gardens, until it was time for my tour of the library, and then I stomped in its direction.

I paused to take in the impossibly long, imposing, grey building. Something about it made me take a deep breath. I thought about the reality of what lay behind its cold stone and many windows: Centuries of knowledge, with all of its wonder, horrors and truths.

I sighed a little in awe, and in slight annoyance too, because I had just seen Alice's honey blonde hair glinting in the sunlight, as she stood outside, welcoming new students, and distributing hand-outs. I greeted her politely as she passed me my library information pack. I had determined to be, at least, civil to her, if there was even the slightest possibility that she might be able to put me in the path of any more events offering complementary refreshments.

As soon as enough students had assembled for the tour, she led us inside the library.

My heart stopped. I froze, transfixed and chastised. The prickle hummed lightly, then purred, pressing its lips to my neck like a tentative lover, deeply aroused, but politely cautious.

The library could not be real. It was, surely, some enchantment. Rows of old, precious books stretched from the floor to the elegant, vaulted ceiling, and further in each direction than the eye could see. The space was so tall that a dark, wooden mezzanine level provided a small interruption to the ubiquitous shelving, about halfway up the wall. Small busts of important people were scattered about the shelves. Scholars perused dense, weighty tomes, at reading tables, scribbling furiously in their notebooks, discovering their passions and their truths. Though the lighting was dim, a deep, golden glow seemed to radiate from the spines of the books themselves, bathing the place in a regal light.

For a moment, I desperately wanted to share the sight with Liam, and then remembered that I might never see him again. My sadness did not last long, however, as Alice began to lead us from one area of the library to another, informing us of where certain sections of particular interest were located, and explaining the protocol for requesting valuable items for study.

As we moved towards a back corner, I began to hear a slight, rustling sound. The prickle raised its head from my neck, craning towards the noise, curiously. The rustling sound grew a little louder, and only then did I realise that it was actually *whispering:* A dry, unearthly whispering, emanating from the bookshelves… Hundreds of voices, repeating a list of names, some familiar and others that I had not heard before. "*Cú Chulaind, Echu, Badb, Brigit, Nuadu, Lug, Medb, Bres, Midir, Macha, Fúamnach, Étaín…*"

I gasped sharply, looking around at the rest of the tour group, for any sign that they could hear the whispering too. Of course, they could not. Alice, however, was studying my reaction, a knowing smile playing about her lips.

"This is where you will find the books on Irish myths and legends," she announced, staring at me, as though I were the only one to whom the information might be of interest.

What *did* that blasted girl know about me, and how?

Far too soon, the tour of the library was over, and I found myself blinking back out in the sunshine, as my eyes readjusted to natural light.

The tour group dispersed, but Alice grabbed my arm and said: "That little reception I told you about is at six o'clock. You *will* join us, won't you?"

"Yes," I replied, with a slight shrug, designed to dislodge her hand from my person.

"Great," she called as she left, "See you later!"

I pondered what to do for the next couple of hours, and soon decided that I wanted nothing more than to be back in the library. Though it was only my second time inside, plunging back into its, vast, solemn cocoon felt like coming home.

I did not need to consult a map to find my way back to the section that I longed to explore. The crackling whispers grew louder and louder, as I approached, filling my mind with the appellations they chanted: *"Macha, Diarmait, Gráinne, Derdriu, Noísiu…"*

"Can I help you?" came a small, hushed voice, startling me from my reverie.

I looked about, astonished, but saw nobody in my vicinity.

"Down here!"

I looked down, and there he was: A little fellow, barely taller than my knee, with those unmistakeably enormous, ancient eyes. One of the small ones!

"Hello," I exclaimed, a little too loudly. He furrowed his brow in disapproval, and I remembered that we were in a library. "What are you doing here?" I asked, lowering my voice.

"I could ask you the same thing," he replied, cheekily, "I'm always here. I don't see *your* kind around here too often, though."

My kind? I was intrigued by his words, but not as curious as I was about his presence in the middle of a city.

"This seems a strange place for you to make your home," I observed.

"I did not make it so. It simply is." Then, he looked over at the bookshelves with irritation, and pressed his tiny finger to his lips. "Shush," he ordered sternly, "She knows very well that you're here!"

The whispering ceased immediately.

"Are there… more of you here?" I asked, peering, with increasing interest, at my surroundings.

"Oh no, that's just the books," he replied nonchalantly, "Rowdy bunch. Always desperate for attention. May I procure a volume or two for you to peruse? What did you have in mind to read today? 'The Boyhood Deeds of Cú Chulaind', perhaps? Or 'The Cattle Raid of Cooley?'"

I now wanted only to speak to him further, and to better understand how he had come to be here, so far removed from nature, but I did not want to offend him by rejecting his offer, so I thought about it for a moment, and responded:

"Do you have any material relating to The Dagda?"

He nodded decisively. "Certainly! Just take a seat, and I'll be with you in a moment."

I sat down at a nearby reading table, still not quite able to believe what I was experiencing. What followed was more astonishing still. With unnatural speed, he leaped up to the second row of books, scaled the edge of the bookshelf skilfully, plucked out a small volume, and jumped back to the floor, with the grace of a cat.

He presented the book to me with a flourish. "I'll be here if you need any further assistance."

I wondered if he was planning to stand there, and watch me as I read, but then realised that he had quite disappeared from sight.

Whatever next, I mused. Then, I opened my book. It was a collection of old stories about The Dagda. I was intrigued to discover that he was also known by other names, such as 'Echu Ollathir', and that he was often described as a large man, or even a giant, which bore no resemblance to the spindly fellow that *I'd* encountered. I wondered if it was not only the small ones who had lessened in size with time, but the Great Ones too. He was associated with fertility and strength, as well as magic and wisdom, and had the power to control life and death, time, and the weather. I wondered if he still possessed all of those abilities, or if his magic had diminished with his stature. He was known as a great god and father figure. That did not surprise me. I had seen the respect that he commanded, at the gathering of the immortals, back in the woods.

I lost myself in the stories of his nature and deeds, and by the time I remembered to glance at my watch, it was already six o'clock. Part of me never wanted to leave the library, but the hollow, gnawing feeling in my stomach dictated otherwise. I jumped up, and went to replace the book on its shelf.

At that moment, the small one reappeared and snatched it possessively out of my hand. "Leave that to me," he instructed authoritatively, "I do hope we'll see you here again."

"Yes, thank you, I expect you will," I answered with slight amusement, and hurried away to the reception at the history department, fantasising about what sustenance it might provide.

As soon as I arrived, Alice accosted me. "Kathy! So glad you could make it! I was afraid you might not come!"

"Sorry I'm late," I muttered, "I lost track of time at the library."

"Ah, yes," she smiled, "It's a very special place, isn't it?"

I narrowed my eyes. Was this a hint that she knew something about the magical aspects of the library, or was I just being paranoid? "It's beautiful," I responded flatly.

"Let me introduce you to everyone!" She placed an arm about my shoulders protectively, and led me here and there, introducing me to various faculty members, and other students. The friendly girl who had been sitting with Alice, and given me directions to the notice board on my first visit to the college, was named Samira. She was still friendly. Dr. Herbert gave me a broad smile and a wave, between stuffing a pork pie into her mouth. I eyed it covetously.

As though reading my mind, Alice drew me towards the platters of food displayed on a long table. "Why don't you help yourself to a snack, and I'll get you a drink? Red or white?"

"White, please," I murmured robotically, my attention entirely taken by the thought of eating imminently.

I picked up a plate, and surveyed the spread. There was smoked salmon on soda bread, quiche, pork pies and sausage rolls, spicy chicken legs, scotch eggs, stuffed mushrooms and peppers, a cheese plate and a large green salad.

I struggled to prevent myself from dribbling greedily as I piled my plate with everything I could see, and tucked into the feast, turning my back to the congregation so that nobody was forced to witness my voracity. Alice reappeared with a glass of wine, and I attempted a thankful nod between mouthfuls of mushroom.

Alice watched me curiously. I wished fervently that she would go away and leave me to my meal.

To my relief, she said: "Well, I'd better get back to the party. Please, eat as much as you like. You barely had any lunch! Come and find me when you've had your fill!"

I managed an awkward smile of acquiescence, through my chewing. I ate and I ate. I ate as though I had never eaten before, and might never eat again. I ate until my stomach hurt, and beyond. When I could not physically cram another morsel inside me, I washed it down with a swig of wine, and contemplated surreptitiously filling my bag with food for later. I decided against it, lest it was observed.

Dr. Herbert approached me. "Nice to see you again… Kathy, was it? Are you having a good time?"

"Yes, thank you," I replied with a genuine smile of replete satisfaction, "The food is excellent!"

She agreed enthusiastically, as she picked up a chicken leg to nibble. "How has your day been?" she asked.

"Great! The library is the most wonderful thing I've ever seen, and I'm very much looking forward to beginning my lectures."

"That's nice to hear."

I would have liked to speak to Dr. Herbert further, but Alice popped up again, exclaiming: "Kathy, you *must* come and meet my friend Paul!"

After a further couple of hours of conversation, the numbers of attendees began to dwindle, and somebody began to pack away the food leftovers into tinfoil parcels.

"Would anybody like to take some of this home?" she called out, "It'll only go to waste."

"I'll take some," I replied a little too quickly, "For… my flatmate."

The woman passed me several silver bundles, and I eagerly squirreled them away in my bag.

"A few of us are going to continue on to Temple Bar for drinks," said Alice, "Will you join us?"

I found myself longing to agree. I couldn't bear for the day to be over, and I had so much enjoyed the atmosphere in Temple Bar during my brief stay. Reluctantly, my mind acknowledged the reality of my lengthy bus journey back to Tom's house, and my excruciating lack of funds for drinking in pubs, so I declined.

As I trudged to the bus stop, I forced myself to dwell on all of the positive things that had happened that day. I had a feeling that I was going to enjoy my course, I couldn't wait to spend more time in the library with my new little friend and, most importantly, I had a bag full of food.

When I arrived back at my accommodation, and turned my key in the door, I heard Tom's voice call out: "Oh, she's back! Kathy, come here!"

I walked cautiously towards the living room, which I generally avoided, for it was his domain, and his company held very little appeal. I pushed open the door, and Tom handed me the phone. He was completely naked. My mouth fell open.

"It's your sister," he snapped, apparently entirely unabashed.

In shock, I lifted the receiver to my ear and stammered: "H- hello?"

"Hello, Kathy," said Aoife, "You're home late. Are you well?"

"Oh, erm… yes. It was my college induction day, and there was a small gathering afterwards, to welcome new students."

"I see. I hope you're not spending too much money. I won't be able to send you anything more until next month."

"Y- yes, I know. Don't worry."

"I had the baby."

"What?"

"I had the baby yesterday. She came a little early, but she's fine."

She. At least she had a girl. Less chance of it growing up to be a rapist. "Oh… um… congratulations, I suppose."

"Thank you. I'll call her Eili after our mother."

"That's nice," I replied, although the thought of Alan Lynch's spawn being named after my beautiful mother made my skin crawl.

"Well, anyway, I just thought I'd let you know that you're an aunt."

An aunt? That infant is no niece of mine! "Okay. Thank you."

"I'd better go. People are waiting to use the hospital phone."

"Of course. 'Bye, Aoife."

She hung up. Tom walked right up to me and snatched the receiver back, his floppy manhood dangling inches away from me. I felt ill. He said nothing further. He sat down in his armchair, and continued to watch a football match. I rushed out of the room, and raced up to my attic, my heart pounding. Aoife had a daughter, and my landlord had no personal boundaries. At least I had food. I pulled a scotch egg out of my bag, and tried to forget all else.

CHAPTER TEN

In the weeks that followed, I became increasingly aware of Tom's strange behaviour. I could hear him pacing around the house at night, and up and down the stairs, over and over and again. He would go into the bathroom, lock the door, and not emerge for hours at a time. I attempted a timid knock, once or twice, genuinely afraid that he might have died in the bath. I did not receive a response, but he would emerge some time later, as though nothing had happened. He always smelled of alcohol, and his voice was usually slurred. In between his bizarre, indoor perambulations, and lengthy sojourns in the bathroom, he remained cocooned in the living room, with the television on. I could hear him shouting violently, on a regular basis. I could not always make out his words, but I assumed that they were directed at the outcome of various sporting events. He barely spoke to me, which was something of a blessing, but sometimes, when our paths crossed, he looked at me, with such a hateful snarl, that I felt uncomfortable. I could only surmise that he loathed having a lodger, as much as I despised being his, but had made the decision to endure it grudgingly, for the sake of more drinking money.

Occasionally, I had the feeling that somebody had been in my bedroom, when I returned home from college. I had few possessions, and they did not always seem to be quite where I thought I had left them. I wished that my little attic had a lock on its door, but was afraid of what his reaction might be, if I were to ask him for one.

I had supplemented my meagre collection of biscuits with a little fruit and dried meat for, what I hoped was, a more balanced diet. I still did not have enough to eat, and the squirming gnaw of hunger had become my constant companion. In fact, it had found its own voice, in the same way that my anger once had.

I felt fortunate that the more intellectual parts of me, at least, were receiving plenty of nourishment from my lectures, and long evenings at the university library. My new little magical friend continued to act as my personal librarian… Only when the mythology corner was utterly deserted, of course. Though nobody else could see him, they would have noticed books flying about the shelves, as he fetched and replaced them for my inspection.

I'd asked him if he had a name.

"A name?" he'd responded in astonishment, "That's far too grand a thing for one such as I. I am… books. I am what remains of the power of the books: The important magic and rituals, and eternal, ubiquitous truths, preserved in the books."

So, he was another little memory: A remnant of spells and magic that were once great, but were now small, and lived on, just a little, by having been written down for posterity. I began to think of him as Mr. Books in my mind, though I did not dare to call him by that appellation to his face, lest he thought it childish or mocking.

I often saw Dr. Herbert in the library, and she usually acknowledged me warmly, and sat at the other side of my reading table to work. I noticed that she always cast a curious glance at what I was reading. I thoroughly enjoyed her lectures. She brought the anthropological interpretation of myths and legends to life, with her passion and excitement. Mr. Books would appear only briefly, when she was there, to chastise the paper inhabitants of the shelves for their raucous whispering, so that I could concentrate on my study without any unnecessary distraction.

One evening, Dr. Herbert and I packed up our belongings, and left the library at the same time.

"You have quite the love for mythology, don't you?" She remarked, once we had left the quiet building.

"It's a great interest of mine," I replied.

"How did it come to be such a passion?"

I faltered for a moment, knowing that I could not say: "Well, I've met some of the characters, and I long to know more of their histories." Instead, I said: "My mother used to love the old tales, and read many of them to me when I was a child." It was not a lie.

"How wonderful that she gave you such a gift," smiled Dr. Herbert, "These things should not be forgotten."

"How accurate do you think they are?"

"What do you mean?"

I paused, searching for the right words. "These tales and traditions were written down by... mortal men. Do you think that what remains to us, for our study, contains the truth of what our ancestors really believed?"

She raised her eyebrows, and I realised that I had betrayed myself slightly by using the term "mortal men", as though I were aware of some alternative. I hoped that she would ignore it.

"I think," replied Dr. Herbert, thoughtfully, "That we need to read between the lines of what is recorded, to hypothesise- to the best of our ability- what the truth of the original beliefs might have been. The Latin alphabet came to Ireland with Christianity, and educated monks wrote down the traditions of the Pagan people that they met. They could not call an old god a god, because for them, there was only one. So, for example, when you read a tale of a woman who is portrayed as a mortal with magical attributes, you can often surmise that the original myth was about a goddess, and her story usually says something about her divine functions, which might relate to fertility, or creation and destruction: The domains of the gods."

I nodded eagerly.

"Don't worry, Kathy," she added, "I know it sounds complex, but we'll be exploring all of this in more detail, as the course progresses."

"Thank you."

"Feel free to come to me anytime with more questions, though. It's good to see somebody so thirsty for knowledge, and eager to understand these matters. Only by the efforts of people like us can the tradition survive."

I grinned at her gratefully before departing, and contemplated our discussion as I walked to the bus stop.

"Do you remember Mr. O Mordha's roast lamb?" asked my hunger.

Be quiet, I snapped inwardly, We'll have a snack when we get back to the attic.

"The cakes that Aoife used to make for your birthday were good, weren't they?" continued my hunger, completely unabashed, "Oh, look at that fast food place across the road. I bet they sell fish and chips! Fish and chips would be nice, wouldn't they?"

Shut up! I've heard quite enough from you!

My hunger's voice receded to a churlish and persistent, gurgling grumble, which made it hard to focus on loftier matters as the bus crawled back to Tom's house.

When I finally arrived, I could hear the dull roar of a televised match, and Tom's swearing emanating from the living room, as usual.

I scurried upstairs, and opened my dresser. My biscuits were gone. My dried meat was gone. Only one, solitary apple sat in the drawer in which my food had been. Sharp tears sprang to my disappointed eyes, their bitter taste spreading down my face in moments.

"Our food!" shrieked my hunger, "Where's our food? What has he done?"

With a matching screech, I bolted downstairs and threw open the door of the living room, not caring if I found my landlord in a state of undress.

"You stole my food," I yelled, my body trembling with rage, and hot tears still spilling down my face.

Tom barely looked up, and regarded me with his customary snarl. "What are you babbling about, girl?" he hissed drunkenly.

"I had biscuits, and meat, and fruit in my room, and now they're gone," I cried, "How dare you? How *dare* you steal from me?"

"I don't know what you're talking about, you ungrateful bitch," he slurred, "You need your head examined."

My mouth opened and closed several times, in astonishment. Then, I saw the empty packet of biscuits lying on the floor by his feet.

"This," I yelled, my fury renewed. I picked up the empty packet and threw it at him. "These were *my* biscuits, and you stole them!"

"They were *my* biscuits," he retorted, "You think you're the only person in the world who ever bought a biscuit? Get out, and get back to your attic!"

"Y- y- you *thief*," I sobbed, running out of the room, and hurtling up the stairs, to throw myself across my bed.

"Close the bloody door, you lunatic!" he bellowed.

With a scream of frustration, I summoned the prickle from within me, and sent its invisible arms flying back down the stairs, to slam the living room door closed, with all the force of my anger.

I heard a crashing, splintering sound, loud enough to wake the dead. I heard Tom swearing loudly.

I froze, waiting for his furious footsteps to sound on the stairs. I waited, and waited. They did not come. The swearing grew more incoherent, and trailed off. I wondered, for a moment, if whatever I had sent downstairs had actually hurt him. I waited, longer than was entirely morally acceptable, to creep down and check. I saw the broken shards of what had once been a door. I heard him snoring loudly. I was less relieved than I should have been. I tiptoed back upstairs, and wept quietly as I ate my apple.

The following day, I passed him on my way out of the house.

He was standing in the hall in a dirty, insufficiently fastened dressing gown, staring at the remains of the door.

"Do you know what happened to this?" he growled.

He doesn't remember! "I think you fell into the door," I replied, coldly.

"Must've been some fall," he mused, seeming genuinely shocked, and not in the least suspicious.

The prickle purred with a slight chuckle of dark satisfaction, as I left for the bus stop.

That morning at university was not an easy one. It began with one of my favourite lectures by Dr. Herbert, but while her appealing voice rang out with interesting facts and musings, an unwelcome inner speaker insisted on drowning her out.

"Do you remember the stews that your mother used to make? They were so warm and comforting," babbled my hunger.

Shut up.

"Her apple pies were good as well. Remember the picnic that Liam made you for your birthday? He made chicken, and sandwiches, and…"

I told you to shut up. I found, to my shame, that in that moment, the memory of the food was more painful to me than that of my last, pleasant interaction with Liam.

"Mr. O Mordha always made delicious biscuits, didn't he? Oh, and the food at the reception on induction day was nice, wasn't it? A slice of that quiche would go down well…"

SHUT. UP.

I had a few free periods before my next lecture. I went to the library, hoping that Mr. Books would not silence the whispers too soon, as they struck me as the only noise that might drown out the incessant whining of my hunger.

Alice was there. I had seen her in the library on several occasions, since the term began. She always appeared excited to encounter me, and always lingered, fidgeting a little, even after she had clearly finished her study for the day. I assumed that she was hoping I might leave with her, so that she could interrogate, or examine, me further, in that annoying way she had. I always kept my head firmly ensconced in my books, and waited until I could be reasonably sure that she was gone, before taking my leave.

Mr. Books avoided her in the same way that he did other students and staff, which put paid to my brief suspicion that she had any magic herself.

"Kathy," she whispered, that day, "How lovely to see you! Are you well? You look a little troubled."

I sighed defeatedly, reluctantly thankful for the distraction of potential conversation. I mentally scanned the happenings of my recent existence, and decided that quite a lot of it was fit for human consumption, with the exception of a few carefully omitted details.

"My landlord is a bit of a creep, and has begun stealing from me."

"Oh no, how dreadful! Can't you move elsewhere?"

"I don't really have many options. My room is cheap."

"Don't you receive a student grant?"

"I decided to accept my place at college at rather the last minute. The deadline had passed to apply for help."

"I'm so sorry," she consoled me.

At that moment, I became aware of Mr. Books' disapproving little face, peering at me from behind a shelf, and decided to conclude the conversation, and concentrate on some study.

"Oh well," I shrugged, "Next year should be better. I'll apply for student housing and assistance in advance, then."

I wandered over to the bookshelves, and ran my hands across the well-worn spines, debating inwardly which whispering volume to select.

I had seen the tale called 'The Wooing of Étaín' before, and had briefly wondered if it had anything to do with the Étaín *I* knew. I had been too hurt and angry, by even the thought of her, and her triumphant face in Liam's arms, to investigate further. Today, my hand lingered on it for a while, with a little morbid curiosity.

"A pizza," mused my hunger, "An enormous pizza, with extra cheese, and olives, and mushrooms, and ham, and…"

Shut up.

"How about a burger? A burger piled with bacon, and topped with a fried egg?"

Shut up.

"Cauliflower cheese! We haven't had cauliflower cheese for ages. That would be nice, wouldn't it?"

Right, 'The Wooing of Étaín' it is. Now, shut up. I picked up the slender book, and returned to the reading table.

The tale began with Midir, a man of the *síd*. I took this to mean that he was an immortal figure, his godhood not acknowledged overtly by the medieval Christian writer, but barely disguised.

Midir sought to wed the fairest woman in Ireland, whose name was Étaín. Her father demanded that impossible tasks were completed in return for her hand, but Midir accomplished them and returned home with his new bride. However, Midir already had a jealous wife named Fúamnach, who was wise and clever, and a powerful sorceress.

"Ha! 'Wise and clever'," I muttered, without realising that I'd spoken aloud, "That doesn't sound like the crone *I* met!"

Alice's head snapped up from her study, her gaze at its most penetrating. "What did you say?"

I felt a burning flush of panic rise to my cheeks. "Nothing," I insisted quickly, "I said nothing."

Alice nodded, and appeared to return to her book, though I had a crawling feeling that her eyes were still on me.

With a deep breath, I continued to read.

Fúamnach resented Étaín, and turned her into a pool of water. Midir left in grief. The pool of water stagnated, and produced a worm, which then turned into an enormous, purple fly. The fly found Midir, and he recognised it as Étaín. He was comforted by her buzzing, and kept her near him. When Fúamnach heard of this, she flew into a rage, and conjured a terrible wind to blow the fly away. It was blown around by the enchanted wind for many years, unable to have a moment's rest, until it fell into the cup of a queen. She drank the fly, and became pregnant with the next incarnation of Étaín. When this Étaín grew up, she married a king of Ireland called Echu Airem, but Midir heard of this and wanted her back, so he set out to woo her. He tricked her into several meetings, but eventually revealed to her that he was once her husband, and begged her to go to into the *síd* with him. He recited a beautiful poem, describing the otherworld, and promising her all of its wonders, if she would but go with him. Étaín replied that she would go, but only if her current husband, Echu, gave his consent. Midir then set about tricking Echu into a series of wagers, until he was promised an embrace from Étaín if he won the game. As soon as her arms were around him, Midir carried her off through the air, and took her to his own realm. Echu was furious, and demanded that all of the *sídhe* be destroyed until he found his wife. Eventually, Midir reappeared with fifty women, who were all identical to Étaín. A grey hag was with them, and she told Echu that he could have Étaín back, if he could choose the one that was really her. Echu remembered that his wife's special skill was the serving of beverages, and asked each of the fifty lookalikes to perform the task. He chose the one whose bearing most resembled his wife's, and declared that he was satisfied. Midir and the others disappeared. Some time later, Midir visited Echu again, and revealed that Echu had selected and lain with his own daughter, who had been born and raised after Étaín was taken away into the *síd*. Echu was distraught, but did not seek revenge, or pursue Étaín further, because he had declared his honour satisfied and was now bound by his word.

I sat back, astonished, countless questions teeming in my mind. This account suggested that, far from Étaín pursuing Fúamnach's husband relentlessly, he had pursued her, and every man she had encountered had longed to keep her for his own. Was she indeed, then, as the Étaín I'd met seemed to believe, a precious symbol of sovereignty? A consort desired by any who would have power? Why was she now such a petty, manipulative creature, desperate for validation? Where was Midir? Why had they been parted again? Was she no longer important, because the concept of the union between king and fertility goddess had strayed so far from men's minds?

"How did you end up the way you are, Étaín?" I mused.

Alice's eyes were suddenly on me, with renewed intensity. "What do you mean?" she demanded.

I groaned inwardly. I had inadvertently muttered my thoughts out loud again. "Nothing," I repeated tersely, "I meant nothing."

She surveyed me, as though calculating a particularly tricky arithmetic equation. "I saw a food company giving out free samples near the cafeteria," she announced, "Shall we go and get some before they're all gone?"

"Yes!" squealed my hunger, "Oh, I wonder what samples they have. Will they have pasta dishes, or baked potatoes, or ice cream?"

"Okay," I relented. Again, I was in no position to ignore the possibility of free food.

Mr. Books appeared, as I replaced 'The Wooing of Étaín' on its shelf. He looked a little surly, presumably irritated that Alice and I had begun to converse again and disturb his peace.

"It's okay, we're just leaving," I whispered.

"Did you say something?" asked Alice.

"No," I replied.

"What were you reading, Kathy? 'The wooing of Étaín', was it?" she asked me, as we walked to the cafeteria.

"Yes," I replied guardedly, "Why?"

"Do you know a different version of the tale?"

"No. Why do you ask?"

"It's only that... I heard you muttering a few times, while you were reading, as though there were aspects of the account that you didn't agree with. I wondered if you knew another version of the story."

"No. It's the only one that remains, as far as I'm aware."

"And you don't know anything further about it, from... anywhere else?"

"I don't know what you mean."

"Very well," she sighed, sounding somewhat unsatisfied.

The free samples were none of the things that my hunger's imagination had conjured. They were a new brand of cereal bar. They did not look particularly appetizing, and the staff who had been hired to distribute them looked bored and dejected, as though they had received very little interest in the products.

"Free cereal bar?" asked one of them, in a hopeless tone of expected rejection.

"Yes please," I replied enthusiastically.

She appeared pleasantly stunned. She removed a bar from a box of ten, then thought better of it, offered me the whole box, and handed a second box to Alice.

My hunger jumped up and down with glee. "We're going to eat," it sang, "We're going to eat!"

Alice surveyed the packet, as we walked away, and sighed slightly. "Oh, they contain raisins. I hate raisins. You'd better have mine as well."

I wondered if she genuinely disliked them, or if she was being kind, because I had alluded to my financial difficulties. I decided that I didn't much care, and gratefully accepted the offering, stashing it in my bag with near-reverence.

"Shall we go for some lunch in the cafeteria?" she suggested.

"Oh, no thanks, I'll just eat some of these cereal bars," I responded, then felt slightly ashamed of my circumstances, and added: "I wouldn't want them to go to waste. Just think of the starving people in Ethiopia!"

I was pleasantly surprised that she didn't press me further to join her. I hurried away to sit on the grass beneath a tree, and devoured two of the bars in a row. I desperately wanted to inhale a third, but cautioned myself that I needed to make them last. Aoife would be sending me some money in a few days' time, and I might be able to survive until then, with less physical discomfort, if I rationed out my new provisions.

When my lectures finished for the day, I made the unusual decision to go for a walk, instead of holing myself away in the library. The air was cool, and the fingers of Autumn had tinged the trees with russet tones, but the sky was bright and clear, and I thought that a turn around Temple Bar might offer a nice distraction, and put me in a better frame of mind to deal with Tom and his decimated door, later.

As I wandered into the area, the intoxicating life and colour of the busy square filled my senses comfortingly. Some shops were still open, and I floated in and out of a few, fingering eccentric clothes and accessories that I could never hope to afford.

A sign outside a bar advertised 'two for one' drinks. I was extremely tempted to take advantage of the offer, but thought better of spending my last few pounds on something so frivolous. As the shops began to close, and the excitement of the evening rose in the voices of nearby revellers, I resigned myself to sitting on a step in the square, and watching the passers-by. I wondered where they were going, and what minor adventures might await them.

Eventually, as the evening drew in, I decided to trudge back to my bus stop, and enjoy one more cereal bar in the gloom of my attic, before sleep did me the favour of stealing some of the unwanted time between my dismal incarceration and my next lecture at university.

I left Temple Bar by one of the alleys which was less well populated by visitors. I passed some industrial dustbins, looming outside the back door of an unremarkable building, and heard a small noise.

Curious, I peered around one of the bins, hoping to see a cat, or a dog, or even a fox, but instead found myself staring at another little magical being: a small one. I gasped. I should not have been surprised, considering the existence of Mr. Books, but what alarmed me most about this little fellow, cowering behind a hulking bin, was his appearance rather than his presence. He was a pitiful, bedraggled creature with a hollow, haunted expression, and all colour missing from his deep, jaded eyes. His look of despair reminded me of the small ones that Liam and I had found, lost in the woods, so many moons ago, after some enchantment had so cruelly robbed them of a part of themselves.

When he saw me, he sprang back in fright, and trembled pitifully. "Please," he begged, "No! I have no more to give!"

"Don't be afraid," I said, gently, crouching down to make myself seem closer to his size, and less of a threat, "I mean you no harm. What can I do to help you?"

His almost vacant, yet fearful, eyes merely widened, and he fled so quickly that I could not even fathom in which direction he had gone.

I thought about waiting, in the hopes that he might come back, and allow me to provide some comfort or aid, but there was only so long that I could stand around in an alley, and his terror had seemed so acute that I thought it far more likely that he had found a better place to hide, out of my reach.

The encounter perturbed me. I wondered what might possibly exist in the middle of the city to cause so much damage and distress to a little magical creature.

I pondered it on the way back to Tom's house, and continued to do so as I carefully slid my precious cereal bars, one by one, under my bed in the attic, hoping that his rough hands would be far too large to prise them out. I mused on it when I woke, and on the way to college in the morning.

As soon as I had time to go to the library, I rushed there, hoping that the mythology section would be empty, and I might have an opportunity to speak with Mr. Books.

Fortune was on my side, and he appeared promptly, as soon as I approached my now-customary reading table. "How can I help you today?" he enquired, courteously.

"I- I was actually hoping to converse with you a little," I ventured, nervously.

"Converse?" he repeated, frowning. "This is not a place for conversation. This is a place for reading."

"Yes, of course. I realise that, but something happened last night, on which I thought you might have some light to shed."

"Something happened in the library?"

"No, not in the library, but…"

"Then, how could it be any concern of mine?"

"Please listen," I implored him.

He pursed his lips, entirely unconvinced that he wanted to do so, but he remained silent so that I might speak further.

"I met another one of your kind last night," I began.

"Another one?" he parroted, confused, then nodded as if some truth was dawning on him, "Ah, in another library?"

"No, in an alley in Temple Bar. He was… hurt. Damaged, somehow. I wondered if you knew of any threat to magical creatures, that might explain how he came to be in such a sorry state."

"Threat? The only threat is forgetting. As long as people remember the timeless truths, I will remain. I think I used to be something else… something bigger, but I have forgotten what that was. It is of no matter to me now."

I realised that he truly did not understand what I meant. His only concern was preserving the knowledge of what had once been. The traumatised little fellow from the alley may have been similar in appearance, but whatever fate had befallen him was something entirely alien to Mr. Books' reality.

I waited and waited, but the envelope I was expecting from Aoife, containing money for the next month, never came. I rang her to check that she had sent it, and she assured me that she had. I believed her. Whatever else she might be, she had always been organised and dutiful. She rebuked me for my failure to enquire as to the wellbeing of her offspring. I apologised mechanically, and exchanged as many pleasantries as I felt were absolutely required.

She rang me back later to inform me that she had checked with the post office, and that the registered envelope she had sent had been marked as delivered. Its disappearance might have been a postal error, of course, but a far darker, and more likely, explanation was beginning to occur to me.

"Tom," I said, interrupting him in the kitchen while he was rummaging through the fridge for beers, "You haven't received any post for me, have you?"

He froze, and I knew instantly that he had. "No," he barked, avoiding my gaze.

"I was expecting something from my sister. I wondered if you might have… kept it for yourself by accident, not realising that it was mine?"

"I said no!"

"It just seems a little strange, because it was sent by registered delivery, and the post office swears that they obtained a signature for it, at this address…"

Tom slammed his beer down on the putrid countertop, and spun 'round to face me, now defensive. "And, just what are you accusing me of, girl? You'd better be very careful…"

"I only wondered if you might be able to look through your recent post again, in case it got mislaid. Otherwise, we'll have to assume it's been stolen by the postman… or …someone else, and we might have to get the police involved…"

"Are you threatening me?" he bellowed, angry spittle bursting from his mouth, and spewing me with droplets, "Do you want a roof over your head or not? I got an envelope in the post, containing my rent, so I took what was mine."

My hands balled into fists, with cold fury, as he admitted it. "That envelope contained far more than I owe you for the rent."

"No, it didn't."

"Yes, it did. I have nothing else to live on. Please give it back."

"The extra was for repairing the door."

"*I* didn't damage the door!" It was not *entirely* a lie. Although they could be commanded, there were times when my powers felt less like a part of me, and more like some other entity that had claimed me for its host.

"You live under this roof. You have to contribute to the upkeep."

"Those are not terms that we ever discussed."

"Not my problem if you've forgotten."

"I haven't forgotten. No such conversation ever took place."

"Prove it." With that, he snatched up his beer, stormed into the living room and slammed his shiny new door behind him.

I stared at it, longing to smash it again. It wouldn't bring my money back.

For the first time since I had started college, I wondered if I had the stomach for it that day. I decided that, even if I sat there blankly and did not absorb a word of a single lecture, it would be preferable to remaining in Tom's festering abode, so I went.

I crawled into the comforting arms of the library, flopped down at my reading table, and allowed the familiar whispers of the books to wash over me.

Mr. Books appeared on cue, silencing them with a stiff reprimand, and enquired: "What would you like to read today?"

"I don't think I want to read today. I think I just want to sit here, if that's okay."

His little brow furrowed in confusion. "But the library is for reading."

"Is the library not for reading and thinking? After all, without thinking, there would be no remembering or writing."

He nodded slowly, musing on what I had said. "Yes, perhaps you're right. Reading *and* thinking."

"So, today, I would just like to think." In truth, I did not want to think at all, but I did want to be somewhere quiet and safe.

"Very well. Let me know if you change your mind, and require any reading material."

"Thank you. I'll do that."

He was gone as swiftly as he had arrived.

"Who are you talking to?" asked a familiar voice.

Alice. Of course it was.

I had not noticed her approach, and Mr. Books had apparently not sensed it either. Perhaps I had so confused him, with my talk of thinking, that he had not been on guard, to his usual extent, allowing our exchange to continue longer than was prudent.

"Nobody," I replied.

"But, I heard you conversing with someone," she insisted.

"Perhaps I was absently talking to myself."

"Really? You were leaving long pauses, and replying, as though to another voice…"

"I'm a very strange person."

She looked surprised by my response, and unsure of how to proceed. "Are you okay?" she asked simply.

"Not exactly. My landlord has now stolen money from me, leaving me in a very difficult situation."

"That's appalling," she exclaimed, "Have you spoken to the police?"

"I fear it would be very hard to prove, and more trouble than it's worth."

"He shouldn't be allowed to get away with it, though."

"No, he shouldn't," I muttered darkly, "And, when the time is right, I'll make sure he doesn't."

Alice looked impressed. "Well, I saw how you dealt with the boy who stole your bag. You can clearly look after yourself."

"As I told you, it was just kickboxing."

"Ah, yes. Kickboxing." Her tone teetered between sarcasm and amusement. "You must be very skilled. I could have sworn that the thief had been thrown to the ground before you'd even caught up to him."

"My instructors always praised me for my agility," I responded stoically, though I was in no doubt that she was mocking me.

"Are you planning to continue your training?"

"In kickboxing?" I hadn't even thought about it. "I really can't afford classes at the moment."

"But, classes are free to students of the university, at the gym. They might have kickboxing classes there."

My eyes widened. "Really? I'll go and find out! Thank you!"

"Kickboxing?" repeated my hunger, "Can we eat it?"

Shut up.

Mr. Books materialised behind Alice, positively scowling. I could almost imagine exactly what he was grumbling inwardly:

"Reading and thinking, *not talking*."

I went straight to the gym. It hadn't even occurred to me that being a student might have perks like free activities. The centre had a pool, exercise equipment and various smaller rooms for training sessions. I went to the reception desk to ask about kickboxing classes.

"Yes, we run those twice a week," said the young man behind the desk, "Are you a member?"

"I'm a student at Trinity College," I replied, "I was given to understand that I could attend classes, free of charge…"

"No problem! Membership is free for students. You just need to sign up. You can then attend classes, use the training equipment and swim whenever you like. Would you like to do that now?"

"No," replied my hunger, "I'd like a cheese sandwich."

Shut up.

I nodded enthusiastically at the receptionist, thinking about what a difference it might make to my mood to have something cathartic to do, and something to punch whenever I thought of Tom.

When I left the sports centre, I bumped into Alice again. I wondered if she had deliberately wandered that way, hoping to meet me after I'd investigated the classes.

"Success?" she asked.

"Yes." I held up my newly printed membership card, proudly.

"Great! Why don't we go for a swim together tomorrow, at lunchtime?"

I shrugged. "Yes, why not?" I couldn't imagine how she could interrogate me whilst doing lengths in a pool, so the idea seemed relatively benign. In fact, apart from her slightly too-keen interest in my secrets, *she* seemed quite benign. After all, she had tried to help when my bag was snatched, she had put me in the path of free food twice, and had recommended the gym to me. She did not appear to mean me any harm.

So the following day, we met for a swim.

"Are you a strong swimmer, Kathy?" asked Alice, as we struggled into our swimsuits, "I'm not, if truth be told. I should really practise more."

"I used to swim in a lake near my house in Kerry, when the weather was warm," I replied, "But I haven't been for years…" My voice trailed off. Of course, it was something that Liam and I had enjoyed doing together on our excursions in his father's boat, when we were so much in love, and happy together.

"Are you okay, Kathy?"

"Yes, I'm just feeling a little nostalgic for home. Let's go!"

We walked out of the changing rooms to the pool area, and climbed into the cool water. I enjoyed the delicious shiver, as my skin adjusted to the change in temperature. We began to swim. It occurred to me that going up and down the lanes, indoors, was not quite so enjoyable as floating around the lake in the woods, on a sunny day, but it was nonetheless calming and peaceful. I closed my eyes, revelling in the feeling of weightlessness as I swam.

Alice was a lot slower than I was, so our lengths soon became unsynchronised. Just as I had reached the shallow end, and was preparing to turn, I heard her cry out. I spun 'round, and saw her small hand disappearing beneath the water at the deep end, followed by an enormous, panicked stream of gurgling bubbles… Then, nothing.

The oblivious lifeguard was fiddling with her Walkman.

Alice might be drowning! Despite my speed, I was not sure that I could swim to the other end, in time to save her. My instincts overcame my sense, and my mind pulled the dormant arms of the prickle to attention, then flung them out over the watery expanse and plunged them deep into the pool. They scooped Alice up, and tossed her out of the water, with sufficient restraint so as not to hurt her. Then they retracted, and curled back up safely inside me.

Alice sat bolt upright, looking in all directions, in astonishment. There was nobody anywhere near enough to her, to have performed the rescue by mortal means, least of all me.

I clambered out of the pool and went to her, hoping that the trauma of her near-death might have sufficiently confused her, as to allow me time to make up a plausible excuse.

The lazy lifeguard then noticed that something had happened too, and rushed over, babbling apologies, and enquiring as to Alice's wellbeing.

"I'm fine," she assured us, getting to her feet, "No harm done. Who saved me?"

"It was a man," I said quickly, "He was near you at the time. I don't know where he's disappeared to, now."

"I didn't see anyone," remarked Alice, knowingly. I realised that, far from looking frightened or confused, she appeared positively delighted. I, however, was terrified.

She knows. Damn her, she knows! But what does she know?

"Well, I think that's enough of that for today," she grinned, "Shall we dry off and have a hot drink?"

I nodded mutely and followed, noticing the confident, self-assured swing of Alice's hips, and observing that her gait was not at all that of one who had recently been in mortal peril.

She couldn't have…? Could she? Could she have faked the whole thing, to trick me into using my magic… Into confirming her suspicions, as to what she had witnessed, one the first day we met?

I tried to tell myself that my cynicism was just that, but her elated and satisfied demeanour left me uneasy.

As we walked from the gym to the cafeteria, I suddenly felt faint. Spots rose to my eyes, and blinded me for a moment. I wobbled, and felt Alice's arm grab mine to keep me upright.

"Kathy! What's the matter?" she exclaimed with concern.

My sight returned, and sounds flooded my ears, as I steadied myself.

"That's what happens when you don't feed us for days, and then exercise," my hunger rebuked me.

Shut up.

"I- I'm alright," I insisted, shakily.

"What a pair we are, drowning and fainting! We're definitely in need of tea and cake," commented Alice jovially, but she linked my arm for support for the rest of the journey to the cafeteria, and I was glad of it.

When we sat down, I pulled out my purse, hoping to find enough change for a cup of tea.

"Put that away," instructed Alice, "This is on me."

I tried to protest, weakly, but she was having none of it, and strode off purposefully, in the direction of the counter. She returned with a large pot of sweet tea, two cups, and an entire plate of cream cakes to share.

My hunger grew eyes, which immediately popped out of their sockets on stalks. "Cakes! We're going to have cakes!" it squealed.

"Dig in," said Alice, as she poured our tea.

"Thank you." I reached for a cream cake, determined to restrain myself, and take dainty mouthfuls of the treat, but my appetite overcame me, and I devoured it in two, gluttonous, shameful, bites.

Alice politely averted her eyes, but did ask: "Have you been eating enough? You look even thinner than you did a few weeks ago."

I hung my head. "It's been… difficult. As you know, my money was stolen, and I…"

"Have you thought about getting a part-time job?"

"It has crossed my mind. At first, I was determined to resist the idea, because I was afraid it might interfere with my study, and my time in the library, but now things are more desperate, it might be my only option. I wouldn't even know how to start looking for something, though. Is there a notice board?" I thought about Tom, and added: "Not that I've had much luck with those…"

"Well, I work in a pub in Temple Bar. I think you might fit right in there. They're very flexible with hours, and they pay well."

"Really? But I don't have any experience…"

"We'll show you the ropes. There's really nothing to it. As I said, I think you'd *really* fit in. Would you like me to arrange a trial shift for you?"

"Yes please!"

"Great, I'll let you know tomorrow." Alice frowned. "You know what? I don't think I'm in the mood for something sweet after all. I'm going to get chips instead. Finish the cakes, will you?"

"Okay." I was sure that she was just being kind, by orchestrating a situation which allowed me to eat more, without embarrassment, and when she later insisted that she couldn't finish her chips, and invited me to do so, I was doubly certain. I was so overwhelmed by the generosity of the meal that it did not even occur to me to wonder why she hadn't questioned me further about her impossible rescue at the swimming pool.

True to her word, Alice bounced up to me the following day, and cried: "It's all set! Are you free to do a trial shift at the pub this evening? They'll pay you for it in cash at closing time."

I was a little surprised by the short notice, but I agreed enthusiastically. My current situation could not continue. If I didn't start earning some money soon, I would end up too weak from malnutrition to even get to college in the morning.

Alice and I met when our lectures had ended for the day, and walked over to Temple Bar together. She led, as we threaded our way through the narrow alleys, surrounding the square.

She suddenly stopped and called: "Here we are!"

I was astonished to see that we were standing outside a pub. I could have sworn that the alley was completely empty when we'd entered it. I was even more surprised to note that it was the same little bar that had so caught my attention when I'd first arrived in Dublin, but had failed to find a second time. It *was* very hidden away. I concluded that I must have glanced down the alley, on my search that evening, and simply missed it.

An old sign hung over the door, bearing the appellation: 'The Horse and Hag.' It seemed a slightly odd name, but no stranger than those of some other drinking establishments I had seen.

"Shall we?" Alice pulled the door open, and stood back to admit me.

I entered slowly, feeling a little timid. The first thing that struck me was how much more spacious and atmospheric in seemed inside, than its outer appearance suggested. The entrance led to a large, main bar, decorated sumptuously in dark wood and elegantly faded, velvet curtains and tapestries. A few patrons were drinking at cosy little tables. I could see a corridor off the room, leading towards another area at the back. An enormous bar, stocked with countless, fascinating bottles of all different colours, loomed to the left, on which a middle-aged black woman was leaning. Her face was creased, and kind.

Alice tugged me in her direction and introduced her as Evelyn, the landlady.

"Pleased to meet you, Kathy," smiled Evelyn. She had an accent, though I could not place it.

I reciprocated politely.

"Your food is ready."

I frowned. "But… I didn't order any food…"

Evelyn laughed. "I don't let anyone work behind my bar without having had a good meal, first. Have a seat wherever you like, and I'll bring it over."

Alice and I sat down in a nearby snug, cocooned in rich, red velvet. "This is very kind of her," I observed with a little suspicion. I was sure that Alice had said something to Evelyn about my levels of starvation, and the two of them had concocted a plan to feed me.

"Oh, Evelyn is great," replied Alice breezily, "So, what do you think of the place?"

"It's really not what I expected," I breathed, "It looked so small and run down outside, but inside it's…"

"Yes, it's quite something, isn't it?"

I nodded, grateful not to have to find the right words myself.

At that moment, Evelyn came back with meals for both me and Alice. Each plate contained thick slices of aromatic roast chicken, crisp roast potatoes, broccoli and cauliflower cheese, all glistening with a hearty helping of gravy.

I stared at the landlady, my jaw wide with disbelief. "A- are you sure…?" I gasped.

"Eat up," instructed Evelyn with a twinkle in her eye, "Come and find me when you're finished." She presented us with cutlery, and bustled off.

I stared at the food for a few more, exquisite moments, before remembering my manners, and calling out: "Thank you!"

I tucked into my meal, simultaneously wanting to ingest it in instants, and savour every mouthful. It seemed the most blissfully delicious thing that I had ever tasted.

"She's a good cook, isn't she?" commented Alice.

I nodded vigorously, my mouth far too full of tender, succulent chicken to speak.

When I had cleaned my plate, I took it behind the bar, and easily found the kitchen, where Evelyn was busy stirring something with a mouth-watering aroma, in a large pot.

"Thank you so much for the wonderful food. What would you like me to do now?"

She rubbed her chin thoughtfully. "Go and ask Alice to show you the basics behind the bar."

I obeyed. Alice taught me to pull pints of beer and stout, and how the cash register worked, and where the drinking vessels and measures for spirits were to be found.

Every so often, she paused to serve a customer. Eventually, she suggested that I should try it. The next time somebody walked up to the bar, I took a deep breath, tried to cultivate a confident and competent air in all of an instant, and asked:

"What can I get you?"

"Two pints of lager, please," responded the customer.

I filled the glasses from the beer pump, presented them to him, took his money, succeeded in giving him the right change- with just a moment's hesitation- and he walked off, apparently satisfied.

"You're a natural," smiled Alice. I noticed that she was filling a number of curious, old-fashioned goblets from a bottle of mead. She carefully loaded them on to a tray. "Now, would you be so kind as to take this tray to the back room, for some of our regular patrons?"

"Back room?"

"Yes, it's just over there, to the left." She gestured helpfully.

"Of course," I agreed, and picked up the tray. I walked in the prescribed direction, and found myself in a corridor, following the rich aroma of thick cigarette smoke, and the sound of laughter, into another spacious room. This one was quite different from the main bar. Although it was similarly decorated, it was lit only by glowing candelabra. Soft fur throws, and thick cushions, were strewn about the space, giving it a luxuriously decadent atmosphere. The prickle fidgeted curiously, spreading tendrils of excitement down my spine.

A group of patrons was casually arranged about the room, sprawled comfortably on the furniture. Strange, old-fashioned music was wafting from somewhere, its curling, ethereal notes barely audible over the din of lively conversation.

There was a large, central table of intricately carved wood. I went to place the tray of mead upon it, and the closest members of the group looked up at me in unison.

The tray connected sharply with the floor. The mead splashed my feet. The metal goblets rolled about, noisily, on the wood.

Immortals. There were immortals among them. *Great Ones.* Not individual incarnations that I recognised, but there was no mistaking those timeless eyes, impossibly beautiful faces, and that intoxicating quality that shimmered in the air around them.

As I stared at them, Alice materialised beside me with a triumphant smile. "You know them for what they are, don't you?"

I nodded dumbly.

She giggled delightedly. "I just *knew* you'd fit in!"

CHAPTER ELEVEN

"Well, well," exclaimed one of the Great Ones, surveying me with a keen interest, "And who do we have here?"

He was slender, with a lustrous mane of auburn hair, curling to his shoulders, and a particularly playful expression on his exquisite face. He cut an eccentric figure, dressed in a waistcoat, complete with a pocket watch, and an old-fashioned shirt with billowing sleeves. His elegant fingers were curled around a decorative cigarette holder, from which a delicate wisp of smoke emanated. He was half-sitting, half-reclining, in a large, antique chair, with one leather-clad leg casually flung over one of its arms.

"I'm Kathy," I replied, finally locating my voice.

"They call me Bres," he offered in return, "Now, what manner of thing are you, young Kathy?"

A female immortal, who bore too strong a physical resemblance to Étaín for my liking, dislodged herself from her perch on the edge of a velvet sofa, and floated in my direction, her large, ageless eyes bright, and sparkling with curiosity.

"I'd say she's something closer to us," she declared.

"I'd say you're right, Macha," nodded Bres.

"Oh, no, I'm not... an *immortal*," I corrected them quickly.

Bres narrowed his eyes, though his expression remained jovial. "Are you quite sure?"

"Well... no, I suppose I can't be entirely sure, but I *have* almost died on several occasions..."

"Quite the mystery," observed Macha, clapping her hands together gleefully.

Another excruciatingly beautiful female, with chestnut hair, rippling to her dainty waist, and a spirited expression, rose to her feet and introduced herself as Medb.

There were mortals among them too, who smiled at me pleasantly enough, but resisted the urge to make my acquaintance, as though they knew and accepted that their names and company were inconsequential in comparison with those of their otherworldly companions.

I became slowly aware of another male figure, watching me with particular interest. One of *them*. His form was slender, but strong. His hair shone like dark silk, spilling endearingly across his face and ending at his finely chiselled jaw. His eyes were timeless pools… Perhaps even just a little wider than the others', and radiating a light that was his alone. His cheekbones would have been the envy of even the most skilled sculptor. He too wore a mixture of old-fashioned clothing and leather, but in a less elaborate style. He was seated opposite Bres, in a rich, soft chair.

As he noticed me noticing him, I felt the prickle rise to my cheeks in the form of a furious flush. His face broke into a smile, and his eyes remained fixed on mine, as though I were the only living thing that remained in the universe.

"Hello, there. They call me Sam," he said casually, his voice soft and cool, like satin and spring water.

For a moment I was distracted from my reverie. "Sam?" I repeated. *What an odd name for a god!*

His smile broadened a little with amusement, as though he could read my thoughts. "Oh, it's short for something very long and boring."

A searing feeling in my face suggested that my flush was deepening. I could not think of a thing to say. I nodded, and looked away hurriedly, though I could feel his eyes upon me still.

The butterflies deep inside me, that I had thought dead, began to awaken, as though from a long sleep, and though they were as yet too weak to fly, or even flap, their tiny wings trembled a little with a curious excitement.

"What on earth is going on in here?" grumbled Evelyn, striding into the chamber, and noting the spilled drinks on the floor, "There's nobody behind the bar, and look at this mess!"

"I- I'm so sorry…" I began.

However, Alice jumped in, and explained: "Kathy was just a little startled to meet our 'friends'."

"Didn't you warn her?"

Alice dropped her head sheepishly. "No. I wanted it to be a surprise…"

Evelyn tutted loudly. "Foolish child. Well, you can stay here, and clear this up. Kathy, come with me to the bar."

I hesitated for a moment, torn between duty, and that feeling of longing to be with them, that the Great Ones inspired. The prickle wanted to stay. It yearned for them. It craved them. Its empty fingers stretched towards their light, sickening for a touch or taste of it.

I, on the other hand, was still aware of the fact that I needed this job, so I reluctantly followed Evelyn back to the main bar.

"I'm sorry again for spilling the drinks…" I began.

She waved her hand, dismissively. "Never mind that. It's Alice's fault, really. Always has to create some sort of drama, that one! Are you alright?"

"I'm fine. I was just… shocked for a moment. I never thought to encounter their kind in a pub!"

"So, you *have* met them before? Alice told me you'd said a few strange things, that made her suspect as much."

"I haven't met… *those ones* before, but…"

"You've met others of their kind?"

"Yes, but in deserted woodland places, which is where I assumed that they belonged."

Evelyn shrugged. "Forces such as those are everywhere… *belong* everywhere."

"So… they come to the pub a lot?"

"Oh yes, they're usually here. Been here for years. They just arrived one day, and made it their own. I could sense that there was something different about them, as soon as I saw them. Before I knew it, there were rooms in the building that hadn't been there before, everything had been decorated to their taste, and they were holding court in the back. When they wanted company, one of them would go out, and come back with attractive, human playmates to carouse with."

"And…" my brow furrowed, "What do they *do* here?"

"Well, they drink, and smoke, and dance, and sing, and…"

"But, what is their *purpose*?"

She shrugged again. "They haven't mentioned one to me. They just want to enjoy themselves, I suppose. Being immortal must get long and boring."

"Where do they go when the pub closes?"

"They stay as long as they like, and then they go wherever they go. I've never thought to ask."

Something else occurred to me. "So… you, and Alice, and the other customers who look human… Do you all have magical powers?"

"Ha!" Evelyn's laugh was distinctly derisive. "No. What on earth would make you think that?"

"But, you can all *see them*!"

"Of course we can, as long as they let us."

"So… you don't have to be a seventh son of a seventh son, or…?"

At that, Evelyn's eyes widened in astonishment, until it hit her that my question was in earnest, at which point she threw her head back and laughed loudly. She laughed, and laughed, and wiped the tears from her eyes, proclaiming:

"What nonsense! Mind you, some of them do get a bit high and mighty, and attached to their lofty notions. At the end of the day, it's all up to them: Who sees them, and who doesn't see them; who finds the pub, and who doesn't find the pub…"

"You mean to say that they magically control who comes the place?" No wonder it had proved so elusive when I'd first arrived!

She nodded. "Doesn't bother me. They pay me well enough to make it worth my while." She chuckled.

I shook my head in amazement. Suddenly, I heard the words I had said to Aoife, before I'd left home, ringing in my ears: "I'm expecting to have a far more… normal life in Dublin." *I should have known better.* I couldn't help laughing a little, too.

Alice reappeared presently, stowed away a bucket and mop, and began to wash the goblets I had dropped.

"I'm going to get on with the cooking," announced Evelyn, "I'd better not come back and find the bar unmanned again!"

I shook my head, meekly.

She bustled into the kitchen.

"Alice," I exclaimed, as soon as she had gone, "Why on earth didn't you tell me? You've been sniffing around me for weeks, in the most bizarre manner. You obviously saw me use my powers, the day we met. Why didn't you just *tell* me that you knew about magic, instead of making me so uncomfortable, for all of this time?"

She looked genuinely regretful. "I'm sorry. I suppose I just wanted to be certain that I *had* seen what I thought I had, before opening up to you. Otherwise, you might have thought me mad. When I first saw you, you almost reminded me of *them*. Then, I witnessed your fight with the bag snatcher, and I was sure I had seen something supernatural, but I couldn't quite believe my eyes. I thought that if I spent time with you, you'd let something slip, and I could tell you about the pub, and about them, but you always seemed so guarded…"

"So, that day we went swimming… Did you pretend to get into difficulty, to trick me into using my powers again?"

Alice now looked suitably ashamed. "I really hope you believe me when I say how sorry I am. I just wanted to find out, once and for all if you were magical, and then…"

"And then, once you got your confirmation, you brought me here, to frighten the life out of me with shock, instead of explaining it to me first?"

"You had muttered some strange things in the library, as though you knew other gods. I didn't think you'd be afraid. I thought it would be a wonderful surprise!"

I wasn't yet sure if it was wonderful or not. The prickle certainly seemed to think it was, but I was cautious. After all, my prior dealings with Great Ones had not been, what you would call, unequivocally positive.

"So," she continued, "*Are* you one of them?"

"Of course not," I snapped.

"But, you *are*… something else. Something magical? What *are* you, exactly? *They* seem as confused by you as I've been."

I shrugged. "I'm a girl who has powers. I don't know anything more."

"Surely, your parents must know why you're… different."

"I've never met my father, and my mother died too soon to tell me anything relevant about myself, so whatever they knew is destined to remain a mystery."

She gulped. "I'm so sorry. I didn't mean to…"

I sighed. "It's fine. So, how did you become involved in all of this?"

"I think it was by chance, really. I was walking down the alley one day, last year," recounted Alice, "And I suddenly noticed 'The Horse and Hag.' Medb was standing outside. I stopped to stare at her, for I had never seen anything so beautiful, and she asked me if I wanted a job. I would have said yes to anything she asked me, in that lovely, silken voice."

"So, is it *them,* or Evelyn, that I have to impress, if I want to get this job?"

Alice laughed. "Oh, you've got the job. Don't worry about that."

As if on cue, Evelyn emerged from the kitchen. "Kathy, why don't you pour yourself a drink, and enjoy it in the back room? Alice and I will finish up here."

"Are you sure?" I asked, trying to disguise the longing in my voice. An eager part of me pined to go back and be with the Great Ones, more than anything. Even the more cautious part of me was, at least, curious, and wanted to examine them further, for signs that might clarify their purpose or motivation.

Evelyn nodded kindly. "It's your first night, and you've done well."

When I returned to the lavish, back room, things appeared to have become livelier still, in the intervening hours of alcoholic refreshment. Bres was skilfully singing a song. It was not one I knew, but I recognised the sound of the old language. Two human girls sat at his feet, watching him adoringly, while one plaited the other's hair. Medb was taking part in a card game, her eyes gleaming competitively. Macha was ensconced in the corner, reclining in swathes of velvet, while a human boy fed her grapes, and caressed her resplendent face. Sam was clapping along to Bres's song. Another mortal girl was perched on the arm of his chair, surveying him with a craving awe.

As soon as he noticed me, he leaped to his feet with a broad smile. I could not be sure if he had deliberately dislodged his admirer, but she toppled to the floor unceremoniously, and crawled off to join another group, looking disappointed.

"Kathy," cried Sam, "I was hoping you'd return. Come and join us!" He deliberately moved an empty chair beside his own, and gestured for me to sit.

I felt the irritating blush spread across my cheeks again, and the internal squirming of butterflies, as I made my way to his side. The prickle purred.

He sat back in his chair, stretching his legs out and crossing his booted ankles elegantly. He fixed me with a playful smile, his wide eyes full of the past, and the future, and all of the earthly elements, and flickers of unearthly things that all of my language could not describe.

"So, tell me, Kathy," he asked, "Where do you come from, and why do I find you so fascinating?"

"I- I…" I stammered, my blush burning like flame, "I come from Kerry. Do you know it?"

He laughed. He was a god. Of course he knew it. He knew everywhere.

I truly desired to physically pick up my own foot, and stuff it into my mouth, and so far down my throat, that I would suffocate, and die, and never have to utter another, embarrassing word in Sam's presence, ever again.

I was almost relieved when Bres interrupted: "Pay no attention to him, Kathy. Won't you join me in a song?" His tone was almost covetous.

"Leave her alone, Bres," snapped Sam, "We're having a conversation."

To my astonishment, Bres raised his hand, and a bolt of light whirled in Sam's direction, hitting him squarely in the jaw. Sam looked merely irritated. He flung a small magical blow back at Bres, in return. Bres growled, and reciprocated with a larger bolt. As it flew from him, its power singed the hair and shoulder of one of the girls sitting at his feet, and she squealed and leaped away, her eyes full of tears.

Before I knew it, the invisible fingers of the prickle had darted protectively from my body, and slapped Bres across the face, with a force that shook him.

"What on earth is wrong with you?" I demanded, explosively, "I've never seen such a petty, irresponsible use of magic! You should both be ashamed!"

The whole room was immediately silent. Gods and mortals alike were staring at me, open-mouthed, and still as stone. I was suddenly fearful. I could not believe the foolishness of what I had done. Though they may have been squabbling like schoolboys, they were still immortals, and a rebuking by a lesser being, such as myself, was unlikely to be appreciated. I contemplated the likelihood that they might kill me. Even at my strongest, I could not hope to be a match for one of them, let alone a room full of them.

Then, Sam began to laugh. It was a chuckle at first, then an uncontrollable, echoing burst of unbridled mirth. "Bravo, Kathy," he cried, "You're quite right!" He began to clap.

Soon, Macha and Medb were laughing and clapping too, and their mortal companions followed suit. All eyes were still on me, but I could read warmth and admiration in their expressions.

Finally, even Bres sniggered a little, reluctantly at first, then with somewhat more jollity. He rose to his feet and, with a comically exaggerated flourish, bowed low before me, and faced me with a rueful smile.

"Well, that told me!" he exclaimed. To his credit, he then went to the girl he had injured, to make his apologies and enquire as to her wellbeing.

Sam surveyed me with amusement. "Well, now look what you've done. You've made me find you even more fascinating."

I opened my mouth, but only something akin to a strangled gulp came out. I took a deep breath, and composed myself. I looked frantically about the room, hoping to spy something about which I could make some inconsequential conversation, in order to change the subject.

That was when I became aware of a tall figure, in the opposite corner. He was clearly another immortal, but I had not noticed him before. His hair was very long, and dark, and he was shrouded in an enormous cloak, so that little was visible of him, other than his head. He did not look as though he had been laughing or clapping. He was watching the scene with a sombre, almost furious expression. Perhaps I *had* made an enemy, after all.

"Who's that?" I asked.

"Oh, that's Nuadu," replied Sam, dismissively.

"He doesn't look happy."

"He never does. Miserable fellow. Always surly."

I nodded uncomfortably, still unnerved by Nuadu's dark expression.

"So, tell me more about yourself," said Sam. It occurred to me that, perhaps, Alice had been entirely correct in her observation that they found me as mysterious as she did.

Of course, I found myself equally confusing. Frustrated that I had little light to shed on my own nature, and still aware of Nuadu's disconcertingly dismal gaze, I became a little flustered, and muttered:

"I should be getting home."

"Oh, don't go," Sam exclaimed, "You deserve another drink for putting Bres in his place!"

"I really must go," I insisted, finishing the last of my beer, and getting to my feet, hurriedly.

Sam made a playfully disappointed face. "You will come back, won't you?"

"Well, apparently, I work here now, so I expect so."

My mind whirled on my way back to Tom's house, on the bus. I half expected to wake up in my attic at any moment, and find that it had all been an elaborate dream. Of course, I knew that my reality was usually far more outlandish than my dreams.

I put my fingers into my bag surreptitiously, and stroked the bundle of notes that Evelyn had pressed into my hand for my services. I had not been expecting so much. My mind strayed from the memory of Sam's beautiful face, for a moment, to the wonderful provisions that I could buy with my new earnings… but only for a moment. His eyes were imprinted on my vision, like the stain of a too-bright light, that cannot be blinked away.

Bloody Great Ones, I grumbled internally, *Always so maddeningly captivating.* I was not proud of the blushing, gibbering, girlish behaviour that I'd exhibited, when trying to talk to Sam. It was clearly his fault, for his audacious flattery, and embarrassing remarks. What could I possibly have been expected to say? "Yes, I am rather fascinating, aren't I?" *That might have been an improvement.*

I told myself that it wasn't an *attraction* I had, but an understandable curiosity. I wasn't even sure if I *liked* this new group of immortals, and I certainly did not trust them. They appeared astoundingly earthly, hedonistic, and immature, for gods. Even Étaín, though her methods and ideas were warped and unwelcome, had seemed to have a *purpose.* The Dagda had a purpose. Even the small ones in the woods, and Mr. Books, had purposes, or duties, that they fulfilled. However, Evelyn's assessment of the lot in 'The Horse and Hag' was that they were simply there to enjoy themselves. Was there truly nothing more to their existence?

I remembered my meeting with The Dagda in the *síd*, when he had tried to explain his reasons for wishing all of the old gods, and their remnants, to find their way back to each other, and some notion of a great and shared destiny.

He had said: "The ones that you know from the woods aren't even the worst of it. Some parts of us are so separate that they squabble amongst themselves, like petty children. Reining them in will not be easy. But we must be made whole, or we serve no purpose. What good are we to the land, or to man, or to anything, for that matter, if we are off serving tiny little fragments of ourselves?"

Squabbling amongst themselves, like petty children, sounds about right, I mused, thinking of Bres and Sam. While Bres had started it, taken it too far and felt the full weight of my outrage, Sam had not been entirely innocent in the matter, either. He had retaliated, albeit mildly. Is this really all that they did with their powers? Throw them around the back room of a bar… when they weren't acting as magical bouncers, deciding who entered the pub, of course? It seemed a very limited life for such potentially mighty beings.

Naturally, the following day, I rushed to the library to begin researching my new immortal acquaintances. Mr. Books appeared in his usual spot, and offered his assistance.

I chose to ask for reading material on Macha first. When my small friend reappeared, with a book containing a relevant story, I hesitated slightly, before dismissing him.

"Was there something else?" he enquired in his usual, slightly impatient tone.

"I was wondering…" I began.

"Yes?"

"Can you think of a long name from the old tales, that could be shortened to 'Sam'?"

He pursed his lips. "'Sam'? That doesn't ring a bell! Can you be more specific?"

"Not really…"

"Well, I'm not here to find a hypothetical needle in a haystack!"

"Of course not. Sorry. I'll try to find out more, and get back to you."

"Very well."

"Wait," I continued, "Before you go…"

"Yes?"

I coughed nervously, aware that he had never seemed to appreciate more personal lines of questioning. "Can you… *choose* whether or not to show yourself to people in the library?"

"*Choose?*" he repeated with a frown, "*Choose?* I do not choose. I do not decide. I merely *am*. Few see me. Most don't. That is the way of things."

"Thank you, sorry to have troubled you," I whispered quickly, his desire to be gone not having escaped me.

Perhaps the ability to show oneself to mortals at will was exclusive to the Great Ones, I surmised.

I sat down to read a story named 'The Twins of Macha.'

Crunniuc the widower lived, with his sons, in an isolated part of the Irish kingdom of Ulaid. One day, a mysterious woman arrived at his home. She began to keep house for him, as though she had always been there. She slept with him as a wife does. She was stronger and faster than any man. She brought him great prosperity, and his household thrived. One day, Crunniuc left to attend a fair, organised by the king. His 'wife' was now heavily pregnant. Before he left, she warned him not to say anything foolish while he was there. He dismissed her concerns, but when he arrived at the fair, he could not resist boasting that his wife could outrun the king's horses. He was swiftly brought before the king, and threatened with execution, if he could not prove his boast. The court sent for his wife. She reluctantly agreed to race the horses for her husband's life. However, as the race was about to begin, she went into labour. She begged the assembly to postpone the race until she had given birth. Her request was denied. She raced the horses in agony, and gave birth to twins at the finish line. She then stood before the crowd, announced that her name was Macha, and cursed nine generations of the men of Ulaid to experience labour pains for several days each year.

I raised my eyebrows at the cruelty of the tale. Could this poor, mistreated figure really be the same Macha who had seemed so bright and friendly at 'The Horse and Hag'?

Her revenge on the men of the kingdom in the story, albeit well-deserved, had been severe, and illustrated the greatness of her power. Perhaps there was something darker to Macha than our first meeting had suggested.

"After all, Étaín once seemed benign too, didn't she?" I muttered.

A familiar voice startled me. "I keep finding you in here, muttering about Étaín," whispered Alice, conspiratorially, taking a seat opposite me, "You know her, don't you?"

"You could say that," I replied curtly, still not having quite forgiven the girl for the weeks of interrogation and trickery that I'd endured, while she had tried to get the measure of me.

"Is she like the ones I know?"

"In appearance, perhaps." My tone was still guarded, and unfriendly.

Alice sighed. "Look," she said, gently, "I'm sorry again. Are you… alright after last night?"

"I'm fine," I shrugged nonchalantly, "It was a surprise, but nothing terribly out of the ordinary, in the greater scheme of things."

"Gosh, really?" she breathed, looking impressed, "You must have had such an interesting life!"

"That's one word for it."

Mr. Books popped his head 'round the bookshelf, wearing his typical, disapproving expression. His appearance reminded me that I actually needed to leave the library, in order to attend a kickboxing class at the gym.

"I have to go, Alice," I announced, gathering my belongings.

She looked hurt, and I felt a little sorry for her. After all, these otherworldly matters were relatively new to her, and I could not entirely blame her for her overly excited, and imperfect, behaviour.

"It's not you," I added, "I have training."

Her eyes brightened slightly. "Shall we have a drink at 'The Horse and Hag' tonight?"

"My next shift isn't until Saturday…"

"I'm not working either, but we could still go for a drink!" Her tone was pleading.

"Very well," I conceded. I tried to tell myself that I had agreed to the meeting to placate Alice who had, after all, been kind to me, in addition to being maddeningly cloying and inquisitive. However, I knew, deep down, that a large part of my acquiescence had little to do with her, and more to do with the fact that Saturday seemed like an eternity away, and an irritating part of me was longing to see… *Them* again.

As I wandered to the pub to meet Alice that evening, I found myself in unusually good humour. I had enjoyed my class, and was pleased to be back in kickboxing training. I actually had some money in my purse, and had finally been able to buy lasagne from the university cafeteria for lunch. It hadn't been of a particularly high standard, but had tasted wonderful to me. I now had a simultaneously delightful and uncomfortable, squirming feeling in my stomach, and it was not hunger, but anticipation. I was going to see *them* again. Well, I presumed so. I suddenly remembered that Evelyn had said that they were *usually* there. I couldn't be sure what that meant! Perhaps they *wouldn't* be there! My butterflies suddenly felt empty, and anxious. What if I walked into that extravagant back room, and found it quiet and cold, and devoid of their exquisite faces?

I swallowed heavily, and told myself to stop thinking like a silly schoolgirl with a crush. Étaín had turned against me. The Dagda had left, and never returned. I had got over them, and I could get over this one. *These ones,* I corrected myself sharply, entirely unwilling to admit that there was one beautiful face that I wanted to see above the others'.

As I approached the alley, it also occurred to me that the pub might have disappeared again, but I spotted it as soon as I turned the corner. The prickle curled luxuriantly about my neck and shoulders, whispering excitedly. They *were* there. I just knew it.

Alice was waiting for me at the bar, swirling a straw in her vodka and orange. "You came," She grinned.

"I said I would," I replied a little tersely, and immediately rebuked myself. She could be irksome, but I was sure that she really was quite harmless. *You agreed to come out. Now, make an effort to enjoy it!*

"Very well," I answered my internal voice.

Alice looked confused.

I did not care to explain. "Shall we have shots?" I suggested, brightly.

The shots were served by an attractive girl named Sylvie, who Alice informed me was Evelyn's daughter. I could see the resemblance, though her accent was entirely Irish.

"The first round is on the house," she smiled.

"Well, we'll have to have a second round, then, won't we?" I exclaimed. I had discovered, in recent hours, that I thoroughly enjoyed the feeling of being able to take money out of my bag and actually pay for things, without a sense of terror. I'd warned myself not to get too carried away, but agreed with myself that I had permission to be just a little extravagant for one night.

Of course, I was simply dying to suggest adjourning to the back room, but politeness dictated that I paid some attention to my companion, before getting lost in immortal eyes. The prickle was impatient, but I ordered it to be quiet, and asked Alice the usual questions that one asks an acquaintance. I realised that, until now, I had always been so eager to be rid of her that I had never made any effort to find out what part of Ireland she came from, or where she had gone to school, and so on.

We were downing our third round of shots by the time Sam strode out into the main bar.

"What, no shot for me?" he demanded loudly, his voice dripping with mock-disappointment. He punctuated his question with a playful smile.

I felt cold. I felt hot. I felt stiff and leaden, my mind frantically searching for some clever retort, but finding only the stillness of stolen breath, and the weight of those beautiful eyes, boring through me.

Sylvie saved me by presenting us with three strong shots. We drank them, and the blood rushed back to my brain, from whatever girlish place it had been, as I coughed and spluttered. *How attractive,* observed my internal voice, cringing at the fact that it belonged to me.

"What on earth was *that?*" I asked Sylvie, as soon as I had regained some composure.

She laughed. "Poitín. It does blow your head off, but our… 'special guests' love the stuff!"

Sam smiled appreciatively. "It takes rather a lot of effort to get drunk, when you've been around as long as we have," he explained, "So the stronger the better!"

"I think I'll stick to something a little less…" I began.

"Lethal?" suggested Alice.

"Precisely!"

We giggled.

"Anyhow," exclaimed Sam, his focus on me, "What on earth do you mean by returning here, and not coming straight back to greet us? It has seemed like an eternity since you left, you know!"

"Oh, I'm sure you've managed to keep yourselves entertained in my absence," I responded, surprising myself by actually formulating a sentence.

"Doesn't mean we wouldn't have even more fun *with* you, though." His tone was jocular. "We need someone like you around to keep Bres in check! He receives far too few slaps across the face."

Sylvie's eyes widened, eagerly. "What on earth happened last night?"

Although she hadn't been present when my instincts had got the better of me, somebody had evidently told Alice what had transpired, because she smirked knowingly.

"Well," said Sam, for Sylvie's benefit, moving to the middle of the room, as though he were an actor, taking centre stage, "Bres was being his usual, boorish self, throwing things around the room, hit one of the girls, and *this one…*" He paused, fixing me with a stare, at which my butterflies rippled. "*This one* smacked him across the face, and gave us both a damn good talking to… and quite rightly, too!"

Sylvie's jaw dropped. "Kathy, do you mean to say that you actually walked up to Bres and hit him in the face?"

"Oh, *no*," replied Sam on my behalf, his hands animated, "There was no 'walking up to him' required! She did it *our* way!" He mimicked the motion, with a flick of his wrist.

"Oh." Sylvie looked impressed. Magical powers seemed to be unequivocally admired at 'The Horse and Hag'.

I couldn't help smiling at Sam's theatrical account of the event. It made quite the change to be praised for my abilities, after years of being despised by Étaín, and feared by Aoife. Even Liam had never seemed entirely *happy* about my gifts, or his own. He was always too concerned with what might go wrong. Suddenly, I began to see what might be attractive to the immortals about a light-hearted life at 'The Horse and Hag', after lifetimes upon lifetimes, of more serious concerns.

Sam extended his elbows to me and Alice, as though to escort us both somewhere. "Shall we?" He gestured towards the back room.

Alice took his arm, willingly.

The prickle tried to leap at it, but I slapped it back and pretended not to notice Sam's old-fashioned gesture. I walked ahead. I did not want to know what it was like to touch him. *That way, only trouble lies.*

"Well, well, well," cried Bres as we entered, perfectly resplendent on the same ornate chair that he had occupied the previous evening, "If it isn't my old nemesis, Kathy!"

His tone was warm, and his ancient eyes twinkled with mischief.

I smiled shyly, hoping that I was correct in interpreting his words as a friendly joke. "Hello, Bres."

"Has that scoundrel, Sam, been monopolising you all of this time?"

"I was just filling Sylvie in on your disgraceful exploits from last night," interjected Sam sarcastically.

Bres adopted a scowl, which soon faded into a smirk. "Well, come over here, the lot of you, so that Kathy can experience some *proper* company!" He waved his hand, and several mortals, who were occupying nearby seats, scuttled away into a corner.

I felt uncomfortable at the careless way in which his admirers had been treated, but thought better of creating any further conflict so soon, by commenting on it, and followed Sam and Alice to the empty chairs.

Macha and Medb approached, to greet us, their exquisite faces bright and eager. They did not touch me, but I observed that Medb and Alice exchanged a long, elated look, and that the goddess began to stroke my friend's honey blonde hair tenderly.

"I have a game to finish," said Medb gently.

"I'll see you later," smiled Alice, caressing her light, immortal fingers, before she departed.

Medb returned to the card table, where a group of human companions were waiting patiently for her. She picked up her hand of cards, and surveyed it thoughtfully.

"Oh, Kathy," she called absently, "Could you pass me that cup?"

I noticed that there was an unattended goblet of mead on the corner of a table, closest to me. I dutifully stood up and made to pick it up.

"What are you doing?" exclaimed Medb, frowning as she looked up from her game, "Just… *pass* it to me!"

With a slight gasp, I understood her meaning. She had intended me to send the drink across the room magically, not carry it the mortal way.

I was slightly nervous. I had never really used the prickle for such an unimportant thing. It felt, somehow, demeaning to my power, to even contemplate treating it as some sort of convenient servant.

The prickle, however, did not appear to be in the least bothered by the request. It trickled obligingly from my uncertain hand, scooped up the goblet, and transported it swiftly to the card table.

"Thanks," muttered Medb absently, as though the feat had been nothing.

The prickle returned to me and nuzzled my cheek, apparently pleased and contented to have been helpful.

"You're not used to this, are you?" whispered Sam gently, drawing nearer to me, to keep his question private. His eyes were, once again, on mine, with an indescribable intensity, and his lips just a little too close.

"No," I admitted, "I've always…"

"Been around mortals?"

"Well… mostly."

"Magic is clearly in your nature," he smiled, "You'll come to enjoy it, in no time."

His breath was warm and fragrant in my face, tingling on my skin, as a trembling excitement began to pulsate, somewhere deep inside me. *Those butterflies. Those damn butterflies.* I couldn't bear it. I jerked my chair away, and cried: "I'll get shots!"

Before anybody could answer, I had fled out to the main bar.

For the rest of the evening, I made sure to keep my chair at a certain distance from any of the Great Ones. I desired to avoid that powerful sensation, of wanting to be pulled inside them. The prickle sickened for it, crawling uneasily about my shoulders, and whimpering with desire. I paid it as little heed as I could.

Sam addressed an occasional comment in my direction, but did not attempt to engage me in another more intimate exchange. I told myself that I was relieved.

Bres sang again, and we all clapped along to the intoxicating rhythm. I drank more than I ever had in my life, yet still felt only slightly, pleasantly fuzzy. Medb had won her card game, and nodded with satisfaction, as if that was as it should be. She had immediately come to sit with

Alice. They held hands and exchanged the odd, tender glance. I wondered if it were actually possible that there was something more between them than the simple adoration of a beautiful goddess, by an inconsequential girl.

One of the mortal lackeys scuttled into the room from behind a tapestry, at the opposite side of the room from the door, and whispered to Bres. Bres paused in his song, and turned to survey the room, as though he were deciding something.

He said quickly: "Macha, you go."

Macha looked reluctant. She was on an elegant sofa, sandwiched between a boy and a girl. He was kissing her neck, and she was combing her luxuriant hair.

"Put them down, Macha," snapped Bres, "They'll still be here when you get back."

The goddess sighed, and pointedly ignored him.

"Well, as usual, it seems that I have to do everything around here myself," grumbled Bres, and strode off behind the tapestry.

He returned within minutes, looking entirely unperturbed, and took his seat. I raised my eyebrows questioningly, but Bres's response was to resume his song, so loudly as to drown out any possibility of conversation.

I wondered what was behind the tapestry, and why someone had been needed there, but only for a moment, because I then became aware of Nuadu, glowering in the corner, his face seething and full of hatred. I had almost forgotten about him. I was sure he had not been there earlier. His expression alarmed me.

Bres noticed my interest in the surly, cloaked being, and, as soon as he had finished singing, he cried: "Nuadu, come over here! You haven't met Kathy yet. Don't be so rude!"

Looking as though he would rather cut off his own head, Nuadu stomped in our direction, and bowed courteously, though his eyes were anything but friendly.

"Greetings," he muttered.

As he moved, his cloak fell open, revealing a gleaming silver arm, in place of flesh. I tried not to gasp, but he must have noted my surprise, and yanked the garment closed again with his other hand.

"P-pleased to meet you, Nuadu," I offered, a little nervously.

He nodded briskly, and returned to his corner.

"I'm afraid that's as much as you're likely to get out of him," said Bres, dismissively.

"Miserable fellow," added Medb, in agreement.

I looked over at Nuadu, and felt a shiver slither down my spine.

"It's time I was going," I announced, realising with a surprising amount of regret, how late it had become.

"Oh, can't you stay just a while?" wheedled Bres.

I shook my head, bade everyone farewell, and walked out towards the main bar. As I was buttoning my coat by the door, I began to prickle. Somebody was behind me.

I spun 'round. It was Sam. He was smiling suggestively. "One last shot?" he asked.

"I wish I could…"

Before I could finish my sentence, two small glasses appeared in his hand, one of poitín, and one of something mercifully milder. We drank them. His face was, once again, too close to mine, and I could almost taste the alcohol on his breath. I had found the poitín too harsh, when I had drunk it, but on him, the aroma was heady and sweet, and I longed for my tongue to experience just one, small…

I stepped back. No. I would not kiss him. The fact that I had even considered it was clearly the result of too much alcohol. Why, he was a god, and I was just *me,* and… No. Just no.

He smiled crookedly, his expression both amused, and a little thwarted. "I still find you fascinating."

"Well, yes, I suppose I am," I replied, my tone as nonchalant as I could make it. Inwardly, I jumped up and down, and patted myself on the back for, more or less, remembering the retort that I'd composed on the bus, the night before.

He chuckled. "Goodnight, Kathy."

"Goodnight, Sam."

I pushed the shot glass into my pocket, and hurried out into the night. I slammed the door closed, and leaned back against it, breathing heavily. No. Just no. Any real attraction to an immortal was entirely futile. The Great Ones at 'The Horse and Hag' seemed fond enough of their mortal companions, in the way that a child is fond of its playthings, but will one day outgrow them. I would not let myself become one of those simpering fools, cowering on the floor of the pub, desperate for a morsel of attention from a shining, unearthly being, whose existence I could never hope to understand.

I resolved not to let myself be swayed by Sam's attentions, or his declarations of fascination. I was certain that I was merely some entertaining novelty, whose appeal would fade as suddenly as I had appeared among them. No. I would get over this. I hoped that I would get over it soon, because the thoughts that I currently had of melting into the depths of his eyes, caressing his dark, silken hair, and touching his shimmering body, were utter torture.

I was so immersed in my own thoughts that I almost missed the little being, standing right in front of me: A pathetic, almost transparent thing, with pale, haunted eyes, not unlike the pitiful small one I had found cowering in an alley some time ago. Its terrified gaze met mine.

"H-hello," I said gently.

He studied me, and drew back with a petrified hiss, his head darting one way, and then another, as if deciding in which direction to flee.

"Don't be afraid," I added, "I mean you no harm."

"You're one of *them!*" he shrieked, his voice a tiny whimper. He ran.

I opened my mouth, to urge him to stay, but he was entirely out of sight. I frowned. One of *them*? Who did he mean? A human, or…? I remembered Macha's assertion that she thought I was closer to an immortal than a human. Could it be that this poor little fellow had mistaken me for a *Great One?* If so, there was clearly no more love lost between the supernatural ranks in Dublin, than there had been in the woods of Kerry. I was perturbed. The sorry state of the small ones in the city was unbearable, yet how could I ever hope to help them, if they would not let me get close?

CHAPTER TWELVE

I visited the library after my lectures the following evening. It had been a slightly painful day, racked with the queasiness of a hangover, and concern for the small one I had encountered outside 'The Horse and Hag'. The memory of his visible terror plagued me, but I felt utterly powerless to find him, or intervene in whatever hardship he had endured. I needed a distraction.

I knew that I had heard Medb's name as a child, in one of the old stories my mother had told me about the young hero Cú Chulaind. *Something about a bull*, I thought, but could not quite remember how it went.

Mr. Books was only too happy to oblige, and brought me a book named 'The Cattle Raid of Cooley.' I sat down and began to read.

> Medb was a powerful queen of the Irish province of Connacht. The sight of her was said to rob a man of two thirds of his strength, and it took thirty two lovers to satisfy her sexual appetite.

I raised my eyebrows. "She seems to have calmed down a bit over time, then," I muttered, before continuing with the story.

> Medb and her husband Ailill, the king, began to compare their riches one night, and came to the conclusion that they were equal in wealth, apart from the fact that Ailill had one more bull than she did. Medb would not stand for this, and made enquiries as to where she could acquire a bull as powerful as her husband's. A particularly fine bull in Ulaid was the only one that seemed to fit the bill. She tried to get it, by promising land and sexual favours to its owner, but when her plan failed, Medb declared war on Ulaid, gathered a great army, and marched north. Because the men of Ulaid were incapacitated by the annual labour pains that Macha had cursed them with, it was left up to the warrior Cú Chulaind to defend the province alone, for he was exempt from the curse. Cú Chulaind defeated Medb's greatest warriors, one after another, but she finally succeeded in taking possession of the bull, and then retreated. Back in Connacht, Medb's new bull fought Ailill's bull, and killed it, but then died of its own wounds. And so,

neither Medb nor Ailill ended up with a prize bull, but were equal in wealth again.

I couldn't help smiling, as I noted the connection between Macha's revenge and Medb's initial advantage in the battle. No wonder they were such great friends. My smile grew a little wistful, with the faint memory of my mother's voice, reading the tale to me so many moons ago.

I sighed. I had hoped a story, and a little research, would take my mind off the worryingly damaged small one outside the pub. It had not.

For a moment, I wished that I had interrogated Sam a bit about his name, so that I might research him too, but soon remembered why I hadn't. Getting too close to him felt dangerous. It seemed that I could barely keep my wits about me, unless he was several feet away from me at all times. I chided myself for my weakness. My relationship with Liam was barely cold in its grave. How could I have allowed myself to have those lustful thoughts about someone else, so soon, even for an unguarded moment? Yes, he was a god, with the palpable power and charisma to weaken anyone's resolve. They were all enthralling and intoxicating, to a deeply unfair extent. What hope did any mortal have of resisting their otherworldly charms? Yet, Sam preyed on my mind in a way that Bres, Medb, Macha, and Nuadu, did not, and it was infuriating.

No, I told myself sternly. Just no. Not for you.

I gave up on study for the evening, and took the bus back to Tom's house. I was a little surprised not to hear his drunken shouting as I approached.

I was more surprised to find him stark naked, standing in the hallway. For a moment, I thought he was staring at me, but soon realised that he was staring *through* me, as though fixated on some invisible object on the doorstep.

"Tom," I exclaimed sharply, "What are you doing?"

He showed no sign of comprehension.

I waved my hand in front of his eyes repeatedly. He did not react.

It then occurred to me that he was having a drunken blackout. Perhaps that was why he spent so many silent hours in the bathroom… Some sort of inebriated sleepwalking!

As if he wasn't bad enough conscious, I grumbled inwardly, as I climbed the stairs, leaving him to his bizarre trance.

I unwrapped an enormous baguette, stuffed with cheese, ham and salad, that I had bought myself on the way home, and began to munch contentedly. It had not been long since such a thing would have existed only in my fantasies, and I was still enjoying the novelty of nourishment.

The following morning, I crept out of the house, afraid that he might still be standing in the hall like an ugly, pasty statue. He was not. However, the carpet looked wet in the spot that he had occupied, and left me in little doubt that he had urinated on the floor. I suppressed an empty retch, and hurried on my way.

Although it was Saturday, I had agreed to meet Alice for a swim, after which I thought I might go to the library, or for a walk, until it was time for my shift at 'The Horse and Hag.'

"You're not going to pretend to drown again, are you?" I enquired with a smirk, as we changed into our swimwear.

Alice did not respond, but quirked her mouth sheepishly.

After we had completed twenty mercifully uneventful lengths of the pool, she suggested that we go for lunch. I agreed, happy in the fact that I still had just enough money from my first night's pay left to do so.

I ordered an omelette and chips, and tucked in enthusiastically.

"So, the other night at the pub was fun, wasn't it?" Alice observed.

I nodded, my mouth too full of fried potatoes to comment.

"They're wonderful, aren't they?" She smiled and leaned her hand on her cheek, a dreamy, faraway look in her eyes.

I swallowed, and began: "Feel free to say if this is too personal a question…"

"Yes?"

"Is there… something between you and Medb? I couldn't help noticing you seemed close."

Her face lit up, and she exhaled deeply. "Oh, yes. We're together. I can't believe how lucky I am."

"So, you mean… *together*, in the way that Macha clearly enjoys spending time with the boys and girls in the back room, or…?"

"Oh no, Medb and I are very much in love."

"Really?"

She bristled slightly at the incredulity in my tone. "Do you find that so hard to believe? I know I don't have your powers, but she clearly sees something worthy in me, even if *you* don't."

"I didn't mean…" I trailed off, trying to find the right words, "Don't you worry that you might be more of an… amusement to her than a real partner? I mean, look how they treat their other human companions."

"It's different between me and Medb," she insisted, sulkily.

I should have left it there, but I couldn't help adding: "*Love* seems such a mortal emotion, and they're… not. Has it never occurred to you that it may not be a feeling she's capable of having? They must have had countless sexual partners over the centuries. Could any of them really have been that special?"

"How could you possibly know how it is between us?" snapped Alice.

I relented. "You're right. Sorry."

"Anyway," she continued accusatively, "Don't think I haven't noticed the way you look at Sam, and turn a peculiar shade of beetroot every time he speaks to you!"

I snorted dismissively. "Sam? I haven't paid any more attention to him than the others. They're all very beautiful and magnetic, of course, but I wouldn't go down that path with any of them." I felt the blush on my face betraying me as I spoke.

She narrowed her eyes. "And what path is that?"

"Chasing after a god, like the rest of the sycophants in the back room."

"Is that how you see me?"

"Of course not," I replied quickly, "I'm sure your situation is quite different."

She appeared warily appeased, as though she suspected that my words were false but had chosen to be content with them rather than to argue further. She had, after all, spent weeks trying to get my attention. I suspected that she was not willing to give up on the friendship over a petty quarrel, after all of her efforts.

"Shall we have couple of drinks somewhere?" she asked, changing the subject.

"I'm not sure I should be drinking before my shift!"

"Oh, one or two won't do any harm, and you don't have to be at work for hours," she insisted.

I sighed. I knew better than to argue with Alice when she was determined. "Very well. Where shall we go?"

"Pub crawl of Temple Bar?" she suggested, brightly.

"That sounds like more than one or two…"

"Oh, it'll be fine! Just have a mineral if you feel tipsy."

"I really do need this job, you know."

She laughed. "They wouldn't let Evelyn fire you, even if she wanted to… And she doesn't. Haven't you noticed what a curiosity you are?"

I rolled my eyes, wishing that I were just a little less 'fascinating' to the Great Ones. If Sam hadn't been so repeatedly, audaciously forward with me, it would be far easier to ignore him.

As Alice and I left the café, she began to shout and wave. I noticed that her friends, Samira and Paul, were walking across the quad. They saluted her in return, and hastened their pace in our direction.

"Pub crawl of Temple Bar?" asked Alice.

They shrugged in acquiescence.

"Well, it *is* Saturday," smiled Samira, "And we've been studying in the library until now, so I suppose we deserve a reward!"

"Excellent!" Alice clapped her hands happily, and led the way as we walked.

"Are you finally going to take us to this mysterious pub you work in?" Paul asked her, "What's it called again? 'The Nag and Hag'?"

"Oh no," replied Alice, "Kathy is working there tonight, and we can't have the landlady see her drinking before her shift."

"Oh, so *you've* been there?" exclaimed Samira, turning to face me.

I nodded briskly. It was evident that Alice had not shared much with them about 'The Horse and Hag', or its secrets.

"What is it like?" demanded Samira, "Alice is so tight-lipped about it!"

I noticed Alice watching me sideways, her expression tense.

"Most of the regulars are very…" I paused, a naughty part of me enjoying her evident discomfort, as she anxiously awaited the conclusion of my sentence. "…old. The regulars are very, very old. One might almost say, ancient!"

Samira looked disappointed. "Oh, that doesn't sound like much fun at all."

"No, it doesn't", agreed Paul, "I'm surprised that there's such an old man's pub in Temple Bar."

"Indeed. It's an unusual place," I continued.

Alice smirked, fell into pace with me, and muttered: "Very clever," under her breath.

The rest of the afternoon passed pleasantly. We wandered around Temple Bar, visiting various pubs, chatting about university, music and current affairs. I drank two beers and, at Alice's insistence, one shot. After that, I dutifully ordered only cola. It was quite freeing to be with ordinary people, talking about ordinary things.

Eventually, I checked my watch and decided that it was time for me to leave for work. "This has been fun," I admitted.

"We must do it again soon, when you have the evening off to get drunk with us," laughed Samira.

"Will you be in later?" I asked Alice quietly. She shook her head and explained that she had promised to attend a friend's birthday party that night. "See you soon, then," I called cheerfully.

As I walked to 'The Horse and Hag', I hummed a little tune. As soon as I reached the door, however, my cheerful song froze on my lips, as I began to prickle with that maddening, familiar, heady feeling. *They* were there, and the prickle knew it. I took a deep breath before entering.

True to her word, Evelyn presented me with a bowl of stew, and instructed me to eat it before beginning work. It was even more delicious than her roast chicken.

Once I had gulped it down, I took my place behind the bar, and silently reminded myself of where everything was. The main room was busier than I had seen it before, that evening. It was full of noise and laughter, and quite a few patrons who did not in the least resemble the attractive youths who kept the Great Ones company in the back room. I had assumed that the immortals were frightfully selective about who they allowed to frequent the establishment, but it appeared that their preferences were surprisingly broad.

Sylvie came to the bar, and I served her a tray of shots. She took it back to a table, at which she was sitting with a group of friends.

I busied myself polishing glasses, as I waited for the next request. Suddenly, my stomach churned. Those blasted, infernal butterflies were now as boisterous as ever they had been, fluttering in unashamedly dramatic circles, and intertwining with the rippling shimmer of the prickle. My knees faltered a little, and I put down the glass I was holding, afraid that it might slip from my fingers.

Of course, *he* was standing at the bar.

"Hello, Kathy," he said with a smile.

"Hello, Sam."

"Would you care for a drink?"

"I'm working."

"Oh, yes, I see. Well, in that case, I'll have a poitín, if you would be so kind." To my horror and delight, he pulled up a bar stool, and sat down right in front of me, as if he were planning to take his time.

I presented Sam with his drink, and he contemplated it for a moment. He brushed a strand of shining, dark hair out of his eyes, with his elegant fingers. They caressed the sharp curve of his high cheekbone as they performed the small task. The prickle, achingly jealous of those fingers, almost leaped out of my body to touch his face.

No! I snapped inwardly.

An unremarkable, mortal customer then approached the bar. He did not look *at* Sam, and he did not look *through* him, but he paused uncomfortably and stepped to the side of him, as though he knew that *something* was there, but not quite what. As he ordered his drink, he appeared uneasy. He kept his head down, shifted anxiously from one foot to another, and scratched absently at his wrists. As soon as I had presented him with his stout, he scuttled back to his table a little too quickly.

"Wait," I cried, "Your change!"

"Keep it," he muttered uncomfortably. Then, he sat down and looked mildly confused, as though wondering why he had given me such a large tip.

That's interesting.

"What was that?" I asked Sam, "I thought everyone in this bar could see you."

"Oh, it's not quite so simple." He swirled his glass and downed his drink. "Evelyn and Sylvie like to retain some of their regular human patrons, but the sight of us can be a bit… *much* for people. Therefore, we save our true faces for those few who we think will be… suitably appreciative."

"Fawning and sycophantic, you mean?" I muttered before I could think better of it.

Sam's enormous eyes widened, and he laughed, astonished at my impertinence. "You really don't hold back, do you?"

It was currently taking most of my energy to hold back the prickle from jumping across the bar to ravish him, but he wasn't to know that.

Mercifully, the tense moment was interrupted by the radiant arrival of Macha. She glided out of the back room, her bright eyes taking in her surroundings, and she clapped with delight as she reached us.

"Isn't this charming?" she exclaimed. It was evident that she was not in the habit of frequenting the main bar. She slapped Sam's thigh jovially. "So, this is where you've been hiding!"

Sam gallantly rose, and offered her his seat. She sat down daintily, and ordered some mead and poitín.

"Oh, isn't it fun to be out here with all of the... *normal* people, for a change?" she squealed.

I noticed that everyone in her vicinity was staring just a little too hard at their drinks, as though it were vitally important for their eyes not to wander in the direction of the bar.

I leaned towards Macha and Sam a little, and whispered curiously: "So, as far as the other customers are concerned, am I standing here talking to myself?"

Sam chuckled. "No, it's not quite that simple."

"Of course it's not." These Great Ones may seem more straightforward, in their hedonistic desires, than The Dagda and his followers, but how remiss of me to have thought that they would be any less enigmatic when asked a question?

Macha appeared distracted, and began to sniff the air in the spot that I had occupied when I had drawn closer to her. "Kathy, you smell familiar."

My mouth opened and closed for a few moments, entirely unsure of how to respond to such a strange observation. "Well," I answered nervously, "You *have* met me before."

"Oh, I know, but..." She snapped her fingers frustratedly, as though trying to remember the lyrics of a long-forgotten song, "There's something else... You smell of someone I know. You say that you are not of our kind, but you must have tasted one of us most intimately. It's like... a residue. Who was it, Kathy?"

As soon as she said the word 'tasted', I gasped and stepped backwards. Could she, somehow, sense that fragment of Étaín's power that I had taken into myself during the ritual with Fúamnach? Of course, the Great Ones were all connected, so there was no reason why one would not be familiar to another. I could not possibly explain it to Macha, without admitting that I had almost succeeded in devouring an incarnation not unlike her own. How would they see me then? As an enemy, or possibly even a threat?

"I'm not sure what you mean," I said carefully, "I played with, and encountered, a number of magical beings when I was growing up in Kerry."

"But, it's something more than that…" continued Macha, perplexed.

A couple of customers walked up to the bar, paused on the periphery of the space that the immortals were occupying, and skittered nervously sideways. They glanced at each other uncomfortably, then began to examine their hands as they squirmed.

"I think we're getting in the way of Kathy doing her job," announced Sam, "Come, Macha, let's go and rejoin the others."

I breathed a sigh of relief.

She looked reluctant, but stood up to go.

"Do come and see us before you leave, won't you?" called Sam, before disappearing around the corner.

As soon as they had taken their leave, the customers' expressions relaxed and grew jovial again.

"So, what can I get you?" I asked, brightly.

As my shift drew to a close, I fancied that I could almost feel them willing me into the back room for a last beverage. The prickle and the butterflies wanted to go to them, of course. Another part of me was cautious. If Macha recognised the 'smell' she had noticed as Étaín's, awkward questions might ensue. I could lie, but these were powerful beings who might well have magical ways of getting to the truth of the matter. Mind you, if I avoided them, it could further fan the flames of their curiosity.

Evelyn paid me, and offered to pour me a drink.

As she presented me with a beer, something occurred to me. "You and Sylvie," I observed, "You don't seem to be so… overawed by *them* as the other humans who see them are."

Evelyn laughed slightly. "They're very beautiful, of course, and we've come to like having them around, but we have our own gods who could give that lot a run for their money."

"They're not *all* like that, you know."

"What do you mean?"

I sighed, surprised to feel a little protective of figures like The Dagda, who seemed to have more earnest and significant concerns. "They're not all defined by getting drunk in the pub. Some of them want… something more."

"Well, they probably won't turn up around here then, will they?" she chuckled.

"Probably not." By now, the prickle was practically strangling me with desire to follow the magic, and I decided to give in.

I took my drink to the back room. As I approached, I heard a song. For a moment, I assumed that Bres was performing again. I wondered why his voice was even finer than it had seemed before.

It was not Bres. It was Sam singing, and playing an old-fashioned, stringed instrument, with a quick, silken touch. I stopped, frozen at the beauty of his words. I could not understand them, but I could sense the truth of them. He sang of joy and sorrow, and love and longing. The haunting melody penetrated the crevices of my mind, and my eyes misted as I recalled every moment of my life: The beauty, the triumphs, and the losses. How could one who was never born, and could never die, express or elicit such excruciatingly authentic emotions?

When his song finished, I felt even closer to tears, for I could not bear to be without the magnificent music. I was on the verge of crying out, imploring him to sing again, when I was interrupted.

"Kathy," said Bres loudly, "My old adversary, do come and sit down!"

I stood still, too overcome to speak.

Sam stood up. "Or…" he said, "Shall we go out?"

I opened and closed my mouth, searching for my words. It was clear that the moment was over, and I would have to bear the grief of the end of his recital. "Go out where? The main bar?" I asked, confused and still distracted.

He laughed, and clapped his hands for attention. Medb and Macha looked up. "Let's go out!" he exclaimed.

Macha leaped from her seat excitedly. "Oh, what a good idea! We haven't been out for ages!"

Medb nodded. "Yes, let's go out!"

Bres thought about it, and concluded: "Very well."

Nuadu merely grunted darkly from his corner, and stormed out of the room. I took it that he would not be joining us.

"Shall we go for cocktails?" squealed Macha.

"I want to go to a nightclub," protested Medb.

"We'll do both," stated Sam.

Bres nodded approvingly.

"Would you like me to go and fetch a carriage?" offered one of Macha's companions. They all agreed enthusiastically, and he ran behind the tapestry, in the mysterious direction from which I had once seen Bres depart and return.

"Kathy, get your coat," instructed Sam.

I obediently walked out towards the coat rack in the main bar, before suddenly stopping. *What on earth are you doing?* I demanded of myself, *This is madness!*

"Kathy," boomed Bres, "Come along! The carriage is here!"

What sort of carriage was it? Some supernatural vehicle from a portal behind the tapestry, that might whisk me away to another dimension for twenty years?

"Kathy," called Sam. His exquisite face peered around the corner to investigate my whereabouts. "Oh, there you are!"

I gulped.

'I must get home. It's late.' Say the words.

My curiosity slapped the words away from my lips, as soon as they began to form, and I rushed towards him. "Coming!" I cried.

To my surprise, what lay behind the tapestry was no otherworldly gateway, but an entirely drab, tiny, empty room, and an unassuming back door. Outside was a horse-drawn carriage, in which the others were huddled expectantly. The fine animals and the driver all looked entirely benign, and of this world. It occurred to me that Macha's boy had merely dashed out to hire one of the carriages, usually favoured by tourists, from a nearby road.

I laughed slightly to myself at my overactive imagination, as I clambered in to occupy the only cramped space remaining. Of course, it was beside Sam, and his proximity was as intoxicating as ever. I tried to freeze my breath so as not to inhale the heady scent of him. I tried to ignore the excruciating tingle on my skin where my body met his. I tried to forget his song. The horses took off, and their gait kept pace with my hammering pulse.

The journey was mercifully brief. The carriage halted near neighbouring Grafton Street. Macha's boy leaped down first, and held the door open for the rest of us to pile out.

"Cocktails first," insisted Macha, gesturing towards a sophisticated establishment, just a few feet away. The doorman anxiously avoided our gaze as we entered.

Inside, a hostess was hovering, waiting to greet and seat patrons. She glanced at us, and then shuffled in the opposite direction, nervously fidgeting with her cuticles.

"A table for six, please," boomed Bres in a loud, authoritative voice.

The waitress flinched, and scratched at her ears as though wanting to claw the sound away. "W- we're full," she muttered, with a shudder.

"What about that place up there?" said Sam, more gently.

She glanced upwards as though she had been asked to look at a crawling mass of spiders, and she shrieked slightly. A large, empty table sat on a mezzanine level at the top of a glass staircase, overlooking the whole bar.

Without waiting for her to respond, Bres strode up the steps and settled himself at the centre of the table. The others followed.

Macha's boy and I were the last to ascend. Before we did, the hostess turned to us, recognition and relief flooding her face. We were things that she could make sense of. However, she continued to twitch spasmodically, and in a frightened voice, whispered to us:

"B- but we don't *have* an upstairs!"

"Things change so quickly these days," I replied breezily, before climbing the staircase, and occupying the last chair. I was not remotely surprised to find myself beside Sam again. At least, there was enough space to pull my seat a few feet away from his.

He smirked, as though the gesture had not gone unnoticed, but refrained from comment.

"Do you do this often?" I asked him.

"What, go for cocktails?"

"Tour the city, frightening the wits out of the general public, I mean."

"No, we don't go out often."

"It seems a little cruel."

Sam looked somewhat remorseful. "They forget about it, the instant we leave," he explained, "As though we were never there. If we showed our true faces to everyone, it would cause lasting chaos!"

I nodded. He had a point. I imagined the entirety of central Dublin in the thrall of my immortal companions, all sense gone from their heads and no desires left to them, other than to serve the gods' every, earthly whim.

"But…" I began, cautiously, "These are not your true faces either, are they?"

I expected him to laugh at my disrespectful observation.

He merely smiled, a little wistfully, and a faraway look carried his gaze away from me, and to something unseen. "Perhaps not. We have had these faces for such a long time that they feel… real. But yes, there was something else once. We were something… other." He looked as though he could not quite recall what that 'something other' had been.

His eyes regained their focus, and fixed once more on mine. "Well, Kathy, you've fascinated me again. How do you know so much of these matters?" he asked, "Who told you of our beginnings?"

His earnest expression left me unguarded for a moment. "Some magical beings tried to explain such things to me when I was a child," I replied, "They were not like you. They were small, and placed no importance on their faces. Then, I met The Dagda, and he told me…"

"*The Dagda?*" hissed Sam. He stiffened, as though a cold breeze had whipped him.

I ceased to speak. What was that expression on his face? Dislike? Bitterness? Fear? Respect?

"You know The Dagda?" His knowing eyes were almost blank with astonishment.

"Did you say 'The Dagda'?" demanded Bres from the other side of the table, his face equally grave, "Why on earth are you talking about *him?*"

Sam gave him a look that was difficult to read. "Kathy knows him, apparently."

Bres raised his eyebrows. "And how do *you* know *him*?" he asked suspiciously.

I was still unsure of how to interpret their reactions. Their unusually stiff expressions could mean that they were impressed, or appalled. In case of the latter, I decided to downplay my history with The Dagda. "I met him in the woods a few times when I was younger." I said nothing of the banquet of the immortals, or of our encounter in the *síd*.

"And, what did he say?" enquired Bres carefully.

"Not much. I found him to be a very enigmatic fellow." That, at least, was no lie.

Bres looked relieved. A certain knowing returned to Sam's eyes. Of course, I had been about to tell him of my conversations with The Dagda, and I was sure he sensed that there was more to my story than I had just admitted. He did not press me further, however. For that, I was grateful.

Macha's boy had been at the bar ordering cocktails for, being human, he did not unnerve the staff. He returned triumphantly, with a large tray of refreshments. We all sipped, and Macha squealed in delight, and professed her love of pineapples, and the atmosphere relaxed. She and her playmate giggled and caressed each other in the corner. There was little conversation among the rest of us. Bres and Sam were unusually quiet. I wondered if they were still unnerved by my mention of The Dagda.

Before long, Medb, who had been looking distinctly impatient, slapped her hands on the table a few times for attention. "Let's go to a club now!"

"Very well," concurred Bres.

I rose, and began to button my coat eagerly. A nightclub sounded good. A nightclub sounded far too loud for any further probing, or uncomfortable conversation.

We strolled out of the building, climbed back into our carriage, which I could only assume had been paid to wait, endured another extremely short, cramped journey around the corner, and then alighted again.

The nightclub was dark and smoky. Bres spotted a table that he liked in an alcove. It was occupied, but when the group sensed his approach, they all scuttled off, eyes downcast, looking uncomfortable and scrubbing at their wrists.

Macha's boy was, again, sent to the bar. It occurred to me that, though I saw myself as being far closer to him than to them, in nature, the Great Ones did not treat me as such. It seemed to indicate a very real hierarchy, dictated by who had powers and who did not.

A DJ was playing moody and melodic music, with a sensual beat. Medb was eager to dance. She and Macha persuaded me to join them. I was shy at first, feeling utterly insignificant beside their luminous, luxuriantly writhing bodies, but as the boy brought me more drinks, I began to truly enjoy myself. The prickle was purring, aroused by every light, fluid touch from Medb or Macha as we danced. Eventually, Sam and Bres joined us. I was somewhat inebriated by now, and found myself smiling at Sam instead of warily recoiling. He appeared to enjoy the attention.

We laughed, and drank, and moved together. I felt as though I were in a trance, enraptured by the rhythmic sounds, and the blur of their beautiful faces bobbing across my vision, the trails of their eyes and skin cocooning me in a web of excitement, and carefree release.

All too soon, the DJ announced, through the microphone, that he had finished his set. The main lights flickered on, denoting that the night was at an end.

Medb pouted, and stamped her foot. Instantly, the lights flickered off, the DJ began to play another song, and everybody resumed their revelry.

I drew close to Sam, enjoying the slight haze on his beautiful face through the drunken filter of my eyes. "Is she... *compelling* the club to continue?" I whispered.

He grinned. "Oh yes, this happens."

I giggled. I watched with slightly guilty amusement as the DJ and the bar staff repeatedly attempted to close the club, then suddenly 'thought better' of it. Medb extended the night for a good two hours.

"Come along, we can't stay here forever," said Bres finally, sounding suddenly bored of the whole affair. He looked a little sullen, and glanced at Sam with something approaching resentment in his eyes. If he'd been human, I would almost have thought he was sulking because his companion had received more attention than he had.

"Oh, just one more song," begged Medb.

"No," snapped Bres, "I've had quite enough."

Medb reluctantly allowed the visibly perplexed employees to go home.

Sam and I laughed as we spilled out into the sunlight, for dawn had come and gone. The carriage was still waiting. I wondered if the driver had actually been paid, or compelled by one of them to do our bidding.

"Will you join us back at 'The Horse and Hag'?" Bres asked me.

I shook my head emphatically, and his face grew even more disappointed. I did not want the night to be over, but it was. I was far from sober, and my eyes were weary. I suspected that *they* had no need of sleep, and I envied them a little.

"My bus stop isn't far," I insisted, "I should go."

"May I walk you there?" queried Sam.

I was surprised by the question. "I can look after myself!"

"Oh, I know," he assured me, smiling, "But won't you let me have your company for just a little while longer?" He offered his arm, his eyes playfully pleading.

I did not have the wits about me to resist. I hooked my hand through his elbow, feeling the soft, luxurious fabric of his jacket, and the prickle of his presence. We strolled away.

"Kathy," he said softly, "Fascinating, beautiful Kathy, I would like to know more of you."

"I would like to know more of *you*," I retorted.

"What do you wish to know?"

"What is your true name?"

He chuckled. "My *true* name is not even a word, or a sound that I could express to you."

"What's 'Sam' short for, then?"

"I would rather be just 'Sam' to you."

I sighed, with a flicker of amusement in my resignation. "How predictably enigmatic."

"What did The Dagda really tell you?" His voice was suddenly just a little more serious.

"Why did you react the way you did when I mentioned him?" I countered.

He sighed, and paused as though choosing his words carefully. Was I actually about to get an answer?

"The Dagda is... different," he began, "He is very powerful. Perhaps all of us were, once, but it has been such a long time, and we have all changed, so very much. I don't think he... *approves* of us. I don't think he is content for us to be what we have become."

"Perhaps he knows that you could be..." I trailed off. We had arrived at the bus stop. I leaned against the railing wearily. I had been about to say: 'more', but I found that I did not want to. I did not want to see Sam's beautiful eyes hurt. I did not want to wound the creature who could sing with such feeling, that I had actually begun to wonder if it were possible that an immortal *could* understand emotion... And in that moment, I did not want him to be *more*. I wanted him to be just 'Sam', with his gentle voice, and capricious smile.

"Yes?" He prompted.

I did not respond. I stared into his eyes, and he stared into mine. I felt my grip tighten on his arm imploringly. I felt the warmth of his breath close to mine. I lost myself in those ancient eyes. I do not know which one of us kissed the other first. It felt as though we had melted into each other in unison. Our lips explored each other's, hungrily, and the taste of him was like nectar and sunshine and... Power. I could taste his power. I could feel mine reaching inside him, somehow, caressing him with its invisible hands. He was hard against me, and his strong arms were around my waist. I could not help myself from sinking into his embrace. I fingered his marble sculpted cheek tenderly, almost unable to believe that I finally knew the touch of his shimmering skin.

A dull roar, and the screeching of brakes, announced the bus's arrival. The last shred of sense, embedded somewhere in my fading consciousness, suddenly cried: *What are you doing?*

I wrenched myself away from him. "I- I'm sorry!" I cried.

He raised his eyebrows nonchalantly. "Don't be! I'm not."

"I- I..." I felt tears spring to my eyes.

He looked concerned. "I really thought you wanted to..." he began.

"I did!" I shrieked, "And it *cannot* happen again!"

"Whyever not?"

"Because you're... *you*, and I'm *me*, and..." I swallowed heavily, about to burst into tears. I rushed for the bus, suddenly certain that I must get away, before I disgraced myself entirely.

It's a bit late for that, observed my inner voice disapprovingly.

It was also too late for the bus, it seemed. The doors had closed and it had begun to pull off again. In utter panic, I called on the prickle. It whirled out of me, and into the bus. It somehow turned the steering wheel of the astonished driver in the opposite direction, and the bus pulled back up to the kerb and opened its doors. I jumped on and fled upstairs. I tried to steady my breathing, and finally dared to glance out of the window. Sam was nowhere to be seen.

CHAPTER THIRTEEN

I slept, despite my utter misery. In fact, I slept through the rest of Sunday, and into Monday morning. I readied myself for college mechanically, my mortification utmost on my mind. It had been such an entertaining evening, and I'd had to ruin it all by doing the one thing that I had promised myself not to, and running off hysterically like a lunatic.

When I arrived at the university, I floated robotically from one lecture to another, until it was time for lunch. I realised that, not having eaten the day before, I was in need of sustenance. It had not occurred to me until then. There were far louder voices in my head, to scold me that day, than my hunger.

As I entered the cafeteria, I groaned. Alice was there, waving at me, and motioning for me to join her. The sight of someone associated with the Great Ones made the memory of my shame all the more bitter.

I bought a bowl of mushroom soup and a ham sandwich, and reluctantly presented myself at Alice's table.

"You look a little the worse for wear," she observed with a cheeky smile, "You must have had a good night on Saturday! I'm sorry I missed it. I hear you all went out…"

I put my head in my hands and moaned deeply.

"What's the matter, Kathy? Are you still hungover… or did you not enjoy yourself?"

"I… *enjoyed* myself too much." It occurred to me that, if anyone could understand, it might be Alice.

"Did something happen?" I watched her examine my expression, as I felt a blush rise to my face. Her smile grew triumphant, and a little mocking. "Oh, I see! Something happened between you and Sam, didn't it?"

"I'm such an idiot," I blurted out, "I kissed him."

She burst out laughing, and I did not blame her, considering I had all but lectured her for her dalliance with Medb, when we had last sat in the cafeteria.

"I know, I know," I continued, "You don't have to say it. And to make things worse, I then told him that it couldn't happen again, began to cry, magically commandeered a bus, and ran off!"

She continued to laugh, but her eyes now had a little more sympathy. "It's understandable, Kathy. It can be very emotionally powerful, being with one of them. Your mind was probably in such a whirl that you didn't know what you were saying. He won't pay any attention to it…"

"But, I meant it!" I interjected, "That *cannot* happen again!"

"Why? You're clearly smitten. It's written all over your face."

"Regardless of that, it's asking for trouble! It's utterly ridiculous! I don't want to… get hurt."

She surveyed me, thoughtfully. "I don't think he wants to *hurt* you."

"He won't be able to help himself! He's not like us! I've known others of their kind, and they can be capable of the most frightening cruelty."

"He doesn't seem like that…"

"There was one I knew who didn't seem like that either."

Alice cocked her head to one side. "Was it… your mysterious Étaín?"

I nodded. "When she needed my help, she could make me feel as though I were the only person she cared for in the world… But as soon as she thought I was in the way of something she wanted…"

"Kathy, you can't assume *everyone* is the same, just because you've had one bad experience."

"But, they *are* all the same, aren't they?" I fidgeted miserably. "At least… they were. I can't be sure how different they are from each other now. Has Medb told you much about their fragmentation from the collective energy that was?"

"She and I don't dwell on the past, and neither should you."

I sighed. "I'm such an idiot."

"Well, I think you're being frightfully pessimistic, and making a problem out of something that should be lovely," she declared.

"No, I'm just an idiot," I grumbled.

She pursed her lips, half-amused and half-frustrated, and shook her head. "We'll see how long your resolve lasts," she concluded with a playful wink.

Her refusal to see the gravity of the situation irked me. I finished my lunch, made my excuses, and paced agitatedly around the grounds of the college, until it was time for my next lecture.

Fortunately, it was with Dr. Herbert, which cheered me a little. She was discussing the theme of the goddess of fertility and destruction. It seemed ironic, after my conversation with Alice, that I was forced to contemplate the fact that a deity could be benevolent, and responsible for abundance and harmony, whilst simultaneously reigning over darkness and death.

I thought of the story of Macha, a generous provider and mother figure, who was capable of the most cruel revenge. I also thought about Étaín again, an innocent maiden, too desirable for her own good because of the kingship she bestowed, and the dark and terrible acts I knew her to have perpetrated.

Dr. Herbert explained that creation and death were part of the same natural cycle. Destruction had to occur to make space for regrowth. The goddess was neither positive nor negative, but held different functions in an ancient mythological drama, symbolising the turning of the seasons, and the inevitable ageing and succession of mortal men.

At the end of the lecture, I did not immediately stand up and leave. I sat, and mused a little. Dr. Herbert glanced at me as she gathered her papers.

"You look deep in contemplation, Kathy," she observed.

"Just thinking," I smiled, "I'm fascinated by the dual nature of divinity. None of the gods were unequivocally benevolent. They were worshipped for both what they could give, and what they could take away."

She nodded. "That's a good way of putting it. Of course, the gods are essentially personifications of nature, and we all know that nature can be sublime and cruel in equal measure."

"True. May I ask you an unrelated question?"

"Of course!"

"This is going to sound a little odd, but can you think of the name of a mythological character beginning with the letters 'S-A-M'?"

She furrowed her brow, intrigued. "Did you see it in a partial fragment of an old text, or…?"

"Something like that."

"Hmmm… Leave it with me! I'll have a think."

"Thank you, Dr. Herbert."

"You're very welcome, Dear." She tucked her rebellious, dark curl into her bun, and hurried off.

I sighed deeply, not least because I was due to work at the pub the following night, and *he* would be there. If only I could avoid him until I regained my sanity, and his interest in me waned, as it inevitably would… At that point, I could carouse in the back room to my heart's content, and all would be well. I was laughably, over-confidently certain of it. The only flaw in my strategy was that I could not afford to quit my job until that blessed day dawned, and it seemed altogether impossible to avoid him at 'The Horse and Hag.'

I stomped glumly back to Tom's house from the bus stop that evening. Even the bag of fish and chips, that I was clutching under one arm, did not raise my recently malnourished spirits as much as it should have.

I plodded upstairs, through the cupboard and up my own little staircase. As I reached the top, I froze.

Tom was in my attic. Tom was in my attic, stark naked. Tom was in my attic, stark naked, and urinating into the drawer of my dresser.

I dropped my fish and chips. I screamed at him in utter horror. He did not hear me. The prickle lunged from me, furiously. Its enormous hands surrounded him, dragged him downstairs and out of the front door, and flung him on the grass in the front garden. It closed the door with an indignant slam, and retracted to rejoin me at the top of the house. I watched from my small window, as passers-by laughed and jeered at him. He, apparently, hadn't even woken up.

I surveyed the sodden, stinking drawer in which I kept most of my clothes. I had to get rid of it, and all of its contents, but couldn't bring myself to touch it without retching.

Again, the prickle obliged, yanking the whole drawer out of the dresser and down to the back yard, where it was dumped unceremoniously in one of the outside dustbins.

I shook with rage, and a bitter sense of loss. My favourite, warm jumper, which had felt so comfortable to snuggle into in winter… Those jeans that fitted like a glove… The one bra that didn't chafe… all gone.

I washed my hands with fervour, for about a quarter of an hour, ate my tepid fish and chips, and cried myself to sleep, bitterly.

I wish I could have seen Tom when he came to, nude in front of his house, wondering if he was having one of *those* mortifying nightmares, and soon realising that he was not.

He was glowering at me in the hallway, in his dressing gown, when I came downstairs.

"What on earth has been going on?" he demanded.

"What do you mean?"

"I- I was locked out of the house, so I came around the back to get in the kitchen door, and found *my* furniture in the bin! How dare you? You'll be paying for that!"

"Oh, you mean the drawer that you *pissed* in? I don't think so!"

He looked as if he were about to slap me. "You're getting madder by the day."

"*I'm* not the one who woke up naked in the garden!"

As he unleashed an explosive tirade of profanities, I rushed out of the house.

The day passed far too quickly, and I found myself on my way to 'The Horse and Hag' for my shift, rather hoping that a car would run me over on my way, so that I had a good excuse to avoid it.

It didn't, and I turned up promptly. The eerie caress of the prickle left me in no doubt that *they,* and most likely *he,* were there, just a corridor away. Evelyn greeted me cheerfully, and fed me a chicken and leek pie. It should have been utterly delectable, but tasted like ashes in my mouth.

"Are you alright, Dear?" asked the landlady, noticing my unhappy demeanour.

"Not really," I replied, pushing the accompanying peas around my plate despondently, "My landlord is being… difficult."

She patted my shoulder with concern. "Yes, Alice said something about that when she recommended you for the bar job. He steals from you, doesn't he?"

"It gets worse." I lowered my voice, so that the couple of customers in the front bar wouldn't overhear. "He drinks heavily, sleepwalks naked around the house, and last night I found him… *urinating* in my dresser drawer."

Evelyn grimaced. "How revolting! You shouldn't have to put up with that!"

"Put up with what?" I was surprised that I hadn't noticed Sam's approach, but there he was, in all of his splendour, looking as maddeningly beautiful as ever.

I was lost for words, and quite sure that the colour in my cheeks was deeper than that of the rich, velvet curtains.

Evelyn filled him in on what we had been discussing.

As Sam listened, the expression on his face changed, from a gentle smile, to something cold and dark. His usually bright eyes clouded over, into a black rage. He was suddenly terrifying, and I shuddered.

"This will not do," he exploded, "Nobody can treat *you* like that! Who is this fellow? A mere, drunken mortal? He has the audacity to treat *you* like that? Why don't you just toss him out of the window for his impudence?"

"I- I can't really just *kill* him," I explained gingerly, still unnerved by the powerful change in Sam's manner, "I'd go to prison."

He tutted. "Ah, yes, these irritating human traditions. Well, you can't possibly *stay* there!"

"I have nowhere else to go."

Sam thought for a moment, with deep concentration. "Evelyn, why doesn't Kathy just take the room upstairs?"

"The room upstairs?" repeated Evelyn.

"Yes," insisted Sam with emphasis, "*The room upstairs*. You know, the one over the kitchen, upstairs from the store room?"

"Oh, *that* room," she smiled, "What a good idea!"

I looked between them, suspiciously. I had a feeling that Evelyn had no prior knowledge of any such room.

"Why don't we go and show it to her?" suggested Sam.

He led, as we made our way into the store room. Sure enough, there was a small, spiral staircase in the corner that I had never noticed before. It seemed as much of a surprise to Evelyn as it was to me. We wound our way up, and opened a door at the top.

Inside was a bedroom. It was light and airy, and simply furnished, though the large, wrought iron bed and the sumptuous pillows and blankets upon it, looked of excellent quality. It had a wardrobe, a desk and chair, and a bookshelf. The floor was of dark wood, like the rest of the building. A cheerful little fire danced in a small but decorative wrought iron fireplace, which was adorned with Celtic knotwork, and depictions of horses and hounds. A thick, fur rug lay invitingly on the floor. I thought it was the loveliest room I had ever seen. It could have been designed especially for me. Anything more opulent would have made me uncomfortable.

"Very nice," observed Evelyn, abandoning any pretence that she was familiar with the chamber.

Sam watched me, his face now gentle again, and his expression almost timid, as though he were awaiting my reaction with trepidation. "So, what do you think, Kathy? Would you be comfortable here?"

I quite forgot myself in my excitement. "It's perfect," I gushed, "Of course I would!"

He appeared pleased. "Good. Now, go and get your things, and come straight back. We can't have you spending one more night in that… *man's* house." There was a flicker of that darkness in his eyes, again.

"I have to work," I protested.

"I'm sure Sylvie will do it," said Evelyn, "You can do her shift tomorrow evening instead. I'll just go and check with her." She went back downstairs.

"So, you see?" grinned Sam, "Everything is resolved! Now, off you go!"

I couldn't help smiling back. I loved the room, and his kindness, but an uncomfortable thought was churning in the back of my mind, and I felt that I must address it before fully embracing my good fortune.

"Sam," I began, "Thank you for… all of this. I really appreciate it."

"I don't know what you're talking about," he said, with a twinkle in his eye. We both knew he had created a room where there was none.

"But…"

"Yes?"

"I meant what I said the other night."

"What, in particular?"

I fidgeted nervously. "After we kissed, I said that it couldn't happen again."

"Oh, yes, I know that. I don't really understand it, but you can explain it to me another time." He did not look heartbroken. I was both relieved, and bitterly disappointed.

"Very well then," I exclaimed, trying to sound as nonchalant as he did, "I'd better go and pack!"

I had never been so happy to see Tom's house. Even if I had believed I had the strength to compel the prickle to return to my attic, gather my belongings and bring them to me in Temple Bar, I would have chosen to come in person, for the blissful feeling of knowing that it was the last time I would have to see the miserable man and his festering abode.

He was rummaging through the fridge when I entered, and did not notice me slip upstairs. I pulled out my suitcase, and crammed everything into it hastily. It did not take long, as I had discarded most of my urine-soaked clothing, along with the drawer.

"Goodbye, attic," I muttered, "I'd like to say it's been nice knowing you, but it really hasn't."

I shut the small door, triumphantly, and clattered back downstairs.

Tom turned, alerted to my presence, and scowled as he noticed the suitcase. "Where do you think you're off to?" he demanded.

"Somewhere you'll never find me, you disgusting creep," I replied.

"You still owe me rent!"

"I owe you nothing," I snapped.

He began to swear loudly.

"Actually," I continued, "That's not quite true. I do owe you *something* for the way you've welcomed me into your home, and the level of respect you've shown me."

There was a loud crack, as the kitchen door ruptured from side to side. There was another crash as the living room door splintered into a thousand fragments. The sound of utter destruction continued throughout the house, as the prickle found and decimated every door in the putrid place.

Tom dropped his beer and began to make petrified, gurgling sounds. He fell to his knees in terror.

"Now," I concluded brightly, "I think the money you stole from me should just about cover the damage, so we're done here. I wish you a long and excruciating existence!"

And with that, I left the house, hopped on the bus, and moved to 'The Horse and Hag'.

As soon as I had folded away my few remaining clothes, and arranged my books on the shelves, I ventured downstairs to see if I could be of any help at the bar. I felt guilty for inconveniencing Sylvie.

She greeted me warmly, assured me that she had been perfectly happy to swap shifts, and invited me to sit down for a drink. I realised that a drink was an extremely attractive proposition, after my eventful day.

"So, I hear you have a room here now," remarked Sylvie, as she poured me a beer, "Fancy that!"

I nodded. "So it would seem."

"I'd love to see it!"

"You're welcome any time." As I sipped my drink, it occurred to me that Evelyn hadn't really been given the opportunity to refuse my installation over her kitchen. "I hope you and your mother don't mind…" I said, tentatively.

Sylvie laughed. "Oh, not at all! Mum said she was glad to have someone keeping an eye on the place overnight, and that it was nice to see one of *them* using their gifts for someone else's benefit, for once." She suddenly paused, wide-eyed, as though she were afraid that she'd said something she shouldn't have. "You… did know about the room, didn't you? Where it came from?"

"It was pretty obvious," I reassured her, "He *tried* to hide it, but he won't be winning an award for his acting skills any time soon."

She chuckled.

As if on cue, the prickle announced that Sam was nearby. He pulled up a stool beside me at the bar, and asked: "Is everything alright with the room?"

I smiled. "It's wonderful. Now, all I have to do is save up for some new clothes, because I binned everything that Tom had tainted with his filth."

"Naturally," nodded Sam, with a dark shiver, "I'm glad you have accommodation more worthy of you now. Of course, you truly belong in a palatial chamber, adorned with jewels and other wonders, but I sense that might not be to your taste."

"You gauged it perfectly."

"Gauged?" he repeated in mock-confusion, still unwilling to openly admit that the room was an enchantment, though he was far too astute not to know that I knew. I wondered if he was reluctant to come out and say it, because he wished to spare me any increased sense of obligation that speaking the words might create. I dismissed the idea, concluding that I was probably ascribing far too human reasoning to one such as he. He most likely just enjoyed the game of his feigned ignorance.

I told him about my parting gift to Tom, and he chuckled approvingly. He asked if I would join them for drinks in the back room. It felt rude to decline, considering what he had done for me, but I was very weary. Besides, I was still determined to limit the time I spent with Sam, however difficult it might be, in the hopes that my longing to feel his skin against mine would eventually recede.

"I would, but…" I paused, "I used up a lot of energy, destroying Tom's house before I left the place today, and I'm really looking forward to a night in my beautiful, new bed."

"Well, I'm glad he got some comeuppance, though if it were me, I'd have made his blood boil from the inside until he was cooked, and fed him to a hungry hound."

I knew that I should be more disturbed than I was, by the casual way in which he spoke of murder. I reminded myself that I could not expect a sense of human morality from one such as he. After all, he was something entirely other, merely wearing a face. It was hard to believe it, though, when the mask he sported was so beautiful, and his songs spoke of the deepest of emotions, and his actions towards me were so kind.

I sighed.

Sylvie left the bar to collect some glasses before closing.

"So," said Sam, "You were going to explain it to me."

"Explain what?"

"Why you don't want to kiss me again." His tone was utterly calm, and his manner entirely free of embarrassment.

A furious flush rose to my cheeks. "I never said I would explain it to you."

"Even so, would you mind?"

"Well… we're… *different*," I muttered.

He contemplated my words for a moment. "Everything is different from something."

"I- I may have powers, but I'm just a girl. How could we ever be expected to truly understand each other? I will age, and sicken, and die, and you will remain as you are. I don't know what it's like to live countless lifetimes, and I never will."

"I wish you could," he observed, staring at me a little wistfully, "I think I would enjoy knowing you in countless lifetimes."

The simple, earnest way in which he professed something of such magnitude made me want to wrap my arms around him, and cover him in kisses.

"But that can never be," I insisted, feeling a little cruel, and deeply frustrated, "And *this* can never be."

He shrugged, looking only mildly disappointed. "If you say so."

I reminded myself again that his words hinted at emotions he could not feel… That I was a new, favourite curiosity to a child, that he believed he would not discard until the end of his days. Days were not the same for children as they were for adults, and days were certainly not the same for humans as they were for immortals.

"I should go to bed," I stated, again irritatingly close to tears.

"Very well then," replied Sam, rising from his stool, "Sweet dreams, Kathy."

I would wish you the same, but your kind doesn't sleep.

I realised that the one thing missing from my perfect, new room was a bathroom of any description. Of course, bodily functions and washing facilities were of no concern to the Great Ones, so the slight omission was understandable. I crept downstairs with my toiletries and brushed my teeth in one of the pub lavatory sinks. I resolved to shower at the gym the following morning. It was a minor inconvenience, in comparison to living with Tom.

When I returned to my room, I took a moment to look out of the window. I soon recognised the street below as the one that led to the back door behind the tapestry.

It was then that I saw them: A group of three, making their way in that direction. One of them was tiny in size, leaving me in no doubt that it was one of the small ones. He did not look faded or forlorn in the way that the last ones had. His gait was steady and I could clearly see a shock of healthy, bright red hair protruding from his hat.

His two companions were taller… Not tall enough to be fully grown adults, but somewhere in between. I frowned. Could they be children? If so, why would they be coming to a bar at night, with a little magical creature? Suddenly, one of them looked up, and I saw his face. These were no children. Those enormous, ancient eyes pierced the darkness, and left me in no doubt that they were something other… Something I had not seen before. As they disappeared from view, I wondered if they had been admitted to the immortal gathering downstairs.

I had never seen magical beings there, other than the Great Ones, but I conceded that they, and 'The Horse and Hag', were still quite new to me. Perhaps other ancient creatures sometimes joined in their festivities. I was very tempted to put my clothes on, and present myself in the back room, claiming to have changed my mind about drinks.

A wearier part of me wanted to enjoy one, peaceful night in my alluring bed. It reasoned that the mysterious figures may not be downstairs at all. They may well have been three beings, entirely unconnected to the Great Ones, enjoying a midnight stroll in Temple Bar. If I turned up in the back room now, for no good reason, what would Sam think? That I had entirely abandoned my resolve to end our bizarre courtship of sorts? Would I have to endure giving another, excruciating explanation of why we couldn't be together? I told myself that, if they were indeed guests of the Great Ones, I would encounter them again. After all, there was really no escaping the place now.

I woke up the following morning, after a truly wonderful night's sleep, and stretched blissfully, like a cat in the sunshine. It was true. I had a new home. An unfamiliar sensation filled me: Contentment.

I looked at my dearest possessions, arranged carefully around the room, and smiled. Liam's little wooden carving sat among my books. I had barely given it a thought as I'd unpacked it the previous evening. I felt guilty for having been so immersed in my new life, that I hadn't wondered, in some time, how he was, or how he was filling his days. Was he alone and dejected in the woods, or had he met someone who could make him happier than I had? A part of me hoped that the latter were true. Another part of me, of which of which I was less proud, was not thrilled by the idea.

I groaned slightly, when I remembered that I would have to shower at the gym, but it was a small price to pay. I got up, and gathered my belongings for the day ahead.

The short walk to the university was a pleasure in comparison with the slow, crawling bus journey I had so despised. I swam and showered, and retreated to the library. I did not have time to investigate any more of my immortal companions in the books that day. I had an important essay to work on for Dr. Herbert, and wanted to get it just right, so Mr. Books spent the morning helping me with my research.

I went to the cafeteria for lunch, and passed Alice on my way.

"Congratulations," she gushed excitedly, "I heard all about your new room, and what you did to Tom's house!"

"When did you hear that? Were you in the pub last night?"

"I was with Medb in the back room," she sighed, dreamily, "You must have been unpacking when I arrived. I didn't know you were there, until Sam came back from speaking to you, but he said you'd gone to bed."

"Was… anyone else there?" I asked, carefully.

"Well, Bres and Macha and…"

"But did you see anyone… *unusual*?"

She frowned and shook her head.

"Never mind," I shrugged. It seemed that I had made the right decision by staying in my room. The small one and the two, strange beings I had seen from the window, must have been on their way elsewhere. Of course, I then remembered that Alice could not see Mr. Books, so it was possible that they *had* been there, but not visible to her. I brushed my thoughts aside. "Would you like to join me for lunch?"

She bit her lip nervously. "I can't today. I have… something to do."

I was surprised by her reaction. She had always seemed eager for my company before. I wondered what could account for her uncomfortable and secretive demeanour. I hoped that she wasn't upset about my room, or jealous of the fact that Medb had not made her a similar offer.

I waved her off, and had lunch alone.

When I returned to 'The Horse and Hag', with a little time to spare before my shift, I raced excitedly up to my new room to make absolutely sure that it was still there. I pushed open the door, and was astonished to find Alice and Sylvie sitting on the bed. I had, of course, told the latter that she was welcome any time, but I had rather expected her to wait until I was present.

"W- what are you two doing here?" I asked.

They looked at each other and giggled.

"Sorry for the imposition," grinned Sylvie, "But we…"

"Oh, just look in the wardrobe," exploded Alice, clapping her hands exuberantly.

Puzzled, I opened the wardrobe door, and my mouth fell open. It had been quite empty when I left, and was now filled with clothes. What was this? Another enchantment? Speechless with surprise, I fingered some of the garments. They were of exactly the style that I favoured: Simple and form-fitting, in muted colours. I noticed that they still had tags on them from a clothes shop. *That's an unlikely level of detail, even for magic.*

"Where did these *come* from?" I exclaimed.

"Sam sent us shopping," squealed Alice, "Do you like them? We have the receipts, so you can exchange anything you're not keen on. We mainly went for the sort of thing I've seen you wear at college, and then added a couple of dresses we thought might suit you for clubbing. I hope we got it right."

"They're… perfect!"

"Oh, good!" Sylvie bounced up and down on the bed with excitement. "After you went to bed last night, he asked for our advice on getting you a new wardrobe, in place of all the clothes you'd had to throw away. So glad you like them!"

"It was very sensible of him to consult us," added Alice, "If he had magicked something up, you'd probably be trailing around in velvet ballgowns, or leather corsets."

I sighed deeply, and sat down beside them on the bed. "It's just… too much. I don't feel I can accept…"

"One does not turn down gifts from *them,*" stated Alice.

I had a feeling she was right. "Thank you both so much for picking out such lovely things."

"You're very welcome!"

"I suppose he paid for everything?"

"Naturally."

I sighed again. "And, I suppose it was all frightfully expensive?"

"Well…"

"I feel… embarrassed," I groaned.

"Don't be," smiled Sylvie, "Money is nothing to them. They probably just conjure it as required. Who knows if it even lasts, once it reaches the bank, or disappears in a puff of smoke?"

"It's still very thoughtful of him…"

"I know! I wish *I* had someone to send my friends shopping for me," she laughed.

"Is he downstairs?"

They nodded in unison.

We all filed down the little staircase, and into the main bar.

Evelyn was waiting. She asked me if I would like my meal now.

"Thank you," I replied, "I just need to go into the back room for a few minutes to thank…"

"Oh, yes, of course," she smiled, "I heard all about it."

I ran down the corridor, then paused to compose myself before entering the chamber. Grateful as I was, I refused to rush in like a simpering fool.

I felt as though his eyes had been on me even before I walked in. They were huge, and hopeful, and full of anticipation.

I went to him, and crouched down beside his chair, a hand on its arm to steady myself. "Sam," I said quietly, "Thank you so much."

"It was my pleasure," he grinned, "Did they buy the right sorts of things?"

"They couldn't have done any better."

He appeared satisfied. "That pleases me."

"You really don't have to keep doing things for me, you know…"

"Why not? It's all very easy for me, and it makes you happy."

"Well… thank you again. It was a very kind thought."

He laughed a little, looking slightly surprised. I suspected that 'kind' was not a word he had been called very often. He patted my hand, and the sensation of his skin rippled through me.

"I have to work," I announced, getting to my feet and taking my leave a little too quickly. In the corridor, I leaned against the wall, tried to steady my breathing, and pressed the hand he had touched to my lips.

Later that evening, Evelyn asked me to take some rubbish outside. As I hauled the bags towards the bins, a small noise from the corner caught my attention. I placed the rubbish on the ground, as quietly as I could, and crept over to investigate.

As I suspected, another dazed, blank, wretched little creature was shivering against the wall. It gazed at me forlornly, all big eyes and terror. It was wearing a hat that I thought I recognised.

"Please, little friend," I whispered, "Tell me what happened to you."

The small one shuddered. "H- h- he," he stammered, his voice nothing but a memory of a breath, "He took… something from me…"

"Who was it? What did he take?"

I heard a door slam. Forgetting not to startle the small one, I ran in the direction of the sound and found myself staring at the same door that lay behind the tapestry in the back room of the pub. "Who's there?" I called. I received no response.

I hurried back around to the front. The small fellow had fled. I raced through the main bar, into the back room. The immortals were carousing as raucously as ever, in their usual places. Only Nuadu stood near the tapestry, looking uncomfortable. I strode right over to him, and placed my hands on my hips in an attempt to look as authoritative as possible.

"You," I hissed, "Was that you at the back door, Nuadu?"

He glared at me furiously, and pressed a finger to his lips.

"I heard the back door slam from outside," I insisted, "Was it you?"

The others now noticed my presence, and my less than friendly demeanour, and grew silent with curiosity.

"Is something wrong, Kathy?" called Sam.

"I- I don't know…" I trailed off. I wasn't exactly sure what I was I accusing Nuadu *of*. Had he seen something? Had he *done* something to the small one outside? Was it all a complete coincidence, and the small one had come from elsewhere? Nuadu continued to stare at me, a grim warning in his eyes.

I swallowed heavily. "Never mind." Turning to Sam, I added: "I'd better get back to the bar."

He nodded cheerfully, though his eyes remained on Nuadu, as I walked away, clearly wondering what had transpired between us.

I left the room. *Just as well I'll be living here now,* I thought. It would give me an opportunity to keep a closer eye on Nuadu, and see if there was any connection between him and the plight of the small, magical creatures in the neighbourhood.

It wouldn't do to start throwing accusations around, unless I was sure, particularly when I couldn't be certain of how the other gods would react. They appeared to treat Nuadu with a certain lack of courtesy, but there was no reason to believe that they would not side with their own kind over me. Though, thankfully, it seemed that that my lovely room had not been created with the assumption that I would pursue some sort of affair with Sam, what might happen if I really angered them, and him? Would the lovely little chamber just disappear, and leave me out in the cold? I determined that I would have to be subtle in my approach, if I wanted to get to the bottom of it.

After work, I retired to my room, and curled up in my soft bed, with a book. My head was nodding and I had almost begun to doze off, when the prickle seized me by the shoulders in alarm, pressing urgent talons into my skin. Something was wrong. Instinctively, I rushed to the window, and looked outside. The two, strange immortal fellows were back, but this time they were dragging the poor small one with the hat down the street. He was squirming and twisting, trying to free himself from their clutches, but was no match for them. I immediately raced downstairs, and out of the pub, to confront them.

"You there," I cried, as I ran towards them, "What are you doing?"

"Taking this one back," replied one of them, "Escaped earlier." Then, he turned to face me, and frowned. "Who are you?"

"Taking him back where?"

"Mind your own business."

"Let go of him this instant," I yelled.

The fellow who had addressed me lifted his free hand, and aimed a magical blow in my direction. Momentarily surprised, I jumped out of its path too late, and it collided with my arm. It stung.

The furious prickle rose from me, and lashed out, knocking him clean off his feet. He appeared stunned, and a little fearful. I realised that he was not very strong.

His companion then sprang into action, aiming a similar blow at me. The prickle batted it away like a mildly irritating fly, and it rebounded and hit him squarely in the jaw. In his surprise, he loosened his grip on the small one.

"Run!" I screamed.

The small one tore away, and his captors made to follow.

"Oh no, you don't," I muttered, and sprang at them both, kicking one in the stomach and knocking the other with my elbow. They staggered backwards, clearly weakened. They may have been magical, but it seemed that I did not even need my powers to beat them.

Stubbornly, they faced me again, and once more, I leaped at them, kicking and punching them both repeatedly until they sagged down against the wall, looking distinctly the worse for wear.

"Please," begged one, "Let us go. We'll leave the small fellow alone."

I didn't believe a word of it, but I reasoned that I'd, at least, given him enough of a head start to find a tiny place to hide, out of their reach.

"Not so fast," I said, raising my hand threateningly. They both gulped. "Where were you taking him?"

"We can't tell you," whimpered the other, "We can't talk about it!"

"You will, if you value your lives!"

They made a break for it, hurtling down the street in the opposite direction from the small one. I let them go. Angry and curious as I was, it did not seem a reasonable course of action to chase them around town, pulverising them for the rest of the night. Besides, my injured arm was sore, and I wanted to take something for the pain.

I went behind the bar, and rummaged about under the counter, where I was sure that I had seen a packet of aspirin. Suddenly, the prickle shimmered, and Sam was there.

"I *thought* I sensed you out here," he said gently, "What are you doing downstairs, at this time of night?" He noticed the searing, red mark on my arm, and froze. "What happened?"

I wasn't sure how much to tell him. I had no idea if the ones I had fought were connected to *these* immortals, or not. I suspected that they might have been dragging the small one back to Nuadu, but I couldn't be sure.

"There was an… altercation outside."

"What sort of altercation?" he asked, "That is not the mark of a human blow."

"No, it was two… magical fellows, up to no good."

"What were they doing?"

"I- I'm not sure, really. Don't worry, I fought them off."

He looked concerned, but held his tongue. I concluded that he could tell, from my tone, that I did not wish to be questioned further on the matter.

"Come here," he instructed me.

"No, I'm fine, really…"

"Don't be silly. Come here."

I sighed, and went to him. He placed his hands on my shoulders, spun me around, and marched me down the corridor to the back room. He kept hold of me firmly. The prickle soared at his touch.

Sam led me to Bres, and said: "Help me to heal this."

Bres raised his eyebrows, taking in my injury. "How did that happen?"

"Never mind. Just do it."

Bres glared at him suspiciously, but put down his cigarette, and placed his hand on my arm. His touch was cool and warm. My skin tingled at the sensation. The pain gradually subsided, and I looked down to see that the blemish was gone. Sam let go of me. Bres did not remove his hand from my skin, though. Instead, it slid down to my wrist, lingered for a moment, and then seized my hand with a surprising intensity.

"You have great power, Kathy. I can feel it," he remarked, "I'd love just a taste."

Sam bristled beside me. "Don't you dare." His voice was quiet, but tinged with a steely anger that chilled me.

"Oh, come on, Kathy. Just one little sip, for your old nemesis," wheedled Bres, his tone playful but his eyes serious as death.

I was not sure what he meant, but I wrenched my hand out of his grasp instinctively.

Sam's stare grew black, and before I knew it, Bres had been flung out of his chair and across the room. He looked up from the floor, with an expression of shock and purest hatred. For a moment, his face contorted with fury, and was no longer beautiful, but a hideous, snarling thing with mighty, snapping jaws.

Medb and Macha were watching, their faces aghast. They looked from Bres to Sam, and back again, as though they could not comprehend how such a thing could have happened.

Sam walked over to Bres and stood above him. His bearing was frightening. "Do not test me," he said darkly, and left the room.

Without a moment's hesitation, I followed him. He was standing in the main bar, his expression stunned, as though he could not believe what he had done. I thought I saw him tremble a little, but could not be sure whether it was with rage or fear.

"Are you… okay?" I asked timidly.

He turned to face me, his enormous eyes bewildered and desperate, and closer to human than I had ever seen them. "I did what I had to," he replied simply. His voice was gentle again.

"Will Bres be angry?" It was a foolish question. I had seen the magnitude of his fury rupture the peace of his exquisite mask, for that brief, awful moment. "Are you… safe?"

"There's not a lot he can do to me," Sam reassured me.

"What did he want to do to *me*?"

"He wanted to drain some of your power into himself."

I felt sick. I remembered Étaín, standing in that clearing, while Fúamnach and I devoured her, and her blank, helpless stare as she became just a little… Less.

It had taken an intricate ritual, and both of our strength, to do it, but then Étaín was a Great One. As a mortal, I might be easy pickings for one of their kind. I shuddered.

Sam noticed my distress with concern. "Don't worry. I will never let that happen."

I couldn't help it. I threw my arms around him, and held him tightly. He embraced me, burying his face in my hair. I could feel his sweet breath on my neck. His power rippled through my body as we held each other.

Suddenly, I did not care about the fact that he was a god. I did not care if I became one of those simpering halfwits, fetching and carrying in the back room. Nothing mattered but how much I wanted him. If it made me a fool, so be it.

"Come with me," I whispered, and took him by the hand, through the store room, up the little staircase, and into my bedroom.

CHAPTER FOURTEEN

I closed the door behind us, and kissed him deeply, winding my fingers through his luxuriant hair. He picked me up with one strong arm, as though I weighed nothing, and placed me gently on the desk, so that my face was closer to his.

To my disappointment, he stepped back.

"I thought you said this couldn't happen," he observed with amusement, and perhaps, just a little astonishment.

"I say a lot of things."

"I don't want you to think you have to do this out of some sense of gratitude…"

I groaned. "Well, this is a fine time for you to develop a mortal conscience."

"I know," he laughed, "My instincts are telling me to shut up and take you."

"Would you please do them the courtesy of obeying?"

He drew closer, then paused. "I want you to know…"

"What?"

His fingers brushed my cheek tenderly, the expression in his eyes still far too human. "You're not one of those… 'sycophants', as you call them, to me. I want you more than anything."

I almost believed him. I reached out for him, and he tumbled into my arms, his soft lips on my neck and shoulders. I moaned, and wrapped my legs around him, pulling him closer against me. We kissed again, and I felt myself melting into him, his taste intoxicating. I wanted to experience every part of him. I wanted to crawl into him, and feel him from the inside out. I wanted… *him*.

His hands caressed my back, and my skin shivered. Suddenly, my vest top had been ripped off, and hurled to the floor, though his hands had not performed the action. I considered reciprocating, and sending the prickle to remove his clothes, but chose to do so with my own hands instead. I wanted to feel… everything. He touched my breasts, and I bit down on his shoulder to stop myself from crying out. I clung to him, and he picked me up again, carried me across the room, and tossed me onto the bed.

I looked up at him as he stood over me, and gasped at the magnificence of his naked body. I implored him, with my eyes, to come to me. Even a moment without his touch seemed unbearable.

He was in my arms again. I pressed myself against him, feeling his hardness and my readiness, and I whimpered with desire. He teased me before he let me have what I wanted, kissing my breasts, and allowing his magic to ripple across me, bringing me such pleasure that I could barely endure it. I tingled in places that I hadn't known existed.

The prickle writhed on my skin. Its tendrils reached out hungrily, for the infinite, intangible parts of him and, when they met, their invisible fingers intertwined as closely as our bodies. It was then that I knew what it had been yearning for, so ferociously: An instinctive connection, the existence of which I could not have imagined… Until now.

I whimpered with desire. I desperately wanted everything he had to give. We gazed at each other, in breathless anticipation, before I finally felt him inside me. The prickle swelled, and I quaked. I felt, somehow, almost devastatingly, close to completeness.

Sam was strong, and sure, and powerful, as he took me, and gave into his own, ravening lust. I could feel something approaching: The inevitable call of impending, glorious release. As we drew close to climaxing, we gripped each other desperately. My nails were in his back. His fingers were clenched around my hips, the might and longing in them pleasurably painful.

The moment came: That excruciatingly beautiful crash of a thousand waves. He roared. I cried out. Our magic exploded from our bodies, in a dazzling blast. The books toppled from the shelf. The window rattled.

We sank into each other's arms, and I burst into tears. I did not feel ashamed of the display of emotion. I had felt the true weight of his countless lifetimes in that moment. I had glimpsed eternity. I wanted my life to stop: Not to cease, but to pause at that ecstatic instant, so that nothing else would happen, or exist, ever again.

I raised my eyes and noticed that he too looked moved. We stared at each other, both wanting to speak, but having no words. He must have had a million lovers, but his eyes told me that he had experienced our union with the same intensity as I had.

We lay there. We lay there for a long time, intertwined and utterly lost in the feeling between us. Dawn came and went. The sky shone brightly. Dusk fell. We barely noticed, utterly entranced by exploring each other's bodies.

Finally, I whispered: "I... have to go downstairs."

"That's not the first thing I expected you to say," he smirked.

I blushed slightly. "I need to... erm... use the ladies' room."

His eyes widened in surprise, then comprehension. "I-I didn't think..." he stammered, looking utterly embarrassed.

"I'll only be a minute."

"Why don't you just... use the one over there?" he suggested, quickly.

I turned curiously. Another door had appeared in the wall. I rose to investigate, and found a little bathroom, complete with a toilet, sink and luxurious bathtub.

When I returned, he smiled playfully. "Is that better?"

I giggled. "Thank you."

"I'm so sorry I didn't think of it before."

"Why would you?"

He opened his arms, and I ran into them, gasping with excitement to feel him near me again.

"You must remind me of these mortal necessities," he observed.

"Very well then. I'm starving!"

"I think I can do something about that."

I followed his gaze towards the window, and noticed a small table with two chairs, laden with fruit, meats, bread, and a bottle of mead. It had not been there before. He sat and ate with me, though I was sure he had no need of sustenance.

"Do you enjoy food?" I asked him.

He smiled and nodded. "It is one of the many pleasures of this world I have come to savour."

After our meal, we snuggled up among the blankets and pillows again, stroking each other's skin and gazing at each other. It occurred to me that the first man with whom I'd had sex in a bed, was anything but a man.

"What are you going to do about Bres?" I asked suddenly, "Will he forgive you for interfering?"

"I'll give him a little time to cool off. I'm sure it will be fine," he replied, attempting to sound reassuring, though his expression seemed grave. "I think you'd better stay away from him, though, unless I'm there."

"Oh, don't worry. I intend to." I shivered.

Sam held me closer to him, his arms protective. I dozed a little, half-waking every so often to feel his caress on my skin. At one point, I murmured:

"I'm sorry, this must be very boring for you."

He kissed my forehead. "Time is of little consequence to me. I don't want to be anywhere else."

I nuzzled his smooth, firm chest, and went back to sleep.

When the following morning came, I awoke, and his beautiful eyes brightened to see mine. I longed to forget about the real world, and everything in it, and just be with him, but I had already lost a day in his embrace.

"Sam," I said, "I have to tell you something."

He looked apprehensive. "Please, please," he begged, "Don't say that this can't happen again!"

I burst out laughing, and he appeared relieved.

"I was going to say that I should really go to college."

"Oh," he answered brightly, "Of course you should! As I said, you must remind me of these things. I don't *have*… things to do, so I don't tend to consider such matters."

I showered and dressed, and he watched me hungrily from the bed. It took all of my strength not to peel my clothes off again, and run to him.

"May I escort you?" he asked.

"Certainly," I replied with a smile, amused by his old-fashioned, courtly turn of phrase.

We walked, hand in hand, to the university, and I marvelled inwardly at how strange it was to feel almost like a normal couple… Apart from the way in which passers-by avoided us, and scuttled away uncomfortably, as we approached. When we reached the gate, he kissed me goodbye tenderly, and then he was gone.

I sighed.

I turned, and came face to face with Alice. Her hands were on her hips, and she was wearing a very deliberate smirk.

"Well, well," she commented, "It seems your resolve failed even sooner than I thought it would! I owe Sylvie a fiver."

I narrowed my eyes. "Shut up," I ordered.

"Now, remind me, how did you put it again? You wouldn't go 'chasing after a god, like the rest of the sycophants in the back room'?"

"Shut up."

She burst out laughing. "I'm happy for you."

I smiled bashfully. "So am I."

She linked my arm cheerfully, and we walked towards the library.

"You must tell me," she said, her tone suddenly more serious, "What happened in the pub two nights ago, after I left?"

"Sam and Bres had… a disagreement. Did Medb tell you about it?"

"She mentioned *something*, but she was quite evasive. I was there last night, and the atmosphere felt very strained. They do have their squabbles, but this must have been something more. You weren't there, I noticed. I expect you had better gods to do… sorry, I mean *things*." She smirked again. "Sam wasn't there either, funnily enough."

I blushed, and she giggled.

"So, what happened?" she prompted me.

"Bres said something Sam didn't like, and he threw him across the room," I recounted, entirely omitting my part in the matter. Something about Bres's intentions towards me, and Sam's reaction, felt too dangerous to be spoken of casually.

"I do hope they'll make up," sighed Alice.

I nodded nervously.

"I'm sure you were of great comfort to Sam afterwards," she remarked, jovial again.

I chuckled. "Shut up."

Alice finally finished teasing me, and went to one of her lectures. I went to the library to continue researching my essay. Dr. Herbert was there and, consequently, Mr. Books was not visibly present. This offered me the rare opportunity to browse the bookshelves unaided, and I lost myself in little tales of truths gone by. I saw no mention of a character whose name began with 'Sam', though. I contemplated asking Dr. Herbert where I would find information on Bres and Nuadu, as these were figures I had still not investigated, and I was utterly suspicious of them both in different ways. However, I then realised that it was time for me to leave the library for a lecture.

I whispered a farewell to Dr. Herbert on my way out.

She looked up with a friendly smile. "Oh, Kathy," she said, "Before you go, I've been meaning to ask you: Are you sure that the name beginning with 'Sam' isn't the festival of Samain?"

I shook my head. "I'm pretty sure it's the name of a god or deity."

"Okay, leave it with me! I'll think further." She waved and returned to her reading.

My lectures seemed more tedious than they usually were that day. The department professor droned on and on about the possible etymology of a certain word in Old Irish, before concluding that nobody had truly got to the bottom of it, and scholars remained undecided.

Another lecturer attempted to engage us in a talk on medieval cooking implements, and showed us slide after slide of photographs of near-identical cauldrons.

One student raised her hand, and asked: "Is there any evidence for the existence of cauldrons?"

There was a shocked silence.

"Apart from the actual cauldrons in these photos, you mean?" replied the lecturer in astonishment.

I groaned inwardly. I had no patience for such nonsense that day. My mind was not truly there, and every moment felt like an icy shard turning in my breast.

My heart raced as I made my way back to 'The Horse and Hag' at the end of the day. I had made no plans to meet him but, after what had happened between us, he would be there... Wouldn't he? He had said that he wanted me more than anything...But now he had had me. My wary inner voice cautioned that he might have had his fill. He might have had his fun, decided to give Bres a wide berth, and gone away to find new amusements elsewhere. However, the part of me that had felt what I felt, when I looked into his eyes, knew that he would be waiting... Wouldn't he?

I swallowed heavily as I opened the door, and went to put my rucksack away upstairs. He wasn't in the main bar. He wasn't in my bedroom. He had mentioned that he could sense my presence, which was of no great surprise. The prickle knew that there were Great Ones in the back room. If he was among them, would he come and find me, or would I have to go to him, simpering and fawning like one of the other mortal companions I had so pitied?

I took a deep breath, and crept back downstairs. Alice was behind the bar. The room was otherwise empty. She took one look at me, with my hands clenched anxiously and eyes wide with trepidation, and burst out laughing again.

"He's in there," she smiled knowingly, nodding in the direction of the back room, "He told me to tell you to come and find him as soon as you got home."

I slumped down onto a bar stool. At least he hadn't forgotten about me, but nor was he waiting at the door, as eager to see me as I was to see him again.

"I think I need a drink first," I confessed.

Alice laughed. She poured me a shot, and I downed it in an instant. For a moment, I almost mistook the warm feeling spreading through me, for the effects of the alcohol. Then, I realised that it was the prickle: The prickle, communicating with me in a way that it never had before, cocooning me in an all-encompassing embrace. It was... *Happy*.

"You're back," observed Sam from the doorway.

"You're here," I responded.

We watched each other, neither one of us moving, for what seemed like an eternity.

Alice coughed. "I'll just… go and change a barrel," she muttered, and scampered out towards the store room.

Sam and I held each other's gaze for several more, excruciating moments. Then, his face broke into an indescribably beautiful smile. He opened his arms, and I ran to him. He picked me up, and swung me around, covering me with kisses and engulfing me in the sweet, heady scent of him. The floor disappeared. Time stopped. When our lips met again, a shudder rumbled through the room, as our powers reconnected, reaching for each other too, with invisible fingers.

"I want you," he whispered.

I nodded.

We raced upstairs to my room, and ripped our clothes from our bodies with a hungry mixture of magic, and hands, and teeth. He held me effortlessly, as I wrapped my legs around him. We did not get as far as the bed.

"Now," I pleaded, my lips to his ear, "Now…"

My mouth was on his skin when he entered me, muffling my cries as he moved against me with longing and urgency. I writhed and clung to him, gasping. The pleasure was unbearably intense, as our bodies and our magic collided, building towards something magnificent. Wave after wave of frantic desire coursed through the room, shaking it with voracious power. Then release came: That breathless, screaming moment of unendurable freedom, and agonising ecstasy. We tumbled to the ground. Time stopped again.

I do not know how long we lay there, no longer two separate entities, but some new incarnation comprising the two of us, and our hands, and our lips, and our warm, fragrant bodies. Glimmering fragments of magic played on our skin. The rug on the floor felt soft, and luxurious, against my back. I wondered if he could have foreseen such a moment, when he'd chosen to put it there.

Then, he said: "Well, that was something."

"Indeed."

"Have you had many lovers, Kathy?"

The question astonished me. "No," I replied.

"I'm surprised."

I laughed incredulously, not quite knowing how to react.

"It was a compliment," he added.

"Well, then… thank you." He looked at me expectantly, and I realised that he was waiting for some comment from me on his own prowess. "And your experience does not disappoint," I offered, carefully. If I began to try to explain how he truly made me feel, I worried that I would never stop. I would simply become a gibbering mess, spilling out words of flattery, one after the other for all eternity, and still not quite capturing the truth of it.

He smiled, seemingly satisfied. "Good."

It occurred to me that, though he was wearing the guise of a man, and in many ways behaving very much like one, there was no subtlety or delicacy around sex for him. It just was.

"Will you come down to the back room with me?" he asked, "I'd like to show you something."

I felt wary. "Will it be alright, with Bres there?"

"Oh, he'll behave himself," Sam assured me, brightly.

I longed to go with him immediately, not wishing to be far from his side for any longer than was unavoidable, but I was aware that I was a dishevelled, sweaty mess after our passion, and I could only imagine the mocking expression on Alice's face if she saw me in such a state, so I said:

"I'll follow you down. I'd just like to freshen up first."

"Of course," he smiled, and a moment later, he was dressed and impeccably presented. He left the room with a last, dazzling grin at me.

I pondered the fact that, while he showed no sign of wanting to be away from me, he displayed no fear of it, either. Perhaps that dreadful, craving feeling of parting was the domain of finite mortal life alone.

I showered and put on clean clothes, and made my way downstairs to the back room.

The scene was much the same as it usually was, but for Sam, towards the rear of the chamber, setting out strange wooden pieces on a table. He turned to me as soon as I entered. "There you are," he exclaimed, "Now, before we begin, Bres has something to say, don't you, Bres?"

Bres, slumped in his usual chair, smiled stiffly, like a child who had been told they would be spanked if they did not apologise to Auntie for putting spiders in her hat.

"I'm sorry for that business the other night," he said, without even a hint of authenticity, "Let's put it down to the poitín, and never speak of it again."

I was surprised that Sam had had the authority to elicit the apology, even if it was not remotely in earnest. I'd always had the impression that Bres was a leader, of sorts, amongst the group, but perhaps it was not quite that simple. Of course, nothing ever was.

"Erm… very well," I agreed nervously, and hurried in Sam's direction.

As I passed Bres, however, he whispered to me, so that nobody else could hear: "I didn't know you were *his,* when I said what I said."

I bristled, uncomfortable with the idea of being seen as anyone's possession. I made no reply, and joined Sam at his table. He pulled out a chair for me, and absently waved one of the sycophants away to free a chair for himself.

"How would you like to learn to play fidchell?" he asked.

"Fidchell?"

"It's a game I made up, many moons ago."

I was curious. "Very well," I agreed.

As it turned out, it was a strange, complex game, not entirely unlike chess, but quite its own. I was impressed that Sam's intellect had concocted it. He beat me, game after game, but I did begin to get closer to defeating him as the evening wore on, and he smiled approvingly.

"Sam," I asked later, emboldened by the few glasses of mead I'd had along the way, "Did you tell Bres that I *belonged* to you?"

"I did," he replied, without a hint of awkwardness, "Not that it's any of his business, really, but I wanted to make it very clear that he was to keep his hands off you in future." He paused, watching my expression. "Was I wrong? Do you and I not belong to each other now?"

'Belong to *each other*' sounded quite different. If the words had not been spoken by a god, I would have called it romantic. It was probably the closest he could come to proposing a relationship. My butterflies swooned with the weight of the compliment, diving dramatically into my depths to languish in delight.

"I- I suppose we do," I muttered, hoping that the colour in my cheeks was not as deep as it felt. I hurriedly began to set up another game of fidchell.

He merely smiled brightly, as though we had been discussing something as inconsequential as the weather.

I went out to the bar to buy some shots.

Alice poured them cheerfully. "Is everything alright again between Bres and Sam?" she asked.

"Well enough, it seems." I answered. Bres's apology had been stilted, and awkward. I wasn't entirely sure whether they had been truly reconciled, or whether Sam had coerced him into line by means of some threat.

There were a few ordinary patrons in the main bar now. Two of them walked up to order beverages. The first ordered a glass of red wine.

Alice looked around with irritation. "I think I'm just out of that. I'll have to get another bottle from the store room."

The second customer sighed with impatience.

"You serve him, and I'll get the wine," I offered.

She nodded gratefully.

As I was unpacking a crate of bottles in the store room, I heard voices from the street on the other side of the wall. The prickle was suddenly uncomfortable. It raised its hackles, and growled. I abandoned my task, rushed upstairs to my bedroom, and peered out of the window. The same pair of immortal fellows I had fought two nights ago were out there, but this time they were accompanied by a female who looked similar to them. I wondered how to think of these creatures. They were somewhere between the small ones and the Great Ones... The 'tween ones? They had two small ones with them, who appeared as yet unscathed.

I almost tumbled down the staircase in my haste, and burst out of the pub to confront them, to the faint sound of Alice exclaiming: "Kathy! The wine!"

The magical group was now at the back door of 'The Horse and Hag.' The one who had injured me was knocking for admittance. I pressed myself against the wall, and held my breath, not ready to be noticed. I wanted to see who answered. Somebody opened the door cautiously. Inside was pitch black, and I could not see who it was. The immortal fellow spoke to them, for a few moments. I was not close enough to hear what they were saying. They all went inside, and the door closed again.

My heart thumped in my chest. I should have intervened before they entered. I had a sickening feeling that something awful was about to happen to the small ones. I struggled to breathe. I *had to* go straight to the back room, find the small ones, and confront the immortals. I simply *had to*. I was terrified.

At that moment, the three 'tween ones emerged from the door again, chuckling gleefully. They spotted me immediately and scowled.

"You!" cried one of them, "You'd better not be here to interfere in our business again!"

"What are they doing to the small ones in there?" I cried, "Who's hurting them? Please tell me! Is it just Nuadu?"

"None of your business," yelled the female, and aimed a magical blow in my direction.

This time, I was ready. The prickle sent it straight back in her direction, and followed it with a bolt of its own for good measure. The 'tween one was hurled to the ground.

His companions sprang into action, flinging their pathetic little magical bolts at me. The prickle dispatched them with ease, allowing me time to approach. As soon as I could, I leaped at them, covering them in well-executed kicks and punches. They slumped to the floor.

The back door opened a crack, and I threw myself against it. "Who's there?" I shrieked, "Who are you? Bring back those small ones this instant!"

As if on cue, one of the small ones was shoved unceremoniously though the small opening in the door, out on to the street. Inside still looked black. I could not see a thing. The door slammed shut again.

"I'm coming to find the other one," I warned loudly.

I was about to rush straight back into the pub, but stopped to examine the small one first. He appeared dazed, and his eyes were strangely dim. He was shivering.

"Are you alright?" I asked, anxiously.

"They told me they were taking me somewhere wonderful," he whispered, "But they…" He shrieked.

I became aware that the 'tween ones were beginning to scramble up from the ground, as their injuries healed. The small one tore off.

The three strange beings faced me, with something between fear and hatred in their ancient eyes. The female stepped forward boldly, and flung both her hands at me, unleashing the most powerful blow of which she was capable.

The prickle swatted it back at her, and it hit her in the stomach. She was thrown backwards, with such force that she travelled several feet in the air. The two fellows grabbed her, pulled her to her feet, and they all fled.

"And don't come back," I called.

I had no time to dwell on the incident. I had to get behind the tapestry, and find the other small one. I ran as fast as I could through the main bar, and down the corridor… And straight into a dark, hulking figure.

Nuadu grabbed me by the shoulder. The prickle trembled at his powerful touch. "Don't," he hissed.

"I have to…" I began, urgently.

"I know exactly what you're going to do," he snapped, "Don't."

"So it *was* you at the door. Where's the other one? What have you done to him? You *must* tell me!"

"It's too late for him," said Nuadu darkly.

"Y- y- you… monster!" I cried.

"You don't know what you're talking about," he barked, "If you value your life, you'll leave this alone!"

"You didn't see what I did to the three wretched creatures out there," I retorted, more boldly than I felt, "I can look after myself! Besides, Sam will protect me!"

"If you value *his* life, you won't force him to try."

"He can't die!"

"There are many ways of ceasing to be. If you meddle in this, and set him against the others, you risk losing him as he is. You don't want that, do you?"

I gasped, weakly. "Who do you mean by the others? How many of you are involved?"

"It is enough for you to know this: If *you* get involved, you will regret it. You will regret it in ways that you never believed you could regret. If you have any sense, you will heed my words. Go back to your game of fidchell. Smile at your beautiful lover. Do not speak a word of what you have seen, or what you suspect. If you do, you cannot fathom what might be unleashed." He gazed at me intensely, and I saw something I recognised in his enormous eyes. He was telling the truth.

He let go of me, and walked away.

I pressed my hand to the wall to steady myself. My breathing was too shallow. I felt faint. How could I reconcile the role I had played since childhood, of protector to the small ones, with standing back and doing nothing, when they were being abused, or drained, or whatever horrible fate they were meeting behind the tapestry? My skin crawled. Nuadu had told me to return to the board game. I did not think I could stomach it, or keeping such monstrous things from Sam. He had said we belonged to each other now. How could I lie to him, and not tell him that there were vile, dark secrets in this place?

I did not go to the back room. I walked into the main bar, still deep in thought.

"Kathy," exclaimed Alice, "What on earth is going on? You said you'd get a bottle of wine, and instead, you ran out the door as if you were being chased!"

"I- I thought I heard a fight outside, and I went to help," I said flatly. I did not like the feeling of having to start keeping secrets again, but Nuadu's grim warning had unnerved me. I had no reason to trust him, but something about the gravity of his tone, and the insistence in his eyes, had affected me.

"Oh, of course, because of your kickboxing?" said Alice.

"What?"

"You thought you might be able to help, because you can fight?"

"Oh. Erm, yes."

"Was everything alright?"

I was about to reassure her, but found that I couldn't stomach telling a lie quite that immense. "It's over now."

She noted my demeanour with concern. "Shot?"

I nodded. "Make it poitín."

After I had downed the drink, and barely felt it, I wandered numbly up to my bedroom. I knew Sam was expecting me downstairs, and my butterflies would insist on going to him eventually, but I needed a little time to process what had just happened.

I noticed Liam's little wooden carving on the floor, along with most of my books and toiletries, and felt a deep and crawling sense of guilt. The force of my sexual connection with Sam had, literally, thrown the thoughtful gift from my former love to the ground, like a discarded piece of tat. I picked it up and put it in a drawer, from where it was less likely to be dislodged, and I would not have to look at it.

I sat down heavily on the bed. I had not had a chance to gauge how damaged the small one who escaped had been on his release, but they had thrown him back, and kept the other one. *Why?* It made no sense. Why were those 'tween ones fetching fellow magical beings, and leading them here, like lambs to the slaughter? The only way I could find out was to ask questions. Nuadu would not answer them, and he had convinced me that asking them of any of the others was deeply unsafe.

I suddenly wished that I had *someone* to speak to, who knew of otherworldly matters but was unconnected to 'The Horse and Hag.'

I imagined talking it all over with Liam and Mr. O Mordha in their cottage, but it was a fantasy that felt very far away.

Eventually, my breathing returned to normal, and I decided that I had better rejoin Sam in the back room. He must have been wondering why those shots were taking such a long time to procure.

He was singing, when I returned. His beautiful eyes brightened to see me, and he reached out an elegant hand to take mine. I leaned my head on his shoulder as I lost myself in his exquisite words and voice. The melody rose and tumbled, refreshing me like spring water, and wrenching my heart out like talons of grief. I cried. Nobody batted an eyelid. Most of the other sycophants were weeping too.

Nuadu watched me from across the room, his grave expression a stern warning against choosing not to heed his words. The small one was nowhere to be seen. I decided to keep my silence for now, but I would not leave the matter alone. Somehow, I determined, I would get to the truth of it all.

The following day at the library, I had the most unsettling feeling that someone was watching me. Mr. Books was there, of course, arguing with the whispering bookshelves as usual. However, I had the distinct, prickling impression of something else *other*, lurking just out of sight. My spine tingled apprehensively, as I tried to finish my essay. Finally, the feeling passed. Whatever it had been was gone.

Dr. Herbert arrived, and sat opposite me with a friendly "Hello."

"Where would I find information on figures named 'Bres' and 'Nuadu'?" I whispered.

"Oh, your best bet is the *Lebor Gabála*," she replied with a smile.

I thanked her, and went to locate the item. I read the introduction to the volume before beginning the primary text. It was a book of invasions of Ireland, composed in the medieval period, and largely invented by the author, though some of it was based on earlier mythological tradition.

I flipped through the book, until I found the section on the *Tuatha Dé*, which was a common name for the old gods in medieval texts. Many Christian writers, not wishing to acknowledge their divinity, due to their devotion to the one god, portrayed them as a race of people with magical powers, by that name.

> Nuadu was the king of the Tuatha Dé, and was a just and wise ruler, but when he lost his arm in battle, he was no longer accepted as a leader. Tradition dictated that a king must be free of any physical blemish. The physician, Dian Cécht, made him an arm of silver to replace it, and he became known as Nuadu *Argetlám*, or 'Nuadu of the Silver Hand'. However, he was still not perfect in his subjects' eyes, so he was replaced as king by Bres. Bres was charismatic, and beautiful to behold, but proved to be a selfish and careless ruler. He abused the Tuatha Dé cruelly. The healer finally succeeded in replacing Nuadu's arm with a real one of flesh and bone, and the latter was welcomed back eagerly by the Tuatha Dé, as their rightful king. Bres's kinsfolk, the Fomoire, declared war on the Tuatha Dé. The skilled warrior and hero Lug *Samildánach*, or 'Lug, Equally Skilled in Many Arts' defeated the Fomoire, but spared Bres's life. Lug then took the kingship for himself.

I put the book down with a gasp. I could not assume that this medieval account was entirely true, but I was in no doubt that the resentment between Nuadu and Bres was very real. How had such a wise and just king become the terrifying, dark figure I knew, and why had his arm returned to silver from flesh? What had happened to Lug? I suddenly froze as realisation dawned. Lug *Samildánach*. *SAMildánach*. Sam.

"You know," observed Dr. Herbert, looking up from her reading, "Speaking of the *Lebor Gabála,* it's just occurred to me, the god Lug is sometimes called *Samildánach*. Do you think that could be your mysterious name beginning with 'Sam'?"

I nodded slowly. "I rather think it might."

I had heard of Lug before, in some of my mother's old tales. He was one of the greatest of the Irish gods. I rushed to the bookshelves to acquire a more thorough description of his attributes, desperate to be sure whether or not *my* Sam was once... Him.

The name Lug was not difficult to find.

> He was a warrior, a scholar, a musician and a powerful sorcerer, among his many skills. He was very beautiful. He was said to have invented a game called *fidchell*...

I stopped. It *was* him.

The part of me that still felt wary, and a little foolish, for my feelings towards him, was aghast. It had been difficult enough to accept the fact that I was maddeningly smitten with some deity, that I could never hope for him to love me, and that we could never grow old together, or have anything even approaching the semblance of a normal life. The fact that he had been a mighty king of the gods made my dreams even more pitiably laughable.

It was late when I left the college, having attended several lectures and a kickboxing class. My heart stopped when I saw the familiar figure at the gate. The prickle purred, and hugged itself excitedly. He was waiting for me!

He looked up as soon as I noticed him, and his exquisite face split into a smile of thousand suns in the dusk. I, somehow, found myself in his arms before I could even remember how to use my feet.

"I thought I'd come to you, today," he said after he had kissed me deeply.

"How long have you been waiting?"

"I don't know," he shrugged, "Some time. No time at all. It's all the same to me."

"I- I think I've discovered your 'long and boring' name," I confessed, suddenly shy.

I could not read his expression. He lowered his head, almost wistfully. "Does it make a difference to you?" he asked.

I realised that it really didn't. In that moment, in my painfully short lifetime, he was what he was, not what he used to be. I shook my head. "To me, you're just 'Sam'."

He pulled my hand to his lips, and pressed it there intensely, for a few moments. "I think that pleases me."

As we walked home, it occurred to me to wonder if it might have been him I had felt, watching me in the library. After all, he had a very different concept of time from mine. He might have been floating around the campus all day, keeping a respectful distance until I had completed my work.

"I thought I sensed someone in the library earlier, hiding themselves from me," I said, "Was it you?"

"No," he replied, "Why would I do that? If I came to you, I would want you to see me."

"Of course. Never mind." The strange feeling I'd had perplexed me. I wondered if my misgivings about Nuadu and Bres, and all of the horrible secrets I was keeping, were driving me insane, and the prickle with me.

"Beautiful Kathy," began Sam as we reached 'The Horse and Hag', "I want you."

I squeezed his hand. "I want you too, but I have a shift behind the bar soon."

"I'll be quick," he replied, with a playful smile.

I melted instantly, and smiled back. "Don't be *too* quick."

I raced inside and up the stairs, and he followed.

I made it behind the bar just in time, breathless and exalted by the vigour and beauty of Sam's body on mine. I attempted to smooth my hair, as I greeted Sylvie, who'd had the earlier shift.

"You look… elated," she remarked, "Been doing something nice?"

"I- I- er…"

She laughed. "I'm teasing. I know. *Everybody* knows. You can't keep much hidden around here for long."

Nuadu seems to be doing a bloody good job of it, I thought darkly. I gave Sylvie a bashful smile. "Silly, isn't it?" I muttered.

"What is?"

"Me, getting involved with one of *them*. Where on earth could I hope for it to go?"

She shrugged, as she moved to the other side of the bar. "Nobody knows where anything will go, until it goes. I've known him for years, and I've certainly never seen him like this before: Drinking in the main bar, making bedrooms for people, buying gifts, teaching you to play fidchell… It's all completely alien behaviour for him. I think he has real feelings for you, Kathy."

My butterflies swooned again, taking to hundreds of tiny, internal couches and demanding smelling salts to resuscitate them. "Drink?" I offered casually, my burning face betraying me.

"Please," she accepted with a smile.

Evelyn bustled out of the kitchen, and announced that, though I'd informed her I wouldn't be back in time from kickboxing to eat before my shift, she had left something in the microwave for me to enjoy later.

"You're too good to me, Evelyn," I grinned.

The bar was excruciatingly empty that night. Sylvie only stayed for one, and went out to meet friends. One elderly man nursed a pint of stout for an hour or so, reading a newspaper, and muttering incoherently about the articles it contained. He seemed lonely, and eager to engage me, and I attempted to take a polite interest in his ramblings.

I vaguely understood something about a bizarre death that had taken place in the suburbs. It seemed that a man had been found, mysteriously impaled on the leg of a table, in his own kitchen. I nodded patiently at the customer, but didn't pay it much attention, until he added that all of the doors in the house had been missing.

I froze. That seemed far too much of a coincidence. So, Tom had come to an unpleasant end. I wondered how he could possibly have impaled himself on a table. A drunken accident, I supposed. I tried prise a little sympathy for him, from somewhere deep inside me, but found that I did not have much to give.

The old man said something further, that was entirely incomprehensible, and shuffled home.

I ached for Sam, just a corridor away, but out of my reach until my shift was over. His eyes were the only thing that could make me forget the torture of my misgivings, about the fate of the small one who had disappeared. I knew he was staying away because the manner in which his presence affected the ordinary patrons, made me uncomfortable. I longed to run and tell him that I was alone, and beg him for his company. I resisted the urge. Even if our backgrounds were anything but equal, I was determined to maintain some shred of dignity.

The hours crawled by. I polished glasses. I stocked the fridge to bursting. No requests came from the back room for drinks. It was rare that they did. The Great Ones usually conjured their own beverages, only asking for service as a novelty, when it occurred to them.

I attempted to build a sculpture out of straws. I stacked cocktail sticks in interesting piles. Finally, the moment came. Evelyn bustled out of the kitchen with the meal that she had reheated for me, paid me and told me that I could close up.

I thanked her profusely, locked the doors, and wolfed my food down, eager to be done with it, and meet Sam in the back room. When he saw me, his face lit up.

"Good evening, Kathy," Bres greeted me with a courteous smile, though there was no warmth in his eyes.

I nodded politely in response. Medb, Macha, and some of the sycophants waved, and I hailed them in return.

I made my way to Sam's side, and he immediately clasped my hands in his own. The unbearable tingle of his touch rippled through my fingers, and finally woke my swooning butterflies. They fluttered excitedly. I longed to pull him away, and upstairs to bed, but decided that desperation was not a flattering shade. I simply refused to throw myself at him again, god or not.

He had no such qualms. "I would like to be alone with you," he announced, "Would that please you?"

My butterflies promptly fainted again. "It would."

As we made our way upstairs, I whispered: "You don't have to be quick this time."

He grinned.

CHAPTER FIFTEEN

We lay on the bed, in the afterglow of our passion. Tiny tendrils of magic shimmered in the air... Memories of the explosively powerful fusion we had shared. He was propped up on one arm, stroking my stomach, his wide eyes staring down at me, filled with all the colours of this world and the other. I reached up and fingered his silken hair.

"I find you intoxicating," he remarked.

He finds me intoxicating?

I turned what, I can only imagine was, an interesting shade of puce.

"Thank you," I muttered quickly. I racked my brains for a change of subject. "Tell me more about Nuadu."

Sam groaned. "Oh, must we really talk about *him,* at a time like this?"

"None of you seem to like him, and he strikes me as a most unhappy fellow. Why do you think he stays with you?"

"We have been together for such a long time, I don't think it has occurred to either of us to depart," mused Sam, with a faraway look, "He was not always miserable. He was truly great once. A mighty force, and a loyal ally."

"What changed?"

"We both did... but not in the same ways." He looked uncomfortable, "Over time, we all grew lesser... a shadow of what we once were. I found a new way to be. He found another."

"So, there was a time when you were friends?"

"That is not a word we would use, but yes, something like that."

"And what about Bres?"

"Oh, there was a time when Bres was our most sworn adversary. I showed him mercy once, many moons ago, and he stayed. We hated each other, but he stayed, and he stayed, for he had nowhere else to be, and as the years wore on, the memory of the enmity grew less, and things between us became a resigned... companionship of sorts.

The familiarity of hatred can become fondly nostalgic, given enough time, and we have had a great deal of that. Bres grew to enjoy his changed existence, and taught me to take pleasure in it too. Nuadu never came to terms with it, and became, somehow, far from us, as ages passed, though he was still there. Medb and Macha came later… Both lost, unsure of how to be what they now were. We showed them that there was still satisfaction to be had, and delight to be found, in lesser things. And so, our lives became as you find them. They have been this way for such a long time that the memory of what was lost has dimmed."

"So you are… content with things as they are?"

"I give it little thought, but I am not dissatisfied." He paused and caressed my shoulder thoughtfully. "More precisely, I have not *been* dissatisfied, but since I encountered you, I have felt… different. I believe that I am happy now."

My butterflies shuddered at his words… Not with fear, or anxiety, but with the unbearable weight of the truth of them. They were silly things, fluttering around inside me, filled with girlish thoughts, and at the command of my every whim… But even their tiny minds were beginning to understand the seriousness of it. I was falling in love. I was falling desperately, hopelessly, frustratingly in love.

"When I'm with you, I'm happy too," I confessed.

The brilliant smile that illuminated his face at that moment may truly be the most beautiful thing I have ever seen. "Well then, we should celebrate," he declared, "Let's go dancing!"

"Now?"

"Why not?"

I couldn't think of a reason not to, so I agreed. His spontaneity and excitement were endearingly infectious.

"I'll need to get dressed," I observed.

He pulled me to him for a passionate kiss. "You do that. I'll send someone for a carriage," he said, leaping out of bed and instantly appearing groomed and attractively attired.

"If we're just going around the corner again, do we really need one?" I called, but he was gone.

I laughed and shook my head. Their quaint traditions were amusing, though somewhat mindboggling. I selected one of the more revealing items from my new wardrobe, dressed, and brushed my hair. I paused for a moment to study my face in the mirror. It was a little flushed, which was not surprising, given that I had been tumbling about in an amorous heap with Sam until very recently. Perhaps there *was* something about my features that was just a little closer to theirs. Suddenly, I did not feel so plain as I usually did. I wondered if my reassessment of my looks was based on my true reflection, or on the way that Sam's eyes made me feel when they were on me.

I shook off my reverie, and hurried downstairs. Sam was waiting for me at the bottom. He picked me up from the last step, spun me 'round, and placed me on the ground. I giggled.

"Alice has just turned up to see Medb," he announced, "They're going to join us. Does that please you?"

"Yes, that sounds lovely," I replied. Almost anything would have pleased me in that moment, but I imagined that a night out with Medb and Alice would be fun, and I was genuinely happy at the idea of their company.

Sam smiled. "Good! They're waiting in the carriage."

We left the pub from the front doors, of which I was glad. I had no desire to see Nuadu's scowl, or Bres's now cold eyes, or walk through that tiny, dark room behind the tapestry, into which the small ones had disappeared, and emerged changed, or not emerged at all…

Alice was waving cheerfully from the carriage. I selfishly decided to put my dark thoughts aside, and just enjoy the adventure ahead. There was little I could do about it now, in any case. Sam helped me in, slammed the door behind him, and the horses trotted off into the night.

As Macha was not with us to insist on cocktails, we went straight to 'The Hazard', which was the nightclub that Medb liked. It was pulsating with music and life. Flashes of brightly coloured light throbbed in time to the beat, turning our hair pink, then blue, then green. It was late, and the dancefloor was a swarm of intoxicated youths, moving in passionate, writhing admiration of the DJ. Sam sought out the alcove which we had occupied between dances on our last visit, and again, the people who had been sitting there gathered their belongings, in something of an uncomfortable frenzy, and scuttled hurriedly away. Alice offered to procure a round of drinks, and disappeared to the bar. The rest of us sat down.

Sam kissed me, and stroked my thigh. Public displays of affection were very new to me, but I found that I didn't care. He had said I made him happy, and my heart glowed.

Medb smiled at me. "He's really quite taken with you, you know," she observed as if Sam were not even there.

I was glad of the flashing lights to cover my blush. "I- I'm fond of him too," I replied shyly, feeling that some response was expected.

She nodded approvingly. "You make a handsome pair," she continued, "You look well together."

"Th- thank you?"

I was overwhelmingly grateful to spot Alice returning with a tray of beverages. She sat beside Medb, and they touched and kissed each other too. They looked happy. I could not possibly know if Alice experienced the same things when she looked into Medb's eyes, as I did when I gazed at Sam, but the manner between them seemed intimate, and real. I began to think that Alice had been right: She was not a plaything, or a curiosity, to Medb, but a real partner. *Or perhaps, that's what you'd* like *to believe,* whispered an annoying inner voice. I told it to shut up.

I excused myself to visit the ladies' room, and Alice offered to accompany me.

"You do realise," she remarked, as we washed our hands and smoothed our hair in the mirror, "That we are essentially on a double date…"

"… With two ancient and immortal beings," I added. We both laughed.

"It's so strange," I mused, "And yet it feels oddly normal."

"I know what you mean," smiled Alice, preparing to return to our table.

I had noticed a splash of beer on my top, and was attempting to dry it. "I'll see you outside," I called. I was left alone in the bathroom.

I muttered obscenities about my clumsiness, as I scrubbed at my clothing. Suddenly, I became aware of a strange feeling. At first, I thought that the hand dryer had malfunctioned, and was sending out an intensely penetrating cold blast, but soon realised it was something more: A deep, familiar prickle. Not the gregarious prickle, that wanted to laugh and dance with the Great Ones at 'The Horse and Hag', or the passionate, hungry prickle that yearned for Sam, but something far more solemn, and reverent. Its hackles rose, and I was left in no doubt that a powerful immortal was not far away.

Then, I saw his reflection in the mirror behind me. It had been some time, but I recognised him immediately. The spindly man with the all-knowing eyes: It was The Dagda.

"Hello," I greeted him in surprise, "The washroom of a nightclub is not a place I'd have expected to meet you."

He looked serious. If I hadn't known better, I would have thought that the expression in his eyes almost bordered on concern.

"What are you doing, Kathy?" he demanded.

I raised my eyebrows. "Doing? I'm just trying to deal with this stain..."

"That is not of what I speak! What do you mean by keeping company with the likes of *them*? These are the sorts of beings that I warned you about, Kathy: Capricious and self-serving!" He stepped closer. "And I can smell one of them on you. Do you have any idea how dangerous they could be, to one such as you?"

I frowned, astonished. "Are you... *worried* about me?"

"You should be worried about yourself," he retorted, "Do you know what they could do to you? Sap your strength to fortify their own, the way they do to every other magical creature that has the misfortune to cross their path, and not for any noble purpose, but merely to feed their insatiable greed?"

"Well, Bres said something, but he seems to have backed off, and I suspect that Nuadu is the one harming other magical beings, but I'm well-protected, and I am trying to figure it out…"

"You know nothing of these matters," snapped The Dagda, "Only the silken story they choose to tell you, with the pretty mouths in their shining masks. Do not be fooled, Kathy. They are not to be trusted. Not a one of them. I will be back to deal with them, once and for all, before long. In the meantime, they are no fit company for you."

Deal with them once and for all? I repeated, inwardly. What did he mean?

"And just how are you planning to 'deal' with them?" I demanded, sounding braver than I felt.

"Not a one of us should be degrading ourselves, parading around in these silly faces and human guises. All must be made whole: As it was when things were as they *should be.*"

I gasped. Did he want to take my Sam away, and make him part of that nameless, faceless thing that once was? Did he want to rip Medb out of Alice's arms? I had seen wisdom in The Dagda's plan, once, but now, I could not possibly conceive of Sam not existing as he had become… Never touching him again… Never seeing his smile. Not letting Sam be 'just Sam' seemed unimaginably cruel.

I felt a lump in my throat. I did not want to anger The Dagda. I did not want to be against him. Something about him had always made me feel a certain warmth, and he clearly did not wish me harm. Furthermore, I did not know if I had even remotely the power to challenge him… But why was it that his lofty plans always seemed to involve bothering those I cared for?

"I- I can help," I cried, "I'll find out what they're doing to the small ones, and I'll put a stop to it. I'll stop them using their powers for anything… wrong, or silly. Then, you can just leave them alone."

"You? You alone will stand against *them*? This is foolishness, Kathy."

"I'll do it. I *have* to believe I can make things right."

He sighed. "If you truly wanted to make things right, you would heed my advice. I see you are already far too deep in their thrall for me to expect any sense from you."

I was offended. "Thank you for your concern," I replied coldly, "I've survived without it until now."

He looked… Hurt. A small, too-human flicker in his eyes was genuinely hurt. I felt guilty. His visit had seemed to serve no other purpose than to warn me of the danger he considered me to be in, though I could not imagine the nature of his interest in me. Before I could say anything to soften my harsh words a little, The Dagda was gone.

When I returned to the alcove, I positively flung myself at Sam, wrapping my arms around his neck as tightly as I could, and burying my face in his shoulder. *The Dagda will have to prise my hands off you himself, if he tries to take you away!*

He held me, and kissed my neck, mistaking my gesture for normal, exuberant affection, and not desperation and fear. "Alice bought more shots," he said, brightly.

I drank, and then I bought shots, and I drank some more, hoping that the oblivion of inebriation would blot out The Dagda's unwelcome visit. I began to feel hazy, and a little blurred around the edges, and Sam's arms around me were the only real and safe thing in the world. Medb suggested dancing, and we weaved our way onto the floor. The crowd parted obligingly as we went, instinctively avoiding the Great Ones, but sufficiently dulled by intoxicating substances not to appear particularly perturbed by their proximity.

We danced, and we danced, until Medb had finally had her fill of compelling the revelries to continue beyond their usual hour, and we burst back out into the daylight and climbed into our carriage.

As the clip-clop of the horses' hooves pranced on the cobblestones, taking us home to 'The Horse and Hag', I thought how glad I was not to be leaving my beautiful Sam behind at a bus stop, after an awkward kiss, this time. I was looking forward to falling asleep with his sweet, fragrant body against mine, and dreaming of him.

When we arrived back at the pub, the others automatically went in the direction of the back room, presumably intending to continue the party. "I'm exhausted," I confessed, "I think I'll go to bed."

Medb bid me a friendly goodnight, and Alice hugged me. They drifted off together, their hands intertwined.

"Would you like me to join you?" asked Sam.

I nodded. "Very much, but I'm afraid I will doze off before long, so don't let me stop you from enjoying more drinks with the others, if you prefer."

He pulled me to him, his arm around my waist. "You please me more than anything, whether you are awake or not. I will come with you."

I kissed him deeply, for saying exactly what I had hoped, but had not dared to imagine, he would say. As my lips melted into his, it occurred to me that I might have just a little more life left in me than I'd thought.

He gathered me into his arms, like a weightless bundle, and carried me the whole way upstairs, and into my room.

I awoke at midday with a start and, pausing only to devour my beautiful lover's mouth for an unbearably brief moment, declared that I had better go to college, and try to salvage something of the day's learning. I showered, dressed, grabbed my rucksack, melted into Sam's exquisite embrace again, ripped myself away from it with difficulty, and rushed downstairs.

"See you later," I called, as I ran.

"Until then, beautiful one," he called back.

I arrived at the university, just in time to attend my lecture with Dr. Herbert. She was discussing Irish gods and their other Celtic counterparts. There was a great goddess of fertility named Epona, it would seem, of whom depictions and inscriptions remain on the continent. In Ireland, she had been said to correspond to mythological figures like Macha and Étaín, whose divine origins were hinted at in the medieval manuscripts, by their magical attributes, and an association with horses. Though Étaín's equine attributes were less obvious than the others', she bore the epithet *Echraide,* or 'Horse Rider', in some of the old texts, suggesting a connection. These goddesses were also associated with a character from Welsh mythology, called Rhiannon.

Dr. Herbert went on to point out that some of the gods were more obviously direct counterparts of each other, even sharing similar names. Two of the examples she gave were that of the Gaulish god Lugus, who corresponded directly to the Irish Lug, and the Welsh Lleu, and that of Nodens, who was worshipped on the continent and in early Britain, and corresponded to Nuadu in Irish tradition.

I was fascinated. I wondered if there were incarnations of something like Lug Samildánach in other Celtic countries, or whether they had become something quite different, over time.

When the lecture was over, Dr. Herbert looked up at me and waved. "Did the Lebor Gabála solve your mystery, in the end?" she asked.

I nodded. "It did, thank you."

"Oh, good!"

I was suddenly prickling uncomfortably. I turned around, expecting to see a magical figure behind me, but saw only my usual classmates, filing out of the lecture theatre. I was still certain that someone was there... Hiding. Watching. It was the same feeling that I'd had in the library, days ago. I shuddered, and hurried out of the building.

I hugged my coat, and took a few deep breaths of fresh air, trying to shake off the unpleasant, crawling sensation. Somebody tapped me on the shoulder. I shrieked, as though I had been stabbed, and leaped a whole foot into the air.

"Oh, gosh, I'm so sorry, Kathy," exclaimed Alice in alarm, "I didn't mean to scare you!"

"I- It's okay," I stammered, "I'm feeling so jumpy today. Must be the hangover. I'm impressed you made it to college too!"

She laughed. "To tell you the truth, I had a long nap before visiting the pub after hours, last night. I often stay up very late with Medb, so I've had to alter my sleeping patterns, to get some rest in at odd times. Otherwise, I'd never manage to get here in the morning!"

"Makes sense," I observed, "I might need to start doing the same thing. I'm so tired, my mind is playing tricks on me." *Or am I being watched?*

"I bet you haven't eaten anything. Shall we go for a bit of late lunch?"

"Yes, let's do that," I agreed enthusiastically, "A meal, and a very strong cup of coffee, might be just the thing." I linked her, and we walked to the cafeteria cheerfully.

The unnerving, prickly sensation did not leave me after lunch. It followed me to the library. I paused, again looking around for any visible sign of a supernatural being nearby, but saw none. I could not help feeling as if something was toying with me... Teasing me... Taking pleasure in my discomfort at its presence, as it remained just out of sight.

I made my way to my reading table, and Mr. Books presented himself, shushed the noisy inhabitants of the shelves, and asked if he could be of assistance, in his customary fashion.

I prickled and prickled, and shifted my weight uncomfortably from one foot to the other. "Have you seen anyone... strange around here lately?"

"Strange?" he repeated, "I do not think I am the one to gauge what manner of person *you* would find *strange*."

"Has there been anyone here who can see you?"

"No, not for many moons. Apart from you, of course."

"Never mind," I sighed, "I have an essay to write."

"I'll leave you to your work, then."

I sat down, took out a pen and paper, and had one last look around for anything out of the ordinary. Suddenly, the strange feeling was gone.

I returned to 'The Horse and Hag' that evening, weary and perplexed by my paranoia. Why would anyone want to spy on me? I briefly wondered if it was The Dagda, but soon dismissed the idea. He did seem oddly interested in my movements, but I suspected that he had far more important things to do than lurk around the university, watching me. That was not even the part of my life to which he objected. Besides, it really didn't seem like his style. Nuadu had warned me not to speak to anyone about the small ones. Had he been keeping an eye on me, to make sure that I was heeding his words? I dismissed that notion too. The only ones to whom I'd considered speaking of it were here in the pub, not at the college.

I ordered a drink from Sylvie, as I mused. The prickle, suddenly happy again, began to squeeze the life out of me, and I knew that Sam was close. His arms encircled me before I'd had time to turn around.

"Hello," he said simply, his breath against my neck.

My butterflies swelled inside me.

"Hello," I replied. I did not turn to face him immediately. I closed my eyes and enjoyed the feeling of his unexpected embrace.

"Will you take your drink through to the back room, and join us?"

"I will."

Bres was singing, and I made a great show of clapping and cheering approvingly when he finished. I had noticed him grow distinctly surly towards me since his altercation with Sam, and though the intentions he'd had that night unsettled me, I had decided that some rapprochement might be in order, for the sake of an easy life.

Nuadu watched me darkly from the corner as I applauded. I could not help thinking that there was a little sadness, mixed with the loathing in his stare, that night.

Sam and I played a game of fidchell.

Macha squealed and giggled from somewhere in a tangled mass of bodies on the sofa. I did not examine the scene too closely, out of some sense of propriety.

Medb was playing cards, and winning repeatedly. I wondered if any of her companions had ever dared to beat her, and concluded that she probably wouldn't have stood for it.

"Would you like us to be alone now?" asked Sam. I thought I heard hope in his voice.

I nodded, smiling. He took my hand and led me from the beautiful chamber. I looked back, and remembered my first glimpse of it, in its lavish, faded splendour. What a place it was: A magnificent, secret den of beauty and pleasure, hidden away in the corner of an unassuming little bar.

My heart quickened as we reached the staircase, and we both broke into a run. He seized me eagerly as we entered the bedroom, and we toppled to the floor. I unbuttoned his tunic with trembling fingers, and he peeled off my top without the aid of his hands. I gasped as I felt his touch on my bare skin. My lips reached for his, and we kissed longingly, ravenously, taking our time to enjoy the sensation, and the delicious anticipation of what was to come.

Suddenly, I heard a noise outside the window, and instinctively pushed him away. I ran across the room to investigate. The 'tween ones were outside. All three of them… And they were leading another small one towards the back door.

"I don't believe it," I muttered angrily, "This again!"

In an instant, Sam was at my side. "Kathy, what is it? Is something wrong?" He watched the small figures in the street below.

"This time, I'm really going to teach them a lesson," I hissed. I grabbed my top from the floor, and put it back on. I made to run to the door, and felt Sam's strong hand on my shoulder, pulling me back.

"Leave it," he said simply.

"I will not leave it," I exclaimed, "Do you have any idea what those little beasts are doing…?"

"Please leave it," begged Sam, "Don't go."

"Let go of me," I cried, and he released his grip defeatedly.

I raced downstairs and out of the pub. Before the 'tween ones had a chance to notice my approach, I dispatched one of them with a swift kick, and the others with a mighty blow from the prickle.

They soon leaped upright, and faced me with three, defensive glares.

"Run!" I screamed at the small one, "Run for your life!"

He looked at me, puzzled. "But, I'm going to take tea with the great gods," he answered, "It's going to be lovely!"

"You're going to be drained of everything you have," I shrieked, "Get out of here!"

I blocked a tirade of little magical blows from the infuriating trio, and sent them all flying backwards.

"Run!"

This time, something in my tone resonated with the confused small one. He looked uncertain for a moment, then dashed off, and disappeared from view.

The three, scowling 'tween ones had not yet given up. One of them pelted me with blows from a distance, while the other two tried to rush me from either side.

"I've had just about enough of this," I announced, and felt the true depths of the prickle uncurling themselves from somewhere deep within me, sliding up through my body, like a twisting dragon, and flowing from me with a white-hot rage. A blast emanated from me. The ground shook. The 'tween ones were forced back through the air, like little rag dolls, bouncing off walls and colliding sharply with the cobblestones.

The back door of the pub was thrown open.

"You really need to stop meddling in my affairs," observed a familiar voice from inside.

He came into view, his hands clasping each side of the door frame, angrily. He wore a sneer of contempt on his exquisite face, and his eyes glittered with malice.

"You!" I cried.

"Yes, me," replied Bres, "Now, will you please do me the courtesy of leaving well alone, things that are none of your concern?"

"It *is* my concern," I insisted, "I won't have you hurting the small ones! Are these miserable wretches luring them here at *your* bidding?" I gestured towards the three, who were still immobile on the ground after my attack.

"Enough," snapped Bres, "Really, Sam, can't you keep your little amusement under control?"

I was suddenly aware of Sam, standing just behind me.

"You don't speak of Kathy like that," he retorted, with a flash of that deep anger that I'd witnessed when he had thrown Bres across the room.

With a frustrated snarl, Bres stormed back inside.

I followed immediately, afraid but determined to confront him, and glad of the sound of Sam's footsteps echoing mine.

He pulled the back door shut behind us, and grabbed me again. "Please Kathy," he implored me, "Just come away, and let him calm down…"

I shrugged his hand off, and exploded into the chamber that had looked so beautiful just a short while ago, but now felt cloying, and sickeningly artificial.

"What have you been doing to them, Bres? Have you been 'tasting' their powers, the way you wanted to sample mine? Draining them dry, leaving them withered husks, robbed of all sense? Is that it? You greedy, disgusting thing!"

He was standing at the central table. He slammed it with his fists, sparks of his magic erupting from his hands as they collided with the wood.

"I'll see you dead," he growled.

Sam stepped forward and stood between us, bristling with anger. "I'll see *you* dead before I let you harm a hair on her head! I spared your life at The Battle of Mag Tuired. I won't make the same mistake again."

To my utter astonishment, Nuadu walked down and stood beside Sam, he too facing Bres with a dark fury.

"You'll have to get past both of us if you want to hurt her," he declared, "I don't fancy your chances!"

"You?" squeaked Bres mockingly, "Do you think I am afraid of *you*? Why, you don't even have an arm! I've taken a kingdom from you!"

Nuadu squared his shoulders. "And I took it back."

"And lost it again, to this one, you damaged fool!" Bres flung his animated hand towards Sam.

"And I was happy for him, or anyone else worthy, to have it!" thundered Nuadu, " Not *you,* you worthless piece of scum!"

Macha and Medb looked genuinely terrified. Macha crawled into a corner, as though she were hoping it would swallow her up.

Medb approached, shakily. "There must be a way to resolve this," she said, a pleading desperation in her voice, "After all, what will we be if we do not have each other?"

"The only way to resolve this is for *her* to go," yelled Bres, pointing an accusing finger in my direction.

"She's not going anywhere," stated Sam.

"Oh, you say that now, but you just wait and see how quickly her appeal fades when all of *this,*" Bres smashed the table again, for emphasis, "All of *this* starts to disappear! Everything the powers *I've* collected have brought us. Everything I've shared with *you*!

"I have my own powers," roared Sam, "I have no need of you!"

"You could barely put one foot in front of the other, when we lost what we lost," sneered Bres, "The once great Lug, stumbling around in a fog, not knowing what to be. *I* brought you back to life! *I* did! And this is the thanks I get?"

Nuadu growled. "You repulsive, crawling creature. We should have cut your head off when we had the might to do it."

"You stubborn old fool," retorted Bres, "You coward! You could have enjoyed all of this. You could have had your hand back, if you'd only had the bravery to do what I have done!"

"What *you* have done is weakness itself! Sapping little bits of magic from others who were once like you, to keep your beautiful faces, and your fine chairs, and the love of the witless mortals you drag in here for your pleasure!" Nuadu spat in disgust. "But perhaps I *am* a coward. How many years has it been, that I have watched your low deeds, hating every minute of it? I know not. The fact that it has taken the courage of a young girl, to bring this matter to a head, should make us all ashamed of ourselves!"

"I've taken nothing that we didn't deserve," said Bres, his voice now more controlled, "I haven't destroyed anything real... Just moved a little power from one place to another. Don't you see? Medb is right. We can't turn against each other. That's what *she* wants." He fixed me with a glare again, so cold as to freeze the blood. "*She* came in here, with her mysterious magic, and her beguiling face, and she spoiled the harmony that we've created."

"That harmony is nothing but a filthy lie," hissed Nuadu.

Sam's shoulders were tense, as he listened to the exchange. His face was almost forlorn, as though some truth had been ripped from his consciousness, and had left him with a void of uncertainty.

Eventually, he found his voice again. "Kathy is right," he said sadly, "And so is Nuadu. We have let this continue for far too long. We have learned to grow comfortable with it, and live only for ourselves... But there are others worth living for too."

He turned to look at me, and his eyes were almost timid. Afraid.

"So," I finally breathed, having remained silent, in astonishment, as the heated exchange unfolded, "It was all of you. You *all* knew. Even… *you?*" I felt my heart become very heavy, as though it had been transformed to lead, and sink with a dull thud to the bottom of my stomach.

"I…" he began.

"You see?" cried Bres, "You see the loathing in her eyes? She doesn't even want you anymore! Let's just get rid of her, and be done with it, and never speak of it again!"

"You won't touch her," warned Sam, darkly.

Bres shrieked with frustration. "You fool! You still defend that mortal slut? You hopeless, witless fool!"

He raised his hand and unleashed a powerful bolt, coursing in Sam's direction.

Sam conjured an equal blow to meet it, and their magic collided in mid-air, sending ripples through the room.

The sycophants, who had mostly been cowering under tables during the argument, fled down the corridor in terror.

I followed suit. I did not care about the danger of the magic. Any fear of injury was the furthest thing from my mind. *He knew. He knew the awful things that were happening, and he did nothing to stop it.* How could I reconcile this knowledge with his tender eyes, and unfaltering loyalty to me?

Suddenly, I needed air. I needed to escape.

I could still hear shouting from the back room as I ran for the front door.

"Kathy," cried Sylvie, "What on earth is going on?"

I barely heard her, and made no reply.

I burst out into the cool evening, and struggled to catch my breath. I slumped to the ground, and hugged my knees. I don't know how long I sat there, before the back door opened. I felt sick. Was it Sam, who I didn't know whether to hug or hit? Or Bres, come to kill me? I was unsure which possibility seemed worse.

It was actually Nuadu.

He walked slowly towards me, his eyes grave. "I told you that you would come to regret it, if you meddled in these matters," he said.

"I had to know. I had to stop it. The small ones are my friends, and I promised The Dagda…"

"The Dagda?" he raised an eyebrow, "What does *he* have to do with any of this?"

"He knows what you've been doing, and he's coming for you." I snapped.

"Let him come, if he must," shrugged Nuadu, "It is probably for the best… Though I suspect you are not so eager to bid your lover farewell."

"I really don't know anymore," I whimpered, my voice weak.

"I will tell you something," he continued, "It may comfort you, or not. I hold Lug, or 'Sam', as you know him, in the highest regard. Yes, he has become twisted by Bres's lies and manipulation, but I do not believe that he ever held a small creature in his hands, and drained the life from it himself."

"B-but he let it happen, and enjoyed the spoils."

"True, but I don't believe he understood the full horror of it. Perhaps he did not allow himself to dwell upon it, which was weak, but we are not accustomed to weakness, and we do not deal with it well. The way Bres puts it, that he has merely been 'moving some power around, from one place to another', is easy to accept for one who is longing to accept *something*. And, whatever he has been in recent lifetimes, I think Lug has become something else entirely, under your influence. I looked at him today, and saw a flash of the hero I once knew. I was proud to stand beside him."

"Really?" My leaden heart leaped just a little with a fragment of hope that Sam could be redeemed.

"I would see you keep him," nodded Nuadu, "But of course, that choice is yours."

"So," I began, suddenly trying to remember all of the questions I had longed to ask someone who would speak the truth to me, "Those creatures, who are something between you and the small ones… The ones that brought Bres his victims. What are they?"

"Precisely what you say they are. Something in between. We have all lost something. Some more than others. Others even more than that." He looked wistfully at his silver arm.

"But didn't your physician heal your arm completely?" As soon as I had uttered the question, I regretted it.

Nuadu did not seem to mind. "He did, but our magic faded as we grew lesser, and his with it. I was remembered as Nuadu Argetlám, and to that I returned."

"Why do those… 'in between ones' do Bres's bidding?"

"Why does anyone do his bidding? He has created a beautiful fantasy. A court of delights. They long to be a part of it. He will never admit them, but he gives them hope that one day, he will. They dream of it, for they have forgotten what to be, but have not quite forgotten how to want, and the emptiness and craving of it sickens them."

I almost pitied the wretched 'tween ones…. Almost.

"So, why were you at the door when the small one escaped?"

"I was freeing him. I do not know if it is merciful or not, to let them back out into the world in that sorry state, before Bres has had a chance to devour the last morsel of them, but it seemed the only small kindness I could do."

"I see."

"I will not let it happen again," he assured me, "Your bravery has summoned my courage. I will put a stop to this. You can leave. You are truly in danger now, and I would see you go far away from Bres's wrath."

"I thought you said you would like to see me stay with Sam."

He nearly smiled. "Sometimes, we would see more than one outcome. It is a frustrating constraint of the mortal realm, that only one is possible. Perhaps you could take Lug away. He would go with you. Of that, I have no doubt."

"And you would stay?"

"I would make sure that the dark deeds that have taken place here do not repeat themselves," he said, "That is, if I have the power to do so." He looked down, disapprovingly, at his silver arm.

"You shouldn't doubt your strength because of that," I told him, "The value of any being is determined by far more important things than a limb."

"It seemed so important, once…"

"And, as you said, things have changed. Surely, you must now see that what you look on as an affliction does nothing to dampen what you can achieve. I have done what must, but Bres would have killed me on the spot, if I hadn't had your support."

"*You* have done *far* more than what you must. You should be proud of yourself."

"I'm not really sure what I feel about myself, or anything…"

I swallowed heavily. What I wouldn't have given for Liam or Mr. O Mordha's wise counsel. They had always seemed to know the right thing to do.

"Thank you, Kathy," said Nuadu, almost kindly.

"For what?"

"Helping me to find belief in myself."

"Thank you, too."

"For what?"

"Standing up for me, and telling me the truth."

"There is… another that you should also thank for his loyalty," Nuadu pointed out.

I gulped again.

As if on cue, the back door opened once more, this time very slowly. It was *him*.

"I'll take my leave of you now," said Nuadu quietly, "I know that you have much to discuss. Please do not forget the things I have said."

I nodded, and he was gone.

I turned to face Sam, with a maddening mixture of eagerness and dread.

He walked towards me calmly, crouched down against the wall, and adopted a similar pose to mine. He remained a few feet away, as though he knew that his proximity would not be entirely welcome.

"I have never known regret," he said, earnestly, "But I know it now."

"Really?" I asked, my tone as devoid of emotion as I could make it.

"Yes."

"What do you regret the most?"

"Keeping things from you. Not putting Bres in his place. Seeing that disappointment in your eyes," he murmured, "I've asked him to leave."

"And has he?"

"Not yet."

My breath hissed through my teeth, tensely. "So, when you tried to stop me from confronting him earlier, did you just want to ignore the problem, and for things to stay the same?"

"No. I wanted to keep you safe."

"And if, as he says, the glamour he has built around this place begins to crumble, what will you do?"

"I will do nothing. I will just… be."

"Will you promise that?"

"I will swear an oath on anything that you choose to name. My honour, my destiny… My very existence."

"I suppose I should, at least, thank you for supporting me against him earlier," I sighed, remembering Nuadu's words.

"You should not thank me for anything. I should thank you. Bres claims that he brought me back to life, but you have done so in a way that he never did."

My butterflies longed to flutter, but the leaden weight of my heart still pressed cold against them.

"Do you no longer want me?" he asked.

"I- I'm not sure."

"I suppose I deserve that. But… is there a little hope?"

"Perhaps… if you are in earnest." I longed to burst into tears, and crawl into his comforting arms. I resisted the temptation, and tightened my grip on my knees.

"I am. But, if things happen as Bres warns," mused Sam, "If the glamour fades, and things are no longer as you've known them to be… Will it change the way you see me?"

I laughed harshly, and mirthlessly. "I wish that I could expunge every magical particle from your body, and drag whatever shred of you remains, away with me for a life of peace, in the most remote cottage I could find."

"If you were there, I think that would please me."

I cried unashamedly now, large tears spilling from my eyes and landing on my jeans. "But that can never be."

"At least," he observed, with just a shadow of his usual, playful smile, "Your words give me hope that you have not ceased to want me entirely."

"That's never been the problem," I muttered.

He shifted his body a little closer to mine, still suitably wary of my reaction.

I looked up at him, his beautiful face a blurred mask through my tears. "Never again?" I whispered, "You swear it?"

"I swear it."

I lowered my face to my knees, racked with sobbing. I cried with sadness, and disillusionment, and a certain relief. I had always known that I could not expect him to understand a mortal concept of right and wrong. I could not deny the flashes of callous disregard for others I had seen in him, time and time again, and I had still chosen to belong to him. I had accepted that I was a fool, and claimed him as my own, regardless. I had finally tasted the bitter reality of what I had always known to be true… But I had also come to see something else in him: Devotion… To me, at least. He had taken my side. He had promised to do better, for me. It was more than I had ever expected from him, when he'd first bewitched me with his smile.

"Come here," I murmured.

He was on me in an instant, his arms around my trembling shoulders, and his breath on my hair. I turned to him and kissed him. I kissed him because he seemed in earnest. I kissed him because I needed comfort. I kissed him, hoping to forget my disappointment, even for a moment.

It felt different now. Somehow, less blissful, yet more passionate. I could sense that we both longed to lose ourselves in each other, just as much as gain any enjoyment. Our lips met ravenously. Our fingers craved the other's skin with a new desperation. Before I knew it, we had begun to tear each other's clothes off in the alley outside 'The Horse and Hag'.

"Stop," I whispered, "Not here… people will see."

"Nobody will see. I will make sure of it."

I believed him. I allowed him to pick me up and take me against the wall. It began to rain softly. We moved against each other, our pace frenzied, and our mouths melded together. People passed by occasionally, but as he had promised, not one of them so much as cast a glance in our direction. Sylvie came out and looked up and down the street with concern, at one point. She shrugged, and returned to the bar. It was simultaneously strange and exciting, not to be seen.

When we came, we held each other as though we were both afraid that the other would disappear if we let go. We stared into each other's eyes, and screamed into each other's mouths, with the intensity of it. It was the second time that my power had shaken the ground that evening.

"Nuadu is a good friend to you," I observed, as I caught my breath, "He spoke well of you when I was appalled, and helped to change my mind."

"I must thank him profusely for that."

I suddenly felt almost shy. My desire for Sam, and the distraction of our pleasure, had made me unguarded. Now, I realised that I was standing, naked, wet and shivering, in an alley. I began to pull my clothes on frantically, mumbling:

"I need a bath."

"Of course." He picked me up, before I could protest, carried me back into the pub, and up to my room. Somehow, the bath was already full of luxuriously warm, fragrant water before we had even approached it. I undressed, and climbed in wearily, allowing the heat, and the gentle ripples, to soothe my shivering skin, and with it, some of the darkness from my mind.

He knelt by me stroking my hair, while I drifted, and let myself relax.

Suddenly, my eyes snapped open in realisation, and I seized his hand urgently. "You must swear one more thing," I begged him.

"Anything," he replied.

"You must stop using your magic for silly, frivolous purposes."

"Such as?"

"Unnecessary things, for your personal gain."

"If you say so. But, I assure you, my own powers have not been robbed from other magical creatures…"

"It's not that. The Dagda is coming for you, and I do not want him to have any excuse to take you away."

"I will not leave you for a thousand of his kind."

"He may not give you that choice. You *must* promise me."

"I promise I will try," he conceded.

CHAPTER SIXTEEN

When I woke in the morning, he was gone. I blinked in confusion, my eyes searching the room for any sign of him. I had fallen asleep in his arms, the night before. I was sure of it. It had not been a night for laughter or celebration, but for tender feelings and tentative forgiveness. We had held each other solemnly, missing the more carefree times we had shared, but appreciating the magnitude of the fact that we had both chosen each other in a time of adversity. He had been so willing to say anything to regain my favour. I had truly believed it was important to him. And now, he was gone.

I leaped out of bed, and struggled into fresh clothes, my heart pounding. Had Bres spirited him away, by some trickery? Had The Dagda come for him in the night? Had he simply changed his mind, and decided that his promises to me were too great a sacrifice to bear?

I ran downstairs, and heard the murmur of low voices in the main bar. I was surprised and curious, given the early hour. The prickle embraced me with warmth and relief, and I pressed my hand to the wall for support, as I exhaled deeply. It was Sam and Nuadu. They were sitting at one of the tables, speaking quietly and seriously, over cups of mead.

Sam rushed to me as soon as I approached. He threw his strong, protective arms around me with a kiss. "Dear one," he said, "I'm so sorry not to have been there when you opened your eyes, but Nuadu and I had important matters to discuss."

I nodded. "Of course. Are you talking about Bres?"

"We are," confirmed Nuadu, "And of The Dagda. Lug told me you extended the same warning to him last night."

"I did. I won't have any more secrets between us."

"That is as it should be," replied Nuadu, "I regret having urged you, so harshly, not to speak out about your misgivings before."

"I know you were trying to protect me."

"Even so…"

"Kathy," interrupted Sam, "We are going to call a meeting in the back room soon. We plan to confront Bres, and tell him that his behaviour will no longer be tolerated. We will have a new order here."

"What if Medb and Macha don't agree?" I had no idea whether the female immortals' roles in Bres's dark deeds had been passively complicit, like Sam's, or more actively hedonistic.

"We hope to convince them. A more tempered existence does not have to exclude pleasure or joy."

"He will not make it easy," muttered Nuadu, "But we must try."

"So, we are agreed then?" concluded Sam.

Nuadu nodded gravely, and stood up.

Sam extended his hand to me.

"You want *me* at the meeting?" I asked in surprise.

"Of course," he replied.

I experienced a shudder of foreboding, but knew that if I did not attend, I would drive myself half-mad with curiosity, so I walked with them, down the familiar corridor and into the back room.

The sycophants had not returned, and the room was in disarray. The beautiful furniture had been smashed, and curtains had been ripped down and shredded by furious hands. I was in no doubt that it was the work of Bres's petty, childish anger. Macha and Medb were sitting together on two of the last remaining chairs, their eyes wide and fearful.

"You're back," cried Macha gratefully, as we entered.

Bres was reclining in his usual seat, looking spent after the destruction he had wrought. He surveyed us with a lazy resentment.

"What is *she* doing here?" he demanded, his mouth contorting with distaste at my presence.

"She has every right to be here," snapped Sam, "I won't hear another word about it. Now, we need to talk."

Bres stood up slowly. "No. *You* need to listen. This could all be restored. I could make it what it was, with a snap of my fingers. All you have to do is let me manage my own affairs, and we can have it all back."

"And, by 'your affairs'," replied Nuadu, "I suppose you mean, stealing and draining power from others, to top up your own, failing strength?"

"I will never mention it again," said Bres, "You will not have to know about it. You will not even have to think about it. I will keep it so separate from you that, in time, you will forget about it entirely."

"Absolutely not," thundered Nuadu, "We will not let you continue with this."

Bres raised his eyebrows incredulously. "Not *let* me? I'd like to see *you* try to stop *me* from doing anything, Argetlám!"

"We will both stop you," said Sam, "We have defeated you before, and we can defeat you again."

"Oh, and are you quite sure of that?" smirked Bres, "After all, I have been feeding on the weaker ones for lifetimes, while you've sat about and let me do almost everything for you. Are you sure that you want to go about, making threatening promises you can't keep?"

Sam squared his shoulders. "We were always more powerful than you. Perhaps we forgot it for far too long, but now, something has awoken. A veil of artifice has been pierced. I remember things of my former self that I had thought dead, and I know that Nuadu feels the same. Do you really wish to test our resolve?"

"It would be an entertaining battle, certainly," answered Bres, sounding more jovial, "But no. I do not want enmity. I just want us all to enjoy our endless lives together, in peace and camaraderie… Even you, Nuadu. Don't you see that there is no need for these harsh words? *She* has twisted you, and turned you against me."

"You have done that all by yourself," snapped Nuadu, "I would have peace between us too, but I will not have it at the expense of others. We stood for something once. Kingdoms rose and fell at our command. We made important decisions. Look at us now. We are pathetic. If our power fades, so be it. I would rather see us lesser still, living with honour, than clinging to a faded dream of greatness when our deeds are anything but great."

Bres clicked his tongue, disapprovingly. "Don't you ever just want to be happy? Is there something so wrong with desiring a little joy and contentment? Humans have no shame about pursuing these things. Why should we?"

"Because we should be... more."

"Well, it's not our fault that we're not. It's theirs! Mortals! *Her* kind!" Bres narrowed his eyes at me. "*They* forgot us, *they* put a new god in our place, *they* wrote us into their stories as lesser than we were, and we paid the price!"

"That is no reason to turn on your own kind," reasoned Sam, "I have come to see that some comfort or contentment, gained at the expense of ripping the life out of your weaker kinsfolk, is very hollow indeed. We will not stand for it anymore."

Nuadu nodded in agreement.

"And, what about the two of you?" Bres gestured towards Medb and Macha, "Will you insist on remaining silent, like two witless hens, while these preening cocks dominate the proceedings?"

I saw Medb's eyes sparkle with anger. He had phrased his question well, hoping to elicit that combative sense of competition, that had sent her ancient guise to war for the sole purpose of equality.

Macha, too, bristled. I wondered if the memory of the hardships, that the whims of men had wrought upon her, were gnawing at her a little.

Nuadu growled. "Do not dare to cloud this matter with talk of gender. It, like everything else about us, is merely an illusion, and you know it."

"An illusion we have worn for so many lifetimes that Macha and Medb seem to have embraced their supporting roles wholeheartedly," replied Bres, with a sly glance at the goddesses, "It seems that only *I* remember they have their own strength, and their own will."

He was clever. He was very clever. He was goading them, and trying to turn them against Sam and Nuadu. I could see how his words might have addled the wits of even the greatest minds.

Taking a deep breath, I stepped forward. "You may choose to accept your guises, but does that mean that you must accept utter cruelty as well? Medb, I have seen the way you look at Alice. You have emotion. You have the ability to be moved... To be kind. Perhaps these feelings are new to you, in the greater scheme of eternity... But can't you see them for what they are? A great reward, not a great loss? You may have been deprived of riches, and glory, and power, but you have gained something far more valuable in return."

I saw Medb's expression soften.

"And you, Macha," I continued, "I see a great light in you. In Bres, I see only darkness."

Bres grimaced. "Without darkness, there is no light."

Sam squeezed my hand so tightly that I feared he might break it, but I gripped his in return, with equal ferocity. "We had to carry both of those things within us once," he said, "We had to carry them for a very long time, because that was the essence of us."

I was reminded of the words of the goddess Brigit, many moons ago, at The Dagda's feast in Kerry. Of creation and destruction, she had said: "Both must be, and we must be both."

Sam paused for thought, then continued: "But we have changed. Everything has changed. Perhaps there is no longer room, in the beings that we have become, to contain both in equal measure. Perhaps we grew closer to the ones who once worshipped us, adopting too many of their habits, but too few of their gifts. Perhaps we have to allow new feelings to become a part of us: Compassion, friendship, and regret. Yes, regret too. Bres is right that there is no light without darkness. And yet, perhaps we can use those less palatable aspects of our weakness to show us the way to a different sort of joy and fulfilment."

"Well spoken," remarked Nuadu.

"We are *gods!*" yelled Bres, "Gods! Compassion is not for ones such as we! We are... *everything*. We deserve... *everything*."

"But we cannot have it anymore," insisted Sam, "And I have learned that there are things I value more than greatness... Things I will continue to exist for, whatever I become."

My eyes filled with tears.

"So, this is it?" rasped Bres in a low voice, strangled by his own indignation, "Will you all stand against me, at the beck and call of this mortal wretch, who cannot possibly hope to understand what we have endured?"

"Why not stand *with* us, Bres?" asked Medb, suddenly, "Why not let go of some of the things you crave, in favour of harmony and amity?"

"I will sacrifice *nothing!*"

"We have already sacrificed so much," came Macha's tentative voice, "And we have continued to exist. Perhaps we will barely notice a little more loss, as time passes…"

"Fools! All of you!" cried Bres, "I will not degrade myself by staying here a moment longer. You will regret standing against me, and *you* most of all." He took a few steps towards me, and fixed me with a stare so painfully black that I stumbled a little. His mask slipped, and for a moment, I saw that horrid, crawling, gnashing thing I had once glimpsed behind his face. "I will take everything you hold dear. I will destroy it before your eyes. I will leave you begging for death, and still, I will not take your life. I will leave you with a gaping chasm where your peace used to be… And you will rue the day you came here."

Sam and Nuadu stepped forward protectively, but found themselves looking at an empty space where Bres had been.

He was gone.

Macha raised her hands to her face, aghast. "What do we do now?"

"I don't know about anyone else, but I could do with a drink," sighed Nuadu.

Sam nodded, and absently raised his hand, as though to conjure refreshments. I took hold of his fingers and closed mine around them. "Don't," I said, "Let me get them."

I walked out to the bar, and tried to keep my hands from trembling, as I poured out cups of mead and shots of poitín. The confrontation could not have gone worse, and his departure, though a temporary relief, terrified me. The vicious, vengeful threats he had made were bad enough. Even worse was the knowledge that he was now free to hunt the small ones at his pleasure, far away from our interference.

I retired to my bedroom later, to shower, change and contemplate my impending doom. The atmosphere in the decimated back room had been grave. Sam and I had tried to play fidchell, but our hearts hadn't been in it. Medb had attempted to interest Macha and Nuadu in a card game, with little success.

I was distractedly brushing the same strand of hair for the hundredth time, when I felt a chill. I prickled apprehensively.

The Dagda was standing by the window. "Well," he observed, "It seems you have finally learned the truth."

I did not bother to ask how he knew what had happened. I merely nodded miserably.

"I hope you now understand why I warned you to stay away from this lot."

"B- but," I protested, "It will be different now. They have promised to be different." My shoulders fell. "The only problem is Bres."

"That one is a problem, certainly," he agreed, "But the *only* problem? I think not."

"What do you mean?"

"Do you really believe, child," he began, exasperatedly, "That the others will suddenly turn from centuries of pettiness because you desire it? They are monstrosities. Warped, pathetic things that should not exist as they are. If they are now capable of a little mercy, or a small amount of care, it only brings them further from their destiny, not closer. You defile them more by seeking to impose your values upon them."

"But, if they do no harm, why can't you just leave them alone?" I cried, my emotion getting the better of me, "Besides, I notice *you* are still wearing your human face. Why should you keep it, and seek to deprive others of theirs?"

"That is my burden to bear, for as long as I must negotiate with the others. I will be the last to let go of the artifice, but mark my words, it will come to pass."

"It's not fair! They don't want to go! Please don't take them away!"

"They do not know what they want. I think this has far more to do with *your* desires than any true concern for them." He sniffed the air. "I can sense that you still keep one of them close to you. I suspect you do not want to lose him. You are selfish, and mortal, and that is at it should be… But you are more than that too, and I implore you to try to see the truth of the matter with the gifts I gave you."

"Gifts… *you* gave me?"

"I spoke in error. You see how degraded my kind has become, that even I cannot choose my words with accuracy?"

"Enough of this enigmatic nonsense," I exploded, "You will tell me what you meant, or you will go away and leave me alone!" I stamped my foot, and the prickle roared for emphasis. The floor trembled.

"Do you seek to impress *me* with that part of yourself?" snapped The Dagda, his eyes now angry, and his composure all but gone, "Foolish child. See how they have already corrupted you, with their capricious displays of power? The magic you have comes from *me*. You will not intimidate me with your tantrums, using a part of yourself that *I sired!*"

"Sired?" My mouth fell open.

"I have said too much. I became emotional. It was wrong of me to say it." He looked close to stamping the floor himself.

"But you said it. *Sired*. I know what that means. Are you saying that you're my…"

"Do not use the word," he implored me, "I despise the mortal stench of it. I abhor the fact that I have never been capable of utter dispassion when it comes to you."

"So, it's true." I dropped my hairbrush. That part of me that had longed to go with him, when I'd first met him in the woods, knew it. The part of me that had wondered at his interest in me knew it. The part of me that had always found something oddly familiar in the depths of his ancient eyes knew it.

"But…" I breathed, "I thought that my mother was the magical one. The small ones said…"

"Yes, she had powers too." A flash of pain darted across his face, as though I had raised such an excruciating memory that he could not bear it. "Do not ask me anything further. I will speak no more of it."

"But… you *must* tell me *something…*"

"I must do nothing. This is why I never intended you to know. You will expect things of which I am no longer capable. I turned my back on those parts of my existence, and I will not succumb to them again… even for you."

"But…"

"Silence. I will say only this: You must let them go. You must let *him* go. You must leave, and cease to seek out what can only bring you tragedy and torture. I am not proud of the part of me that cares for you, but I would see you live a happy life, unburdened by the affliction that I… we… gave you."

"I believe your concern is real, but you barely know me, and you have no idea what will make me happy," I protested, "If you want to help me, you will stand against Bres, and make sure that he can never hurt anyone again. As for the others… Well, I fought for the small ones in Kerry to be allowed to remain as they are, and I'll fight for these ones too."

"So, you defy me?"

"So, you will not help me?"

"I have tried. I have tried many times."

"And yet, you will not come to my aid in any way that I actually want," I groaned.

"I cannot place what *you* want over what is best."

"And, who are you to say what is for the greater good? Another, fallible incarnation, with feelings of your own, to which you've just admitted? Why should anybody believe that your will is the only path to follow?"

"You are overwrought with emotion," he said, "There will be no sense from you now. I shall take my leave, and speak to you again, when your passion has not deprived you of your wits."

"No! Wait!" I cried…

But, he was gone.

I walked down to the back room, and collapsed heavily into a chair. The Great Ones watched me with interest, noticing the change in my demeanour.

"Are you alright, Kathy?" asked Sam, "Has something else happened?"

"Not really." *You said you would keep no more secrets.* I sighed. "But, apparently, The Dagda is my father."

Everyone stared at me in silence for a few moments. Then, Macha clapped her hands, sprang to her feet, and cried: "The Dagda! *That's* it! *That's* who it was that I sensed in you!"

"Ah," I replied, weakly.

Then, she frowned. "But… no. That's not all. Now that you say it, I *can* smell him, but there is something else too. Something so very familiar, and yet I just can't quite…" She sat down heavily in her chair again, her face a mask of dissatisfaction.

Things could get no worse, I reasoned. "It's Étaín, isn't it?"

To my surprise, she shook her head. "No, not her either. How frustrating!"

I shrugged. It was the very least of my worries.

Some days later, Sam and Nuadu bid me farewell at the university gates, the former with a tender kiss, and the latter with a curt nod. They now insisted on escorting me to and from college, the terrible memory of Bres's threats against me ringing in our memories. I had drawn the line at them following me around the campus all day and they had eventually conceded that, if he came for his revenge, even Bres was unlikely to do so in a crowded place.

The atmosphere at 'The Horse and Hag' had been strained. I had finally explained something of what had happened to Evelyn and Sylvie. It seemed that they'd had no knowledge of Bres's dark deeds, and were both deeply disturbed that such things had been happening on their premises.

Alice had been to see Medb but, otherwise, the back room had remained free of the gods' mortal companions. Sam and Nuadu had refrained from magically repairing the damage to the furniture, at my insistence, though I privately wondered if any level of restraint would dampen The Dagda's zeal to release them from the incarnations I knew.

I tried not to think what atrocities Bres might be out inflicting on creatures smaller than himself. I had no doubt that he would make his move on me, and I longed for it, and dreaded it, it in equal measure. It would likely end in, either his ultimate defeat, or my untimely death. Though I was still quite certain of my mortality, I was not sure what to call myself now I knew I was the daughter of a god. Was I human? Was I something... Other?

"To me, you are just 'Kathy'," Sam had reassured me, and I'd smiled at him, and kissed him deeply in response, charmed by the reversal of the turn of phrase that had become so meaningful between us.

It was comforting to be back at college. My concentration had suffered, but sitting in a theatre full of uncomplicated people, and listening to the familiar drone of a lecture felt safe, and just a little... normal.

Normal, that is, until I, once again, had the uncomfortable sensation of being watched. *Who is it?* I wondered, as I shifted uncomfortably in my seat, the prickle guarded and snappish.

Bres? I stiffened, then dismissed the thought. The feeling of being spied on had begun some time before the showdown at the pub, and Bres had seemed far too comfortable in his showy chair to run around the city, watching me.

As always, the feeling left me as quickly as it had come, and the rest of the day passed uneventfully. As I walked back out to meet Sam and Nuadu at the gates, I took in my surroundings in a way that I had not done since my first visit to the campus. The infuriating transience of happiness had been playing on my mind, and I had promised myself that I would take more time to appreciate beauty and importance, even in the things I saw every day. I studied the old stone walls, and could still almost hear them heaving with their wealth of secrets. I marvelled at the architecture of the gates, which had once seemed to me like a portal to another world.

Nuadu waved, and Sam opened his arms to me. I rushed to him, and soon forgot all else in his embrace.

I was working in the bar that night. I had convinced the immortals that playing magical bouncers was an inconsequential use of their gifts, and now almost regretted it, as the main bar was full to the brim with revellers who had never quite managed to find 'The Horse and Hag' before, and, as a result, I was rushed off my feet. I had conceded that some glamour to stop ordinary patrons from stumbling into the back room was wise, as much for the mortals' sanity as anything else.

I had wondered if I should be allowed to keep my bedroom, being, as it was, another frivolous enchantment.

"But, I made it for *you*, not for me," Sam had protested, "And you *are* The Dagda's daughter. I'm sure he would not begrudge you a room." I hoped that he was right, because a selfish part of me really did not want to give it up.

"I said, *two pints of stout, please!*" bellowed an impatient customer. I sighed and picked up the glasses.

Some time later, I finally found a mercifully free moment to take out the overflowing rubbish bag. As I deposited it in the bin in the alley, that maddening, prickly feeling returned. I saw nobody nearby, but was in no doubt that I sensed the same presence that had been watching me at college.

"Who's there?" I demanded, more bravely than I felt, "Show yourself!"

I heard a chuckle.

"I can hear you," I exclaimed, "Now come out and face me, immediately!"

Three familiar heads popped around the corner, wearing wicked little grins.

"You!" I cried. It was the 'tween ones. Bres's creatures. "Have you been following me?"

"Oh yes," the female informed me, triumphantly, "We've been watching you ever since he asked us to, haven't we?" The others nodded eagerly. "And you never saw us, not once, did you?"

"*He?*" I repeated, warily, "Do you mean Bres?"

They giggled maliciously, confirming my suspicions. "He will reward us well, won't he?" They all nodded again, in unison.

I froze. Clearly, he had contemplated the possibility that I would set myself against him far earlier than I had. That night when he'd wanted to sample my powers had changed everything. I had thought his desires tempered by Sam's authority, but he had just been biding his time, learning about me, fixating on me… Oh, he was clever.

"What have you told him?" I asked, in terror.

"Everything," squealed one of the fellows gleefully, "All about your fine university, and your lecturer that you like so much, and your little friend in the library. He knows *everything*!"

Some of Bres's parting words to me came flooding back: "I will take everything you hold dear." I felt cold. *Oh no. Mr. Books.*

With a thundering roar, the prickle blew the three little spies away. I had to get to the library. I knew I should fetch Sam and the others, but there was no time. I raced down the alley, and in the direction of the college.

The statuesque gates were locked for the night, but the prickle broke the chain as if it were melted butter. The library too was shut, but I blasted the doors open with ease, and made my way cautiously into the familiar, but now petrifyingly alien, building. Many of the lights had been turned off overnight, and the shelves cast hulking, eerie shadows on the walls. It was difficult to make out my path between them, so my movements grew slow and wary.

I crept further and further, towards my reading table. I began to hear the rustling noise of the whispering books, but they sounded different. Their words were frantic and garbled. They made no sense. It was gibberish they were whispering… Utter nonsense. The wisdom, and the truth of them, was gone. Panic seized me. Something was very, very wrong.

And then, he stepped out from behind the bookshelf. For a moment, relief washed over me, believing him to be safe… Until I drew closer, and saw that dazed, haunted expression on his little face, and his almost transparent skin. His empty eyes. He stood before me, his brow furrowed, and in a tiny, whisper of a voice, he asked:

"Did I know you?"

"It's me. Kathy," I gulped, blinking back the tears, "Don't you recognise me?"

"I- I think I used to know things, but they seem to have gone." He paused, a terrified, stricken shadow crossing his face. "He *took* something…"

I burst into tears. "I'm so sorry, my little friend. I'm so, so sorry."

"He took something from *her* too…" he continued, in his now barely audible, faraway voice. He was looking over into the darkness with dread.

I followed his gaze. There was something on the floor. I felt ill, and suddenly wanted to run far, far away. I told myself to be brave. I walked forward, and found myself looking down on what, at first glance, seemed to be a pile of clothes. That is, until I recognised the oversized cardigan, and the two, dark, frozen eyes staring sightlessly from its midst. Dead eyes. Horrified eyes. Eyes that had seen something so dreadful before sight left them, that it was still there, imprinted on them like a reflection that had not left a mirror.

I crumpled to my knees, fighting the urge to vomit. "Dr. Herbert," I whispered, "No! Oh, please… no!"

It was then that I heard a voice I knew, booming from behind me.

"Well, I promised I'd make you regret it," drawled Bres, "How am I doing so far?"

His deliberate footsteps approached me. I knew I should jump up and fight, but my body was convulsing in horror, at the corpse before me, and I couldn't feel my legs.

He did not get too close. Instead, he circled me, pacing around and around me and the grisly mess on the floor, his hands clasped thoughtfully behind his back, as he expounded:

"It's been hard to get you alone, you know. Your valiant protectors have been doing a *very* good job." His tone was mocking. "I thought I might get impatient, waiting for my chance, but it all worked out exactly as I'd hoped in the end. I instructed those three little pests to tell you of their spying. I was *sure* you'd come running when you heard I knew about your little library friend. You're simply *too* predictable."

Ye gods, he *was* clever. Far too clever.

He continued: "You know, it actually crossed my mind that you might be too cautious to come alone, but I've clearly overestimated you. I thought you might bring your lover along, and that I would have to be content with watching you weep over the body from afar. Dr. Herbert, was it? She was an attractive woman. Almost a shame, really. Oh, well. She was only too happy to follow me in here, in the dark, when I showed her my pretty face. Regretted it in the end, I'll warrant… And here you are, entirely at my mercy. Don't you just love it when a plan comes together?"

A thousand obscenities to shout at him flooded my mind, but not a one of them seemed grave enough for what he had done. I had no words.

"Nothing to say, Kathy? Funny, that. You had plenty to say for yourself in the back room the other day, but perhaps you can't be bothered, now that beautiful Sam and your surly, new friend Nuadu, aren't here to be impressed."

He waited, and sighed, as though he were a little disappointed that he hadn't succeeded in goading me into a petty retort. "Never mind. Nothing that you have to say is of any consequence to me."

Then, he walked towards me, and crouched down in front of me, meeting my horrified gaze with his crawling, greedy eyes. "There is *one* thing that I want from you, though."

The prickle lunged at him, blasting him in a panicked fury, but his own power glowed, like searing embers, around him, and the blow barely shook him.

"My last meal did me the *world* of good," he purred, "That little fellow had far more in him than they usually do. I have no fear of *you*, today."

He grabbed me, roughly, with his strong hands. I struggled against him, and the prickle fought, but his grip barely loosened. Suddenly, I felt very strange… As though his fingers had, somehow, burrowed into my flesh, into my body, into my very core. They grew teeth, and tongues.

Though I could not see them, I could feel them lapping at me, and heard a repulsive, sucking sound as some tiny fragment of my inner self was pulled away. Then another, and another… Tiny tendrils of my most intimate parts swallowed, stolen, gone. I screamed, and writhed, and tried to summon my powers. Layer after layer was devoured. I could feel the very depths of the prickle, curled up tightly somewhere deep and dark, resisting, whispering: *You will not have me.*

I thought I heard another voice. I could not process it. My mind made no sense. It was a swirling, jumbled thing, trying desperately to summon its courage, and…

With a colossal thud, Bres was thrown off me, and across the floor of the library, skidding on Dr. Herbert's blood as he went. Sam and Nuadu were picking me up from the floor.

Sam's anxious face was in mine, crying: "Kathy! Kathy! Please speak to me, Kathy! What has he done to you?"

I clung to him, trembling, as some semblance of order began to return to my thoughts.

"H- he… *took* something from me," I muttered, weakly. Then, everything went dark.

Darkness. Shouting, angry voices. Light. Magic. Darkness. A strange, shimmering feeling of being there, yet not quite there. Then, darkness again.

Daylight came, and I found myself in my bed, cradled in his arms like a most precious butterfly, his touch gentle so as not to break me.

"Kathy, are you awake?" he asked.

I nodded. I knew that something was wrong. Something had happened. What was it? Suddenly, memories of the library began to flood my mind like an unwelcome recollection after a night's heavy drinking. Mr. Books. Dr. Herbert. *Me.*

"Did it really happen?" I whispered.

"So, you remember?"

"I- I think so… You and Nuadu arrived, and… it's all a bit of a blur after that. What happened? How did you find me?"

"I think *you* found *me*," he murmured, "At least, a part of you did. The magic that has intertwined with mine, in those intimate moments. Since we first lay together, I have almost felt as though a tiny fragment of you lives inside me. It cried out, and I knew I had to go to you. It showed me the way."

"Yes," I mused, "I felt something, that first time, too… Saw things that I could not know… as if a small part of you had been imprinted on me, somehow… So, you carried me back here?"

"We… *took* you back here."

"Magically."

"I think The Dagda would understand."

"I have not seen you do that before."

"There are things… parts of ourselves, that we had forgotten. We are beginning to remember, now… "

"And what happened to Bres?"

"He ran away. We wanted to go after him, but it was more important to bring you home and make sure you were safe. What did he do, Kathy? Did he take your powers?"

I paused to take stock of what I could feel. With relief, I sensed the great ball of the deep prickle, still nestled inside me, growling like a protective tiger… But there was something missing. That light, familiar sensation that played around my shoulders, and trickled up and down my spine… That comfortable prickle of *being* was so faint that I could not be sure if it was really there anymore, or merely a memory, like an amputated limb that still itches.

"No, not everything," I replied, my voice shaky, "He didn't get deep enough… But, *something* is gone." I burst into tears.

He held me, his grip stronger now that he was sure that he was not cocooning an empty shell that might crumble to dust.

"That's good," he assured me.

"I- I…" I stammered, "I don't know how to be without it."

"You're still you. That is enough."

I crawled further into his embrace, wanting to feel him all around me, instead of the emptiness of my own skin. I cried and I cried, and he stroked my hair, and pressed my hand to his lips. I do not know how long we lay there.

I tried to reach the prickle, buried inside… To stroke it, to coax it out, to make it one with my consciousness, but it stayed put, like a wary dragon deep in its cave. *You let him taste us. You let his filthy tongue in here, where it did not belong, licking us, chewing on us, wearing us away.*

I'm sorry, I replied silently, I'm so sorry.

As soon as I was well enough, Sam carefully led me downstairs.

Sylvie was behind the bar. She asked how I was, in a slightly frightened voice. She had clearly been told something by the Great Ones, but I couldn't tell how much she knew.

As soon as I saw Nuadu, Medb and Macha, they rebuked me, and rightly so.

"Why did you not come for us?" demanded Nuadu, "Why did you go running off on your own, when that is just the thing we have been trying to avoid?"

"I wish I hadn't," I said, simply.

"You could have been killed," cried Macha.

Medb agreed grimly. "It was certainly ill-advised."

"I know," I replied.

"She has been through enough," chided Sam, protectively. "None of this will talk will change what has happened."

I felt that I deserved a telling off, but appreciated his support. "What do we do?" I asked, "We can't keep avoiding him. Look what he's done! We must seek him out, and not let him continue on this rampage!"

Nuadu nodded. "It will not be easy. He is strong now, and concealing himself from us. We cannot determine his precise location."

"He hasn't finished with Kathy," muttered Sam darkly, "I'm certain of it. He wants her, and he will not have her. We *must* find him."

"How?" I asked.

Nuadu frowned. "Let us think on it, Kathy. You should rest."

He was right. I still felt physically weak, and I longed to crawl back into bed.

"Shall I come with you?" asked Sam.

"I would speak with you first, Lug," declared Nuadu. I assumed that he wanted to discuss some strategy between them to find Bres, or draw him out.

That was important. I longed for Sam to join me. His arms almost made up for the empty, aching loneliness where my active prickle had been. However, I said:

"You should talk. Join me later."

"Very well," agreed Sam, though he looked reluctant to leave my side.

"I'm sure Bres won't come for me under this roof," I reassured him with feigned nonchalance.

He nodded, and kissed me. "I will know it if he does. I will come to you soon."

As I trailed through the main bar, feeling empty, naked and terribly alone, I spotted the payphone by the door. I looked at it, wondering if it might be alright to ring Mr. O Mordha for a quick chat. I wouldn't tell him anything. I wouldn't worry him... But just the sound of his comforting voice... His warm, kind, uncomplicated voice, might make me feel a little better... I thought about it, and thought better of it, and thought about it again...

Before I could reason any further with myself, I popped some change into the coin slot, and dialled the familiar number.

It rang and it rang, for what seemed like an eternity. Perhaps he was out. *Good. Just as well,* I told myself. It had been a foolish idea. I should never have done it...

Suddenly, a voice answered the phone. It was not Mr. O Mordha.

Ye gods!

"Hello?" repeated Liam.

Silence.

"Who is this?" he demanded, sounding irritated.

Silence.

His voice came again, this time his tone more tentative. "Kathy? Is that you?"

How does he know?

I almost slammed the phone back down. I almost put on a deep voice and barked: "Sorry, wrong number!"

Instead, I stood there, witless and frozen, breathing hard into the receiver like some lunatic.

"Kathy?" he asked again.

"Yes," I blurted out, "Yes, it's me."

"Is everything alright?"

"No, not really." I burst into tears, frightened, embarrassed, forlorn, and utterly ashamed of myself.

"Please calm down, and tell me what's happened!"

The whole sorry mess tumbled out of me in a garbled stream: "There are Great Ones in the pub, and one of them has been hurting the small ones, and I challenged him, and he hates me, and the 'tween ones have been spying on me, and the library is enchanted, and he drained Mr. Books, and he killed Dr. Herbert, and he tried to take my powers, and now the prickle is hiding and won't come out, and I feel so empty, and The Dagda is my father, and he's trying to take them away, and I don't want them to go, and…"

"Good grief," muttered Liam, "I know you're upset, but could you please take a deep breath and start again, because I really didn't understand a word of that?"

I paused, and did as he instructed. I inhaled and exhaled slowly, and then I told him everything. Well… Almost everything.

"I'm so sorry," he breathed, the concern in his voice audible, "It sounds like it's been awful for you. I imagined that you were up in Dublin, having the time of your life, drinking and dancing, and making new friends…"

"Well, there *has* been… a *bit* of that."

"Shall I come? Can I help?"

I did not answer immediately, remembering how the prickle had always been strengthened by his touch, and how he had healed me after Étaín's fire. Perhaps he *could* help… But how could I ask him to put himself in the way of such danger?

"I- I don't know," I croaked, weakly.

"For once in your life, Kathy, just say yes or no. If you want me, I'll leave the cottage this instant, and travel to Dublin. Shall I come?"

"Yes." As soon as I had said it, I regretted it.

"Right," he concluded, and the line went dead.

What have I done? I should have rung him back immediately, and told him I had changed my mind, and that he should stay away. I should have stopped him. Oh, how I wish I had stopped him.

Instead, I sank down to the floor of the pub, and put my face in my hands, wanting to disappear. The bar was so crowded that nobody noticed.

Moments later, Alice rushed in, and saw me in a crumpled heap. She bent down and hugged me tightly.

"I'm so sorry," she said, tears in her voice, "I just heard about Dr. Herbert. I can't believe it! You must be heartbroken. I know she really took you under her wing. Who would *do* such a thing?"

I knew I had much to tell her, but I was still horrified, and preoccupied by the latest mistake I had made.

"Alice, I've done something incredibly stupid," I admitted.

"What?" she asked, pulling me to my feet, and leading me to an empty booth, "What is it?"

My elbows slumped on to the table. "I was missing home, and I rang my ex, and I told him everything that's happened, and now he's on his way here to help me." I swallowed heavily. "I haven't told him about Sam."

Alice raised her eyebrows. "That doesn't sound… great. Can't you call him back and tell him not to come?"

"I should have. I'm pretty sure it's too late now. He was about to leave the house. I'm such an idiot!"

She patted my arm comfortingly. "Don't worry," she soothed, "It might be a bit awkward, but I'm sure they'll behave themselves, and it will be okay."

"Nothing is okay," I sighed, "I still haven't told you what happened in the library."

CHAPTER SEVENTEEN

When Sam emerged from the back room, he appeared surprised, but hopeful, to see me sitting with Alice.

"I thought you were going to bed," he said, "Are you feeling better?"

I laughed mirthlessly. "Not really."

Alice looked uncomfortable. "I'll leave you two to talk," she whispered, and squeezed my hand supportively. Then, she disappeared down the corridor to find Medb.

Sam took the empty seat she had occupied, and instinctively stroked my hair. "You appear thoughtful," he observed.

I sighed deeply. "I have to tell you something."

"Yes?"

"A… friend is coming to visit me from Kerry."

"Is it… a good time for that, with everything that's been happening?"

"No. I should have put him off. I was feeling homesick when we spoke, and I stupidly told him to come, and now there isn't much I can do about it."

Sam studied my face a little too keenly. "Is he… a lover?"

I felt myself turning red. "He was."

"Ah. Do you plan to sleep with him?"

"No!" I exclaimed, "Of course not!"

Sam nodded, and mused: "I think that I am glad of that. It sounds foolish, but I would prefer not to share your affections."

It occurred to me that monogamy was unlikely to be common practise among his kind. I shook my head, wearily. "My affections are yours."

He picked up my hand, and pressed it to his lips. "Will he be disappointed if you don't sleep with him?"

"I… don't know."

"I'm sure he will be."

I smiled weakly at the compliment. "There is another reason I asked him to come," I confessed, "When I was growing up, he always had the ability to strengthen my magic, and he has some healing powers of his own. I wondered if he might be able to help me recover from Bres's assault."

"Oh, so he is one of us?"

"An immortal? Oh, no. He's just a boy… But he *is* the seventh son of a seventh son of a seventh son."

"How mysterious," pondered Sam, "I have never heard of a mortal with the gift of healing. If he can help you, I welcome his visit, of course."

I leaned my head on his shoulder. "Thank you. How was your talk with Nuadu?"

"Interesting… But, that can wait. You look tired. Shall we go to bed?"

"Yes, please!"

He helped me upstairs, then I undressed and crawled under the covers. He snuggled up beside me. I had thought that I would fall asleep in minutes, but found myself excited by his taut, alabaster skin against mine, and his sweet, intoxicating breath on my neck. I kissed him deeply, and pressed myself to him, feeling his arousal.

His hands were on me in an instant, hungrily exploring my body, while I moaned, and wrapped my leg around his hips. He thrust himself inside me, and we moved together, our maddening pleasure escalating as we writhed. We clung to each other feverishly, when sweet release came, and his power roared with satisfaction. I felt a deep thud inside me, as my buried magic responded to our ecstasy in spite of itself, but it did not reach out for him, or ripple against my skin.

I kissed him again, my heart racing, then drew back and timidly asked: "Did it feel… different for you?"

"Yes," he admitted, "But no less wonderful."

I could not tell if he was in earnest, or simply being kind. I buried my face in his muscular chest and, before long, sleep found me.

Some hours later, a colossal pounding noise jolted me awake. "What was that?" I cried, rubbing my bleary eyes in confusion.

The din sounded again: A frantic, determined banging from downstairs.

I frowned. "Is that someone knocking at the front door?"

"You did say you were expecting a visit from your… friend," Sam pointed out.

Ye gods.

Liam.

For a shameful moment, I considered pulling the covers over my head, and not letting him in, allowing him to knock, and knock, until he grew fed up and went back to Kerry.

You know very well that is not an option.

I leaped out of bed, pulled on my clothes, and ran downstairs, with Sam in tow.

"Kathy!" bellowed Liam's voice from outside, "Kathy, are you in there?"

"I'm coming," I yelled back.

I found the keys for the door, and went to admit him, my hands shaking so vigorously that I could barely operate the lock.

Sam placed a hand on my shoulder. "Perhaps I should go to the others for a little while," he said, "And give you some time to reacquaint yourself with your… friend."

I nodded, still trembling. "Thank you." I kissed him quickly, and he walked away towards the back room.

"Kathy," cried Liam, "Open the door!"

With a deep breath, I finally succeeded in turning the key, and flung the door open.

And there he was, standing in front of me, against the night, his lovely face and fair hair illuminated by the indoor light. A flood of memories washed over me: Memories I had chosen not to dwell on for quite some time. Everything that had been between us flashed through my mind, from his smile when I asked him if he would like to play again tomorrow, to the touch of his hand, to his horrified face when he realised that he had lain with Étaín.

"Hello, Liam," I said in a small voice.

He stood on the doorstep for a moment, frozen, as if he had no idea how to respond. Then, the stiff expression on his face melted, and he was on me, his arms around my waist, and his face against my neck. His embrace felt so familiar... So natural, that I forgot myself for a moment, and almost kissed him. Then, I took stock of myself and jerked away.

He looked surprised, and a little hurt, but took a few steps further into the pub, and looked around warily. "Are we alone?" he asked.

"There are some... others in the back room, but I don't think they'll bother us for a while."

"Others? You mean, the Great Ones you told me about?"

"Yes."

He shuddered. "Can we go somewhere... further away from them?"

"I can't really leave the building at the moment, in case Bres comes after me again, but we can go to my room."

"Okay," he nodded

I led him through the store room, and up the little staircase. As soon as he set foot in my bedchamber, he began to look even more uncomfortable.

"This is... nice," he observed, though his expression suggested that he found it anything but. I remembered how he had always seemed unnerved by Étaín, despite her charm and beauty. He rubbed his arms, almost as though he were trying to scrub the atmosphere off his person. He could clearly sense that there was something uncanny about it.

"We can go back downstairs if you, prefer," I suggested.

"No, it's okay. This is... fine." He perched awkwardly on the chair.

I sat on my bed, picking at my cuticles nervously.

"How are you feeling?" he asked

"A bit strange," I confessed, "I miss the prickle."

"But it's still inside you?"

"Yes. I know it's *there*... or, at least, most of it is, but it won't communicate with me. I can't summon it at all."

"Would you like me to help you try?"

I was eager for it, but remembering how affectionate he had been downstairs, I was not sure that touching him again so soon was a good idea.

"Thank you. Maybe later," I said.

"So…" Liam's voice trailed off, as though he had been hoping that words would come to him if he began to speak, but they had not.

I cleared my throat. "How have you been?"

"Fine, thank you."

"And your father?"

"He's well."

"Good, good."

"Finding out about The Dagda must have been quite a shock."

I nodded. "It was at first, but it also explains a lot."

"Did he tell you how he met your mother?"

"No," I sighed, "He doesn't seem to want to talk about her at all. I was hoping to persuade him, but we got into an argument about… the ones downstairs, and he left."

"He wants them to join his collective?"

"Yes, but I won't let him take them," I said, fiercely.

Liam raised his eyebrows at the change in my tone. "You seem very protective of them."

"I am."

"But… didn't you say they that knew all about their friend, Bres, and the fact that he was stealing powers from weaker immortals? They don't sound worth your loyalty."

"Things are different now," I insisted.

He looked unconvinced.

I changed the subject. "You must be tired after your journey. I can go downstairs for a while, if you'd like to take a nap."

Liam looked at the magical bed suspiciously, and grimaced with distaste. "No thanks. I'll just find a hotel nearby… But I wanted to look in on you first, to see if you needed anything."

"Thank you for coming."

"No thanks required."

Suddenly, I had the uncontrollable urge to ask him a question, though I wasn't entirely sure why it mattered: "D- did you come to the coach station?"

"What?"

"Before I left Kerry, I gave your father a note…"

"I know."

"Did you come to the station to say goodbye? My coach left early, and I wondered…"

He sighed deeply. "I got as far as the corner, and then turned back. I couldn't bear it. I was a coward."

"No you weren't. You were hurt!"

"I was heartbroken," he blurted out.

"I'm sorry."

"It doesn't matter. We're together now."

"I- I…" I stammered, "I shouldn't have asked you to come here. It was selfish of me. Bres is very dangerous, and…"

"I wouldn't be anywhere else.".

At that moment, a knock sounded at the bedroom door.

"Come in," I called.

Don't let it be Sam. Don't let it be Sam. Don't let it be Sam.

Of course, it was Sam.

"Well, well," he smiled, studying Liam inquisitively, "I hope I'm not interrupting."

"No, of course not," I replied quickly, an intense blush rising to my cheeks. "Liam, this is…"

"Lug Samildánach," interjected Sam loudly, presenting his hand to Liam in greeting, "Pleased to make your acquaintance."

Liam eyed him, as though he would prefer to touch a wasp's nest, but reluctantly shook his hand.

"Hello," he replied, coldly.

Sam strode over to me, and casually took a seat beside me on the bed. Liam bristled.

"So," said Sam, "Kathy tells me you might be able to help her with her powers."

Liam shrugged. "I will gladly try, but I have no idea if I can do anything."

"Strange," observed Sam, "I can't sense any magic in you at all, but Kathy assures me that you have performed impressive feats in the past. You will have my gratitude, if you can be of assistance to her."

"I came here for *her*," responded Liam tersely, his tone leaving me in no doubt that what he truly wanted to say was that Sam's favour was irrelevant and unwelcome.

"I see," said Sam, his tone guarded. The slight had not gone unnoticed. "Where are you planning to stay? I'm afraid we don't have much room for you here…"

"I was just about to go out and look for a hotel."

"I can recommend one," I muttered, "I'm sorry I can't take you there myself, but…"

"Of course. You're in danger."

"I should stay with Kathy, but I could ask someone else to escort you, if you wish," offered Sam politely.

Liam shook his head. "That won't be necessary."

"Very well, then," concluded Sam, "Shall we see you out?"

Liam's eyes narrowed. "Kathy, would *you* like me to leave?"

I swallowed heavily. The tension in the air was almost tangible. "I suppose we should both get some rest," I said, in what I hoped was a diplomatic tone. I went to the desk, picked up a piece of paper and scribbled down the hotel address and directions. "It's just around the corner."

Liam took the note and pocketed it. We walked downstairs silently, and I opened the front door, desperately racking my brain for something to say.

"Goodnight, Kathy," said Liam, completely ignoring Sam, "I'll come back tomorrow."

"Okay. Goodnight. Thank you."

He paused for a moment before departing, as though wondering whether or not to kiss me goodbye. He thought better of it, and took off down the alley in the direction of the square.

I locked the door behind him, and sighed deeply.

"So," began Sam, "How was it to see him again?"

"Fine," I lied.

"Shall we go back to bed?"

"Actually, I quite fancy a drink."

Morning came, and I woke and cringed as I remembered the awkward exchange between Liam and Sam. *I wish I hadn't told him to come.*

Sam kissed me and asked how I was feeling.

"Okay," I replied, "More or less."

He suggested going downstairs to find out if the others had had any further ideas on how to find Bres, and I told him that I would wash and dress, and follow him down.

I wanted a little time to process my thoughts, so I filled the bath and relaxed in it for a while. He hadn't said so outright, but I knew that Liam had not been happy the night before. I wondered if he had travelled to Dublin expecting a romantic reunion. I wondered if he suspected that Sam was more to me than a mere acquaintance. I couldn't help thinking that the latter's behaviour had been a little territorial, introducing himself by his full name, as if to intimidate Liam, and rushing him out into the night so soon. Then again, Liam had been positively rude in his lack of courtesy towards Sam. He had not made even the slightest effort to conceal his contempt.

I groaned. Today is going to be fun.

I eventually made my way downstairs. Evelyn was opening the bar. "How are you, Kathy?" she asked, "I hear you suffered a dreadful loss. Your lecturer was murdered? I'm so sorry."

"I've been better," I confessed.

"Well, don't worry about work until you're feeling up to it." She patted my arm kindly.

"Thank you so much."

I wandered into the back room. The Great Ones were talking animatedly.

"Kathy," exclaimed Nuadu, "We have a plan."

I gasped. "Really? What are we going to do?"

Sam clasped my hand. "We're going to go out for a little while. Don't worry, we won't be long."

"All of us?" I asked.

"Not you," replied Nuadu, "You're far too weak, and your magic isn't even working properly."

I opened my mouth to protest, but he glared at me sternly and I thought better of it.

"Macha and I will stay here with you, Kathy," declared Medb, "Don't worry. I'm strong. You will be safe with us."

Sam drew me aside, and spoke quietly: "I don't think Bres is likely to come back here, but just in case, please promise me that you will stay by Medb and Macha until I return. If you go upstairs, and anything happens, I don't know if they will be able to sense your distress the way I can."

I nodded. "Where are you going? Are you in danger?"

"We'll be fine. You will understand everything soon, dearest one." He kissed me tenderly, and left with Nuadu, by the back door.

Though his words had been confident, I could not help worrying that if Sam was out antagonising Bres further in any manner, he might be in harm's way. Medb and Macha too seemed more distracted than was usual, and I wondered if their unease was an indication of concern. However, they did not share with me what Sam and Nuadu were actually doing, and I did not press them to do so. The goddesses and I had been waiting anxiously for some time, attempting and failing to distract ourselves with light conversation, when Evelyn popped her head around the corner.

"Kathy, there's someone here to see you," she called, "Shall I show him in?"

I nodded tensely. It was not the ideal time for Liam to arrive, but at least Sam wasn't here to antagonise him further.

He stumbled into the back room, his eyes wide and fearful as he took in his bizarre surroundings. His gaze lingered on Macha and Medb with little admiration. His lip curled slightly, in a suspicious snarl. Then, he saw me, and his expression softened.

"Kathy," he said, "How are you today?"

I shrugged. "The same."

"Can we... go out to the other bar?" He cast a meaningful glance at my companions, indicating that he would prefer to speak to me alone.

"I have to wait here for now," I explained apologetically, "Something is... happening. Liam, I'd like you to meet Medb and Macha."

"Hello," he said, warily.

Macha clapped her hands and squealed with delight. "Is this your former lover, Kathy? How pretty he is!"

I blushed, and Liam looked as though he would welcome the sudden arrival of an earthquake.

Medb smirked, shot me a sympathetic look, and greeted him politely.

"You must come over here and tell me all about yourself," gushed Macha, "I hear you have a most distinguished lineage, for a mortal. Did you come here because you still want Kathy? I hope you weren't too disappointed to hear about her and Sam…"

Oh, no. Oh, please, no.

Liam exhaled heavily and froze, as though she had thrown a brick at his stomach. "Sam?" he repeated, his voice icy.

"Yes, Sam. Or did he introduce himself as Lug? He told me that you met last night."

Liam turned to look at me, wearing the strangest expression. For a moment, I almost thought that he was about to laugh. Then, his eyes glazed over, and I could not read anything further in them.

"What is she talking about, Kathy?" he asked, his voice unnervingly quiet, "What nonsense is she speaking? It's as though she thinks that… *you* and *he*… I mean, what a ridiculous notion! You wouldn't…"

I opened and closed my mouth, but no words came. I could feel the burning colour of my face betraying me. I lowered my eyes.

Then, he did laugh. It was not a happy sound, but harsh, and shallow, and incredulous. "It… It *is* nonsense, isn't it, Kathy? Surely, there's no way that you would…"

"L- let's talk about it later," I muttered.

"No, let's talk about it *now*. I want you to tell me that she's mistaken. It simply can't be possible that there is something… *between* you and…" He trailed off with something approaching a retch.

"Liam, I…" I began.

I was interrupted by a loud noise, as the back door opened and slammed shut, and shouting filled the room. Sam entered, hauling two of the 'tween ones, followed by Nuadu, clutching the third. The creatures howled, and struggled, and spat, and swore at their captors. Medb and Macha rushed forward to assist, and the three wretched things were soon wrangled onto chairs, and warned very sternly by Nuadu not to move if they valued their lives. I knew how frightening his threats could be. The 'tween ones remained sulky, but settled down.

Sam turned around with a triumphant smile, and announced: "There! Now, we have the creatures that do Bres's bidding! He has clearly been communicating with them since he left, and he's far too lazy and self-important to do his own dirty work for long. If we deprive him of his instruments, we may draw him out." Then, he noticed Liam. "Oh, *you're* back," he observed, "Have you had any luck in helping Kathy with her powers yet?"

Liam stormed out of the room, towards the main bar.

"Has everything been well?" asked Sam, puzzled.

"Y- yes, fine," I replied, "B- but… I'm so sorry, I have to go."

I chased after Liam, and found him sitting in an empty booth, quivering with rage. I had never seen such darkness in his eyes.

He looked up at me as I took a seat opposite him.

"Tell me it isn't true," he said, his voice like the calm before the eruption of a volcano.

"I- I…"

"I said, tell me it isn't true."

"I didn't want you to find out like that," I blurted out, "I should have told you. I'm sorry."

Liam swore, and punched the wall. "You're sorry? You're *sorry?*"

"I am."

"Sorry for what, exactly?" His tone was sarcastic. "Sorry for getting over what we had so quickly, or dragging me up here like a fool to be laughed at by your new boyfriend and his reprehensible companions, or keeping secrets, or…?"

"I know. I've done everything the wrong way. I should never have asked you to come."

He buried his face in his hands. "When you left, I tried to understand. I told myself that you needed to get away from Aoife, and Étaín, and Alan Lynch… But I *knew*, or at least, I *thought* I knew, that you loved me… That what we had was as special to you as it was to me."

"It *was*. It is. I never expected this to happen."

"Do you love him?"

I gasped at the question. "What?"

"Do. You. Love. *Him?*"

"I- I…"

He punched the wall again.

"You know, it's one thing for you to have moved on, but… with a creature who is not even human? Some entirely amoral entity from a bygone era? *Really?* I know you're impulsive, and you don't think things through, but honestly, I thought that even *you* would have enough sense not to get involved with something like *that*. I mean, where are you going to live? In the *síd?* Or here, in that mockery of a room that I don't even think is real?"

"I know. It's complicated."

"Complicated? *Complicated?* Yes, that's the word for it, if 'complicated' means ripping my heart out, and destroying your own future in the process."

"I shouldn't have dragged you into this. I never wanted to hurt you."

"You know, Kathy, I used to believe that, but now I'm beginning to think that you're callous. Callous and cruel."

"If I could turn back time…"

"Oh, that's a good idea. Why don't we find out if I can heal your powers, which is clearly the only thing you wanted me for, and perhaps you can turn back time?"

"That's not fair. I was sad, and lonely, and when I heard your voice on the phone, I missed you… But I shouldn't have told you to come. I know that."

"Lonely? You don't seem very lonely to me!"

"I feel so strange without the prickle… As though I've lost my best friend."

"I know the feeling."

I winced. "I will always be your friend."

"I think you might want to look up the definition of that word in the dictionary."

"I'm sorry."

"Look," he sighed, his eyes downcast, "I just don't think I can be around you right now. I need to go."

"I suppose that's fair. Will you come back?"

"I- I don't know." He stood up and strode out of the pub, almost bumping into Alice as she arrived for her shift.

She ran over to me, curiously. "Was that him?"

I nodded miserably.

"How did it go?"

"Well, let me put it this way. Before he arrived, I had imagined what I thought was the worst case scenario. I was wrong."

"Oh dear," she sympathised, "How are you feeling?"

"Like a truly dreadful human being," I replied, honestly.

Some time later, I concluded that continuing to repeat Liam's harsh words, over and over again in my head, would drive me mad and do him no good. I remembered the situation in the back room, and decided to see how Sam and the others were faring with the 'tween ones.

They were scowling and wriggling on their chairs, like feral kittens, and the Great Ones were seated in a circle around them. As I watched, it became evident that some interrogation was being attempted, but the trio appeared anything but cooperative.

"Where is he?" demanded Nuadu.

"I'm not telling you, and you can't make me," retorted one of them churlishly.

"You don't want to see what I could do to you," threatened Nuadu.

Sam got up, and came to my side.

"How are things going?" I asked, though it was really a rhetorical question.

He sighed wearily. "It's been like this since you left. We can sense Bres's presence in the city, but he is still trying to conceal himself from us, and we cannot pinpoint his location. These weaker ones were far easier to track down. If we can't make them tell us where he is, he will most likely try to contact them eventually. We may be able to track him when he does. Oh, by the way, was everything alright with Liam?"

"No, not really."

"What happened?"

"He was… unhappy to hear that you and I are together."

"Ah, so he *was* disappointed that you weren't planning to sleep with him."

"Perhaps… something like that. He left."

"For good?"

"I don't know." I glanced over at the 'tween ones. "Anyhow, as to the matter at hand: The longer they are gone, the more likely Bres is to notice, and suspect that we have them. He *is* clever. If they would cooperate, we would have a far better chance of catching him off guard. Would you mind if I tried to question them for a while? I have had dealings with them before."

"Be my guest," exclaimed Sam, gesturing for me to take his seat.

I sat down and stared at the unhappy trio intently. The others watched.

"Well, well, well," I began, looking them in the eyes, in turn, with each repetition, "Here we are again. You remember me, don't you?"

They sniffed, sulkily, in unison.

"I see that you do. Now, you know I can hurt you, because I've done so several times."

"Wasn't that bad," snapped one of the fellows stubbornly.

"Well, of course not," I agreed, "Because those were just warnings. You don't want to see me lose my temper."

"We're not scared of any of you," he retorted, "We were dragged in here ages ago, and not a one of you has done anything to us yet. I think you need us too much to harm us!"

"Ah. Well, let me tell you a secret: The others are far more powerful than I am. They could blast you into next week with their magic. However, they have promised to stop using their gifts for silly, inconsequential little things like you. That's where *I* come in. I have made no such promise. I can bounce you off these walls for the rest of the day, and nobody will do a thing to stop me… But I don't want to do that. I'd like to have a proper chat with you instead. What do you say?"

The female scowled. "I say you're mean and nasty, and you stopped us from getting our reward!"

I nodded. "And, what reward was that? You wanted… 'this', didn't you?" I raised my hands to indicate our surroundings, "You wanted to be in here with us, enjoying *this*, didn't you? Now you *are* here, why aren't you glad?"

"We thought it would be fun," grumbled one of the fellows, "We were promised drinking, and dancing, and music, but this isn't like that at all!"

"No, it's not like that at all," concurred the other, "This is boring and horrible."

The female stamped her foot. "I bet it was more fun when *he* was here. *He* will start a new court, somewhere much better than this, and we will be the most important members!"

"I see. So, that's his plan." I paused. "Sam, would you be so kind as to honour us with a song? Something jolly."

Sam stared at me, surprised, but acquiesced, and began to sing. The melody he chose was not of the twisting, heartbreaking kind he usually favoured, but lilting and uplifting. It was no less beautiful. The joy in his voice radiated through the whole back room. The 'tween ones still looked defiant, but I noticed that their little feet had begun to move to the rhythm, in spite of themselves.

I stood up. "Now, I'm going to go out and ask Alice for some drinks, and then we're all going to have a nice conversation, aren't we?"

I read a small amount of uncertainty creeping into their expressions. *Good.*

Nuadu caught my eye, and favoured me with a rare smile, as I departed.

Alice poured out several little cups of mead, and I returned to the back room with the tray. Sam was still singing, and the 'tween ones were looking at him with something akin to reluctant awe. Their enormous eyes brightened still further, when they noticed the beverages I was carrying.

"For us?" gasped one of the fellows, excitedly.

I nodded.

"You drink first," ordered the female warily, "You might have put anything in there."

"Certainly," I agreed, taking a sip and passing her the cup, "But why would I do that? If I wanted to hurt you, why would I poison you, when throwing you around the room would be so much more amusing?"

She shrugged and began to gulp greedily.

Before long, their faces were merry and slightly flushed.

"Medb, shall we dance?" I suggested.

The goddess rose obligingly, and we moved around the room, in time to the music, swirling and spinning. Before long, Macha had joined us too.

"This is fun, isn't it?" I observed. I turned to face the 'tween ones. Their dangling legs were now positively animated as they watched us, as though longing for permission to join us in our prancing. "Have you ever had this much fun with *him?*"

They shook their heads, reluctantly.

"Now, all you have to do is tell us where he is, and we'll have an even grander party!"

"He's…" began one of the fellows.

"Shush! We mustn't," hissed his companion.

"Very well. Perhaps you've had enough of the music. Sam, you can stop now."

"No!" cried the third, "Please don't stop! I'll help you find him!"

"Oh, good," I exclaimed, "Then, the revelries can continue." I raised a cup of mead, spun around Macha to the beat, and came face to face with… Liam.

Oh, no. No. No. No.

His horrified face looked as though it had been slapped. Without a word, he turned and left.

"Don't stop singing," I called frantically, as I ran down the corridor after him. Liam was almost at the front door. I grabbed his arm, and he turned to face me.

"Please, don't go!"

He showed his palms and sank into a nearby seat, his face blank and stunned, and his manner utterly defeated. "I- I just don't believe this," he breathed. His voice was not angry anymore, merely devastatingly astonished. "I came back to say I was sorry for having been so unkind. I regretted my jealousy. I thought I had left you upset, and angry with yourself… But, I find you drinking and dancing! Cavorting with those… *creatures. Celebrating!* Are you really so cold?"

I groaned. "It's not what it looks like."

"Oh? So the custom among the immortals is to carouse and make merry, as an expression grief?" His tone was mocking.

"Please, listen to me. You have to understand. We have been trying to get those three you saw brought in earlier, to tell us where Bres is. Threats were of no use. Reason was of no use. The only thing they responded to was fun and distraction, so I created it to make them talk. What you saw *did not* reflect my mood. I am wretched, truly wretched, to have caused you pain… But I have to try everything to find Bres. He must be stopped… and it worked! They were just about to tell me where he is… and then…"

"I walked in?" Liam guessed.

"Yes," I sighed, "Please tell me you believe me."

He took a deep breath. "I suppose it makes more sense than you actually having turned into a monster."

Suddenly, Sam rushed out of the back room, and placed his hands urgently on my shoulders. "Dearest one," he said gravely, as Liam shuddered, "They've spoken. We know how to find Bres. We must go at once, before we lose the element of surprise."

I gasped. "Liam, I'm so sorry… I have to leave."

"No, Kathy," said Sam, " I don't want you to come. You're too vulnerable."

"I'm coming," I insisted, "After what he did to me, and Mr. Books, and Dr. Herbert… Don't you dare try to leave me behind!"

Sam pressed my hand to his lips, in reluctant acquiescence. "Very well. I understand."

"I'm coming too," declared Liam, rising decisively to his feet.

"What?" I gasped.

Sam frowned. "*You?* Don't be ridiculous!"

"I'm coming, Kathy," repeated Liam, in an authoritative voice, "This Bres threatens the small ones, who are my friends… and you. Remember how many times I have been a strength to you against the Great Ones? My presence might be the only way to tap into your powers, and I could not live with myself if I let you do this alone."

"She won't be alone," Sam pointed out, "We will protect her."

My eyes filled with tears. Even after everything I had done, my dearest friend would not abandon me. I did not deserve such loyalty.

"Let him come," I said, quietly.

"Of course," replied Sam, "If you wish it… But are you sure?"

I was not remotely sure, but there was no time to think. I nodded.

"Well then, let's go."

When we rejoined the others, they were similarly disinclined to have me and Liam accompany them on their mission.

Sam informed them that it did not seem to be the time to argue with our resolve. "Besides," he added, "What guarantee is there that this is not a trap? Bres is very clever. He may well have instructed his lackeys to send us on a wild goose chase, to lure us out, and leave Kathy here unguarded. She and her friend will be safer with us."

"You have a point," agreed Nuadu reluctantly.

"Let's not waste any more time, then," I said, with determination. I walked in the direction of the back door, and waited for them to follow.

Sam shook his head. "We must go by other means."

Magically.

I went to him, and he took my hand. Macha reached eagerly for Liam's and he accepted it with an uncomfortable swallow. I instinctively reached for his other hand, and felt him relax slightly at my familiar touch. The Great Ones bowed their heads, in solemn concentration, and the room began to melt away.

"Hey! What about us?" cried one of the 'tween ones indignantly, but her voice was soon lost in the void of what had replaced our surroundings.

At first, it felt a little like crossing into the *síd,* as reality, and the ground beneath my feet, disintegrated into a swirling mass of colour and the simultaneous absence of it. Then, small fragments of time and space began to whip past my face, their dance exhilarating, like sparkling particles of nothingness, moving either very quickly or very slowly. There were no recognisable shapes, only a blur of strange sensations, and the comforting warmth of the hands clasped in mine. Something inside me lurched, and churned, as though my lost dragon of power had begun to wake from its slumber. Its fingers crept tentatively outwards, recognising the possibility of some connection. Something it wanted to explore… Then, after what felt like moments, or an eternity, there was something solid beneath my feet again... Faces around me. My skin felt empty, as the curious but cautious tendrils of the prickle retracted.

The place in which we found ourselves was vast, and almost familiar. Velvet and tapestries adorned the dark, crumbling walls. The floors were wooden, but felt weak, and I could see deep chasms in places where they had fallen away. There was intricately decorated furniture, and a few candelabra, alongside debris and decay, and an unclean stench in the air.

It seemed as though Bres had decided to recreate some version of the back room of 'The Horse and Hag', in a derelict building, but had not had quite the power to seal the cracks and hide the true, decrepit nature of the space.

He was there, reclining in his usual chair. The look of surprise and alarm that darted across his face at our appearance could not be feigned. This was no trap. However, he recovered his composure quickly and sprang to his feet.

"Why, how kind of you all to pay me a visit," he gushed, "Had I known you were coming, I would have tidied up a little." He gestured around his new abode. "There's still a little work to do, but in time, it will be grander than a palace. I've just been *so* busy, and my helpers seem to have mysteriously disappeared. You haven't seen them, have you?"

His tone left me in no doubt that he'd just realised exactly how we had found him.

"We don't have time for this, Bres," said Nuadu, grimly. "We have come to end this, once and for all."

"End what? End *me?*" squeaked Bres in mock-astonishment, "Those times are over. There isn't one among you who can vanquish me."

"But all of us together might," replied Sam.

Bres snorted. "I see you've brought Kathy. Very kind of you to oblige. I very much enjoyed the nibble of her I had on our last meeting, but I hadn't quite got to the main course when you interrupted. I'm looking forward to tucking into *you* again," He flashed me a lascivious smile.

"You won't touch her," yelled Sam, hurling a blast of light at Bres, who quickly stepped out of its path with a smug smile.

"Stop it, Lug," warned Nuadu, "He's goading you. He *wants* you throw things around, until you weaken yourself."

Bres raised his hand, and I suddenly felt pain spread across my body, as though the memory of the greedy fingers, with which he had violated me, were searing through me. I screamed. Slowly, my body began to creep towards his. My feet were not moving. My mind did not desire it. He was compelling me… Dragging me to him, as though I were a puppet on a string.

Sam roared, and aimed another attack at Bres. Nuadu, Medb and Macha followed suit. He reeled slightly, as some of their magic hit him, and retaliated with a few blows of his own to keep the rest at bay.

I continued to glide towards him, my body frozen, my will numb.

"Kathy! No!" Liam seized my hand, and pulled me backwards.

There was a roar. It was not another angry voice, but the furious sound of a mighty beast, uncurling its wings, rising up through me, and exploding from my skin, smiting its enemy with a ferocious blast. Bres rocked dangerously, and his uncanny hold on me snapped. The crumbling walls began to weep rivulets of loose plaster. The damaged floor-boards cracked further. The force of it hurled Liam entirely across the room, and into Bres's clutches.

"Well, now," he exclaimed, smiling as though he could not believe his good fortune, "Who do we have here? Another valiant protector of Kathy's, it would seem… But, oh. He's human. How disappointing. He won't provide much sustenance. Oh well, we can still have fun in other ways!"

He pressed his fingers around Liam's throat, as though to break his neck.

"No," I screeched, rushing forward, "Leave him alone!"

Sam lunged at me, holding me back with his strong arms.

"Liam!" I wailed, "Liam!"

"Such passion! It seems she cares for this one," smirked Bres, "Don't worry, Sam. I think I'll keep him."

"No," I pleaded, and strained against Sam's grip on me.

Bres's eyes met mine, and his lips curled into a luxuriant smile of purest cruelty… And with that, they were gone. The space in which Bres had stood, and from which Liam had stared at me, with such bewilderment and fear in his eyes, was empty.

"Where has he gone? Where has he taken him?" I cried

"I don't know," muttered Nuadu darkly.

"But… you're gods! You must be able to find him!"

"I cannot sense him," confessed Medb.

"Neither can I. There is nothing that we can do for now," whispered Sam, "We should go home."

"No!" I shrieked, "I won't leave until he brings him back!"

"He won't do that," sighed Medb grimly, "However much you plead. Sam is right. We must go from here."

I continued to scream, but Sam's grasp on me was too tight to resist, as the place we stood began to shimmer again, and we melted away into the nothingness.

I barely remember the journey back. Just movement, and darkness, and my lonely cries into the void. By the time I was fully aware of anything around me, I was back at 'The Horse and Hag', squirming on the floor, racked with sobbing, while three, bewildered Great Ones peered down at me, and Sam knelt by me, still holding me but looking somehow lost and powerless. It was the first time I had not felt comforted by his touch, and he sensed it. I was also dimly conscious of the 'tween ones, watching me curiously from behind the others.

"Where has he taken him? What is he *doing* to him?" I croaked, almost unable to breathe with the suffocation of my own tears.

"I don't know," replied Sam, helplessly.

Macha crouched down and stroked my hair. "I wish the pretty boy had not been taken away."

I just cried harder. "Why didn't you... *do* something? Any of you? Why didn't you... *save* him?"

"What could we have done?" she replied simply, "If we had made a move, Bres would have killed him where he stood."

"She's right," agreed Sam, gently, "At least there is hope that Liam is still alive. Bres blames you for all of this conflict, and may well be glad of a hostage to dissuade you from acting against him."

"And, he wants your magic," added Medb, "I think he might keep your friend alive, to lure you to him."

"Then, that's what I must do," I decided, jumping to my feet decidedly, though my legs felt unsteady, and my stomach churned, "I must offer myself in return for Liam!"

"No," cried Sam, "You will *not* do that!"

"B- but don't you see? It's all my fault! If he hadn't been there... If I hadn't told him to travel to Dublin... If I hadn't let him come to confront Bres..."

"It was his choice to come," Sam reasoned, "He *wanted* to help you with your powers... and it worked! You threw Bres's control off you, as though it were nothing!"

"And hurled my dearest friend into his arms," I wailed, "It's all my fault!"

"Kathy," said Nuadu grimly, "You have more power in you than a thousand of the small beings Bres feeds on, put together. If you give yourself to him, who knows what terrors he will unleash? Is the life of one boy really worth the pain he will bring to so many, if he fortifies himself with your strength?"

I fell back down to the floor, at the weight of his words.

"Besides," continued Sam, "Do you really think Bres is one to honour an agreement? If you go to him, he will take you, and kill your friend as well, just to see the look of horror on your face before he drains you dry."

"Then, what am I to do? *Sacrifice* him? No! I won't! Not Liam! We could face Bres again. All of us..."

"And he will snap Liam like a twig before we can make a move... That is, if we can find him at all. He will hide from us with far more care, now that he knows we are hunting for him."

"We need time to consider the situation, before acting," declared Nuadu, "Kathy, I cannot hope to understand your human grief, but I would see the boy rescued if possible. However, if we are to even contemplate such a thing, it will take clear thoughts and steady nerves. You must compose yourself, and not give yourself over to such emotion."

I looked up at him and the others. He was right. He could not hope to understand. None of them could.

CHAPTER EIGHTEEN

I went to bed. I told Sam that I wanted time alone to compose myself, as Nuadu had suggested. In truth, I merely wanted time to feel the excruciating truth of what I had done. I did not want comforting words. I did not want caresses, or concern. I didn't deserve them.

Mr. O Mordha crossed my mind, waiting anxiously at the cottage for his son's return. Their bond was such that, even in his haste to come to me, I knew Liam would not have left without a word. He would have told his father that I was in trouble, and that he was going to me. Mr. O Mordha knew the sort of trouble I had a tendency to get myself into.

He must be worried. He must be frantic. Have I killed his son? Has my selfishness killed his son?

I thought of Cú Chulaind, waiting sadly on the doorstep, wondering why his master had not returned.

If only I hadn't told him to come. If he hadn't been there, Sam and the others would have broken Bres's spell. They would have protected me. Then, they might have weakened him enough to capture or bind him in some way, or simply devour him the way Fúamnach and I would have done to Étaín, if I hadn't stopped it. I would have had no qualms about watching Bres go that way. But no. I had let Liam come. I had selfishly wanted him to fortify my own powers… And, look what they had done.

I could feel them in me, more alive now, but still a deep grumble rather than a playful caress. I almost did not want them. I didn't deserve them. All I had ever done with them was to hurt him again, and again, and again… And he had still come back, and walked straight into his doom, hand in hand with me.

I wept, and I wept, and when I could weep no more, I wept again, and when my utter desolation had wrought every saline drop from my wretched body, I contorted myself into the tightest ball I could, and rocked forlornly in the gloom as evening drew in.

"I'm sorry, child," said a familiar voice.

I gasped, my sore, swollen eyes barely able to discern his familiar face in the darkness. The Dagda. *My father.*

"You know?" I gulped, my fragmented mind in no fit state to compose a more suitable greeting.

He nodded. "I would not see you so unhappy. I grieve for you, as for a small part of myself."

"Can *you* find him? Can *you* take me to him?"

"I will not do that."

"You mean... you *do* know where he is? Tell me! I have to find him!"

"He has gone into the deepest parts of the *síd*. Dangerous parts, that are not for you to walk."

"If you don't take me, I will travel down to Kerry, and walk into the *síd* myself, through the only gateway I know."

"You would have no luck of it. The realm he now inhabits is beyond your reach."

"I don't believe you. You're just trying to protect me."

"Believe what you will. Wander the otherworld for days... years... a lifetime. You will not find him, where Bres has taken him."

"But *you* could."

"I will not take you there."

"You must!"

"I must do nothing. This is a tragedy entirely of your own making. I warned you, child, not to interfere in these matters. I *warned* you that these companions of yours would bring you only despair. And what did you mean by dragging your human friend to that confrontation, when you knew that he had no magic with which to protect himself?"

"But he *does* have magic! He *does!* He healed me when Étaín's enchanted fire had almost swallowed me whole!"

He sighed. "Foolish child. That power was not his. *I* gave it to him. I saw you in that moment, hurt and damaged, and that part of myself that I so despise longed to go to you, but I feared that my presence would not be welcome. I sent my energy through him, to soothe your pain."

"You?" I cried, my sadness almost evaporating with the shock of it, "*You?* Why did you never tell me?"

"I did not want you to know. The secret of your parentage is one that I still regret not having kept."

"But, what about all of those times that my power was strengthened by Liam's touch? He must have… something…"

"He gave you confidence," replied The Dagda simply, "His support boosted your courage, and allowed you do things of which you were always perfectly capable. His lineage gave him the ability to see things that most do not, and enticed Étaín with the promise of old traditions that she longed for, but there was nothing more to it than that."

"But, I *felt* something. I felt something powerful, when he took my hand, or sang with me, or…"

"You had a great connection. A very special link that few share. I felt that myself, once, though I have put those thoughts aside. A bond such as yours has a certain power, that does not come from magic. It is something all its own."

"So… I took him there for no good reason at all? I took an entirely human man to a supernatural battle?"

"And I know you regret it. I regret it too. You exist as you are because I could not control my own passions… And now, you must see why my kind cannot remain here as they are. Liam would be safe and well, if it were not for how far we have fallen."

I drew back with a hiss. "Are you actually trying to convince me of your purpose again, at a time like this? Are you refusing to save the life of an innocent man to… teach me a lesson?"

The door opened.

Sam was standing there, staring at my guest with an opaque expression on his face. He did not move.

The Dagda did not appear in the least surprised to see him.

"Lug," he greeted the new arrival, nonchalantly.

"Echu," nodded Sam in return, his voice cautiously muted, "I did not expect to see you here."

"It has been a long time."

"Indeed."

"Echu?" I repeated, puzzled, "Weren't you once married to Étaín?"

"That was Echu Airem," snapped The Dagda, "Do I look like an Echu Airem?"

I swallowed heavily, and was silent.

"I hope you're pleased with yourself," he continued coldly, turning to Sam, "I hope you're proud of everything that has befallen Kathy since you wove your spell around her."

Sam bristled. "I assure you, there has been no such enchantment."

"What would you call this?" The Dagda gestured around the bedroom.

"I call it a place to keep your daughter safe, which is more than you have provided."

"You will only bring her sorrow."

"What will bring her sorrow is if you stand against me."

"Look at her now," said The Dagda, grimly, "Pitiful. Broken. Unhappy. That is no fault of mine."

"I have done *everything* I could to protect her," protested Sam.

"He's right," I cried, running to him loyally, and taking my place at his side, "He is not responsible for any of this! *I* went to the library alone, and had my powers defiled. *I* brought Liam to Dublin. *I* did… and now, *you* could help me, but you refuse!" I pointed an accusing finger at The Dagda.

"How is it you think he can help?" asked Sam, his voice tentative.

"He knows where Bres has taken Liam, and he refuses to bring me to them."

"It is too dangerous," insisted The Dagda, "They are in those places that are not spoken of in the stories… Those places that most of our kind have begun to forget. Places that will feed his power, and weaken Kathy's… And, for as long as he is there, he is no threat to *anyone* else out here. She must let Liam go."

Sam's eyes were grave, as he registered some deeper understanding of the words. "He's right," he said.

"What?" I turned to him, appalled by his betrayal.

"He's right," repeated Sam, "If Bres and Liam are concealed in such a place, they are lost to us, and if you follow, you will be lost to us too. I will not have that."

The Dagda raised his eyebrows. "Well, on one thing, it seems, we agree."

I ran to him, and threw myself on the ground before him. "You *must* take me," I cried, "You *must!*"

"I will not."

"He would keep you safe," said Sam, gently pulling me to my feet. "He would protect you, and I understand what it is he feels. I once had a mortal child too: A great hero of Ulaid. I grieved when he was gone. I will not ask The Dagda to put you in danger."

The Dagda gave him a strange, knowing look, which was difficult to read. "So, we are agreed then?"

"And… you will leave it at that?" Sam's expression too was confusing, as though some unspoken understanding had just taken place between them, to which I had been not been party.

"Keep her safe, and we will leave it at that, for the time being."

"Then, we are agreed."

A stiff handshake took place between the two of them.

"What do you mean?" I demanded, "What is going on?"

"Farewell, Kathy," said The Dagda, "Be well."

He disappeared.

"What was that?" I exploded, turning to face Sam, "What agreement did you just make? I don't understand…"

He did not answer immediately, as though he were choosing his words carefully. "I believe that your father agreed to interfere no further in our life together."

"I heard him say no such thing!"

"When you have known someone forever, you do not always need so many words to convey your meaning."

It sank in, momentarily, that when Sam said 'forever', he meant it literally. "That's all well and good," I ranted, pacing frustratedly around the room, "But I don't believe him about the *síd*. I don't think he's telling us the truth! I'm sure there must be some way to get to them, and he is keeping it from me for some maddening reason of his own."

"He just wants to keep you safe, as I do, dear one."

"Do *you* know how to find them in the otherworld?"

"I do not. There is no way," Sam assured me, "None."

"Promise me! Promise me that you know of no way to reach them, however perilous."

"I swear it."

"It sounded as though The Dagda knew how to get there."

"As you've said yourself, he is an enigmatic fellow."

"I'll go and ask Nuadu, and the others," I suggested, "One of them might know something helpful."

"Their answers will be the same."

"Even so, I will ask them."

"If you wish."

I took a few minutes to wash my face before presenting myself downstairs again, after so many hours of crying. When I emerged from the bathroom, Sam had left. I assumed that he had gone ahead to join the other immortals. I sat down in front of the mirror to brush my hair, and sighed.

I could not leave it like this. I could not leave Liam to this cruel fate. I feared that he might already be dead. I remembered Dr. Herbert's horrible, staring eyes, gazing lifelessly up at me in the library. Human life was of no consequence to Bres. No life had any meaning for him, apart from his own, warped existence. However, while there was even a chance that he had kept Liam alive as future leverage against me, I could not abandon him.

I was certain that The Dagda had not been frank with me. I remembered the respect he had commanded among his immortal companions in the woods of Kerry. I recalled Sam and Bres's reaction when I had first mentioned him. They feared him. They admired him. He was powerful... And *I was his daughter*. Some of that growling, churning magic within me was his. I had walked into parts of the *síd* before. Who was to say I could not walk along its other paths and find my way, fortified by the powers my father had given me? After all, nothing had killed me... Yet.

I took a deep breath, and went downstairs.

Alice was closing the bar. "Are you staying for a while?" I asked her.

She nodded, her face concerned. "You don't look well, Kathy."

I opened my mouth to tell her what we had done, and what I had allowed to happen to Liam, but no words came out. I could not stomach a retelling. The very thought of it made me want to vomit… Made me want to pound my fists against every available surface, until they were nothing but bloody stumps… Made me want to tear at my own hair. Medb could tell her later.

Suddenly, a thought occurred to me. Alice was a year ahead of me in her studies. There were things that she might know. Mr. O Mordha had once told me that there were *sídhe* all over Ireland. Perhaps I did not need to travel to Kerry to find a doorway.

"Alice," I asked in a deliberately casual voice, "Have you made much of a study of *síd* mounds, or ancient burial sites?"

"I've had a few lectures on them, and done a little reading. I'm no expert, but…"

"Do you know of any around here?"

"Well, of course, the best known is Brú na Bóinne, in Co. Meath, which isn't far. It's absolutely full of prehistoric tombs and settlements. Some of it is even older than the Egyptian pyramids! Newgrange is the most famous… Surely you've heard of that? There are even references to it in some of the old stories. They say it's very powerful, and a portal between realms. I'm surprised you haven't been there. I visited on a school trip when I was little."

"We never had much money for such things," I replied.

"Shall we go, one weekend, when we both have the day off? It's an amazing place! I'd happily see it again."

"I'd like that," I replied, a little sadly.

"So, why all the interest in burial mounds? Is it something for college?"

"Yes," I lied.

I offered to pour some drinks for the back room, while she went to Medb. I took my time about it, deep in thought. I knew what I had to do…

But, they would never let me go! The Great Ones would refuse to allow me to walk into any further danger, and they were strong enough to stop me. I knew that Sam, at least, could sense whether or not I was in the building, and track me through that indescribable part of ourselves that we had exchanged when our bodies were one.

It would take a distraction of some magnitude to evade him for long enough to get where I needed to go. Alice had been right in her assumption that I had heard of Newgrange: An impressive, ancient monument, in which the sun shines through a window to illuminate the inner chamber, but once a year, on the winter solstice. However, I had not realised its proximity to Dublin.

If there was anywhere that an entrance to the Otherworld might be concealed, it was surely there. Of course, now that Bres was safely tucked away in another realm, I could suggest returning to my lectures. They would not expect to see me again for hours, which would give more than enough time to get into the *síd* from Brú na Bóinne. However, the thought of delaying my departure, until even Monday morning, felt unbearable. With every moment that passed, Liam might be closer and closer to meeting his demise. I slapped the bar in frustration, then picked up the tray and carried it into the back room.

Within moments, the 'tween ones were on me, skittering around my legs, and tugging at my jeans. I wondered why they were still there. I supposed that they had nowhere else to go, or that they had been so enthralled, by the taste of merriment I had given them to loosen their tongues, that they could not bring themselves to tear themselves away from its memory.

"You promised us a party," cried one, sulkily, "You said the revelries would continue, and then you went away and left us all alone, and nobody has sung us a song since you came back!"

"We were good," continued another, "We helped you! We told you what you wanted to know! Where's our reward?"

"We want a party," cried the third, "Where's our party?"

"You want a party," I repeated slowly, an idea dawning on me. "Then, a party you shall have!"

I went to Sam first, and embraced him hungrily, in a way that I had not done all day. There was no artifice in the kiss itself, although my stomach quaked with the guilt of my impending betrayal. His beautiful eyes bathed me in their light as I drew back, and he stroked my cheek.

"Are you feeling better?" he asked, hopefully.

I smiled at him, my arms still around his neck, feeling his sweet breath on my face. I wanted him. Oh, how I wanted him… Particularly in case it was the last time I would have the chance to know him. I might be dead soon. I longed to feel him against me, to be pulled into that intoxicating place that existed only between us, to explode with him, and curl into him so tightly that we felt like a single being… But there was no time for that now.

"I'm fed up of being sad," I declared, "And the three little ones over there are pestering me for some amusement. Might a distraction not be as well, for all of us?"

"Of course," grinned Sam, "Anything that will alleviate your pain. Would you like me to sing?"

I nodded. "I would… But first, do you think you might clear up the mess that Bres made of this room? I would have a happy time in a beautiful place again."

He raised his eyebrows. "Are you sure we should use magic?"

"If you truly believe that you've made a deal with The Dagda, why not? If he's not going to bother us again, is it so wrong to have a little fun with our gifts?"

"As you wish," he agreed, brightly.

I next approached Macha, and said: "Do you think you might like to go out and find some companions for us in here tonight? The place has seemed terribly empty of late."

"Really?" she squealed, excitedly.

"Absolutely. As many as you can carry," I joked.

She clapped her hands gleefully, and dashed straight out to hunt for lovely youths.

Medb and Alice were curled up together on a sofa in the corner. As I made my way towards them, Alice looked up at me with a sort of horrified sympathy.

"Kathy, I'm so sorry… I had no idea…" she began.

I swallowed heavily, determined to hide my distress, and keep thoughts of Liam at bay, for as long as I had to. "Thank you," I replied, quickly, "We've decided to have a party. Will you stay?"

She looked utterly astonished. "Are you sure? Are you... alright?"

"I need to blow off some steam, before I go mad," I explained.

"Okay. Whatever you need," she muttered with concern.

Nuadu suddenly materialised beside me, and unceremoniously herded me away to a private corner.

"What is going on?" he demanded, "Lug tells me you're planning a celebration, and encouraging him to use his powers for some frivolous decorating endeavour? Are you quite well?"

"You told me to pull myself together." I shrugged. "I think a bit of escapism might help. It's not that I'm no longer sad about Liam, but my tears cannot help him. I want a night to forget myself in drinking and dancing, and perhaps I will be better able to think of a way to save him tomorrow!"

"If you insist," muttered Nuadu, "I will stay out of the way." *Good.* His expression was grim and mistrustful. I was sure that he suspected something, but I hoped that it would not occur to him precisely what form of trickery was afoot.

I ran upstairs to change. Although I knew I would regret it later, when I had to clamber through a tangle of ancient tombs in the dark, I put on my prettiest dress, and then quickly filled my rucksack with a torch, a bottle of water, and all of the money I had saved from my earnings, and stowed it surreptitiously by the front door of the bar.

The lights in the kitchen flickered off, and Evelyn came out. "Oh, hello, Kathy," she said, "I was just about to go home. You look nice! Are you feeling better?"

"Yes, thank you," I beamed, "We're having a party. Will you join us?"

She looked surprised. "Well, you *must* be feeling better! I expect I could join you for a drink or two..."

"Excellent," I called, and scampered off down the corridor.

Sam had outdone himself with the back room. It had never looked more sumptuous or inviting. I gasped, taking in the resplendent tapestries, rich velvets, and dancing flames in the candelabra. It was not quite the same room that Bres had made, and I was glad of it. My love's thoughtful touches and details were even prettier.

"What do you think?" he asked, a little triumphantly.

"It's beautiful." I kissed him deeply. "*You're* beautiful."

"As are you, dearest one," he murmured, his strong arms around me.

I never wanted to leave them, but I eventually pulled myself free and went to the 'tween ones. "Do you have any… friends?" I asked them.

"Friends?" They repeated in unison.

"Are there… others like you, who you could summon to join us?"

Their little faces lit up. "Yes," they nodded eagerly, "Yes, we could do that… But you must tell them all that it's *our* party."

"Oh, naturally."

Macha soon filed in, with a dazzling array of new human consorts. She must have been very lonely since the sycophants left, for there were dozens of them: Eager boys and girls, crying out in wonder at the resplendence of their surroundings, and sighing lustfully at the Great Ones' exquisite faces, as though they might die of such longing.

"Let's have music," I cried brightly, clapping my hands, "Music and drinks! Make it poitín!"

Sam began to sing and play, instantly enrapturing the room with his powerful gifts. Medb obliged by conjuring poitín for everybody. I gratefully accepted a shot, but passed it to Sam instead, and he drank it between verses.

I felt a tug at the hem of my dress. "Our… 'friends' are here," the 'tween ones informed me.

"Wonderful. I'll let them in." I followed them out to the back door, behind the tapestry, and admitted their guests. I had never seen such a fascinating array of strange little creatures, in a variety of shapes and sizes, all enormous eyes and eager faces, as they stepped into the back room and saw the revelry they were about to enjoy.

"Dancing," I called, "There must be dancing! But first… More poitín!"

I paid special attention to Sam when handing out the drinks, making sure he got two for every one the others had.

"It *is* hard to get drunk, when you've been around as long as we have," he chuckled, "But I fancy I might succeed tonight!"

Good. I kissed him quickly, and went to join in the dancing, skipping and leaping with throngs of assorted immortals, and humans alike. Our footsteps rattled the floor.

I had never seen the space so crowded, or so full of laughter, noise and merriment. It was a positive tangle of dancing bodies and good cheer. As time passed, and I ensured that all present were furnished with a steady stream of strong libations, the pace of Sam's music increased, and the dancing grew even more frenzied.

This was it. The party was at its pinnacle. I knew that my best chance was to go, before any lull in the merriment had the chance to occur. It was time.

I paused, for a moment. at the door, watching the scene wistfully. It occurred to me that I had never truly cast a spell. When I had taken part in Fúamnach's ritual, she had set the pieces in motion. She'd had her objects of significance, and a pattern of her own to follow. Of course, I had performed small, magical deeds, but had never really created something where there was none, following a series of actions, step by step, to ensure my will was done. The web of artifice I had spun about the back room that night, using the glamour of duplicity, was perhaps the closest I had come. Fúamnach had had her instruments, and… Perhaps I had mine. An idea suddenly dawned on me. I dashed upstairs to grab a few more items I now thought I might require, and stuffed them into my rucksack by the front door.

Though I knew I was pressed for time, I took one last peek into the back room. I wondered if I would ever see the place again… See any of them again… See *him* again. I longed to go to him and finally tell him that I loved him, but I could not risk his attention on me now, so I whispered it into the air, far too quietly for anyone to hear over the cacophony I'd created.

Then, I retrieved my rucksack and slipped out into the night.

I ran to the nearest taxi rank, my heart pounding, certain that I would hear Sam's frantic cries at any moment, calling me back. No sound came.

I leaped into the back of a cab and breathlessly ordered: "Brú na Bóinne, please."

The driver turned to look at me in astonishment, as though trying to gauge just how drunk I was. "You mean… the tourist attraction in Co. Meath?" he cried, incredulously, "But… that must be an hour's drive away, and it's the middle of the night!"

"Are you going to take me there or not?" I snapped.

"It'll be expensive!"

I took out my money and shoved it in his direction. "Will this be enough?"

He shook his head in disbelief, but put his foot on the accelerator and drove away.

During the journey, I tried to process the fact that I was most likely speeding towards my death… Or worse. Words of Bres's echoed in my ears: "I will leave you begging for death, and still, I will not take your life." Was it to be eternal torture in the *síd,* then, rather than oblivion? I was not dissuaded. I knew nothing, other than that I *had* to reach Liam. I simply *had* to.

Yet, what I was doing didn't feel quite real. I might never see Sam again. I could not quite believe that likelihood, though I tried to prepare myself for it, in as sensible a voice as my mind could muster.

Would The Dagda pine for me as a father bemoans the loss of a daughter, the way Sam had grieved for his mortal son? I remembered the tender look in his eyes when he'd mentioned him. I wished that I had taken the time to ask him about it…To share his pain, and provide what little comfort I could. I wished that I'd had time for so many conversations with him… So many nights and days lit by his smile, and strengthened by his touch.

We had agreed to belong to each other so easily, despite my doubts about my mortality and his eternal nature. He had said that he wished he could know me for many lifetimes. I was sure he had never considered the possibility that he might not even know me for one. *He* would grieve for me. I was in no doubt of it. I did not know if that pain was anything akin to that of mortals', in times of loss, but I wished that I could have spared him even a moment's unhappiness either way.

What I wished for him did not matter. What I wished for myself mattered even less. I had no choice.

"Here you are," announced the taxi driver, screeching to a halt and extending his hand for payment.

Already? Had it really been an hour already? I suppose that a part of me had never wanted the drive to end… Never wanted to face what I was about to face.

I paid the man, and left the car, and he drove away. I blinked repeatedly to acclimatise my eyes to the darkness around me. I remembered my torch, and pulled it out of my pack.

Though it was small, and not very powerful, it illuminated the outline of an enormous structure, separated from the world around it by imposing gates and railings. I hoped that I would be able to break into the complex magically, as the climb over the security barriers looked all but impossible. Now that the prickle was not as it had been, I was not sure how to control it, or ask it to perform the simple tasks that had once come to me so naturally.

Suddenly, I felt very, very silly, and terribly alone, hovering out in the middle of nowhere before dawn, where nobody could be expected to find me.

I had to try.

I put my hand against one of the fences, and compelled it to break. Nothing happened. I took a deep breath, as though trying to draw oxygen into my very core, that my sleeping dragon might breathe the same air as I did, and somehow, be at one with me.

I tried again. I focused on the fence… Considered how weak it was in comparison to what I knew I could unleash. I was suddenly distracted, wondering if the party was still going at 'The Horse and Hag'. Had they noticed I was gone yet? Would they think to look for me here? Would Sam be able to sense my whereabouts from such a distance?

Would Alice give something away of our conversation about *sídhe,* and alert their suspicions? Of course, with their powers, they could be here in moments…

I shouted in frustration. I *had to* get through, and into the otherworld, before they found me.

Try again. I struggled to remember how the surge of power had felt when I'd last confronted Bres. I tried to imagine Liam's hand in mine, as my magic defeated Étaín's watery serpents, and flames. Suddenly, there was a deep rumbling sound inside me, and the fence was blasted open. Shards of it scattered noisily on the ground. I was in.

I hastily scrambled through the gap I had created, and rushed to the nearest wall I could find to hide myself, lest a night security patrol should suddenly appear to thwart me.

After a few minutes, I turned on my torch again, and peered around the corner from where I had concealed myself, near the entry kiosks. All was still. All was dark.

The complex was immense, comprising sombre, silhouetted mounds and stones, further than the eye could see. There was something there. Something deep, and very real. Truth. Eternity. I could feel it in the sudden, new weight that my dragon now carried inside me. I could sense it in its contented growl. This was familiar. I belonged here… Or, at least, that explosive, half-buried part of me did.

I implored it to show me the way: To direct me through the great, hulking shapes, now looming against the tiniest hue of blue in the sky, that indicated dawn was approaching.

Where should I go?

I began to walk, hoping that some instinct would propel me towards a gap between the worlds. I passed small structures, and mounds so large that I first thought them to be vast hills… But they were things that had been made with hands, and tools, and devotion. Something began to whisper to me. It was not the prickle, but an uncanny stream of voices from my surroundings. I did not know the words, and yet I *did* know them, like the buried truth of Fúamnach's chant. The earth and the stones were telling me their story… A story of immeasurable length. A story of thousands and thousands of layers of time, and space, and belief.

My pulse quickened. I knew where to go. Somewhere deep within me, something spoke to its kin, and I understood. I barely needed my torch to light the way, as my very soul propelled me towards the stones, and the inevitability of my path grew firmer in my mind, like a choreographed dance practised so many times that it is second nature to perform it. I did not pause to consider the magnitude of my actions, as the whispering escalated and drew me to a certain mound. I knew that feeling. It was the crossing point. Without a moment's hesitation, I stepped into the *síd*.

Reality dissolved, and time and space danced before my eyes… Fluid concepts that had no set place in the in-between. Then, as quickly as it had disappeared, the world re-made itself around me. It was not my world. I knew its cool heat, and its light shadows, and its colours that were not those of the rainbow. I had never been able to remember them in the mortal realm, but I recognised them immediately, like the faces of old friends, that night… Or was it day? I had expected to find myself deep in the earth, but there was a sky above me, holding both the sun and the moon, and simultaneous, shimmering waves of both of their kingdoms.

I did not see Bres or Liam, nor had I expected to. The Dagda's words had suggested that locating them would take further exploration of their world than I had ever attempted, when stepping in and out of its peripheries.

If only he had come with me, to lead me to them. If only I had his solemn wisdom, and his knowledge of this place, to guide me… *Enough of that. You have only yourself, and you have to do what you must.*

I began to walk. There was no path. I found a raging sea in front of me, which suddenly became a field under the watchful eyes of the strange, dual sky. I stepped onto it, afraid that it would turn to water once more, and swallow me in its thrashing waves. However, the ground felt firm beneath my feet, a flawless blanket of green. I pressed on.

There was something ahead, and then nothing ahead, and then something ahead of me again. The field became a forest: A thick and inhospitable tangle of trees. It took all my strength to push the branches aside, and scramble through even a few feet of it. I felt claustrophobic and disorientated, as the dense foliage swallowed me. I could no longer see the light blue or velvet midnight of the sky. A strange, panicked sensation gripped me.

My head began to spin. My breathing grew laboured, as though the air was no longer fit for me to breathe.

I sat down to rest for just a moment, too overcome by the atmosphere to walk on. *But you* must *walk on*. I pressed my hands against the soft grass, and now found it hard as stone. I was on a rocky clifftop, overhanging a vast drop: An abyss. A chasm with no end, only a foreboding, black nothingness between me and whatever lay, or did not lie, at its bottom.

Ye gods, must I throw myself in there?

I closed my eyes against the thought, fervently hoping that when I reopened them, my surroundings would have returned to that pleasant field.

They had not. However, I was no longer alone.

I had never thought I would see her again. I had certainly not expected to encounter her here. Yet, there she was, radiant and resplendent as ever, her hair a cascade of perfect strawberry blonde, and her sweet face bright and flawlessly poised to greet me. Only those eyes… Those enormous eyes, churning with both light and darkness, were the sole hint at the complexity of her true nature.

"Kathy," she exclaimed, "How lovely to see you!"

I scrambled to my feet hurriedly, moving away from the precipice, and pressing my back to the rock wall that now lay behind me.

"Étaín," I nodded nervously.

"I just *knew* I'd find you here," she smiled, her tone saccharine and melodic, "We can't leave poor Liam in the clutches of that wicked Bres, can we?"

"I've come to rescue him," I said, I supposed a little redundantly. Why else would I be climbing across an enchanted landscape, hours after his abduction?

"Oh, good," she cooed, "I've tried myself, but Bres won't give him up to me."

I was astonished. Was she still labouring under the illusion that Liam would accept her advances one day, and rule Ireland at her side… Or could it be that she actually *cared* about him, as more than a pawn in her archaic ritual?

"You know it's *you* Bres wants," she added.

I nodded grimly. "Étaín," I began, "I left Kerry. I left Liam. I am no longer in your way. I have a new lover. If you care about saving Liam, is it even remotely possible that you might consider working together, and not killing me along the way? I need help. I have no idea how to negotiate this place, or reach Bres."

"But of course, Kathy. That's why I came. If we're being entirely frank, I will confess that I have little concern for your wellbeing, but if Bres gets what he wants, then I can have my Liam, so I shall see to it that you reach him."

"And… *Is* he your Liam?" I wondered if he had his own secrets about his life since our parting, then quickly dismissed it, remembering his reaction to my relationship with Sam. What was it he had called him? "Some entirely amoral entity from a bygone era." No, Liam had not accepted Étaín.

"I will make him see," she vowed, "He needs me now. Only I will be able to help him, when we deliver him from this place."

I waved my hand, impatiently. There was no time for her enigmatic nonsense. "Look, Étaín, if I take on Bres, can you keep Liam safe?"

"I will," she vowed, "But I must warn you, he is not as you knew him."

"What do you mean?"

"For you, only hours have passed since you last saw each other. For him, time has escalated a little differently."

"How differently, exactly?"

"It is hard for one such as I to say, but he is much changed." She almost looked a little sad. "But, not to worry. All could be restored."

I rolled my eyes at the familiar turn of phrase.

"It sounds as though there's no time to waste," I concluded anxiously, "Which way should we go?"

"Why, that way, of course," she smiled, pointing at the inviting green field which now sprawled out before us once more.

We travelled through grass, and wasteland, and fearsome flames that did not scorch the skin. Our surroundings changed from moment to moment. Trees engulfed us. The earth was barren. The co-existence of multiple states in one space was something that had been explained to me by The Dagda, but to watch it rippling back and forth, in front of my eyes, was astounding.

Still, the air felt heavy and unfamiliar to my lungs, and to Étaín's slight irritation, I was forced to stop along the way to pause and draw breath.

She tutted quietly. "What a shame you won't be at your best when you encounter your adversary," she observed, sounding positively chirpy, "Our kind draws strength from time spent in the *síd*, you know. I fear you and Bres will be woefully ill-matched, by the time you find him."

"Wonderful," I muttered sarcastically. I was under no illusion that she would do anything to help *me*. She was probably looking forward to watching Bres suck the life out of my living carcass, before she whisked Liam away to safety.

Still, the bravest part of me was heartened. Liam was alive. Liam was alive, and I finally had someone on my side, albeit temporarily, to whom that actually mattered.

And so, our journey wore on. We passed glistening waterfalls, so beautiful that I wept with despair, and the grisly spectre of old bones, so chilling that I sang with joy. My emotions swirled back and forth with the changing of the landscape. I was moved, but out of synch with the place in which I now truly knew I did not belong, divine parentage or not.

Whatever force had decreed that I would spring from a mortal womb, breathe oxygen and, one day, die, had left its mark on me. Though I appeared slighter than Étaín, my footsteps were heavier in the sand, as though that earthly part of me were a burden I was dragging, and it grew heavier with every step I took further into the *síd*.

"Where will you take Liam when you leave?" I asked Étaín, gasping painfully from the effort of uttering the words.

"Where I must."

"Ah, naturally. Thank you for the clarification."

"It is none of your concern where I take him," she said, "You will have Bres to deal with and, in the unlikely event you survive that encounter, you have another love to return to, do you not?"

I nodded. "But not until I know Liam is safe."

"Oh, he will be safe."

"And what if he still refuses to become your king of the land?"

A certain softness crept into her voice. "He will never be at risk from me."

For a moment, I saw something tender flicker in her eyes. We continued to walk.

We saw others from time to time. Small ones, here and there. A scattering of other beings who were a little larger, in a variety of shapes and sizes. A few Great Ones… Not incarnations known to me, but no less exquisite. All of them went about their business, and paid us no heed. Some were riding horses in the sea. Some were swimming in the grass. I suspected that their experience of their surroundings was something quite different from mine.

Finally, Étaín turned to me, and said: "We are not far from them now. Are you ready?"

I did not feel ready. My body and mind were weary, and my lungs ached. Our surroundings had begun to change again, into something quite sinister. Gnarled tree branches stretched, like misshapen skeletons, in all directions. There was a certain stillness, as though what little air there had been had almost disappeared. I gasped for breath. I held my stomach, begging that powerful, sleeping giant inside me to teach me how to be in this realm… To help me to exist, at least long enough to do what needed to be done.

"You foolish child," thundered a familiar voice, "You defy me again! I told you this was not a place to which you could travel, and here I find you, a spluttering mess, barely clinging to life, and making your way into even greater danger… with *this one?*" He fixed Étaín with a furious stare. "How did she get here?"

Étaín looked suitably chastised. "I did not bring her to the *síd,* Echu," she assured him in a small voice, "She found her way inside alone. I merely… guided her a little."

I nodded miserably, feeling my throat closing around my airway, like an impenetrable, suffocating door.

The Dagda sighed exasperatedly, and took my arm. I immediately felt a little better. I gasped, as the fingers of the atmosphere released their grip on my throat, and my lungs filled with something akin to air.

"You will leave this place with me immediately," he ordered.

I wrenched my arm from his grasp. "I will not! Not without Liam!"

"Do you have any idea what he has endured?" hissed The Dagda.

"No, but I intend to find out!"

"Believe me girl, you do not wish to see what he has become. The sight of it will appal your mortal eyes, and never leave you a moment's peace. Death will come soon for him, and it will be a kindness. You must come away."

"I will *not!*"

His eyes grew dark. "Never has any cursed beast, of this world or the other, had the misfortune to have such an obstinate child as you are! Come, then. See the truth of the matter, if you will not be dissuaded, but do not tell me that you were not warned."

"Finally!" I cried, triumphantly.

He shot me a disapproving glance, silently rebuking me for my insolence, but offered me his arm again. "Come, walk with me. You will have need of my strength, if you have even the slightest hope of enduring what is to come."

His touch was comforting, in spite of his harsh words.

We made our way forward, through the warped remains of what had once been vegetation.

Our surroundings changed again. There was a path beneath our feet, and little stone dwellings on each side. Behind them were farms, with animals I recognised. It seemed something of a village… But only for a moment.

The landscape soon became a mysterious, whispering thing, full of wispy, black shapes, darting about in a disorderly fashion, and entirely impossible to define.

Suddenly, I stopped.

"What is it now?" asked Étaín impatiently.

"I feel something... Someone." My body was certain of a fourth presence. It was not that prickly feeling that had been lost to me, but a deep, primal craving, calling out, yearning for something of itself that was within reach.

"Someone else is here," I said.

"It's me," he said, stepping out of the shadows.

Sam.

CHAPTER NINETEEN

"You!" bellowed The Dagda, before I'd had a chance to react, "You wretch! You excrescence! You vowed to me you would keep her away from here! I only left her with you because I believed you would keep her safe! I only agreed to leave you in peace in your pathetic, degenerate excuse for an existence, because you *swore* that you would *keep her safe!*"

"I tried," said Sam, simply. His voice sounded resigned, and solemn. "I tried. Short of locking her up, and restraining her by magical means, I tried everything to keep my word to you. I even betrayed her for the sake of her safety, but I should have known that her will was too strong to be bent to our desires." Then, he looked at me.

Instinctively, I ran to him, and he enfolded me in his arms, though the intensity of his embrace felt, somehow, muted.

He must be angry.

"I'm sorry," I whispered, "I'm sorry for manipulating you, and orchestrating the distraction... But I knew you would never let me go."

"I'm sorry too," he murmured against my hair, "I should have..." His voice trailed off.

As I stood there, holding him, something about his words, and his very presence, began to trouble me. I drew back from him, cautiously. Something did not make sense. He avoided my gaze, as though he knew exactly what I had just realised, and could not bear to see the recognition in my eyes.

"Y-you're *here,*" I stammered.

"Yes."

"B-but you told me you didn't know how to get here."

"Didn't know how to get here?" repeated Étaín incredulously, "You do know who he is, don't you? Even the smallest and most insignificant of us can travel into the *síd!*"

I narrowed my eyes. "You *swore* to me that you could not get here…"

"I did," he replied.

I gasped, and stepped backwards. "And you lied."

"I did. I betrayed you. I told you untruths. I did it because I did not want you to risk your life."

"And, what about Liam's life?" I exclaimed, "You could have come for him. You could all have come for him! Why on earth did you not? Or… does a mortal life not matter to you at all, unless it is mine?"

He made no immediate reply.

"If that very thing matters to *you,* Kathy," interrupted Étaín, with saccharine-tipped infuriation, "May I suggest that we get on with the rescue?"

"You're right," I muttered, turning away from Sam and taking The Dagda's proffered arm again, this time as much for emotional as physical support. "I don't have time for this."

We walked on, Sam trailing behind. A part of me wanted to look back at him. A part of me wanted to do anything but. I would have to deal with him later… If there was a later.

The ground beneath our feet gave way to a floor. Suddenly, there was no sky, but an elegant, vaulted ceiling, and a room that felt all too familiar.

I stiffened. Though the space was grander, and even more lavishly adorned, I realised that I could almost be walking through the back room, as it had been when I'd first arrived at 'The Horse and Hag.'

I was in no doubt that this was Bres's lair.

There he was, in his usual pose on his magnificent chair, his auburn hair rippling in the candlelight, and his beautiful face watching us with an expression between amusement and curiosity.

"Well, well, well," he exclaimed, addressing himself directly to me, "Another visit! I *am* honoured. And, who have you brought with you this time?" He surveyed my companions. "Greetings, Echu. How did one such as you get dragged into this?"

The Dagda's ancient eyes glittered dangerously. "I have… an interest in this matter," he replied guardedly.

"How mysterious! Étaín… Well, I know why *you're* here. She's been simpering around me for… oh, I don't know, however long it's been, begging to have that mortal back. My, you just know everyone, don't you, Kathy?" He then turned to Sam. "And here you are, of course, running around after *her* like a faithful pup, as usual. I'm actually a little surprised you brought her here. I thought you cared for her safety."

Sam bristled, but remained silent.

"I came here for Liam," I announced, my voice shaking a little in spite of myself.

"Ah, yes, was that his name? I've been calling him all manner of things… My pet, my plaything, my worthless cur… We've been having quite the time of it. Well, I'm sure he'll tell you all about it when you see him… oh, wait. That is, if he still has a tongue. I can't quite recall how far we got during our last game of 'pull the body part from the boy'…"

"You monster!" I yelled. I felt my power grumbling and surging within me… About to boil over, and lash him with its invisible hands.

"Now, you just hold your horses, Missy," smirked Bres, "If you don't play nice, I won't fetch him for you."

I paused, struggling to calm my magic. "Where is he, then?"

Bres clapped his hands for attention, and a gaggle of smaller immortals slithered out of the shadows, heads bowed in reverence, prepared to do his bidding.

"Bring him in," commanded Bres.

"Who?" whispered one of his lackeys.

"Him!"

"Who?"

Bres clicked his tongue irritatedly. "The prisoner!"

"Oh, *him!*" They scuttled off, obligingly.

Bres rolled his eyes. "You just can't get the staff these days."

After what seemed like mere moments and a vast eternity, his attendants returned, dragging something behind them. They lay it at their master's feet, and returned to the shadows.

It was not Liam. It was a large, dark lump of sorts, but I could not quite make out its precise nature, in the dim light.

"What are you playing at, Bres?" I cried exasperatedly, "Where's Liam?"

Bres stood up and placed his foot squarely on the thing on the floor. It emitted a low, agonised groan. "Oh, dear. It seems she doesn't recognise you, my pet. What a shame! Perhaps you are not so pretty as you once were."

My blood froze.

Ye gods…

I stepped closer to the lump, and Bres let me. I could now see that it was moving… Spasming a little, as though racked with pain. It was… A creature of some description, or at least, it had once been. Its skin was charred, as though it had been roasted. I suppressed a retch at the smell of it. It had two legs, though they were broken and mangled into a pulp, from which its feet hung limply, at an impossible angle. One of its arms had been torn clean off at the shoulder, leaving an open wound of bone and sinew protruding from its torso. The other arm was barely clinging to the body by a gory thread. Its fingers and ears had been chopped off more cleanly, but its bald, scabbed head looked as though it had been shorn by the talons of a hunting bird. I thought it had no eyes. The socket closest to me was empty, and gouged. Suddenly, one familiar, bright blue eye popped open, and fixed itself on me from the other side of its mutilated face, and I screamed.

I screamed and screamed, and recoiled from the disfigured wretch, and ran back to The Dagda.

"I told you that you did not want to see," he said, quietly, though he took my arm again.

I clung to him, afraid that my legs would fail me. "Liam…" I whimpered, "Oh, no. No… Please, no…"

"Oh dear," observed Bres, though he sounded anything but perturbed, "I worry that I may have gone a little too far. You probably won't want him back like this… And there I was, hoping to strike a bargain. Perhaps I should have left a little more of his pretty face intact…"

"What bargain?" I demanded, through my tears, "What do you want for him?"

"You know what I want."

I breathed as deeply as I was able, in the confining atmosphere.

Étaín turned to me, with an expression in her eyes that I had not seen before. "Please, Kathy. You must save him," she implored me.

"If I come to you, will you swear to let him go with Étaín?" I asked, quietly.

"I will."

"Very well."

"Kathy, no!" yelled Sam, hurling himself between me and Bres protectively, his hand raised to strike my enemy with his magic, "I will not let you have her!"

Bres pushed down on Liam's stomach with his boot. "If any harm comes to me," he warned, "I just can't be sure that my foot won't go right through the middle of this fellow…"

The Dagda tightened his grip on my arm. "Let him do it, Kathy. It would be merciful to let him go. What sort of life do you expect him to have, like this?"

"B- but, you healed me after the fire," I whispered, "Can't you heal him?"

The Dagda shook his head. "I can help you because you come from me. My strength is your strength. My power helped to create you. It will not be the same for him."

"What about you?" I turned to Sam. "Can't you do something? You and Bres healed my arm after I…"

"Kathy, that was a mere scratch, and it still took both of us to do it," he said, sadly.

"But, *I* can help him," protested Étaín, "Please believe me. All could be restored…"

"Is she speaking the truth?" I asked The Dagda.

He did not answer my question. "I will not let you do this," he insisted.

I didn't trust Étaín, but if there was even a fragment of a hope that she could save Liam, I knew what I must do.

I closed my eyes. My powers rose in me with a ferocity that I had never felt, searing my blood as they poured from me. I cried out as they erupted, crashing through the shell of my body, knocking even Sam, The Dagda, and an astonished Étaín, away from me.

Within moments, I was at Bres's side. "Here I am," I declared, "Close enough for you to kill, if any one of them acts against you. They are no threat to you now. Give Liam to Étaín."

Bres laughed delightedly, with a little surprise, as though a part of him had really not expected me to give in so easily. "And you will not resist me?"

"I will not."

With a flick of his wrist, the living carcass that was Liam sped across the floor, and into Étaín's waiting arms. She caressed him gently, and whispered to him as though he were a frightened child. Whatever her intentions were, I knew, at least, that she did not wish him harm.

The others watched in horror.

"So, you see?" Bres slid a finger down my neck, and my skin crawled. "I have kept my word. Now, it is time for you to keep yours."

Though my mind despised it, my power hungered at his touch. It could sense something… Almost taste something… A small and precious part of itself, that lived within him now. I swelled with longing, and the tendrils of my magic crept up through me, like twisting vines, longing to be made whole, craving the power they had lost. *Remember the words,* I told them, *You understood them when they were spoken to you. Help me to remember…*

Bres's eyes glittered greedily as he ran his hands down my body.

"Wait!" I cried.

"What now?" he sighed, impatiently.

Slowly, I removed my rucksack, and opened the zip. "Will you not let me say goodbye to a few of my favourite things, before you do what you will with me?"

"Are you serious?"

"Please… Just one, small indulgence before oblivion, or torment, or whatever fate you choose for me?"

He shrugged. "If you insist. Might be entertaining, I suppose… But be quick about it… And then, you will not resist me?"

"I will not."

I removed a book from my pack. "My first book of fairytales, from my mother," I explained. I held it to me briefly, and placed it on the ground.

Next, I produced the little wooden tree that Liam had carved for my birthday. "A gift from a dear friend," I said. I held it to me, and then placed it on the ground.

I pulled out the shot glass that Sam had conjured the first night I had almost kissed him. "A memory of happier times," I sighed. I pressed it to my lips, and placed it on the ground.

"Get on with it," groaned Bres, sounding bored.

"Just one more item," I assured him. I took my hairbrush out of the bag.

Bres looked at it incredulously. "This… mortal tool of personal grooming is *special* to you?"

"No," I replied, "It is important, because it carries a part of me as I am now, and I know that I will be something quite different when you have had your fill of me."

He rolled his eyes, and nodded.

I held the hairbrush to me, and then placed it on the ground.

Something happened.

I heard Sam and The Dagda gasp in unison, as they realised what I had done.

My instruments were arranged in a circle, at four points around Bres. He looked down at them, and his triumphant expression suddenly became something other. At first, he looked confused, then utterly astonished, and finally outraged.

His booted foot moved to kick my objects away, but rebounded back into the space I had created for him, unable to enact his will.

"You filthy, lying whore," he shrieked. I could sense fear in his anger. "You treacherous bitch! You me gave your word! Undo this hex at once!"

"I'm not destroying anything real," I whispered to him quickly, "Just moving a little power, from one place to another. See how you like it," I stepped back.

Come to me, I told the prickle, *Remember the words*. The ravenous, cavernous thing inside me twisted and churned, desperate for the connection it craved. It rose from me like the branches of a tree, curling up through my throat, sprouting from my mouth, growing teeth and tongues in its voracity. Its rumbling became a whispering. Its whispering became a song. It was not my voice that spoke the words… Or rather, not words, but the truth of the words. It was another sound, timeless and eternal, encircling my victim in its web.

Bres struggled and writhed. His face contorted into a hundred expressions… A thousand guises… A million masks. Some of them were excruciatingly beautiful but, oh, some of them were terrible too.

The chant swelled then, as though the magic were no longer coming just from me, but lilting and rising with the weight and power of other strands, all intertwining to weave their will around the sacred space.

I recognised them. I knew them. Sam and The Dagda were chanting too, adding their strength to my hungry dance. As the tendrils of our magic lapped at him gluttonously, and pierced the shell that he was wearing with their jaws, he was torn away, piece by piece. His guise dissolved. He was a crawling mass. He was a transparent phantom. He was swirling nothingness… And then, he was gone.

Or… Not *truly* gone. As the prickle devoured the very last morsel of him, and rubbed itself contentedly about my shoulders, like a well-fed cat, I knew that I was whole again. Yet, there was something else within me too. Fragments of *his* power. *His* strength.

Suddenly, I realised that my breath was steady. My body was stronger. The *síd* was no longer an inhospitable place. I felt right. I felt comfortable. My skin rippled and writhed, with all of the sensations I had grieved for during our parting.

I looked down at The Dagda, and saw a new expression on his face: Pride.

Sam's gaze was on me too, and I saw both awe and regret in his beautiful eyes. I did not go to him. I could not afford to think about him yet.

I rushed to the tortured, fragmented thing that had once been Liam. Étaín was still cradling him, her lovely face earnest and sad.

His lips, so swollen, and matted with dried blood that they appeared welded shut with gore, slowly cracked open.

"Kathy," he croaked, the very sound of his voice sore and raw, and full of agony, "Why did it take you so long to find me?"

"I- I came as soon as I could," I told him, "But we are in the *síd*. How long has it been for you?"

"Weeks? Months?" he paused. "I have forgotten. There is no day or night here."

"I know. I know." I raised my hand as though to pat… somewhere on his body comfortingly, but saw only wounds and bone, and parts of his insides that I could not bear to touch. I withdrew my hand, and looked away.

"You can barely bring yourself to look at me."

"That's not true," I lied, forcing my gaze back to his mangled form, with a shudder.

"You have done this, and you cannot bring yourself to look at me. Is the truth of what you have caused too horrible for you to see?"

I gasped, astonished by the seething venom in his tone. He was right, of course. This was all my fault… But it had never occurred to me that *he* would see it that way. That he would blame *me* for what he had endured.

"We have to get him out of here," I said. I looked at Étaín. "Can you really help him?"

"I can, if he will allow it."

"Stay away from me," hissed Liam, "All of you. I will have no more from any of you. Just leave me here to die. It would be kinder… Although kindness is something I no longer expect."

"Liam…" I protested, tears spilling from my eyes at his distress.

"I mean it. Go away. I never want to see you again."

"You *don't* mean it," I murmured, "I will not leave you here."

I turned to the others. "Can you… transport him somewhere? Can you carry him without causing him any further pain?"

"Where shall we take him?" asked The Dagda.

"Take him home," said Étaín, "Take him home, to where it all began."

"His father can't see him like this," I exclaimed, "We must take him somewhere safe… Somewhere hidden, until I can find a way to heal him!"

"You?" cried The Dagda, "How do *you* propose to heal him?"

"Don't underestimate me. You didn't think I could do *this* either," I snapped. I knew that I would probably not even have reached Bres in the *síd* without his help, but he allowed me to have my moment of satisfaction.

"You *must* listen to me," begged Étaín, "I am the only one who can help him."

"You say a lot of things," I sighed dismissively, "Take him to 'The Horse and Hag.'"

"Please… no…" pleaded Liam's hoarse, broken voice, "Not there… Not that place…"

"I will find a way to heal you, Liam," I assured him, "Rest now."

I nodded to The Dagda. He raised his palms, and Liam floated up from the ground like a distorted mass of snapped twigs. The Great One pressed his hand to him, with the lightest of touches.

Sam took my hand, and I instinctively accepted it.

The splendid, wretched room, in which we were standing, began to melt away. The experience of magical travelling felt different this time. The speed, and sway, and colours of it were familiar, as though I knew the path to take, rather than simply being led. My new powers recognised it, and had no fear, as though they were simply walking from one room into another.

When my bedroom materialised around us, I breathed a sigh of relief. I could not quite believe it, but it was over… And I had survived.

But, oh, when I looked at Liam, as The Dagda lay him gently on the bed, my relief turned to bitter bile in my mouth. The horrid, mangled mess of him seemed even more repugnant against this comforting and familiar backdrop. I snatched my hand away from Sam's, angrily. I had forgotten his treachery, for a moment, but the haunted, hateful look in Liam's remaining eye soon brought it crashing back into my consciousness.

I was angry. I was suddenly very angry, and I needed to express it.

"Will you stay with him?" I asked Étaín, "Keep him… as comfortable as possible?"

She nodded. She was standing over the bed, looking down on Liam with true tenderness in her eyes. I envied her the ability to gaze upon his mutilated form with no revulsion.

I nodded at Sam, and stormed downstairs.

He followed.

"Walk with me," I instructed him, and left by the main door. I had wanted to feel the fresh air of my world on my face, but it was different now. My lungs were not so hungry for it as I had expected them to be. I had changed. Even so, I wanted to get away from the pub. My words were for Sam alone.

I walked, and I walked, and I took in the familiar sights and sounds of Temple Bar, and he walked beside me, until I finally stopped, threw myself back against a wall, and asked: "Was any of it true?"

He looked puzzled. "What?"

"All of your fine words, about compassion, and friendship, and a new way of being. Was any of it true?"

He considered the question before responding. "I… wanted it to be."

"But, it was all about me, wasn't it? You wanted me, and you were clever enough to find the right words to say. Well done. I had really begun to believe that you were capable of emotion. I was almost about to tell you I loved you."

"I wish you had."

"I was almost about to tell you I loved you," I continued, "Because I actually thought, for one foolish, idiotic moment, that you might be able to feel it in return."

"I think I might."

"No. It's not love that you feel. It's only desire. You would be happier if I had left Bres to tear the heart out of every magical being he could lure into the back room, and things had remained as they were. You would be happier if I had not gone into the *síd,* not rescued Liam, and not learned the truth of your betrayal. There is no compassion in you. Only a hollow, selfish thing, instructed by your wants and pleasures."

"That isn't true. I care for you. I wanted you to be safe. You are the dearest thing to me."

"I wish I could believe that," I sighed, still hating to see any hurt in those beautiful eyes, "But, how can I, when, at every step, you have tried to stop me from doing the right thing, and only stepped in when you were afraid that I might be taken away from you… That you might be deprived of your plaything before you had finished with it."

He smiled, and it was almost the carefree, playful smile that had melted my heart so many times, but there was little joy in it now. "If I had wanted a 'plaything', I could have had my pick of the women of Ireland. I wanted *you.*"

Again, I longed to believe him. "And your deal with The Dagda," I cried, "What was that, exactly? That you would stop me from saving Liam, in return for him leaving you to your life of decadence and revelry?"

"No. I just wanted him to leave me to a life with you. I do not think I value my existence, such as it is, for its own sake anymore. I thought it pleasant enough, until you came. When I touched you, I realised how empty I had been without you. *You* are what I wanted, and as long as Bres was in the *síd,* you were safe from him."

I screeched in frustration. "*You* wanted. What about what *I* wanted? *I* wanted to atone for my mistakes. *I* wanted to save the life of someone dear to me. I know that we are different, and I cannot expect you to feel those desires in the same way that I do… But I thought I could trust you to tell me the truth, and not try to impose your will over me."

"All of this is new to me," said Sam, earnestly, "Give me time. I will try to make you happy. I may be able to understand what you want, in time."

"How much time? A year? A decade? A lifetime?"

"I do not know."

"And that's the problem, isn't it? I don't *have* time, the way that you do. My life is like sand, trickling through an hourglass. How can I condemn myself to an entire existence of heartbreak, after heartbreak, as you take the easy way out of every situation at the expense of anything that threatens what *you* want?"

"All I want is you."

"That is not enough. I need you to want more… but you can't, can you? The Dagda is right. He tried to thwart me too, but at least he has the decency to hate that part of himself, that wants to protect me at all costs. He knows that your kind does not have the breadth, or the limitation, or whatever it actually is, to experience emotions in a true and noble manner. You were not intended for mortal dealings, and in whatever consciousness you have, which almost resembles a mind, they become distorted, and warped, and petty, and no good can come of them." I softened a little. "It's not even your fault."

He nodded, thoughtfully. "I cannot be what I am not… But for you, I wish I could."

I actually did believe that. He was nothing more, and nothing less, than I had first thought him to be. I had told myself that he was not for me. I had told myself that he could not feel things in the way I did. I had told myself it was madness… And then, I had convinced myself that I had been wrong about everything, because I had wanted to be. Oh, how I still wanted to be wrong. I had reasoned with myself that the connection we had made up for his limitations. How I wished I could reason with myself further, and convince myself that I could still be his. Now that I had known him, artifice or not, there were things that I could not forget: His touch. His scent. His smile. Our bodies erupting together, as our feelings and magic connected. Those fragments of ourselves that existed in each other still. The heartbreaking beauty of his song. His tender caress, and those strong, comforting arms that were the safest place I knew. Those eyes.

I burst into tears. Without hesitation, he came to me, and gathered me up, pressing his face to my neck. "I wish I had not hurt you again," he murmured.

"I know," I sobbed, and held him so tightly that I thought my heart might explode.

I pulled his face to mine and our lips melted into each other. I buried my hands in his silken hair. He kissed the tears from my face. I felt his sweet, maddening breath on me. My pulse quickened.

"Make it so that nobody can see," I whispered.

And, there, against the wall, we tore our clothes away. Our fingers intertwined, and our desire grew breathless and hungry. Our bodies became as one… Ravenous… Desperate for each other. It was not quick. I never wanted it to end, and I sensed that he felt the same.

Once again, I wished that time would cease to exist, so that I could lose myself forever in the sorrowful joy of it. I did not want to think about what would come afterwards. When the excruciatingly beautiful climax came, the wall shook, and the prickle purred, as it wound itself around us, as though trying to cast its own spell. It never wanted the moment to end either… And it did not end. Not for quite some time. The crashing waves of pleasure and pain washed over us again, and again, and again, as we kissed, and clung to each other, and fragments of our magic swelled and swayed with our passion.

When it was finally, truly over, he said: "I know that you think nothing of it was true, but it was real for me."

"It was real for me too," I replied sadly, "But now that I have walked between two worlds, I know that two truths can exist in one space. Ours will never be the same."

"I wish that they could be."

"So do I." I paused. "I've just realised… I remember it this time."

"Remember what?"

"The otherworld. When I went into the *síd* before, I could never recall what it looked like when I came back, but I remember it now."

"It must be due to your new powers. You have become something closer to us."

"Not close enough." My head drooped.

He fingered my cheek fondly. "I wish that I did not exist, so that I might never have hurt you."

"Don't say that. I would not wish the memory away, for all of its torture."

We held each other for hours or moments. I could not be sure which. If we had embraced for an eternity, it would still not have been long enough.

Eventually, the grim fingers of reality began to prod at my consciousness, and I felt suddenly ashamed of what I was doing, when my friend was lying, crumpled and shattered, in my bed, barely clinging to life. "I should go and check on Liam."

He nodded. "You go. It will be easier for you to leave me, if you walk away alone."

My tears threatened to choke me again at the empathy in his reasoning. Perhaps there *was* something just a little selfless in his feelings, after all… Towards *me*, at least. Something not entirely for his self-gratification… Something remotely approaching that mortal concept of… love. Maybe I had not been entirely mistaken after all…

"Well, this is another fine time for you to develop a mortal conscience," I sobbed.

"I know," he laughed. It was a chuckle tinged with sadness. "I would do anything for you."

"I almost believe you."

"If you believe anything, please believe that."

I hesitated.

"Go now," he said, "Your friend has need of you."

I nodded wordlessly.

I went back to 'The Horse and Hag', the prickle on my skin feeling unbearably empty without him, and made my way upstairs. Étaín was still sitting patiently by the side of the hideous, broken thing that was Liam. To my surprise, The Dagda was still there too, gazing out of the window, as though deep in thought.

"How has he been?" I asked.

Étaín looked genuinely sad. "He has not spoken. I have done what I can to ease his pain, but I can do no more until one of you will hear me." She slapped the bedcovers in frustration.

"Liam?" I said, reluctantly approaching him, and trying with all of my might to keep the horror out of my voice. "Liam?"

He made no reply.

"Okay, what is it, Étaín?" I sighed, wearily, "What do you think you can do to help?"

"When the old king dies, the young king takes his place. What is destroyed can be reborn."

"Perhaps I should have specified that I would prefer the less enigmatic version."

"When the king of the land accepts the goddess, he is granted health, vitality and abundance."

"Thank you, that was much clearer," I muttered sarcastically, "Look, are you proposing another ritual?"

She nodded.

"And you think it could save him?"

"I do."

I walked over to The Dagda. "What do you think? Is there any merit to her words?"

"Perhaps," he admitted, "She knows more of it than I do. That sort of tradition is truly her domain."

If I understood her correctly, Liam would have to subscribe to her notion that he was the rightful king of the land, in order to receive the benefits she could grant. I wondered if he could be convinced to participate. Then again, in his current state, I concluded that very little participation might be required. If he was angry that we had imposed more magic upon him, so be it, if there was any chance that his health might be restored. I sighed, suddenly feeling a little like Sam and The Dagda, forcing my will on my friend, when he had specifically begged us to leave him alone.

I told myself that this was an entirely different case. He was badly damaged, and not in his right mind. I could not take the things he had said in the *síd* to heart. He had endured weeks, or even months, of the most gruelling torture, and could not be expected to have a clear head. Trying to save his life *had to* be the right path.

"Very well, Étaín," I said, "What will you require for the ritual?" I tried to ignore Liam's eye, glaring at me with a feral fury.

"I think we should go somewhere that is meaningful to him," she replied, "Somewhere with water. We should go to the stream in Kerry, where you played as children."

"Oh, the one you tried to drown me in?"

"Yes, that one," she agreed, without any hint whatsoever of regret or embarrassment.

It occurred to me how strange it was that I now found her not in the least threatening.

"Will you come?" I asked The Dagda.

He nodded.

"I would like to say goodbye to my friends in the pub," I told them, "I do not think I will be coming back here."

The Dagda raised his eyebrows, and I swallowed heavily as I thought of Sam. I hated to give my father the satisfaction of having been right, and I hated the thought of leaving even more, but I had made my decision.

I trailed downstairs, casting a wistful glance at everything in the main bar. I would miss this place, but knew I could never return. I could not face the university with the empty, walking husk of Mr. Books haunting the library, and the memory of Dr. Herbert's corpse beside him… And how could I ever hope to live anywhere in reach of Sam without wanting him? My resolve would wither as soon as I remembered his smile, or his touch, and I would run to him in a masochistic frenzy, and the cycle of crippling disappointment would never end. My eyes filled with tears.

Sylvie and Evelyn were behind the bar, deep in conversation.

"Oh, hello, Kathy," exclaimed Evelyn when she saw me, "Where have you been? I haven't seen you since the party."

I wondered how long it had been since the party. I had only been away overnight, but my visit to the Otherworld meant that any number of days may have elapsed in Dublin in the meantime.

"I was… helping a friend with something," I said carefully, "I'm afraid I have to go back to Kerry unexpectedly."

"Oh? When will you be back?"

"I don't know that I will."

"I'm sorry to hear that. Is everything is alright?"

"It's not, but I hope to remedy that."

They both frowned, curiously.

"If you need to talk about anything…" offered Sylvie.

"Thank you," I replied, "Thank you both for everything. You've been so kind…" My voice trailed off, as my tears began to fall.

"Oh, Kathy…" They came out and hugged me tightly, in turn.

I squeezed Evelyn's hand. "I'll be fine. I always am, in the end."

I turned and walked down the corridor, into the back room.

"Kathy," cried Medb, "You're back!"

"How long have I been gone?"

She shrugged, and I remembered that a concept of time was not among their gifts.

"Where have you been?" asked Nuadu.

"I've been in the *síd.*"

Macha gasped. "Did you find Bres?"

"I did."

"And…?"

"He's gone… Well, gone as you knew him."

They all looked frightfully impressed.

She pulled out a chair. "Sit down. You must tell us all about it."

"I'm afraid I don't have time," I said, with earnest regret, "I'm leaving for Kerry soon. I have come to say goodbye."

"Oh," Macha looked disappointed, "Will you come back?"

"I don't think so."

"Can we have another party first?" asked one of the 'tween ones, hopefully.

I shook my head. Their little faces crumpled with disappointment, and I almost felt pity. "Perhaps the others will throw a party," I suggested. It occurred to me that I would like to think of them all enjoying themselves after I left, as though I had never brought them such conflict. I would always hold the happy memories of this place in my heart, and it would be nice to think that merriment existed as it once had, in this little corner of the world, even though it was no longer the right place for me.

"We will be sorry to see you go, Kathy," said Nuadu, "Please know that I hold you in the highest regard. I have never met one, man or other, with a braver spirit than yours."

"Thank you, Nuadu."

He hesitated, as though he were trying to decide whether or not to say something further. "What about…?"

As if on cue, Sam stepped through the back door.

We looked at each other for an agonising, eternal moment, our eyes locked in a pressure that seemed almost tangible, as though a beam of emotion were passing between his head and mine.

His face fell, as he read my expression. "You're leaving," he said.

"I am."

"Forever?"

I could not speak. I nodded, afraid that if I opened my mouth, I would say: "I love you. Please come with me. It doesn't matter who you are." I could not let myself speak those words. It *did* matter, even though so much of me still did not want to believe it.

"Are you ready, Kathy?" called The Dagda, entering the room. He grew silent, as he realised that he had interrupted a tense and important moment.

Sam barely noticed him. "Please don't go."

"I have to."

He stepped closer to me, and I could see the real, unfeigned pain on his beautiful face. He seemed, somehow, more human than I had ever seen him. Smaller. Fragile. More emotional… As if the true weight of the tragedy of parting had robbed him of a piece of himself.

"I do not think that I want to spend eternity without you," he said, simply.

My body trembled, as tears threatened to engulf me entirely, and drown me from within.

"You don't have to," The Dagda told him, "You could just let go."

I spun 'round indignantly. "This again? Really? *Now?*"

The Dagda looked suitably chastised, and took a step backwards.

However, Sam stared at him, with a certain light of curiosity in his eyes. He laughed mirthlessly. "Is it really so simple?"

"It could be, if you wish it," replied The Dagda.

"Leave him alone," I snapped.

"If it is his will to return to what he was, you should not deny him the chance."

"I do not want to live in a world without him in it."

"But, you will be gone," sighed Sam sadly, "And I do not think that I want to live in a world without you beside me."

"Are you serious? You're not really thinking of…?" The pace of my words quickened: "This is madness! You're sad now, and you don't want me to go, but before you know it, you'll have forgotten all about me, and you'll sing and dance with Macha and Medb, and you'll play fidchell with Nuadu, and you'll be fine!"

He shook his head. "I will not forget. There are some things that even one such as I does not forget… It is an eternal burden of loss and regret. If you are no longer there to brighten my days, I think I would be free of it."

"No!" I cried.

He turned to The Dagda. "What do I do?"

"Simply let go," he answered, "Let go of your face, and your torment, and that burden you carry, and be what you once were."

"I think that would please me."

"No," I repeated, "Not now. Think on it for a while. You may feel differently, with a little time."

"Ah," he said, with a gentle smile, "Time is for your kind. It brings you peace. It will hold no such comfort for me."

"I can help you, if you wish it," offered The Dagda.

Sam nodded. "Thank you." He looked back at me, still smiling, his enormous eyes lit with a warm glow. "Whatever you must do next will be easier for you, if you know that I am truly gone."

"No, it won't!"

"You know it will."

For a moment, I considered his words. Would it be easier to go back to Kerry, and do what I could to atone for my crimes against Liam, if I knew that Sam was not here, dejected and alone, and wishing for me to come back? Perhaps so…

I saw him notice the change in my expression, and he nodded.

"No," I pleaded again, "Please! I cannot bear to watch you disappear."

"Then, don't." He opened his arms, and I fell into them, my face pressed against his chest.

He held me tenderly and whispered: "Make me one promise. Visit the library before you go."

"What are you talking about?"

"Please. Just promise me."

"I promise," I sobbed, "But, please don't…"

"If I could love, I would love you." He paused. It felt as though an eternity had passed before he said: "I think I am ready now."

He held me to him, tighter than he ever had, his arms that protective cocoon in which I felt safe, and warm, and complete. He held me to him with a strength that came not from his magic, but from something other… That rare bond, which has a power all its own.

He held me, as the feeling of his touch grew lighter and lighter… until I could not be sure if he was still there, or if it was the memory of his arms that I sensed around me. Suddenly, I did not care that he was a god. Nothing mattered but how much I wanted him. He was just 'Sam' to me…

I opened my eyes, about to tell him that I had made a mistake, and that I'd been wrong, and that we were meant to be together, and we could somehow make it work, and that I would never leave him…

But the words froze on my lips.

He was gone.

I sank down to the floor.

A moment passed. Forever passed. It was all the same to me. He was truly gone.

"Will any of you join him?" The Dagda asked Nuadu, Medb and Macha.

The goddesses gasped in horror.

"I would go, Echu," said Nuadu, "But I will wait until all of us are ready. I will see to it that we come to you in time."

"Very well," agreed The Dagda. "Noble Nuadu, you were always the best of us. I regret the fact that we failed you when you needed our support. We placed importance on traditions of vanity, and the artifice of a hand, when we should have been heartened by your valour." He paused. "What of you three? Would you like to leave these little bodies, and become one with all the greatness of the universe?"

"That sounds quite nice, doesn't it?" replied one of the 'tween ones.

"Yes," agreed his companions in unison, "The greatness of the universe. We like that. That is where we should be."

"Can we have a party before we go?" asked the first.

"Yes," said Nuadu, "Why don't we have one, last party before we go?"

"I will see you soon, then," concluded The Dagda.

I felt his strong hands, pulling me to my feet. "Come, child. We should leave."

"He's gone," I whispered, weakly.

"I know. Now, come along. Liam and Étaín are waiting."

Liam.

In a numb, blank daze, I made my way back to my bedroom. The bedroom *he* had made for me. The bedroom in which he had held me as I slept, and welcomed me to a new day with a smile, the light of his beautiful eyes brighter than the morning. I barely felt the floor beneath me. I barely felt that I existed. I floated, like a spectre, up the staircase, and through the door.

I walked to the window, and pressed my hands to the cool glass, desperate for the sensation of something tangible. I screamed.

"Good grief, what is it?" exclaimed Étaín.

"He's gone." I burst into tears, and let my head fall against the window pane with a thud. "He's gone…"

I felt The Dagda's hand on my shoulder. "Child," he said gently, "You weep for Lug, as though he has died a mortal death. He is *not* gone. He has merely returned to what he was. He is all around us, in everything you touch, in the very air you breathe."

His words were of little comfort, though I knew them to be true. Lug may have passed into another form of existence… But Sam was gone.

"I have to go to the library," I said, suddenly.

"What?" gasped Étaín, with impatience.

"I promised him. It's the one thing he asked of me. I must go to the library before we leave."

"Why?"

"I don't know… but I promised!"

"Well, be quick about it then," she snapped, "Echu, can you transport her, so that Liam does not have to suffer the further delay of her plodding there on her mortal feet?"

"I don't think that will be necessary," I said.

I closed my eyes and concentrated, and my mind fell away, as though the gaping jaws of an open door had presented themselves to my will. I stepped in. Colours whirled, and time stopped. I knew the path to take. I stepped carefully through the invisible threads of time and space, focusing on where I wanted to be…

And, suddenly, I was there. The dim lights and muted sounds of the library flooded my consciousness. I took a moment to adjust to the change in my surroundings, and suppressed a dark shudder as I remembered the last time I had been in this place.

Why had he wanted me to return here? Was it his revenge for my having chosen to leave him, that he had sent me back to the scene of such loss and horror, as a malicious parting gift?

No. I almost wished I could believe it, for if I had any reason whatsoever to despise him, it would make the loss just a little less excruciating… But there had been no cruelty in his eyes. No resentment in his embrace… Only the purest, sweetest, most heartbreaking devotion. There was something here that he had known would bring me comfort. I was certain of it… But what could it be?

Slowly, I made my way through the towering bookshelves, and the whispering of the books in the mythology section began to reach my ears. I could not make out their words at first, but as I drew closer, I realised that they now made sense again. Gone was the garbled gibberish they had hissed at me when Bres had lured me to him that night. In its place were the words they had always spoken:

"Cú Chulaind, Echu, Badb, Brigit, Nuadu, Lug Samildánach, Medb, Bres, Midir, Fúamnach, Étaín, Macha, Derdriu, Noísiu…"

I smiled a little. At least *something* was as it was supposed to be.

Suddenly, he stepped out of the shadows. "How can I help you today?" he asked, brightly.

I gasped. "Mr Books!"

Gone was the haunted, lost look from his eyes. Gone was his transparent, drained demeanour. He appeared just as he had when we first met, and his eyes sparkled with all of the important truths he carried.

"*What* did you call me?"

"Sorry," I laughed, delightedly, "Never mind. You look… well."

"If you say so," he replied, with a disapproving frown.

"But, how…?"

"Was that a question?"

I paused, and attempted to compose my thoughts more coherently. "When I last saw you, you did not seem… quite yourself."

He nodded, thoughtfully. "It has been a strange time. One of the gods came, and I'm not entirely sure what happened, but I found myself in some sort of… fog. Then, another one came and he… *gave me* something, and I have been feeling perfectly well ever since."

"What did he give you?"

"Something… of himself." He frowned again, as though he could not quite make sense of it.

Then, I knew the truth of it. Sam had given some of his own power back to the little fellow, to restore him. I had not realised that such gifts could be given as easily as they could be taken away… Yet, somehow, he had done it.

I longed to run to him, breathless and overjoyed, and throw my arms around him, and kiss him as though nothing else mattered in the world but the two of us…

But he was gone.

"Thank you," I whispered. I had no idea if he still had ears to hear me, or eyes with which to recognise me, but I had to believe that some fragment of the one I had known would sense my gratitude, and my affection.

"For what?" asked Mr. Books, looking further perplexed.

I did not tell him I was truly thanking somebody else. I smiled at him. "For being you."

"Can I actually interest you in any reading material today?"

"No, thank you. Not today."

"Very well, then. Let me know if you change your mind." And with that, he popped out of sight, and into my memories. I continued to smile, though my feelings were bittersweet. I was heartened to know that my little friend would continue as he was, ready to engage the next student who was not quite human, with those truths that should not be forgotten. I hoped that, whoever they were, and whenever they came, they would have a better time of it than I had.

Whether the compassion he had wished to possess had finally found a home in Sam, or he had done it just to make me happy, I only cared that he had done it, and I loved him all the more.

But, what of *my* compassion? Poor Liam had waited long enough for my attention, and now he would have it.

"Kathy?" said a familiar voice, "You're back! What on earth happened? You disappeared for days!"

"Alice!" I was simultaneously frustrated and pleased to see her. I had not liked the idea of leaving without saying goodbye, but I was guiltily aware that I had already neglected Liam for far too long.

"Are you alright? You look as if you've been crying."

I sighed, and hugged her tightly. "I wish I could stay. I wish I could explain everything to you. I would love the ear of a friend more than anything right now… But I have to go. It's important."

"Ah. You're in the middle of one of your magical crises, aren't you?"

I nodded miserably. "Thank you, though."

"For what?"

"For being my friend, and for all of the things that happened because of you. However painful and heartbreaking they may seem to me now, I would not give them back."

"I'm worried about you."

"Don't be. I always endure."

She hugged me back, and squeezed my arm warmly.

"Hold Medb close," I added, "Tell her you love her. She may not say it back, but you might, one day, regret it if you don't."

"Okay, Kathy," she said, looking puzzled, "You take care of yourself, won't you? See you soon?"

"You take care of yourself too."

I saw her concerned expression melt into utter astonishment, as I began to dissolve before her eyes.

"*There* you are," exclaimed Étaín, when I crossed back into the bedroom, "Can we finally leave this place, or is there a neighbouring hedgehog you'd like to feed before we depart?"

"I'm sorry," I said, "I'm ready now."

CHAPTER TWENTY

There had been a time when I wondered if I would ever see the woods again. It had not been that long ago, though it felt as if an eternity had passed since I bade the small ones farewell, and took that coach to Dublin, and to my destiny… And to my utter undoing.

As I stepped out of the magical doorway I had made, a familiar scent flooded my senses. The grass was soft beneath my feet. The majestic trees I knew so well towered comfortingly above us, like kindly giants. The sky was clear, and a fresh breeze caressed my face, as though welcoming me home.

The prickle played about my shoulders like a squirrel on a branch, excited by the reunion with our special place.

And there it was: The little stream. The stream I had fallen into, many years ago, startled by a dog, before a boy fished me out and made fun of me for my foolishness.

The Dagda had lain Liam gently on the emerald carpet of the woods, at the water's edge. I looked at the misshapen, shattered husk he now was, and thought that I would give anything to hear him make fun of me again.

Purest agony is something to be felt, not to be seen. Yet, to look upon his face was to witness that very, twisted pain. His eye had become a pool of darkest horror, and within it flickered a raging and unhinged hatred, against the dying embers of everything he had once been. His lips were drained of all colour, and cracked and blackened by rivulets of gore. His body still bore the gouged, blistering marks of his ordeal.

"Has he spoken yet?" I asked Étaín, quietly.

"Not a word."

Fighting the urge to vomit, I crouched down beside him and asked as brightly as I could: "Do you know where you are?"

His eye flickered in my direction, and I saw the festering rage in his expression, but he made no reply.

"We're home, Liam. We're home. We're back in the woods in Kerry. Do you recognise it?"

The eye looked away from me in disgust.

I sighed, and rose to my feet. It was of no use. Either something about the transition from the *síd* to our own world had robbed him of his voice, or he was simply determined not to speak.

"Do you need any help preparing for the ritual, Étaín?"

"None whatsoever," she replied, "It is a very simple thing. All he needs to do is accept a drink."

I groaned inwardly. If, as I suspected, he was sufficiently stubborn as to have rendered himself mute, it seemed highly unlikely that he would willingly take anything offered to him by any of us.

Suddenly, the prickle jolted a little in recognition, and extended its curious fingers, as though reaching out for something nearby.

I turned, and saw a strange procession of figures making their way towards us. The small ones were there… But they were not alone. My eyes widened in astonishment. Mr. O Mordha was with them, and Cú Chulaind padded along beside him… And who was that behind them? *Aoife! Ye gods, what is she doing here?* She was staring at me with an expression that was difficult to read, and clutching a baby protectively.

"Kathy," said one of the small ones, as they reached us, "We knew you were coming. We sensed it."

"We knew that something important was about to happen," added one of his companions.

"And you sent for… *them?*" I cried incredulously, gesturing towards my sister and Liam's father.

"Something told us that they should be here."

"I- I…" I began, racking my brain for something to say to Mr. O Mordha. I found no words.

He barely noticed me, as he stared in horror at the hideous thing beside the stream. His kind face crumpled, and he rushed to his son, shouting:

"No! No! Oh, my beautiful boy! Oh, no!" He fell to the ground beside Liam, and wept. "What have they done to you?"

Aoife gasped, and covered her child's face as she turned away from the dreadful scene. "Good grief Kathy, what happened?"

"I- I… There's simply too much to explain… And you wouldn't want to hear it anyway."

She shuddered, and nodded stiffly, as though she thought that I might be right.

"What are you doing here, Aoife?"

"Mr. O Mordha came for me," she said, "He said he'd been told that you were coming."

"Did he say who told him?"

"Well, those little…" she frowned in distaste, "*Creatures,* obviously."

My mouth fell open. "You can *see* them?"

"Yes, yes," she snapped, "It doesn't mean I want to. I've avoided these blasted woods all my life. I never wanted any of that nonsense."

I shook my head in amazement. It made certain kind of sense, really. We did share a mother, and she'd had her own magic, of whatever nature it might have been.

"Why did you agree to come?" I asked.

Aoife lowered her eyes. "I wanted to see that you were alright. You are… alright, aren't you?"

"In comparison with poor Liam, I'm fine," I sighed.

"This is your niece," she announced, bouncing her baby in her arms.

"Hello…" I reached out a tentative hand to touch her soft skin. I saw nothing of Alan Lynch in her face, which was a blessing. "She looks like our mother," I observed.

Aoife smiled a little. "I thought so too."

I was aware that Mr. O Mordha was still sobbing disconsolately in the grass. "I should go to him," I muttered.

Aoife nodded. "Of course."

I approached the heartbroken man, and sat down beside him. "I'm so sorry. I'm so, so sorry."

He looked up at me, his eyes full of tears. "Surely… *you* didn't do this?"

"Of course I didn't… but it was my fault. He was trying to help me when it happened."

His head drooped. "I know my son. He wouldn't have wanted to be anywhere else, if you needed him. He would walk through fire for you."

"I know. I don't deserve such a loyal friend."

"Child," said The Dagda. I had not realised that he was listening. "You malign yourself too harshly. Do not forget the reckless risks you took to save his life. You are a faithful friend to him too."

"But, I was too late," I whispered, "I was too late… And he should never have been there in the first place. It *is* my fault."

"Kathy, why will he not speak to me?" asked Mr. O Mordha, his face forlorn.

"I don't know. He won't speak to any of us."

"Oh, please," he implored, looking up at Étaín and The Dagda, "Please, is there anything you can do for him? I know you for the divine and powerful entities you are. Can you heal him? I will do anything you ask in return."

"I can," replied Étaín, "I am certain of it. I require nothing from you as incentive. All he has to do is accept a drink."

"Where is it?" gasped Mr. O Mordha, "Please, give it to him at once!"

Étaín produced her beautiful golden cup from the folds of her shimmering skirts. She filled it from the stream, and held it to Liam's lips.

With a hiss, he jerked his head away, and the water spilled onto the grass.

"What are you doing, son?" cried Mr. O Mordha, "You must drink!" He turned to the goddess. "Please, please, he didn't mean it… Please try again…"

"Very well," agreed Étaín. She refilled the cup and, again, offered a drink to Liam. Again, he moved his head angrily away from the goblet.

"Could we just hold his mouth open and pour it in?" I asked.

Étaín tutted. "Kathy, you know better than that. He must accept it willingly. I will try once more, but if he rejects me again, I don't think it will ever work."

"Liam, don't be so stubborn," I pleaded, "This is the only chance we have to make you well."

"You *must* drink, son," insisted Mr. O Mordha.

"If you are afraid that accepting the water will make you king," I continued, "Don't be. Your will is strong, and I truly believe you have the power to choose your own path, tradition or not… besides, what's the alternative? To exist like this forever, subject to the decisions we make for you, with no agency of your own? No independence? If you will not drink for me, then drink for your father. Drink for the small ones. Drink for yourself. You deserve a future. You must try."

A solitary tear slithered from his eye, and trickled down his cheek.

"Please," I begged him again, "Drink."

Étaín filled her cup for the third time, and pressed it to his lips. His mouth opened, and the water trickled into him.

Please let it work.

We all waited with bated breath.

We waited, and waited, for what seemed like an eternity.

Then, as I stared at the mutilated stump where his arm had been, the ragged tendrils of flesh began to knit themselves together. Like ruby vines, they curled themselves outwards and caressed each other, forming a solid tapestry around the cold, milky bone. Gradually, the stump reached forward and produced an elbow, from which more flesh and bone protruded. The rapidly increasing limb tapered into an elegant wrist, before sprawling out in all directions to become a hand. Soft, pliant pallor crept over the creation, like a silken web, consuming its prey and melting on contact. Now, the new part had a covering of skin.

I watched, mesmerized. I dared not breathe, lest I should interrupt the magic. I wondered if my eyes were misleading me… Instruments of my jaded, desperate brain, that had collapsed into the realms of fantastical untruth, and created a vision of what I longed to see.

I turned to Mr. O Mordha and saw the hope shining in his eyes, and I knew that it was truly happening.

As we stared on, the blanket of skin continued to grow, shrouding Liam's body in its embrace, and covering the holes and tears in him with its quick, light caress. Hair spilled from his scalp, like a cascade of gold, and a new blue eye blinked from his beautiful face.

I burst into tears, this time with relief. Liam was healed. Liam was back.

I clasped his hand delightedly, and he snatched it away.

"It's okay, Liam," I assured him, smiling, "It's okay! It worked!"

Slowly, his supple, new hands pushed him up from the ground. His lean, strong legs carried him upright. He touched himself, as though making sure that his body was really there. He looked just as he had before Bres had carried him into the otherworld…

No, I realised. Not *just* as he had. There was something new in his blue eyes. A darkness. A shadow. A haunted despair and a… Coldness. Étaín's magic had healed his body, but she had not been able to prise the awful memories from his mind. They were all there, in his bleak expression, ravaging his thoughts with their cruelty.

"Liam?" came Mr. O Mordha's tentative voice, "Are you alright, son?"

Liam swallowed heavily, and stared at his father with very little emotion.

"Liam, will you still not speak to us?" I asked, softly.

"Oh, I will speak to *you*," he replied.

I laughed as tears continued to spill down my face. He could speak!

"I hate you," he said.

My smile froze on my lips. "W- what?"

"I hate you, Kathy."

Mr. O Mordha's eyes bulged in surprise. "You don't mean it, son. You've been through something dreadful, and…"

"Oh, but I do mean it."

"I'm sorry," I told him, "I know it's my fault. I shouldn't have asked you to come to Dublin. I shouldn't have taken you to see Bres. I shouldn't have…"

"I wish I had never met you," continued Liam, "I used to think that what was between us was the sweetest, most beautiful thing in the world. I used to think that the moon glowed just to illuminate us, and that the sun leaped into the sky each morning, eager to bathe us in her light, because our feelings were stronger, and deeper, and more true, than anything else in existence… But I was wrong. Those were *my* feelings. Not yours. I see that now."

"Liam, you're wrong. I love you. You have no idea how dear you are to me."

"But I *do* have an idea. I finally have an idea of how much you value me… and it is not a lot. You left me, and I forgave you. You forgot me, and took another lover, and I forgave you. I walked into danger with you, time and time again, and finally, it destroyed me.

The things he did to me, Kathy. You could not imagine them in your wildest nightmares. You deserve the memories that I have, and yet a part of me would *still* spare you from them.

I begged you not to bring me to that horrible, twisted place in Dublin, yet that is precisely where you took me. You left me lying in that crawling, magical, mockery of a bed while you went about your own business, for what felt like an eternity…

And then, I heard you crying. I thought you were crying for me, but I listened to your conversation with The Dagda, and I knew that your tears were for *him:* That… thing. A friend to the one that did *this* to me. You loved that thing, that was not even a man, and yet you could not bear to look at me."

"I've cried for you too, Liam. You don't know how much I've cried for you."

"You've cried for your own guilt. Every word you've said to me, since you took me from that cursed place, has been about you. *You're* sorry. *You're* at fault. Did you even miss me? Did you rescue me because you wanted me in your life, or because you wouldn't have been able to live with your guilt if you hadn't?"

I opened my mouth to reply.

"Don't answer that," he snapped, "I know the truth. I begged you to let me die. I beseeched you, but you didn't care. You had to save me. You had to find a way to heal my injuries. You had to be the great hero… as soon as it was convenient for you, of course.

And so, here we are. Well done. You fixed everything. It doesn't matter than being in my own body sickens me…

That I cannot bear to look at my own father… That my entire existence, and everything in it, has become a vile and twisted thing. None of that matters, because I look normal again, and it doesn't turn your stomach to see me. You got your happy ending. Well done."

"I'm so sorry," I whispered, "I hate the damage he has done to you… but you couldn't really have expected me to let you die."

He lowered his eyes. "Perhaps not… but I wish you had."

Étaín stepped forward, her expression tinged with regret. "I see that your form has been restored, but you are not whole. I wish I could do more."

"Oh dear," exclaimed Liam sarcastically, "Has my broken shell of a mind rendered me unfit for kingship? What a shame! What will you do now, Étaín… now that I am of no use to you?"

Her beautiful eyes grew wider, and then a little blank. "I do not know."

"You could let go," The Dagda told her, "You could abandon all of this artifice, and return to what you once were. You could be great again, Étaín. What are you now? Barely more than a girl with a pretty cup. You were ready to join me, once… To work together for a shared purpose, until that boy's lineage turned your head, and you began to long for a more earthly union. You must see now that the time for such things has passed. You could be so much… more."

She stared at him with a mixture of fear and curiosity. "I… I don't know, Echu."

He continued: "You have known little peace in this incarnation. You may even have forgotten how it feels, but you could know it now. I only wish we could grant such peace to Liam. I fear we have not done well by him."

Étaín's enormous eyes brightened. "Perhaps we *could* grant him peace… or at least a little serenity. Perhaps we could change his form to that of one who does not feel the pain of thought so deeply, until time has erased something of the horror in his mind."

The Dagda nodded. "That may be well."

"What are you talking about?" I demanded, "We only just got him back, and now you want to transform him into something else again?"

"I do not want to live like this," Liam interjected, "I will accept any form that dulls what I carry."

"But... what would he become?" I asked Étaín, "Would he still live among us? Would he speak, and eat, and breathe? Would he know us?"

"He would know something of himself, but not enough to torture him with pain and regret. He would survive on instinct. He would live in this world, but not among humans. And one day, when his mind has healed, and rid itself of the darkness it now carries, he would return to his true form, and continue his mortal life."

"Do it," begged Liam, "Please, do it. I long for any release from this torture."

"Son..." began Mr. O Mordha, with fresh tears in his eyes, "You would leave me?"

Liam regarded him sadly. "I'm sorry. I'm so sorry, but I can't bear it."

His father nodded. "I know. I can see it in your eyes."

"If Étaín speaks the truth, I will come back some day."

"I hope that I am here to see it."

"So do I."

They embraced warmly, and Liam patted Cú Chulaind's soft, warm head.

I thought that my heart might burst. I ran to Étaín. "No," I cried, "No! You can't send him away, all alone, for who knows how long? We will tend him, and care for him here, and he will know happiness again. I will make sure of it!"

"Kathy," said Liam, "Please. Let me go. Do me this one kindness, and let me go."

"Then, I'm coming with you," I declared.

"I don't want you with me."

"I don't care." I turned to Étaín and The Dagda again. "Please send me with him. Please. I can't lose him again."

"Kathy, what are you saying?" shrieked Aoife, tears spilling down her face, "This is madness! You have me! You have a niece! Don't you want to watch her grow up?"

"I'm sorry," I said in a small voice, "But this is all my fault, and going with him is the only thing I can do to even begin to make it right."

"You see?" sighed Liam, weakly, "Even your reasons for wanting to come with me are only about yourself. *Your* guilt. *Your* penance."

"Do my motivations really matter?" I asked, "I'll be with you. I won't leave you. Is that not enough?"

The Dagda faced me gravely. "Perhaps there is some wisdom in this. You have healing of your own to do, child. It may be your path to recover from what you have faced together."

Liam shook his head. "I don't want you to come. I want to be alone. Go back to Dublin, and make merry with your immortal friends. You will forget me soon enough."

"I won't," I insisted, "I'm coming with you. You don't have to look at me, if you don't want to, but I will be there, and you will know it, and you will not be alone."

"Étaín," said The Dagda, "I am content with this."

She nodded. "So am I. I would not have him be alone, and he loves her. There is no darkness without light, and no hatred without love." As she spoke the word, I wondered if it could be possible that I saw something of it in her eyes.

I looked about, at all of the anxious faces around me, and at the place where I stood. I did not know what was about to happen. What were we going to become? Where were we going to go? Was this the last glimpse that I would have of anything familiar? Would I know it when I was changed? I wondered if anything I had would still be with me… My memories, my pleasures, my losses, and my bitter, aching emptiness? I hoped so. I would not have given them back, for all of the peace in the world…

But whatever the truth of our impending transformation was to be, I could not, and would not, be anywhere else. It was my destiny, and I had made it so. I could not let him walk away, into the next adventure, without me. Besides, where else was there for me to go? Everything in which I had found some brief contentment was gone… Marred… Spoiled… Treading an unknown path with my dearest friend felt safer than any alternative, however much he didn't want me.

Étaín's elegant hands curled upwards in a strange gesture, and something within me began to change. My mind was not quite itself. I knew who I was, and what I had done, but my perception of it seemed a little duller. My emotions were less acute. My body began to ripple and churn, and my hands and feet became a blur. Every particle of me contorted, and became something other. My vision changed, as though a filter had spread across my eyes. I saw new colours. They were not the ones of the otherworld, but nor were they the ones that humans saw. I felt my mouth twist, and protrude into another shape. I looked at Liam and realised what we had become.

"Swans!" cried Aoife, "She's turned them into swans!"

The baby gurgled and pointed at us with a delighted curiosity.

Étaín looked at us with satisfaction. Her face was benevolent, and her beautiful eyes shone. She was every inch the goddess of creation, smiling at her handiwork.

The Dagda gazed at me. "Be well, daughter," he said.

"Echu," began Étaín, "I feel… free. I think I am ready now. I think I will let go, and return to that domain from which I once fell."

The Dagda nodded, and placed his hand tenderly on hers.

As I watched, her shimmering form grew a little fainter. The light in her eyes dimmed. Her cascade of shining hair swirled in the breeze, as though it were growing lighter, and lighter. She began to disintegrate, each fragment of her guise glistening, as it floated upwards, like a mist of tiny stars.

I thought I felt the air around me swell, as though heartened by a new arrival in its endless, timeless lair.

Liam spread his mighty wings, and swooped majestically to the other side of the stream. I fluttered after him. The action of flying felt like the most natural thing in the world.

Aoife burst into tears. She looked at the creature I had become, with more true recognition than I had ever seen on her face when I was her little sister.

"I wish I had told her how sorry I am," she sobbed, "I wish I had made life happier for her. I always knew she was different, but I didn't want to face it. If only I had been more accepting of what she was, things might have been different. I'll do better by Eili. I swear it."

Mr. O Mordha put a comforting arm around her. "You just told her, Aoife," he said, gently, "Look at the expression in her eyes. She still understands your words. I don't think there is anything you could have done to prevent this. There is an inevitability about it. From the moment they met, their course was fated to be something… other. I always sensed it. What matters is that they're together now… and I have a feeling they'll be back."

EPILOGUE

And so, we wait, and we wait. I do not know if the hideous scars of the memories he bears trouble him, or if his mind is at peace in its new guise. I do not know if my presence brings him any comfort. It doesn't matter. His side is the only place for me to be, until the day that the magic fades, and we return to what we were.

Every year, we make a long journey across the skies, to distant lands and different climates. He flies ahead, and I follow. And every year, we return to the woods. The small ones come to us. Though we exchange no words, they know us for who we are… Or were. I have seen them playing with a little girl by the stream. She reminds me of my mother.

All around me, I feel *them* in the atmosphere. I feel them in the warmth of the sun, and the softness of the snow, and the gentle kiss of the rain. I can feel their power growing. Something is happening. They are returning to their lofty domain. They are becoming what they were. And sometimes, I almost think that a certain star is shining a little brighter, just for me, or that the caress of the wind lingers on my face like a lover's tender fingers.

I do not know what my life will be when the day comes for me to resume it. I do not know what year it will be, or how the world might have changed. I wonder how *I* might have changed. Will I ever feel those mortal emotions again? Exuberance, joy or despair? I know I had them once, though I cannot remember what it was like to experience them. I know I had emotions… and music, and laughter, and love too, though the memory of their power has faded.

And, we wait, and we wait, and we wait. I have forgotten much… But there are things that even one such as I does not forget.

THE END

Printed in Great Britain
by Amazon